Enjoy these thre   tar

Maisey
YATES

Married on Paper

Contains

The Argentine's Price
The Inherited Bride
Marriage Made on Paper

May 2014

June 2014

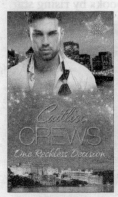

July 2014

August 2014

Maisey
YATES
Married on Paper

MILLS & BOON

Published in Great Britain 2014
by Mills & Boon, an imprint of Harlequin (UK) Limited,
Eton House, 18-24 Paradise Road, Richmond, Surrey, TW9 1SR

MARRIED ON PAPER © 2014 Harlequin Books S.A.

The Argentine's Price © 2011 Maisey Yates
The Inherited Bride © 2011 Maisey Yates
Marriage Made on Paper © 2011 Maisey Yates

ISBN: 978 0 263 24657 5

024-0614

Harlequin (UK) Limited's policy is to use papers that are natural, renewable and recyclable products and made from wood grown in sustainable forests The logging and manufacturing processes conform to the legalenvironmental regulations of the country of origin.

Printed and bound in Spain
by Blackprint CPI, Barcelona

Maisey Yates was an avid Mills & Boon® Modern™ romance reader before she began to write them. She still can't quite believe she's lucky enough to get to create her very own sexy alpha heroes and feisty heroines. Seeing her name on one of those lovely covers is a dream come true.

Maisey lives with her handsome, wonderful, nappy-changing husband and three small children across the street from her extremely supportive parents and the home she grew up in, in the wilds of Southern Oregon, USA. She enjoys the contrast of living in a place where you might wake up to find a bear on your back porch and then heading into the home office to write stories that take place in exotic urban locales.

The Argentine's Price

MAISEY YATES

CHAPTER ONE

"You're buying up my company's stock. Why?" Vanessa clutched her silver purse tightly in her hand and tried to ignore the heat and anger curling in her stomach as she addressed the tall man in black. Lazaro Marino. Her first love. Her first kiss. Her first heartbreak and, apparently, the man who was attempting a hostile takeover of her family's company.

Lazaro's dark eyes flicked over her and he handed his glass of champagne to the slender blonde standing on his left. It was clear from his dismissive manner that he saw the woman as little more than a cup-holder in a designer gown. Well, Vanessa imagined she was a little more than that to him, in his bed at least.

Her cheeks burned, the images in her head instant and graphic. How did he do that? Thirty seconds in his presence and he had her mind in the bedroom.

She stared just past Lazaro, at the painting on the wall behind him, in order to avoid those dark, all-too-knowing eyes of his. She could feel his gaze on her, warming her, turning her blood to fire in her veins. Instant. All-consuming. Still. After all this time. It threw her right back to the summer she was sixteen, when mornings had been all about the hope that he would be there, working on the grounds of the estate. So that she could sit and simply look at him, the boy she wasn't even permitted to talk to.

The boy who ultimately inspired her to break the rules, rules that had been sacrosanct before that.

It was inconvenient that the boy had become a man who still had the power to make her pulse race. Even when he was only a picture in a magazine, looking at him was a full-on sensory experience. In person…in person he made her feel as if her skin was too tight for her body.

"Ms. Pickett." He inclined his head, a lock of obsidian hair falling forward with the motion. Not an accident, she was sure of that. He had that look about him. That sort of hot, can't-be-bothered-to-get-too-slick look. It gave the impression he'd gotten out of bed, combed his fingers through his thick black hair and thrown on a thousand-dollar suit.

And for some reason it was devilishly sexy. Probably because it was easy to imagine what he might have been doing in that bed, what activities might have prevented him from having adequate time to get ready…

She blinked furiously, redirecting her thoughts. She was not going down that rabbit trail again. She wasn't some naive sixteen-year-old anymore, imagining that the fluttering in her stomach was anything more than the first stirrings of lust, imagining that a kiss meant love. No, she wasn't that girl anymore, and Lazaro Marino didn't have any power over her.

She had power. And she would remind him of that.

"Please," she said, turning on her CEO voice. "Call me Vanessa. We are old friends after all."

"Old friends?" He chuckled, a dark, rich sound that made her blood heat. "I had not thought of us as such. But if you insist, Vanessa it is then." His accent had smoothed in the twelve years since she'd seen him, but he still said her name as he always had, his tongue caressing the syllables, drawing them out, making her own name sound impossibly sexy.

Age looked good on him. At thirty, he was even more attractive than he'd been at eighteen. His jaw a bit more square, his shoulders broader. His nose was different, slightly crooked, the imperfection adding to his mystique rather than detracting from his otherwise perfect face. She wondered if he'd broken it in a fight. It wasn't impossible. The Lazaro she'd known had been hotheaded, passionate in every conceivable way. And there had been many times when she'd wondered what it might be like to have all that passion directed at her—and one wonderful occasion when it had been. When he'd made her feel that she was the only woman, the most important thing in his world. Lazaro could lie more effectively with a kiss than most men could with a thousand words.

Vanessa tightened her grip on her purse and took a step back, fighting the rising tide of heat and anger that burned in her stomach, trying to keep herself calm. Unaffected. At least in appearance. "Do you think we could talk?"

"Not here to socialize?" he asked, one black eyebrow quirked.

"I'm here to talk to you, and it's not a social call."

A small smile tipped up the corners of his mouth. "I'm certain you donated to the charity on your way in. Or was that not on your list of priorities tonight?"

Vanessa bit the inside of her cheek, fighting to maintain composure. Taking the glass of champagne out of Lazaro's human cup-holder's hand and throwing the contents of it onto his very expensive suit might be satisfying, but it wasn't what she was here for.

Still, there was no way she was going to allow him to pretend that he was somehow a philanthropic marvel and she was a snobby rich bimbo who walked into a charity event for the company and the liquor and didn't bother to leave a dime.

"I wrote a check as I walked in. You can ask up front if you like."

"Generous of you."

"We need to talk. Without an audience." She flicked a glance at the group he was with. A lot of beautiful socialites, some of whom she recognized, not the sort of women she'd ever been permitted to associate with. Money did not mean class, as her father had always said, and that meant certain people had always been patently off limits to her.

Lazaro among them. Although, for one, heady week, she had defied that command.

"This way, *querida*." He put his hand on her lower back and she cursed the low cut of the gown she was wearing as his palm made contact with her skin. His fingers were calloused, rough from labor still, even after years of white-collar work.

She remembered how those hands had caressed her face, her body. They had been rough then, strong and hot. So very hot. She shivered slightly, thankful that her body chose the moment they stepped out into the chill, Boston air before the reaction hit. At least this way she could blame it on the weather.

The art museum's grand terrace was lit up by paper lanterns strung overhead. A few couples were secluded in dark corners, talking with their heads pressed together, or not talking, enjoying the feeling of seclusion.

Of course, there was no seclusion. There were reporters, there were other people. This was the sort of event her father wouldn't want her to come within a mile of. Discretion was the cornerstone of her father's value system. And of hers.

But she was here. She had to be. She had to talk to Lazaro. As far as Pickett Industries was concerned it was possibly a matter of life and death. She couldn't imagine he had any kind of altruistic motive for purchasing Pickett's shares. In fact, she was certain he didn't.

"You had a question for me?" he asked, leaning against the stone railing.

She turned to him, her face schooled into a neutral expression. "Why are you buying up all of my stocks?"

The corner of his mouth curved upward. "I'm surprised that you realized it so soon."

"Suddenly all of my shareholders are selling to three different corporations, all of whom have one name in common—Marino. I'm not stupid, Lazaro."

"Perhaps I underestimated you." He looked at her, as if waiting for her to be angry or indignant or something. She wouldn't give him the satisfaction.

She pushed down a surge of anger. "I don't care whether you underestimated me. I don't care what you think about me. I care about Pickett and it is in my best interest to try and understand why someone is trying to get to a point where they own equal shares with me and my family."

He paused for a moment, his smile widening, a cruel smile, void of humor, but just as devastating as it had always been. "Do you not appreciate the irony?"

"What irony is that?"

"That *I* can own my share of Pickett Industries. That a storied icon of a company can be passed into the hands of new money with such ease. The American dream, isn't it?"

She looked at his eyes, the glitter in them filled with emotion so dark and deep that she felt it reach into her and pull the air from her lungs. And that was when she realized that it was very likely she'd wandered into a trap. In that moment she wanted, more than anything, to turn and walk away. To leave Lazaro as nothing more than a vivid, unsatisfied memory.

But she couldn't. This was her responsibility. Her mess to clean up. There was no one else.

It's up to you now, Vanessa. Without you, everything crumbles.

Her father's words echoed in her head, filled her, pushed her forward.

"So…this is for your own amusement, then? Something to satisfy your twisted sense of irony?" she asked.

He chuckled, a dark sound laced with bitter undertones. "I don't have time to do things simply to amuse myself, Vanessa. I didn't get where I am by operating that way. My business was not handed to me on a silver platter."

And there was no doubt he found himself superior to her because of that. Fine, he could disdain her for having it easy if he wanted. Pickett wasn't really a silver platter to her. More like silver handcuffs with keys she couldn't access. But she'd willingly accepted the burden. Had done it for her family. For her father, and most of all for Thomas. Because her brother would have carried on Pickett's legacy gladly. He would have made it a success. He would have done it with dignity and kindness, as he had done everything else.

"Then why?" she asked.

"Pickett is dying, Vanessa, I know you know that. Your profits have dropped off in the past three years, so much so that you're now firmly in the red."

Her standard response, the one she'd been placating the shareholders with, rolled off her tongue with ease. "These things happen. It goes in cycles. Production has slowed with the economy as it is, and a lot of our clients are now getting their auto parts manufactured out of the country."

"The problem isn't simply the economy. You are stuck in the past. Times have changed and Pickett Industries has not."

"If Pickett really is dying some kind of slow, painful corporate death, why are you interested in investing your money in it?"

"The opportunity presented itself. I am a man who makes the most of all available opportunities."

Vanessa's stomach tightened as his eyes locked on hers,

the meaning of his words seeming layered in the dim light, almost erotic.

She needed to get out more. She really did. As it was, the four walls of her office were so familiar, her situation was beginning to seem desperate. But that was how it was when one was at the helm of a dying corporation. Lucky, lucky her.

And Lazaro Marino saw it as an opportunity. Heaven help her.

"And what do you intend to do with this *opportunity*?"

"I could put pressure on the board to vote you out of your position."

Vanessa felt as though a bucket of icy water had been thrown in her face. Shock froze her in place, keeping her expression unaltered despite the rolling wave of fear that was surging through her. "Why would you do that?"

"Because you are in over your head, Vanessa. The company has been in decline ever since you were appointed. It is in the best interest of the shareholders to have someone in charge who knows what they're doing."

"I've been working on my game plan."

"For three years? I'm surprised your father hasn't stepped back in and taken control again."

She stiffened. "He can't. When I was appointed CEO he signed an agreement, something the board wanted done to prevent…problems." When her father was in a good mood, he was happy with what she was doing and when he wasn't… well, she wouldn't put it past him to try to oust her himself. No one on the board had wanted the employees, or the shareholders, living with that kind of instability.

Of course, if she didn't turn things around soon that would be the least of anyone's problems.

Vanessa had a degree in business, but a prodigy she was not. She knew it. But she stuck with Pickett out of duty, loyalty to her family, the driving need to make her father happy. How could she do anything else?

Thomas had lived and breathed Pickett, even in high school. Thomas, her handsome brother with the easy smile who had always had time for her, who had shown her warmth and affection, who had remembered her birthday. Who had been the only one able to make their father smile.

And with him gone, she was all her father had left to make sure the company, the family, continued. She couldn't let Thomas's dream die. She couldn't force her father to lose the only thing in the world that truly mattered to him. She couldn't stand to fail at the only thing that made her matter in his eyes.

She couldn't be the one to see it all end, couldn't be the cause of that. She'd let go of vague, half-imagined dreams in order to keep Pickett alive already. She couldn't lose it now. She couldn't see someone else in the position her father had always wanted reserved for someone in their family.

Her great-grandfather had built the business up using family money, and it had been passed down to Vanessa's grandfather, and then to her father. It would have gone on to Thomas next.

The memory of that day was always there, sharp and vivid down to the way the rug in her father's office had made her bare feet itch, to the way her stomach had ached, so intensely she'd been convinced she would die too. Just like her brother.

It's up to you now, Vanessa. Without you, everything crumbles. Everything I've worked for, everything Thomas dreamed of.

She'd been thirteen. All of her brother's responsibilities had been passed on to her that night, the weight of her family's legacy. She'd be damned if she failed.

"It's difficult to compete now that the market has changed. So many things are being done overseas now because there's cheaper labor and lower taxes. It's a hard position for us to be in, but we're committed to keeping the factory here, to keeping the jobs here."

"Idealistic. Not necessarily practical."

He was right, and the worst thing was, she knew it. Had known it from the moment she'd taken her position in the big corporate office. She was fighting a losing battle, and she had been for three long years.

But she didn't want to move the factory, didn't want to eliminate all those jobs. Most of the employees had been with the company for more than twenty years and she couldn't fathom taking that from them. They were her friends in some ways. Her responsibility.

Of course, if the company ceased to exist, the point was moot.

"Maybe not, but I don't have any better ideas right now." It galled to have to say that to him. To be put in the position of having to admit to deficiencies she was far too familiar with.

"As your principal shareholder, I'm not very pleased to hear that."

She narrowed her eyes. "What do you want from me, Lazaro?"

"From you? Nothing. But I very much enjoy the fact that the fate of Pickett is now resting with me."

"Maybe a better question for you is whether this is business or personal."

"It is business. But it is also an interesting quirk of fate, isn't it? Your father once held my future, my mother's future, in his hands. He paid her miserable wages to do work that was so beneath any of you. To keep house and be treated very much as the help. And now I could buy your father ten times over. I have bought the portions of the business that were available."

"So you just intend to lord over us with all that newfound power?"

"As your father has done to others?"

Vanessa bit the inside of her cheek. She knew her father, knew he was difficult at best. But he was all she had, her only family. The most important things to him were their family name, the tradition of the company and their standing in the community. He needed to know that he would always have his place as a pillar of the city, his favorite chair and cigars in his country club.

She wouldn't be the one to lose that for him. Not now.

"I won't say he's been perfect, but he's an old man, he… Pickett means the world to him." And he—they—had lost too much already: Thomas, Vanessa's mother. They couldn't lose any more. It was up to her to make sure that they didn't.

Lazaro looked at Vanessa, her dark brown eyes cool and unreadable, her full lips settled into a slight frown, a berry gloss adding shine to her sexy mouth. She looked every bit what she was. Rich and upper-class, her silver gown hugging her curves without being over the top, the neckline high, the only skin on display the elegant line of her back. Restraint, dignity. That was how the Picketts were. In public at least.

He'd seen a different side to Vanessa Pickett twelve years ago. A side of her that was branded into him, under his skin.

He redirected his thoughts. "What's more important, Vanessa? The bottom line or tradition?"

To Michael Pickett, it was probably tradition. The blood in his veins was as blue as it came. He'd married old money and his daughter was the perfect aristocratic specimen, designed to keep the family name in a position of honor, to keep the family legacy going strong. Likely meant to marry a man of equal stock. That was what mattered to men like him. Not hard work, certainly not any sort of integrity. Just the preservation of an image and a way of life that was as outdated as his business practices.

When the opportunity to buy the shares had come up, Lazaro hadn't been able to turn it down. He hadn't been seeking any kind of poetic justice, but passing the chance up had been impossible when it had landed in his lap.

"I... Of course profit is the most important thing but we—my family—*is* Pickett Industries. We're the soul of the company, the reason it's lasted as long as it has. Without us, it wouldn't be the same."

"Of course it wouldn't be the same. It would be new, modern. Which your father is most definitely not. And you are running things based on systems put into place by him some thirty years ago. It's outdated in the extreme."

Her throat convulsed and a muscle ticked in her cheek. Her delicate hands clung tightly to her purse, the tendons standing out, the effort it took to maintain composure evident. "I don't know what else to do," she said, her voice flat.

He could see the admission cost her. He wasn't surprised by it, though. Vanessa had never seemed the CEO type. At sixteen she'd been sweet—at least he had seen her that way at first. She'd liked to swim in the pool in her family home's massive backyard. The image of her lying in a lounge chair in her electric-pink bikini was burned into his brain, a watermark that colored his view of things more often than he cared to admit.

She'd been intrigued by him from the start, the kid who mowed her daddy's lawn. He'd sensed her attraction right away, her hungry looks open, obvious. He imagined it had been some form of rebellion for her. To be attracted to not just a poor boy, but an immigrant, one who was so far removed from the long, storied lineage of the Pickett family it was nearly laughable.

The fact that she'd managed to burrow beneath his skin,

that the thought of her had made his heart race faster, that he'd looked forward to weeding the flower beds so that he could catch sight of the princess in her tower was even more laughable.

He'd been a fool. That air of sweetness and light had been the perfect way to capture his attention, the kindness she'd shown to him so rare he'd lapped it up like a man dying of thirst. But she'd only been toying with him. And she'd made that clear the evening she rejected him. Later that same night, as a bonus prize to go with the rejection, he'd woken up face-down in an alley, his nose broken along with any of his naive notions of a romance between him and Vanessa, as one of Pickett's hired henchmen warned him to keep away from the precious heiress.

It had been the beginning of rock bottom, both for him and his mother. He at least had crawled his way to the top. His mother had never had the chance. He curled his hands into fists, fought against the blinding rage that always came when he thought of his mother. Of how needlessly she'd suffered.

He chose instead to focus on how far he'd come, how much power he held. Of course, even now, with all of his billions in the bank, he wouldn't be considered good enough for the hallowed Vanessa Pickett. He could have any woman he desired, and had spent many years doing exactly that with women whose names and faces he could no longer remember. But Vanessa was burned into his consciousness. A face he couldn't forget. Kisses he could still remember in explicit detail when far more recent, far more erotic events had faded from his memory.

All the events surrounding her were forever in his mind, etched so deeply, they would never fade. It had shown him that as long as he stayed where he was in life he could be made a victim—a victim of those with money and power, who could hire a group of men to beat up an eighteen-year-old boy, who could get a single mother evicted from her small apartment, get her thrown out onto the streets with no job and no hope of getting a job. He'd vowed never to be a victim again. Never allow anyone to have power over him.

The money he had earned—more than he had ever imagined when he'd started out. But the power, the absolute power that came with admittance into the highest echelons of society—that eluded him. He could not purchase it. It wasn't that simple.

To most on the outside, it would seem he had reached the top, but that was an illusion. What escaped him still was what Vanessa had, what her father had and what they would continue to have even if Pickett Industries went completely bankrupt. A blue bloodline. Family connections that could be traced back to America's first settlers. Not a lineage that began in a hovel in Argentina with an unwed mother and a father whose true identity was a mystery.

He clenched his teeth, fighting against the onslaught of memories brought on by Vanessa's appearance. "Pickett is fixable. And I know exactly what to do to fix it."

Her brown eyes narrowed into slits. "You do?"

"Of course I do. I've made my fortune by turning dying corporations around, you know that, I'm sure."

"Given the constant profiles *Forbes* does on you I'd have to be blind to miss it."

"I can fix the mess," he said, a new idea turning over in his head now, one that made his adrenaline spike and his pulse race.

"By appointing someone new."

"Or not."

"Feeling charitable all of the sudden? I don't buy that, not when you were just dangling the mythical sword over my head."

His heart rate quickened. Right in front of him was the key, dressed in a deceptively sexy silver gown, her dark brown hair swept up into a respectable bun. She was the final step, the way for him to make his entrance into the last part of society that remained locked to him. The way for him to grasp the ultimate power that continued to elude him.

Money was power, but connections combined with money would make his status absolute. It ate at him that there was still a place in society he was barred from. That there were still things outside his control. This was his chance to rise above all that.

And as an added bonus, he would get to see the look on Michael Pickett's face when he took possession of everything the man had always tried so hard to keep in his control. Pickett Industries *and* his only daughter. This was a way to exact revenge on the man who had made Lazaro and his mother unemployable within the circles they'd always worked, the man responsible for their nights on the street in the unforgiving Boston winter. The man responsible for his mother growing weaker and weaker until the strongest woman he had ever known had faded away.

He had watched his mother die in a homeless shelter, without possessions, without dignity.

He bit down hard, his teeth grinding together, the pressure satisfying, helping him keep control over the anger and adrenaline building inside him. He hadn't got where he was by letting opportunities pass him by. He took chances. He made snap decisions with a cool head. It was the secret to his success.

And Vanessa would be the key to his ultimate achievement.

A high-society bride would give him admittance into American aristocracy. He had considered it before, had already considered the advantage of marrying an old-money name to add weight to his own fortune, to improve his status. But every time he thought of marriage, every time he thought of finding a society princess, he couldn't stop himself from picturing Vanessa in her pink bikini. Couldn't erase the memory of stolen kisses in a guesthouse late at night.

Because of that, he'd never entertained the idea of marriage for very long at a time. But now…the idea of Vanessa as his high-society bride seemed too golden to let pass by. It was a chance to have all his needs fulfilled: his need to reach the top, his need for her.

Vanessa, soft and bare beneath him, over him. Touching him, kissing him. Satisfying him.

Desire, hot and destructive, rushed through him at the thought of the chance to have her, to be able finally to satisfy the lust he'd carried with him through every affair, that had plagued him every sleepless night. In that instant, the flood of lust drove out every other thought. Everything was reduced to its most basic principle.

See. Want. Have.

He wanted Vanessa. He had spent the past twelve years with a gnawing sense of unfulfilled desire for justice and for the woman who haunted his dreams.

And he would have her now.

"I'll help you, Vanessa," he said, keeping his eyes locked on hers, "on one condition."

She tilted her chin up, revealing the long, elegant line of her neck. Tender skin he could easily imagine kissing, tasting. "Name your price."

He took a step toward her, cupped her chin between his thumb and forefinger and was shocked by the bolt of electricity that arced between them. She still had power over his body. But judging by the faint color in her cheeks, the tremble in her lips, he had power too.

"Marriage."

CHAPTER TWO

"ARE you insane?" she hissed, looking over her shoulder, checking to see if they were drawing stares. If her father ever heard about her meeting tonight with Lazaro Marino he would very likely explode, just before taking back control of the company, tearing the contract to shreds and dismissing her as a complete and utter failure, both as CEO and his daughter.

"Not in the least," Lazaro said.

Vanessa took a step away from him, her heart thundering in her ears. "I'm serious, Lazaro. Did you by any chance suffer a head injury in the past twelve years? Because while you were never the most sophisticated man I've ever met, you seemed lucid then, at least."

"I'm perfectly lucid," he said dryly. "Don't pretend that you're a stranger to the concept of a marriage of convenience."

Of course she wasn't. There was a reason that every boyfriend she'd ever had had been introduced to her by her father. That there was usually a folder with the man's name stamped on it somewhere in her father's office. The man she ended up with had to be from the right family, with the right reputation. The right credentials.

But she'd never wanted that. A part of her, a part that she kept guarded, locked away so that no one else would ever see, was still that romantic sixteen-year-old girl who believed in love. Who wanted to be loved for who she was, not for her bank balance or for the shape of her body.

Of course, as far as her father was concerned, none of that mattered. Craig Freeman loomed in her future, the man her father had found worthy, the man with the right connections. That part of her life had been selected for her, as her job had been. As so many things in her life were.

Craig had been pinpointed as proper husband material before she'd been old enough to drive.

She'd managed to avoid marriage thanks to college and the demands of running Pickett. Before that, she had worked in most of the positions at Pickett so she could learn the ins and outs of everything, so she hadn't had time to get married. Or even to have a date.

Recently she hadn't had much time to do anything short of commuting to and from her office while taking antacids in hopes of easing the constant burn of stress in her chest.

"Of course I'm familiar with the concept, but that doesn't mean I have a desire to take part in one," she said crisply. That much was true. Marriage of any sort had never seemed like a real problem; it had always been safe in the gauzy future, not something she'd directly addressed. "And I really don't want to marry you." That part she added for good measure, and then wished she hadn't.

"Since when is any of this about want? Do you think I want to get married? To tie myself to one woman forever? Necessity. I've known for a long time that I needed to make a good marriage in order to move freely in all social circles. I hadn't considered you before, but now I see that you'll be perfect. Consider yourself a walking, talking invitation into high society."

Vanessa bit her tongue. "You're sure you didn't sustain a head injury, Lazaro?"

"Quite."

"Because I don't remember you being this much of a bastard either."

"Time changes people, Vanessa. As I'm sure you know. You aren't who you used to be either, are you?"

"No," she said.

Except maybe she was. Being so near Lazaro now made her feel things she'd thought she'd left behind long ago, things she only let herself dwell on when she was alone, in the privacy of her room, in a painfully large and empty bed. Then she let herself dream—about a man who could share not just her bed, but her life. Her love.

But as soon as dawn broke through the curtains, reality returned, and it only hit harder the minute she walked into her office each morning to confront a failing company and her family's heritage slipping through her fingertips because she couldn't figure out how to fix the mess Pickett Industries was in.

And then there was the marriage her father already had planned for her. A marriage to a man she hardly knew, a man she hadn't bothered to get to know, because she'd never been able to face the idea.

When she'd seen Lazaro for the first time, at sixteen, she'd discovered how badly she wanted love, and she'd let herself dream. A mistake. She'd fallen for him on sight, had thought he was special. Unique. But she knew the truth now. Lazaro wasn't unique. He wanted everything he could get. Money. Power. And if he had to use her to get it, he would.

His dark eyes were intent on hers, eyes that used to have a glimmer of humor in them. It was easy to imagine it there. Easy to imagine the boy he'd been. The inky black sky and the outline of the city faded and she was back there, in the summer, twelve years earlier.

* * *

"You aren't really supposed to talk to me." Vanessa looked over her shoulder to make sure her father wasn't watching. Just an instinctive check, because he was at the office, where he always was.

Lazaro smiled, teeth bright white against his bronze skin. Her heart started to beat faster. "Why is that?"

"Because I… Aren't you on the clock or something?"

He looked around the immaculate yard, then back at her, dark eyes locked on hers. It made her stomach tighten. Having him so close…she felt jittery, nervous. But she'd been watching him all summer, had been nurturing her crush on him until it had grown into something more. She lived for him to glance her way, for him to watch her while she lounged by the pool. She longed to see the interest in those beautiful eyes of his.

"I don't get paid hourly," he said, flashing her a grin that made her stomach do somersaults. "I'm done anyway."

"Oh…" she trailed off, all the words in her head jumbled.

"I'll stay until my mother's ready to leave for the day."

Vanessa suddenly felt too exposed in her bikini. She'd picked it partly to draw his attention, but now, with him standing so close, she felt acutely aware of how much skin was on display. She'd never really tried to draw attention to herself using her body, because she hadn't been ready for a man to take her up on the offer.

But Lazaro was different. He made her feel different.

They talked for the rest of the afternoon. About school, how different his inner-city public school was compared to her private all-girls school. But it turned out they liked the same foods, the same music, even though she had to hide hers from her father. She loved hearing how he talked about his mother, how proud he was of her. Vanessa told him how much she missed her mother.

They talked every day that week, sneaking around the

property, evading watchful eyes, and by the end of it, Vanessa was certain she was in love. She also knew that if her father ever found out, Lazaro and his mother wouldn't have jobs anymore and she would be grounded for the rest of her life.

Because while most of the world had modernized, Michael Pickett had not. He very much believed in a class system and in socializing only with those who shared your designated position. She wasn't naive enough to think that her father's heart would soften if she explained that she was really, truly in love with Lazaro.

She was already giving up so much in order to take on the responsibilities of Pickett Industries, already sacrificing so many dreams to major in business when she went to college and spend her life behind a desk, just as her father had done.

Surely that should count for something.

Yes, she and Lazaro had a gulf between them as far as money went. As far as prominence in society went, the gulf was even wider, impossible to bridge. But Vanessa didn't care. She couldn't care. When he looked at her, designer fashions, upscale parties and any feeling of being part of the elite faded completely. The world was reduced to her and Lazaro. There was nothing more.

And that was why risking serious consequences to see him was more than worth it.

It made her wonder what it would be like if it were only the two of them. If she had to leave it all behind for him... she would.

"Meet me tonight. Where no one can see," Lazaro said.

They were hidden in an alcove behind the guesthouse and it was doubtful that they could be seen, but there was always a risk. A bigger risk for him than for her, she knew.

"Okay." She didn't hesitate because she wanted more time with him, craved more time. She wanted to have him hold her hand. To kiss her. To tell her he loved her as she loved him. "Meet me here, at the guesthouse. I can get a key."

She spent the rest of the afternoon trying to decide what to wear, changing her clothes a hundred times. It felt like a first date. She was. Sort of. She'd never been on a date, had never kissed anyone. At her age, she felt like an oddity. Most of her friends at school had done a lot more than that.

But her father kept her on a tight leash, and boys were not something that was supposed to concern her at this stage of her life. Too bad for her father, since he couldn't control her thoughts, and boys had been among her biggest concerns for the past four years.

None of her crushes or interests mattered though, not really. There was a boy, a man really, six years her senior, that her father had his eye on for her—Craig Freeman. His family had all the right connections, the proper bloodline. And the thought of being married off to him someday made her feel like one of her father's broodmares.

She pushed the thought to one side. Craig was far in the future. He was on the West Coast building his name, and as far as she was concerned, having the entire expanse of the country between them was perfect.

And tonight, maybe she would just pretend he didn't exist. Maybe…maybe after tonight she would find the courage to tell her father that she didn't want Craig. At all. Ever.

She looked at the clock and then back at the full-length mirror. Her skirt was too short and her shirt was too tight. That's what her father would say. But she wasn't dressing for her father's approval.

Tonight, only Lazaro's approval mattered.

She left her bedroom light on and closed the door. Her father was at his country club and the odds of him coming home before midnight were slim. Still, she wasn't taking chances.

She slipped quietly through the house and out the door, across the lawn.

When she got down to the guesthouse, Lazaro was there, waiting for her. Relief and happiness flooded through her. "You came."

He smiled that wonderful, knee-weakening smile. "Of course."

She unlocked the door and led him inside. "We can't turn on any lights," she whispered. "Someone might see."

"That's fine." Lazaro took her hand, the shock of his skin against hers making her body jolt. "We don't need lights."

He tugged her gently to him and wrapped his arm around her waist, placed his other hand on the back of her head and tangled his fingers in her hair. She was glad she'd left it down.

He leaned in, his lips feather-light on hers. Everything around her stopped for a moment, time, her heart, everything, as he increased the pressure of his mouth on hers. She closed her eyes, just standing there, letting the sensation of being kissed by Lazaro wash over her.

When the tip of his tongue slid over her lower lip, her mouth parted in shock and he took advantage, stroking his tongue over hers. She wrapped her arms around his neck, boldness surging through her, a desire to make him feel the way she did, hold him captive to sensation, just as she was.

It was nothing like her friends had said. They said it was awkward. Bumping noses and teeth. She'd always heard that a lot of guys were sloppy kissers. But Lazaro was perfect. And there was nothing awkward about it.

And she was so glad she wasn't experiencing this moment with insipid, pale Craig Freeman. He looked as though he would probably be a sloppy kisser. She shoved the thought to one side, firmly planting her mind in the moment.

Lazaro took her hand in his, tugged it lightly as he took a step toward the hallway.

"What?" she asked, feeling dizzy, dazed, her body and soul focused on when he would kiss her again, caress her again.

"Looking for some place more comfortable."

She nodded and followed, her heart pounding in her throat; the only rooms back here were bedrooms, and she really didn't think she was ready for anything that might happen in a bedroom. But Lazaro was… He was different from anyone she'd ever known. She trusted him to go slow. To be what she needed.

He opened a door and looked inside, pushed it open and laced his fingers through hers again, drawing her in with him. She paused in the doorway, looking at the big bed. Her heart thundered hard—nerves, emotion, hormones threatening to wash her away in a powerful tide. He couldn't want to…they'd barely kissed.

He pulled her to him, his hand caressing her cheek. "Just kiss me," he whispered.

Yes. When she kissed him, everything else faded away. Just kissing.

He led her to the bed, his dark eyes serious on hers. She leaned in and kissed him again. He smelled clean. Not fussy and coated in cologne like the guys that went to the country club, but like soap and skin. Like Lazaro.

She'd never wanted anything, anyone, more in her life. She just wanted to stay with him forever, in the guesthouse, away from rules and propriety and all the things she was supposed to want. None of them mattered now. Only Lazaro mattered.

He sat on the bed and she sat with him, accepting a hungry kiss, his hands sliding over her back, down her waist, gripping her hips as he kissed her. Deeply. Passionately. Every thought fled her mind. Everything but how good it felt to have him touch her, kiss her, almost devour her as though she was the most decadent dessert he'd ever had.

She didn't even realize she was falling until she felt the

soft mattress beneath her back, and Lazaro's hard frame over her. She tangled her fingers in his thick dark hair, her thighs parting slightly to make room for him.

Her heart felt as though it was overflowing with emotion, with love. She had to tell him. Had to tell him how much she loved him. How she wanted him forever. No matter what her father thought, or what anyone said. The words hovered on her lips, but she couldn't find the courage to say them.

He knew though. He had to know. She wouldn't be here with him if she didn't love him.

He pushed her shirt up just enough to expose her stomach, the calloused skin of his fingertips pleasantly rough against her tender flesh. She arched into his touch and he took advantage, kissing her exposed neck.

The longing that overtook her was so big, beyond the physical, a deep emotional well that opened up inside her, desperate to be filled, so desperate for all of the attention that was being directed at her.

She was always lonely. Since Thomas had died the void in her life had been vast, her isolation in her own home devastating.

At least it had been until Lazaro. He brought the light back. He held the possibility of a future that wasn't filled with Pickett Industries.

When his hands moved higher, cupping her, she simply enjoyed his touch, tried to push all of the worries out of her mind and simply live in the moment.

He pulled away from her and stood. "What are you doing?" she asked.

"Condom," he said, his chest rising and falling with hard, labored breaths as he reached into his pocket.

A wave of shock rolled over her, making her ears buzz, her throat tight. "I… No," she said, scrambling to sit up. She'd just

had her first kiss, anything more was impossible to fathom.
"No."

She was torn then, torn because in so many ways she
wanted him. Wanted to take advantage of being alone with
him, of having all of his intensity focused on her. Part of her
wanted to make love with him. To take every step possible
to make him hers.

But she wasn't ready. She wanted love before there were
condoms involved. She needed the words. She just did.

And if anyone found out she'd had her first kiss and her
first time on the same night, in her father's guesthouse? She
cringed at the thought.

"What would people think?" The words tumbled out before she had a chance to turn them over.

His eyes darkened, his mouth pressing into a tight line.
A muscle jumped in his cheek. "I don't know, *querida*." The
Spanish endearment sounded like a curse. "They might not
think anything of it. I assumed you had arrangements with
all of the gardeners."

His words were like gunfire, shocking and devastating.
Harsh in the small, quiet space. "I…"

"You certainly aren't the only one of my clients' daughters
I've gotten into bed."

Insults, angry words, curses she'd never spoken out loud
before, all swirled in her head, but her throat was too tight
for her to speak. And in his eyes, she could see her pain mirrored, raw and achingly sad.

He just looked at her for a moment, and she wished she
had the courage to say something. But she just wanted to curl
in on herself and hold the hurt to her heart.

"I think we're done here then." He turned and walked out,
and she just sat and watched him go.

She wanted to go after him. To explain what she'd meant,

because she was certain her words had hurt him in some way. To scream at him for making her hurt.

You'll see him again tomorrow. You can fix it then.

Except she'd been wrong about that. He'd walked out and he'd never come back. All he'd wanted from her was sex. That had been her introduction to relationships. Not exactly sterling. It was a memory, an experience she couldn't free herself from.

And more often than not her mind chose to focus not on the fight, but on the way his mouth had felt moving over hers. The slide of his tongue, his hands on her skin.

Worse than that were the times when she thought about what she'd been willing to do for him. She'd been ready to leave everything behind—her father, Pickett Industries— for him. That had been a moment in time when her future had seemed fluid rather than set in stone, and sometimes she dreamed of what it would be like to have options. To have the unknown stretching before her in a good way, and not in a failing-company, heartburn-causing kind of way.

Her mind was wicked. And treacherous.

Tonight was the first time she'd seen Lazaro in person since he'd left her sitting on the bed in her father's guest-house, although she'd revisited that night a thousand times every time she saw a picture of him, heard him discussed at cocktail parties. The bad boy made good. She'd never been able to truly escape him. Though she'd tried.

She'd only tracked him down now because the ghost of make-out sessions past was trying to stage a hostile takeover of her business—her life. Otherwise, she never would have sought him out again. Ever.

"The way I see it, Vanessa, you have very little choice in the matter if you want Pickett to survive."

"No," she said, "I don't see marriage as a formal business transaction."

"Now, I find that hard to believe."

"Really?"

He nodded. "Are you saying your father has nothing to do with the man you'll marry?" He watched as the light in her dark eyes dimmed. "Are you saying you get to choose?"

She shook her head. "Not… It's complicated."

"Not really."

"I can't," Vanessa said, keeping her voice hard, commanding. The voice she used during board meetings and to men who assumed she couldn't handle being in charge.

"You're already promised to someone, aren't you? Someone with the appropriate bloodlines?" His lip curled into a sneer. "Waiting for one of those golden boys to bail you out?"

"You know my father, he doesn't leave loose ends. Of course there's someone in his plans." The admittance was strange because no one, herself included, had ever voiced it. But no one had ever had to say anything. It was understood. It was as ingrained in her as which fork to use for the salad.

"Do you love him?"

"No." She didn't love Craig Freeman, or even know him, by her own design. She'd taken pains to avoid him, in fact. That hadn't been too hard since he'd been across the country for the majority of their tentative arrangement. He seemed about as interested in the whole thing as she was.

And that was another reason she'd never broached the subject with her father.

"Then why do you have an issue with a business-oriented marriage where I'm concerned?"

Because Craig Freeman could be put off. He was unchallenging. He was a nonentity. In some ways, it had been easier knowing that he was in the not-too-distant future. It took the pressure off her finding Mr. Right when she hardly had enough time to put on lipstick in the morning. Craig didn't make her heart race or her body burn. Lazaro Marino did. And *he* would not be put off by anyone.

Vanessa sucked in a sharp breath. "Before this goes any further, I need to know what this is about."

"Why is it that I can't get business deals with your father's cronies? Why is it that their businesses languish, and yet they sit in their clubs sipping brandy and smoking cigars, ignoring the downfall, rather than pursuing help?"

"Because they're a bunch of stubborn old men who are set in their ways," she said. "Their business models are outdated, just as you've accused Pickett's of being."

"Perhaps. And also because I am not worthy in their eyes. They would rather watch their companies crumble than ask someone like me, with my dirty blood, for help."

"That's ridiculous," she said, even though she knew it was true. Those men would never stoop to taking a consultation from someone so far beneath them in station. That exclusivity was the source of their power, and they weren't about to let it go, no matter how modernized the rest of the world had become.

"It's not. We both know that."

"And you think marrying me will fix that for you?"

He chuckled. "I'm sure the son-in-law of Michael Pickett would be due some respect."

"If my father didn't disown me for marrying you instead of the golden boy he's selected for me," she said.

"Would he?"

She paused for a moment, honestly wondering if he would. She'd been ready to take the chance twelve years ago. More than ready to carve a new life for herself and Lazaro, to leave it all behind.

That dream had ended quickly. Maddeningly, it tantalized

her sometimes when she was in bed, on the edge between sleep and wakefulness. Stupid subconscious.

Finally, she shook her head. "No. He wouldn't. He has too much invested in me. And I own more stock than he does at this point. He can't vote me out of my position, which would mean that if he did disown me he would be separating himself from the company, and he won't do that."

"But if there is no company?" he asked.

If there was no company, her father would never speak to her again. Her life, everything she had worked for for so long, would be meaningless. She would have nothing but her big, empty town house—if she could even afford to keep it—with her big, empty bedroom and her big, empty bed. The thought made her sick, made her stomach physically cramp.

"It's not an option," she said. She refused to think about it. Refused to entertain the idea.

Her relationship with her father was complicated. It wasn't a happy, hugging sort of relationship, but he was all that she had, her only family. He was the one constant in her world. He had always cared for her, he had set her path in front of her and he had paid for her schooling to make sure his goals were met.

And she'd done all she could to earn his approval, done what she could to help fill the void Thomas had left behind. The Pickett heir—the real Pickett heir—hadn't lived to graduate from high school.

It was up to her now. It wasn't a responsibility she could simply shake off or ignore.

"And can you risk that, Vanessa?"

"No." She choked on the word.

"Then marry me."

"It's crazy, you know that, right?"

"More so than the arrangement you already have?"

"Yes," she fired back, brown eyes blazing.

Lazaro's gut tightened. Of course she would feel that way. He was beneath her. He had been a toy to her twelve years ago. Good enough to flirt with, to tease, but nothing more.

What would people think? The look of horror on her face, the incredulity in her voice, was crystal clear in his mind, as though she had spoken it only a moment ago, instead of what amounted to a lifetime ago.

He was the housekeeper's son, and she was the princess of the castle. Years later, now that he had billions to his name and a reputation as one of the world's savviest business minds, she still believed herself above him.

Even as the anger coursed through him, he wanted her. Wanted her with the same burning desire he'd had for her when they were teenagers. Yes, he wanted the vital connections marrying her would provide. But at the moment, more than anything, he wanted her body. He wanted to finish what he had started twelve years ago. He wanted Vanessa, naked, willing, in his bed, crying out his name. His and no other man's. He wanted to brand her as she had done to him with those kisses years ago.

Vanessa's lips on his, her delicate hands skimming over his skin—everything narrowed down to that. The broader goal was lost. There was nothing beyond lust. Simple, pure lust that had been with him since the first moment he'd seen her. A lust that had never released its hold on him. The need to satisfy it was suddenly driving, imperative.

He closed his hands into fists, took in a deep breath.

As much as he wanted that, he had to remember what his real goal was. There would be plenty of time to seduce Vanessa once they were married. It was about business now, and the rest would come later. Business, and dealing with Michael Pickett.

What sweet justice it would be, marrying Vanessa. Having her replace her hallowed last name with his.

How wonderful it would be to see Michael Pickett's face when he discovered his only daughter would be marrying the man he had had beaten in a back alley for daring to touch his beloved princess. For daring to sully her with his hands. A laborer's hands. An immigrant's hands.

Lazaro curled his fingers, forming fists.

The other man's fate—the fate of his much-loved business and that of his only child—was now Lazaro's to decide.

Just as his fate and his mother's fate, had once been Michael Pickett's to decide. And what a decision he'd made. He'd had them evicted. Had made sure they couldn't find work in Boston and that what little they'd had was lost to them.

Now the older man would know what it was like to feel desperate, to have to depend on the whims of someone else. What it was like to have his power stripped from him.

Men like him didn't deserve such absolute power.

"I'm offering you a very simple solution, Vanessa."

"Oh, yes, simple. In what world is marriage the simple solution?"

"In *this* world. Alliances are made by advantageous marriages, it happens every single day. You admitted it is already in your future."

"Nothing was finalized. I believe marriage should be about love."

She looked so sincere when she said it, brown eyes liquid in the dim light. What would Vanessa Pickett know about love? No more than he did.

"Romanticizing an institution has always seemed pointless to me."

Vanessa swallowed hard, her heart thundering, the pulse in her neck fluttering. "You don't seem the type to romanticize anything."

She knew that about him. Had known it the moment kissing had turned into more and he'd produced a condom rather than words of love. Ironic that her very first marriage proposal was from him, twelve years after she'd been hoping to hear it. Of course, there was still no mention of love.

She'd been a romantic then, with all of her heart and not just a piece of it. And she'd learned, at Lazaro's hands, that blind naïveté didn't protect you from cold reality.

And what she had now was cold reality at its finest. A dying business, one that was under her control, the very real danger of losing that control. Worse, of losing the entire company to bankruptcy along with any respect she'd managed to gain from her father. She would be the one to destroy a family legacy that had stood for one hundred years. She was so close to losing absolutely everything, having nothing but a cold, arranged marriage waiting for her when the dust settled.

She also had an out in the form of Lazaro Marino. A deal with the devil, and it would only cost her soul. Well, maybe that was an exaggeration. But from where she was standing, it must look a lot that way. A dark, handsome devil, sure, but the devil nonetheless. And it was truly an exchange of one marriage of convenience for another.

Of course, for better or for worse, the arrangement with Lazaro would never be cold.

No. Impossible. She looked at him, broad shoulders, thickly muscled chest, trim waist and hips. He had a body most women would pay money to get their hands on, and the face of a fallen angel. Perfectly handsome, but with that hint of danger provided by his slightly bent nose and dark stubble. Stubble that would feel rough against her hands, her cheek...

"It isn't as though we would marry immediately," he said, his deep voice breaking through her fantasy.

"We wouldn't?" A stupid response, as though she'd agreed to something when she hadn't done any such thing.

"No. It takes time to plan a wedding. Especially of the calibre I have in mind."

"Oh, you've thought about this?" For some reason that made her stomach tighten.

"Not in a specific sense. But there are certain things expected from a society wedding." His lips curved up into a smile. A smile that lacked humor and warmth. It made her shiver.

She'd never wanted a huge wedding. She'd seen that circus one too many times. Had been a part of it for family friends. Those weddings were impersonal, affairs for the guests and not for the couple, and she'd always found them disingenuous. Although, she was certain, the choice would have been taken from her when the time came with Craig. A big, three ring circus of a wedding, befitting the alliance between the Picketts and the Freemans. The thought made her slightly dizzy. She hadn't given a lot of thought to that eventual union, but all this wedding talk was forcing it to the forefront, making her face something she'd been dutifully ignoring for years.

It had been a foolish thing, keeping that corner of her heart reserved for romantic fantasy. There had never been a hope for that in her future. Never. Lazaro's appearance didn't alter that, it just altered the groom. Craig, with his pale, angelic looks, was after her for the connections she would provide, and Lazaro, dark and dangerous, wanted the same. Neither man offered her love. Lazaro, at least, would help her hold on to Pickett Industries.

"And what do you intend to do with me until the wedding?"

He smiled again, and this time it touched his eyes, lighting a spark in their depths. Heat. She knew the look. She'd been on the receiving end of it before. And it was no less devastating to her at twenty-eight than it had been to her at sixteen.

He extended his hand, his open palm cupping her cheek, and heat spread through her, making her knees feel shaky, her breasts heavy. How long had it been since she'd been so close to a man? And how long had it been since one had made her feel like this? The very few times she'd come into contact with Craig she hadn't felt even the slightest twinge of electricity.

"I'll spend that time seducing my future wife," he said, his voice husky, the remnants of his accent clinging to the syllables, making each word sound like a sensual caress.

She swallowed, her throat suddenly tight and dry as though it had been lined with sandpaper. He was talking about seduction. Sex. It took her right back to that moment, the moment when he'd made it clear that sex was on his agenda for the night, his hand in his pocket, reaching for a condom. She'd been tempted then too, but…she'd loved him then. Or something. She'd been sixteen and sixteen-year-old girls were given to the dramatic when it came to matters of the heart.

That romantic part of herself had always hoped against hope that the man she gave her body to would be a man who loved her desperately, a man she felt the same way about.

It wasn't that that made her want to hold back from Lazaro though. It was the fact that he seemed to command some sort of power over her body, that he could get her hot just by looking at her. He robbed her of all the steely control no other man had ever been able to crack.

That was scarier than anything. That was something she had to master because she was not allowing him to have that kind of hold over her. Not when he already had so much power.

"I'm not just going to jump into bed with you. I don't even know you."

"Sometimes that adds to the fun, Vanessa."

The way he said it, his rich, accented voice caressing the words, made her almost believe it. Made her wonder if love was overrated. "That's not how I see things, Lazaro," she said, her throat so constricted she could hardly force the words out.

"Relax. The courtship will be for the benefit of the media and my future clients. What better than a grand love story to keep everyone fascinated?"

"I don't know if any of my father's friends are old romantics."

"Perhaps not. But the more genuine it looks, the better. It's essential that it look real."

"I don't know..."

"What is it you don't know, Vanessa? Whether you want to embrace success or failure?"

"Why does it have to be marriage?" she asked. "Why can't..."

"Why can't I simply hand you the solution? Why can't I give you the knowledge and help that Pickett Industries cannot afford? Because that's what your father, your family would do for others?"

"That isn't..."

"Nothing in life is free, Vanessa. Nothing."

"I know that," she said, her voice fading. She did know it. She knew the cost of duty over desire better than he realized. Pickett Industries wasn't her dream; Craig Freeman had never been her dream. But running the company, marrying Craig, were what she was supposed to do. This was her duty to her father, to Thomas's memory. And duty was something she'd embraced rather than turning away from. It had taken strength to do that, to deny whatever else she might want in order to preserve her father's respect for her. In order to preserve the Pickett family legacy.

"These are my terms, you can take them or leave them."

Vanessa felt as though the world had just rocked beneath her feet. But it hadn't; the paper lanterns above her head were still steady, the people around them were still talking,

unaware that her life was crumbling around her, that everything she had always believed about herself lay in ashes before her.

She'd never thought she would stoop so low. Had never
thought she would be the one willing to do whatever it took
for the sake of money and power. And maybe if it were only
money and power she wouldn't. Regardless of what Lazaro
said, this did seem different from the friendly, family-made
arrangement she had with Craig. This seemed mercenary. It
seemed... It felt in some ways that she was selling herself.
Her body.

But this was her reputation. It was all she had worked for.
It was her relationship with the only family she had. If she
didn't have that, she would have nothing. Breaking the unof-
ficial engagement with Craig was one thing, losing Pickett,
letting it fall into someone else's hands...that her father would
never forgive her for. And she would never forgive herself.

She couldn't face that. And it was time to step up. To
do what she'd been doing all her life—make the choice that
would best benefit her family legacy and all of the employees who depended on her family for their paychecks.

"I'll take them." Her words sounded flat and harsh in the
silent night air.

"A very wise choice, Vanessa." Lazaro's expression didn't
change, his eyes remained flat and dark, latent heat smoldering there, his square jaw still set firmly. But she could feel
a change in him, a subtle shift in the energy radiating from
him. It resonated in her, caused a response she couldn't ignore or deny.

She looked at the cool, hard man standing in front of her.
To him, this was business. Another way for him to climb to
the top. She just had to see it the same way. She couldn't afford to involve her heart.

"I didn't have much of a choice, did I?" she asked.

"Not one that had a better outcome. And you're a smart woman. You know that the end result is all that matters."

She wanted to be that woman. She tried to be that woman. Because that was the woman who was going to pull Pickett out of the red.

"Pickett Industries is all that matters," she said slowly, feeling the virtual shackles tightening on her wrists even as she spoke the words.

CHAPTER THREE

Surreal didn't even begin to describe it. Waking up and realizing she had consented to marry Lazaro Marino the night before was surreal on an epic scale worthy of Salvador Dali. Given the state of things, she wouldn't have been shocked to see her clock melt off the wall.

But, as surreal as it was, it was her new reality. Nonetheless she couldn't make it feel real. She felt as if she was in a fog that not even driving to work through Boston's harrowing traffic could shake her out of. And when she sat down at her desk it didn't get any better.

It was early, the sun rising pink against the skyline of the city. Vanessa picked up her smartphone and snapped a picture. It was muted, nothing like it would have been if it had been done with an actual camera, something she'd never bothered to buy for herself. It wasn't that she couldn't afford one, but she didn't have time to indulge in any hobby that didn't directly benefit her company.

She would have even less time as CEO of Pickett Industries and fiancée to Lazaro Marino. She looked at her left hand. It was bare, no engagement ring. But there would be one, she had no doubt about that. Lazaro was a man of details and a detail like that wouldn't be overlooked.

She leaned forward and rested her forehead on the cool wood of her desk. How had she gotten so deep into a life that she didn't want? She closed her eyes and took in a deep breath, trying to halt the tears that were starting to form.

She'd made her choice. Long before Lazaro had walked back into her life, she'd made her choice to do what she had to do to keep Pickett Industries in the family. She'd gone to college and majored in business so she could see that that happened, and that she did the best job she could. She'd chosen to put everything personal on hold in order to keep the business afloat.

It was just a part of her duty to Pickett. It felt like more though.

A strange bubble of exhilaration filled her chest because suddenly her future was different. The man standing at the altar in her mind was no longer Craig Freeman; it was the one man who had inspired a kind of reckless abandon in her. The one man who'd made her want to break the rules.

By marrying him, she was both toeing the line and rebelling against it.

That was liberating in some ways, terrifying in others. And what she really wanted to do—hide under her desk until the storm blew over—was impossible because she had to keep it together. She was the CEO of Pickett. She couldn't question her decisions, and she couldn't hide from the hard stuff.

The choice was made. There was no going back. She was committed.

"And possibly in need of being committed, since you're clearly certifiable," she mumbled into the emptiness of her office.

There was the small matter of telling her father that she would not be following his "advice" and pursuing a marriage with Craig. And that Lazaro was the one she was choosing instead. His wrath would be monumental. But she was between a serious rock and a hard place, and the broken marriage agreement, such as it was, would be much more forgivable than the loss of the family legacy.

A sharp knock on her office door had her lifting her head quickly, smoothing her hair. "Yes?"

The door swung open and her heart dropped into her stomach. Whether it had been twelve years or twelve hours, Lazaro still had all the power to make her body hot and achy, to make her lips tingle with the desire to feel his kiss.

"Good morning," he said, coming in without waiting for her permission. She doubted he ever waited for permission to do anything.

"Not especially. What brings you here?"

"I couldn't stay away from my beautiful fiancée," he said, his blinding smile making her stomach curl tightly.

Her stupid, traitorous heart leapt back into her chest and started thundering madly, despite the dry humor in his tone. She cleared her throat. "Right. Why are you here?"

"Because there are details we need to work out."

"Right. Details," she said, her voice hollow.

"There will be a prenup."

"I would hope so," she said, fighting to keep her tone neutral while nerves tightened her throat.

She didn't know if she could go through with it. Marry him. Live with him. Sleep with him. Let her whole life get tangled up in Lazaro.

Speak now, or forever hold your peace.

She looked at him, at the hardened line of his jaw, the glint of steel in his dark eyes. It was too late. If she went back now, he would take everything from her. Everything that made her Vanessa Pickett.

The words stuck in her tightened throat.

"I'm not counting on a lifetime of wedded bliss," he said, his voice dry.

"You aren't?"

"Hardly. But what I am expecting is that you will stand beside me with all the duty and conviction of a politician's wife."

"What exactly does that mean?" she asked, feeling dizzy all of a sudden, fighting to convey only cool composure.

"During a political scandal, no matter how vile, the politician's wife always stands beside her husband because it is about more than marriage. It is her job. This marriage will be your job."

"Planning on creating a vile scandal, are you?" She treated him to her deadliest glare. He seemed entirely unaffected.

"Not in the least. But my point is that no matter what, your commitment to our union must outweigh the circumstances. If at some point we are leading separate lives it is of no concern to me, so long as appearances show a united couple."

She'd been wrong about him being the friendlier option to her arrangement with Craig. As little as marriage with Craig had been truly discussed, she'd assumed he would at least try to be a husband to her. Lazaro wasn't promising that. Not even close.

"Does that mean that even if you cheat on me I have to stay with you?"

"As I will stay with you," he said, his voice hard. "The union, the legal marriage, is what I need. I cannot project thirty years into the future, but I will ensure that you are still with me."

Vanessa was having a hard time breathing. It was as though he'd turned over her solid wood desk and placed it on her chest. Thirty years. This wasn't a temporary arrangement. He was talking about the rest of her life. Shackled to this man.

She tried to imagine turning away again. Imagined telling him the deal was off, and he could take his shares and the entirety of Pickett Industries to hell with him for all she cared.

But she couldn't. The words wouldn't come. They wouldn't even form in her brain in a cohesive manner. The idea of Lazaro losing his hold on her didn't open up a wide arena of possibilities for her life, rather, it showed just how narrow her scope of options truly was. Without Lazaro, the company crumbled. Without the company she had no job, no relationship with her father.

She'd promised her father, the week that Thomas died, that she wouldn't fail him, and she'd set out to make sure she didn't from that day on. She'd dropped out of the photography club she'd been in at school, started doing some basic business courses instead. Done whatever she could to ensure she didn't let her father down.

In her mind, she was a Pickett. She was a loyal daughter. She was the CEO of Pickett Industries. Without that…she didn't know who she was beyond that. And without Lazaro's help, she wouldn't be any of those things. Of course, it was his interference that forced her to choose. But without him, there might not be any choice at all other than to watch Pickett slowly sink beneath the waves of debt, another casualty of a shifting business landscape.

And while this might not have been her first choice for how her life would end up, it was the right thing. At least this way, she would keep the business going. She would have children who would eventually take over.

Her stomach cramped at the thought. Yes, she'd planned on having children someday, but if she said yes they would be Lazaro's children. The room suddenly seemed much too small, Lazaro's presence in it far too big.

Another thought, small and insidious, reminded her of that moment of pure exhilaration when she'd realized that she had changed her future. That she had diverged from the path so carefully laid out for her.

If she said no now, it was back to that path. Everything would stay the same. The thought was suffocating.

She shook her head. "I don't want that."

"What is it you don't want?"

"You have to be faithful to me, Lazaro," she said, her throat tight. The entire conversation made her body feel hot, restless and edgy. She knew that she would be sleeping with Lazaro, and just the thought made her feel charged with adrenaline.

But the sex would be a purely physical act, with legal paperwork to make it all legitimate. There would be no feelings. No love. She didn't even have to ask him about that. The hardness in his dark eyes answered that question.

Fair enough, since she couldn't imagine falling in love with the cold man standing before her. It was shocking enough that her body seemed to respond to him. But she didn't want to share him either. There were a host of reasons why that thought didn't sit well with her, her health being foremost among them. Another being pure, possessive jealousy. But what woman would want to share her husband? None. Love or not.

"You have to give me that at least," she said. "If we have children…I assume you want children?"

"I need them."

He was talking in terms of producing heirs, and in that sense, she needed them too. It felt wrong to think of them that way, when it never had before. She'd always been confident that she would love her children, so it had never mattered if that was part of the incentive for marriage. But now, knowing Lazaro felt the same way made her see just how cold it was. Made her worry that he wouldn't ever see the children as anything more than vessels for his legacy.

Like your father?

She shook the thought off and continued, "If we have children, I think they need to know they can aspire for better than a marriage filled with lies and infidelity."

"I will honor the vows I speak," he said, clenching his jaw tightly.

"Good. Then I'll honor mine. And even if we're a miserable, distant, sexless couple, I will stay with you."

"Inspiring."

"Why should it be?" she asked. "This is a cold, mercenary agreement. I'm not pretending it's anything other than that. I don't want or expect you to fall in love with me, but respect would be nice. I consider knowing that the person you're sleeping with isn't out sleeping with other people to be a great sign of respect."

"Then you will be faithful to me," he said, his voice hard.

"I said I would be."

"And you will not deny me when I come to your bed."

Vanessa put her hand on her stomach, trying to calm the butterflies that were staging a riot inside of her. "After the wedding."

He nodded once, his eyes trained on her face. "After the wedding."

"My father isn't going to like this. I have to… Well, there's the arrangement I mentioned. And his family will be—"

"You are *engaged* to this other man?"

She held up her ringless left hand. "No. But there was an understanding."

"Your father will be grateful to you if he finds out the circumstances surrounding the union."

"No."

"You don't want him to know?"

She shook her head. "No. I can't…I don't want him to know how far things have fallen…how…how bad things have gotten."

"He will have to know what I'm bringing into the union,"

Lazaro said, dark eyes glittering. "I want him to know that I intend to revamp Pickett. I want him to know that I am saving it. That I've done what he could not. If you want to take credit for meeting me while pursuing my help, it is of no concern to me. But I want him to know that I was the one to pull this dying, outdated company into a new life in the modern era." His voice was hard, uncompromising. He knew what it would do to her father to have to accept help, let alone to have to accept help from someone he believed to be beneath him, and Lazaro was relishing it.

Vanessa had never been able to believe what her father said about some people being better than others thanks to their bloodlines. She'd seen too many cruel, horrible people in her social class. People who wasted their money and used those around them with no thought to anyone but themselves. Believing that those people were somehow better than the rest of humanity was depressing.

And when she'd been sixteen, her emotions had been held captive by a boy her father considered to be lower than them. A boy who had grown into the man standing before her.

Looking at him, she felt her chest get tight, pride swelling within her. It shocked her. But she was, she realized, proud of what Lazaro had become, professionally at least.

"Showing you have the real power?" she asked softly.

"Money *is* the real power, Vanessa. Money is how I got into this position, how I managed to purchase Pickett's shares."

"Then why do you care about the rest of it? Why do you need me at all?"

He raised a dark eyebrow. "Because I can have you."

Her stomach tightened. "The proof of how far you've come?" she asked, voice dry.

"Perhaps. But it has very little to do with anyone else's perception. I want every door open to me. I have earned it. Money, I have—I want the social power as well."

Lazaro's blood burned in his veins, adrenaline spiking through him. He wanted everything. To be at the top of absolutely everything. To sit as a social equal with the man who had had him beaten for daring to touch his precious daughter.

And to make Vanessa his. To finally to satisfy his desire for her.

"The old-money society, the American aristocracy, it's as outdated as your father's business model," he said.

"And you'll tear down centuries of it all by yourself, Lazaro?"

"I don't want to tear it down," he said, his voice rough, his accent taking over his words. "I want in."

She looked away, turning her focus out her office window and onto the Boston skyline. "And it frustrates you that you can't do it without help."

Lazaro bit down hard, a muscle in his jaw jumping. "None of this is done out of necessity, Vanessa. It is a bonus. You wouldn't know about the necessities in life, not when your biggest concern is staying employed in a multi-million-dollar position you're not qualified to do. You could walk away and there would be no great tragedy to either of us."

She just sat, frozen behind her desk, dark eyes wide, her mouth pressed into a firm line. She wouldn't walk away. She was too married to the tradition, to the lineage of her family, just as her father had been.

What will people think?

He wondered if she'd had a share in his broken nose if, after refusing him, she had told her father all about how the low-class housekeeper's son had made an attempt to touch her with his filthy, laborer's hands.

He wondered if Vanessa shared culpability for putting his mother and him out on the streets.

That had been the worst part about all of it. As he'd spat blood out onto the grimy pavement in the alley after being beaten by Michael Pickett's men, after he'd been warned never to set foot on the Pickett estate again, been warned that if he so much as looked at Vanessa again, the consequences might be fatal, the very worst part had been wondering if Vanessa had been complicit in it. If she might have wanted her father to make sure she was rid of him.

His mother had lost her job. He'd lost his job. They'd lost their home and his mother had paid the price with her health. Ultimately with her life.

But now he knew that whatever part Vanessa had played in what had happened, she had never intended it. She was thoughtless, but she wasn't evil.

That moment, when he'd been lying in the alley, had been the lowest of his life. But it had been then, jobless, broken and bleeding, that he had vowed to ensure no one else ever held power over him like that again. He would never allow anyone but himself to hold his fate in his hands.

That goal had consumed him, had propelled him from the gutter to the boardroom, had made him millions.

That Vanessa would be the key to unlock the final door, to allow him into the last segment of society where he was still unwelcome, was poetic justice.

He didn't hate her. He had no desire to hurt her or exact revenge on her. But he no longer cared for her. His body still ached for her, that was all.

Michael Pickett, on the other hand, deserved hell on earth and in the hereafter. Taking Vanessa, making her his own, wrenching her from her father's control…the satisfaction in that was endless. The man had been willing to commit murder if necessary to keep Lazaro away from his daughter, and now there would be nothing he could do to prevent him from claiming Vanessa.

"You know I can't walk away. You might not see it as a necessity, Lazaro. But this is my whole life." She met his gaze, her dark eyes glittering. "And I don't think you'll walk away either. You need me, too."

"Do I?"

"Yes, you do."

His gut burned. "You or any other society princess."

"We both know this is about more than that."

Why bother to deny it? "True. It is rather satisfying, the idea of marrying into the family whose floors my mother wasn't good enough to clean."

"What do you mean by that?" she asked, well-groomed eyebrows drawn together.

"I mean, your father fired my mother. We ended up on the streets. So yes, I suppose there is something especially satisfying about it being you."

There was no triumph in her eyes, only shock, sadness. For him? For his mother? It was far too late for that.

"I didn't know."

"Did you think we went on an extended holiday?"

"I didn't know," she repeated, her voice low.

He shrugged. "We'll start with dating, of course."

"What?"

"We need to be seen together, prior to the actual engagement."

Vanessa tried to ignore the knot in her stomach. She didn't know his mother had been fired. She wondered if that had been when he'd disappeared. If that was why he'd never come back after their disastrous almost night together.

She didn't want to ask. Didn't want to let him know she still thought about it. That it still mattered.

She cleared her throat. "And you want us to…date?"

"Of course. I intend to seduce my fiancée with all of the skill that I possess."

He took her hand in his and bent over it, pressing firm, hot lips to her skin. The gesture was light, gentlemanly even. Not even a little bit erotic. At least it shouldn't have been. But it was. It pushed all of her thoughts and concerns right out of her head and caused a riot of sensation through her system, made her entire body weak and energized at the same time. Made her breasts feel heavy as a pulse started to beat at the apex of her thighs.

She hadn't felt this way, not with this level of intensity, since the last time Lazaro had taken her in his arms when she'd been a completely inexperienced sixteen-year-old. And she hated that she still responded this way to him now. He was the man who was holding her future hostage and that she would melt under his touch with absolutely no resistance was appalling.

She pulled her hand back and pressed her palm to her chest, feeling her heart rage against her breastbone. "No seduction required," she said tightly. "You can seduce the media, I don't really care, but not me. I'll do my 'wifely duty' once we're married, but until then, you can keep your lips to yourself."

He tightened his jaw, his eyes dark, glittering. Angry. "Don't worry, princess, I won't defile you in any way."

A stab of regret hit her. For a moment, she wondered if she'd hurt him. But the moment passed quickly. Lazaro Marino didn't do feelings. And the last time she'd turned down his advances he'd walked out of her life. All he saw her as was a body. Well, now he saw her as more than that. A body and a stepping stone on his way to the top.

It wouldn't hurt him to wait.

"One thing you need to know, Vanessa. With me, sex will never feel like duty. I guarantee it." His eyes were hot on her, making her body temperature rise along with her heart rate. His words were an invitation to sin a saint could hardly resist.

Sign me up for sainthood then, because I'm not going there.

She would do what she had to do. She would make this

deal work for both of them, but she wasn't going to fall under
his spell. She'd done it once, and she had no intention of ever
succumbing to his wicked, deceptive charms again.

"Anything else?" she asked stiffly.

"You and I have a date tomorrow night."

CHAPTER FOUR

"Of course you picked Chev's," Vanessa murmured as Lazaro helped her from the limo.

She wasn't happy about it, that was clear. It was written all over that beautiful face of hers, her dark eyes glittering with barely suppressed anger.

"Of course," he said, drawing her to him, wrapping his arm around her slender waist.

It was a cool evening, the cobblestone sidewalk wet from rain that had fallen earlier. But Vanessa's arms were bare, her legs barely covered by the sheer veil of her nylons, killer black heels added to the look, making his mind spin with fantasies that couldn't possibly be legal at this sort of establishment.

Everything about her look was designed to entice. To torment. The formfitting, silken dress she was wearing acted as a flimsy barrier between his hands and her soft, smooth skin. He knew it was soft and smooth. He remembered, in explicit detail, how she had felt beneath his fingertips.

He slid his hand around to her lower back, the deep blue fabric catching on some of the rough patches on his hand, still calloused from so many years of labor. For a moment, his world reduced to Vanessa, to the tease she presented. It would be so easy to tear the gown from her body so that he could touch her, could see just what it would be like to feel her bare skin beneath the palm of his hand.

"This is going to get back to my father in a couple of hours. If it even takes that long."

He felt her tense, the idea of her father seeing them together clearly not something she wanted to think about.

"He won't like to hear about it?"

She shot him a sideways glance. "What do you think?"

He could imagine what Vanessa's father would think. Vividly. Almost like a blow to his face. "He'll learn to deal with it."

"I doubt it."

"Easier to handle than having you deposed as head of Pickett. Or having to file for bankruptcy."

"Possibly," she said, teeth gritted.

Lazaro didn't wait for the host. He opened the door for Vanessa and ushered her into the small, intimate dining room.

"Your usual table, Mr. Marino?" The host approached them and gestured toward the back of the restaurant.

"We'll sit somewhere up front," Lazaro said.

The other man nodded. "Excellent, come with me."

Vanessa turned and gave Lazaro a look that could have frozen fire.

He leaned in, allowing a moment, just a moment, to enjoy her scent. Light. Feminine. The same as it had been twelve years ago. He moved his lips near her ear, brushing her thick, glossy hair back. "The better for us to be seen, my dear," he whispered.

He felt a shudder go through her body. Attraction. Need. The kind that lived so strong in him. She wanted him. Good to know. He didn't want a martyr in his bed. He wanted her hot, begging for him.

"Great," she said, acid corroding the word.

She still didn't want to be seen with him. She was still worried about what people would think. Rage poured into the well of lust that had opened up in him, mixing, mingling, each making the other more potent.

He bypassed the host again and pulled the velvet chair out for Vanessa. She sat, her body held stiffly, her face stony.

Lazaro turned to the host. "Bring whatever you think is best."

"Of course, Mr. Marino."

Lazaro took his seat across from Vanessa. Her facial expression hadn't changed, her bright pink lips set into a firm line, her white-tipped fingernails drumming on the table. He put his hand over hers and halted the motion, curling his fingers around hers.

"You could at least try to look like you're enjoying yourself. Hell, you could actually enjoy yourself, I promise not to tell."

The corner of her mouth twitched. "Sorry if I'm not finding this whole sudden forced-marriage thing all that amusing."

"You use the word *force,* Vanessa, and yet I am not forcing you into anything. There is no way for me to do so. You made the choice, you agreed to it."

"Strong-arm tactics were involved," she said, raising a glass of red wine to her lips.

"Maybe. But you could walk away."

"I can't," she said, balling her hand into a fist beneath his before pulling it back and setting it in her lap.

"Status is so important to you?"

"What about you? That's why you're marrying me."

It was much harder to remember the logical reason behind the union when she was so close to him. Much easier to remember the visceral, base reasons for it. Revenge. Lust.

"Essentially," he said. "But I'm not acting like a victim. I need something, you can help me with it. It's the same for you. So we can use each other, go forward, obtain our goals.

If you want to drag yourself around like a martyr for a few months that's your prerogative."

"That's… I'm not doing that."

"You are. You made the choice."

"So own it?"

He shrugged. "Or make a new choice. Walk away now, Vanessa. I'm not going to force you to stay."

Vanessa met Lazaro's eyes, forced herself not to look away. He was right. It was so easy to blame him. To make all of this his fault somehow. And, well, him buying up all the stocks *was* his fault, but the position she was in wasn't. And agreeing to the marriage had been her choice.

She swallowed, uncomfortable with the revelation. It was more palatable to have it be Lazaro's fault and his alone. To feel as though she'd been forced into it all. It was harder to accept that she'd agreed to it because she couldn't take the thought of failing.

She forced a smile. "You're right."

"It didn't even choke you to say it," he said, his voice laced with dark humor.

"I may not say it again," she said. "But in this instance, you are. I made the choice. I'm not walking away."

She'd chosen this path a long time ago, and while this thing with Lazaro was a diversion, the road would end in the same place. She wasn't turning back now just because things had gotten harder. Picketts didn't quit. She didn't quit. She would see it through.

A server came to the table and set a plate in front of each of them. A whitefish fillet and spring vegetables. Very elegant and perfectly cooked. Exactly what she needed to take her focus off Lazaro for a few moments. But not even a divine lemon sauce could keep her from being aware of him. He was just so very there. So present. Close. And he made her tremble inside. Made her remember what it was like to be kissed with the kind of passion normally reserved for books rather than real life.

She set her fork down and put her hands in her lap.

"Now what?" she asked, looking around the restaurant.

She saw Claire Morgan in the corner, eyeing them both with interest. Claire was a major gossip, had been in high school and still was. And Vanessa was willing to bet that she was holding her phone beneath the table frantically texting people to find out if they knew why Vanessa Pickett was at a restaurant with famed billionaire Lazaro Marino.

"Now we wait for Claire to spread the word?" Vanessa asked, looking back at Lazaro.

Lazaro shrugged. "Her, or anyone else interested in why the two of us might be together. They'll wonder what we're saying." He leaned in slightly and Vanessa fought the urge to jump back, away from him, away from the danger he presented.

He was appealing. Much too appealing. He made her thoughts tangle, and she didn't want him to have that kind of power. If she was going to follow through and marry him, she was going to do it on her terms. That meant not allowing him to reduce her to a mass of quivering female longing just by looking at her.

"Your friend over there is watching us." He looked in Claire's direction. "And there's a table of women in the back corner that have been watching us since we came in."

Probably watching Lazaro, anyway. He was the kind of man that a woman really had to stop and admire. He was everything a man should be. Strong, exuding confidence and a kind of masculine grace. He was also drop-dead sexy, and that certainly didn't hurt his cause.

"They're probably creating our conversation for us," he continued, his voice husky, inviting. It made her want to lean in toward him. To draw closer. "Probably imagining me telling you how beautiful you look. That your lips look far more edible than any dessert they might have here. That your dress, as beautiful as it is, is a crime because it covers up all of your beautiful skin. That I want to spend an hour removing it, teasing you, teasing myself."

Vanessa was held in thrall by his words, her heart pounding in her head. He reached across the table and brushed his hand over her cheek, his thumb skimming her bottom lip. Her lips suddenly felt dry and she slicked her tongue over them quickly. She could taste him. The slight, lingering flavor of him. Just a tease. Enough to make her wish it were more.

"They probably think I'm telling you that I want to take you to my bed and spend hours kissing and tasting every inch of your beautiful body." He leaned back again, a wicked smile spreading over his face. "They have vivid imaginations."

Vanessa blinked. "Oh." She cleared her throat. "They're thinking all of that, huh?" Her face was burning-hot, and she was sure her cheeks were bright pink, a perk of having pale skin.

My kingdom for a little sexual sophistication.

"Probably texting it too."

Vanessa grimaced and picked her fork up again. "I sort of thought as much."

"And by the end of the night it will be common knowledge that you and I are seeing each other."

"At least professionally," she said stiffly. Anything to try and bring back some of her sanity. Because Lazaro Marino had the maddening ability to melt her defenses and she really had to…unmelt them.

"I doubt anyone here thinks this is a professional meeting."

"Why is that?"

"Because you do not look at me the way a woman looks

at an associate. At least I hope you don't look at your associates this way."

"What way?"

A small smile curved his lips. "Did you enjoy dinner?"

"The food, yes." She was almost grateful he didn't answer the question. Because in her head she was doing a really good job of disguising her recurring attraction for him. In reality, she probably wasn't.

She'd rather not have her bubble burst. Her pride had taken enough kicks in the shins in the past couple of days.

"Dessert?" he asked.

That word made a series of erotic images flash through her mind—images of him, his mouth, his hands on her body. Images of the kind of dessert she could only imagine. Heat flooded her face again, making her scalp prickle.

"No, thank you," she said, her throat tight.

The server stopped by the table again, dropping off the check. Lazaro handed the man cash, hardly blinking at the triple-digit cost of the meal. Vanessa normally wouldn't have given it a thought either, but being with Lazaro made her conscious of the cost. There was a time when he hadn't had anything. A time when the cost of this meal would have exceeded his weekly income.

Time certainly did change things.

Lazaro stood from the table, and she kept her focus on a spot of sauce on her plate. Anything to keep from looking at him again. She wanted to, though. Another visual tour of Lazaro was very high on her body's to-do list. But sensible Vanessa wasn't going to indulge in that, because she really didn't want him to know that he held such strong appeal for her. It was a matter of pride if nothing else.

A flash of movement pulled her focus away from the plate just in time for her to see Lazaro's very nice-looking hands drop a very generous tip onto the table. She looked up then.

"That's a nice tip."

He shrugged and extended his hand to her. She looked at Claire, who was pretending to pay attention to her date, but who had one eye on them, then accepted his offered hand as she stood.

"Waiting tables is a thankless job," Lazaro said. "I like to add a thank-you."

"Oh." She dropped her hand to her side and flexed her fingers, trying to erase the impression of his touch.

Lazaro didn't really seem like a generous tipper. He didn't seem generous at all. He'd smashed his way back into her life with all the destructive power of a tornado, and that, combined with his callous treatment of her all those years ago, the insults he'd hurled at her, made it hard for her to attach humanity to him.

He leaned in, his dark eyes glittering. "I've been there, Vanessa. Name the grunt job and I've had it. I escaped it. A lot of people in this position never will. They'll work hard forever just to barely pay the bills. I haven't forgotten what that feels like."

"I…I hadn't thought of it like that." Vanessa had never known what it was like to worry about basic necessities. She'd never even had to worry about the frills in life. A new car at sixteen, vacations to exotic places, a luxury town house as a gift for her eighteenth birthday.

Even now, with Pickett Industries facing bankruptcy, her own position in life wasn't jeopardized in that way. She wouldn't have to worry about being homeless, keeping her car. She'd never had that worry.

Lazaro had.

"Of course you hadn't," he said, his tone dismissive.

She put her hand on his forearm and was shocked by the flash of heat that raced through her. She jerked her hand away. "What does that mean?"

"It means I wouldn't have expected you to have such a far-reaching thought."

"Are you calling me a snob?"

"Do you believe you aren't one, Vanessa?"

The chill in his tone shocked her. The condemnation and anger. "I'm not."

"Because you write checks to charities?"

"No, because…I'm not." She'd never bought into the idea that money or status added to someone's worth, but she did have to admit to herself that she didn't often think too far out of the scope of her own reality either.

She hadn't looked down on Lazaro for being poor. For doing maintenance on the estate to earn money. But neither had she imagined him working toward other things, being unsatisfied, having financial needs that weren't really met by his position. It seemed silly now. Shortsighted.

Lazaro grasped her chin between his thumb and forefinger and tilted her face up, forcing her to meet his gaze. "They're waiting for me to kiss you now," he said, his tone soft again.

"Who?" she asked, her heart dropping into her stomach.

"Our audience."

She licked her lips, the breath shuddering from her body. Her stomach tightened in anticipation.

She swallowed. "Are you going to?"

He dipped his head slightly and her heart felt as though it was going into free fall. "No."

He put his arm around her waist and drew her near to his body, his palm warm and enticing on her waist, his fingers stroking her gently.

"Why not?" she asked. "I mean…we're putting on a… show."

"I'm not going to kiss you, because this is more than just a date." He raised his hand and brushed her hair behind her ear, his eyes locked with hers.

She wanted to laugh, because really, it wasn't a date at all. Parts of her seemed to be forgetting that, her knees certainly had. They were weak now, trembling a little bit. But just because her body seemed to have forgotten didn't mean her mind had.

This wasn't a date. They barely knew each other. She had the sense that Lazaro didn't like her very much, and considering all he'd done to her in the past few weeks, she really shouldn't like him either.

"I'm not going to kiss you because you're my future wife. And I'm showing my respect for you. Discretion," he said softly.

Oh yes, discretion was law as far as her father was concerned. And anyone present who knew her would know that.

"G-good," she said, allowing him to lead her out of the restaurant and into the cool night air. His limousine was waiting for them, idling at the curb.

He opened the door for her and helped her inside, his manners those of a perfect gentleman, the earlier tension absent now.

Vanessa leaned her head back on the seat.

It wasn't a date. They didn't have a real relationship. But they were going to get married. And for one, crazy moment she'd really wished that he was going to kiss her.

Of course, the truth was that even though she'd only seen him in pictures, part of her had been longing to be kissed by Lazaro for twelve long years.

But he held so much power over her. Her professional life, the life of her family's legacy was in his hands. She wasn't going to give him power over her body too. When they were married, she would deal with it.

But for now she had to keep her control. She couldn't forget that this relationship was as mercenary as they came.

And when Lazaro touched her it was too easy to forget. She could never let herself forget.

CHAPTER FIVE

"I HOPE you aren't busy today."

Vanessa jumped and dropped the pen she was holding into the cup of tea on her desk. She looked up and saw Lazaro standing in the doorway of her office.

She looked down into her tea then back up at tall, dark and handsome intruder. "In some cultures it's considered rude to sneak up on people."

"I didn't sneak. You were deep in thought, or something like that." He walked in and put both of his hands on the back of the chair that was positioned in front of her desk. "I wanted to talk to you about your plans for Pickett. Being your principal shareholder, it's very much a vested interest of mine."

"I thought you were going to impart your wisdom to me. That is what you do, right?"

"Yes, that is what I do. Do you know why I'm so good at consulting, Vanessa? Why I make more than any of the CEOs I give consultations to?"

"Why?" she asked, her tone dry.

"Because I'm not stuck in the past. I have no loyalty to tradition or convention. I know how to increase profit, and I'm equipped to see new ways of doing things because the old style of business means nothing to me."

Vanessa gritted her teeth. "Well, tradition means a lot to me. To my father."

"And that's probably the source of most of your problems."

"It's probably also why we've lasted as long as we have," she said stiffly.

"Until now. Now you need change. I'm bringing it. I've been over the expense reports from the past five years, and you might be interested in knowing that there was a sharp decline in sales and production the year before you took over. So it isn't all your fault."

Vanessa bit her lower lip, forcing herself to hold back a string of colorful and inventive expletives. "I know that. I told you changing markets have…"

"Made it difficult to compete. The fact is, Vanessa, if you want to keep the bulk of your production in the U.S. you won't be able to compete. But you can change what you're offering."

"Change what, exactly?"

"The future is in environmental sustainability. Responsible waste-disposal practices, using recycled materials. You might not be able to offer the cheapest product, but you can offer the safest, the most ethical."

"It would require some fairly aggressive campaigning." She started looking around the desk for a pen.

"In your teacup."

She felt the blush creep up her neck and over her cheeks. "I'll just get a new one." She opened her desk drawer and rummaged until she found a non-soggy pen.

"It would require some changes to the factory, to materials, to a lot of things actually. And it will cost."

"I'm not exactly swimming in resources."

"You could take a loan from your future husband."

Lazaro watched as Vanessa's cheeks flushed with angry color. "No."

"We have an agreement, Vanessa. I intend to honor it."

And he intended to let Michael Pickett know just how

much control he was assuming of his assets. That he didn't have just his daughter, but that he'd played the part of savior for the venerable Pickett family business.

"I am not getting myself into that much debt. Not with you."

"Not a loan, an exchange. A fair one, I think."

"Hardly. I feel like you're…buying me." She spat out the last words as though they were distasteful.

"Do you want to back out?"

She snapped her mouth shut, tightened her jaw. "I don't…"

"Because if you do, make no mistake, I don't make idle threats. I will push the board to appoint a new CEO of Pickett, Vanessa."

She curled her fingers around the pen she was holding, angry color spreading from her cheeks down to her collarbone. "Are you always going to hold your power over my head? For the rest of our lives? Because that might be the one thing I just can't deal with."

A stab of regret hit him hard in the chest. Making threats wasn't really his style. But something about the Pickett family, about the whole situation, brought things out in him that were normally dormant. Rage, a reminder of what it was to feel truly helpless, to feel as though his life wasn't really his own, but belonged to those with power over him.

"You don't have to worry about that, Vanessa, provided you don't back out of our agreement."

"I won't," she said tightly.

She looked at him, her dark eyes hard, her lush lips thinned into a tight line. He wanted to kiss her until her lips softened, until she was as desperate as he was. Until she begged.

Later. There would be time later. He wasn't about to let her manipulate him with his desire, even if she was doing it unknowingly. And he was certain she didn't know. She didn't give him any coy looks, no knowing smiles or flutters of her thick, dark lashes.

She blushed easily, her skin turning pink with nerves, embarrassment or anger. Her reactions seemed honest. He wasn't used to dealing with people who possessed Vanessa's straightforward manner. He was used to games, had gotten very good at playing them, at holding his cards close to his chest. Vanessa stripped that ability from him. She brought things to the surface, emotions, he wasn't used to dealing with. He wasn't about to allow her that sort of control. She'd turned him into a blind fool twelve years ago, a stupid boy who'd let the Pickett heiress walk all over him.

He was past that now. He would not be manipulated.

"You're right, *querida*, you won't. Because if you do, I will seize control of everything. I have that power."

"I believe it," she said, her words clipped. "But right now you're in my office. So I think the power might be in my favor."

Pride, unexpected and unwanted, made his chest expand. Pride and a strong measure of lust. He liked it better when she stood up to him. Liked it better when he saw a spark set fire to her dark brown eyes. It made his blood run faster, having her challenge him.

"Going to call security on me?" he asked.

"Do I have to?" She pursed her lips and cocked her hip to the side.

"Only if you can't handle me yourself."

"I'm more than capable. I'm not a little girl."

No, she wasn't. Not even close. His heart thundered heavily in his chest, the desire, the need to reach out and touch her almost overwhelming. But he couldn't afford to feel anything. Not now. Not when he was so close.

He forced his thoughts back on his goal, on his reason for being there. "Good. Busy tonight?"

She crossed her arms beneath her breasts. "I don't know. Am I? Do I have a choice?"

Annoyance surged through him. "Do you think I'm taking total control of your life?"

"I don't know what you expect from a little wife," her words taunting, arousing, infuriating.

His heart thundered hard in his chest. She was making him out to be some kind of a tyrant. She was making him feel like one. He didn't like it, he didn't want her to see him that way, and he had no idea why he should care. When she hadn't seen him as the enemy, she'd seen him as beneath her.

He rounded the desk and she stood, hands on her round, shapely hips, a deadly glitter in her eyes.

"I expect you to attend events on my arm," he said. "I expect to use your connections to make advantageous business deals. And I expect this." He hooked his arm around her waist and drew her to him.

She was breathing hard, her breasts rising and falling against his chest. He realized he was breathing hard too. To hell with fighting it. She was his now, no longer off limits to him.

See. Want. Have.

He put his hand on her face, cupped her cheek, touched her soft lower lip with his thumb. "I want this," he said, his voice sounding rough, strained, even to his own ears.

He dipped his head and kissed her. Her lips parted beneath his. He wasn't certain whether it was in shock or supplication, but he wasn't going to stop and analyze it either.

She would be his now. Finally. His. All the longing, the lust that he'd carried around with him for so many years, aching and unsatisfied no matter how many women had warmed his bed since...

She tasted the same. Just as he remembered. So utterly unique, unforgettable. The only woman who had ever made him lose his head, the only woman who had ever rejected him. The only woman whose memory lingered after years of separation. Most women were a vague impression after a few days. Not Vanessa. She had stayed vivid and powerful in his mind.

And it had only been a shadow of the reality.

Actually kissing her, the velvety slide of her tongue against his, the soft sigh of satisfaction she made against his lips, her fingers curling around the fabric of his shirt as she held on to him, anchoring him to her, that was better than anything in his memory. It made his blood run like liquid fire through his veins, made his body pulse with need, made him hard and aching with the necessity of burying himself inside her.

She stole any semblance of control with the softness of her lips.

He slid his hand around the indent of her waist, the curve of her hip. She had changed physically. Her curves were softer, more womanly. More enticing. He'd been a boy twelve years ago, but he was a man now. And she was all woman.

Vanessa felt empowered by his passion, his anger. He was trying to show her that he had the power, but in one intense rush, she realized that she was the one who held it, because his hands, sifting through her hair, were unsteady, his body was hard with arousal. For her. Because of her.

He deepened the kiss and she took his bottom lip between her teeth, nipping the tender skin, showing him that she wasn't going to be passive, in this or anything else, needing badly to stake a claim on him, as he was doing to her.

A growl rumbled in his chest and he took a step, backing her into her desk. She heard her pencil holder fall onto the floor, its contents scattering. She didn't care.

There was nothing. Nothing but this. This battle of wills

and the all-consuming passion that was taking over her mind, her body.

His fingers crept beneath the edge of her top and she was arched into him, powerless to do anything else. And that sudden loss of control, that concession to his power, made a jolt of reality slap her in the face.

She'd promised herself she wasn't going to let him have this control. She shouldn't feel the way she did, as if she would die if she didn't have him. Inside of her. Now. On the floor, the desk, wherever.

She couldn't afford to give him this part of her, to let him have dominion over her body. He would never love her, and if she gave in to this...she would be vulnerable. She couldn't allow that.

Maybe you can't have love, but you can have this.

Amazing, all-consuming lust.

No. It would never just be that. Not for her. Lazaro was more to her than just a hard body. And she would never be anything more to him than a simple means of feeding his sex drive.

She let go of him and pulled away, her heart thundering in her ears.

He flicked a dismissive glance in her direction, seemingly unaffected by what had just happened between them. Totally unfair, since her world had had another dramatic shift on its axis.

"I can see it won't be a problem," he said.

"What?" she asked, still feeling thick and muddled from the arousal that was crowding all the good, useful information out of her brain and leaving room only for the screaming want that was pounding through her.

"The attraction between us is very strong. That part of our marriage will not be a problem."

As far as physical attraction went, no, it wouldn't be. But

it would be everything she'd never wanted and then some. A man using her because she was convenient. Because she had status. Because she had things he wanted, not because she was who he wanted.

That he was attracted to her didn't make her feel all that special. Yes, Lazaro was a sex god with looks that could not be denied, but men tended to like sex from whoever would give it to them. And after that display he was probably feeling pretty positive that getting it would be easy.

"I have work to do," she said, sinking back into her chair.

"I'll leave you to it then. Are we on for tonight?"

"What are we doing?" she asked, her eyes wandering to the pen still resting in her teacup.

"It's a surprise."

Vanessa watched him walk out of the room and her only thought was that she didn't think she could take another surprise from Lazaro.

Lazaro touched the velvet box in his coat pocket and cursed the flash of adrenaline that raced through him. It *was* adrenaline; it certainly wasn't nerves. He didn't do nerves. He did decisive action. He didn't question, he moved forward with confidence. Always.

That was how he'd worked his way up from the ground level of the massive corporation he'd eventually built up with his ideas on how to reinvent the place. It was how he'd built a career, a name for himself. How he'd netted billions in the bank.

He took advantage of every resource and did what had to be done. As he was doing now.

It was extremely fortuitous that one of the art museum's head curators happened to be on a par with Vanessa's father as far as social clout went. And even more fortuitous that she was a gossip.

It meant that she would tell anyone who was even half-interested that Lazaro Marino had paid to have the museum empty this evening so that he could ask the woman in his life a very important question.

In Vanessa's circle, media exposure was seen as vulgar, common. Anyone could earn that kind of notoriety. The First Families and those like them saw class as something you were born with, not something you could acquire. And anyone who wasn't born with it was somehow less.

The way to spread the word was through careless discretion, nothing half so common as an actual write-up in a newspaper.

He curled his fingers around the ring box and leaned against the terrace railing. Vanessa was due to arrive soon, another detail carefully coordinated with a trail that would be easy to follow.

He heard high heels on marble and looked up. Vanessa was walking toward him, the expression on her face mutinous. She had dressed for the occasion, though, as he'd requested. Red silk this time, hugging her curves. Her lips were painted to match her dress and her dark hair was pulled back into a neat bun. He wished she'd left it down. He enjoyed the feel of the silken strands sliding through his fingers.

He tightened his hold on the ring box. This was what it was about. The ring. Taking his place in the world. The truth was, he didn't give a damn about what anyone in high society thought of him. But he wouldn't be seen as beneath anyone, as some sort of trash from the *barrio* they could despise and lord their power over. He wouldn't be beneath anyone. And Vanessa was the key.

"What is this?" she asked, looking around the terrace. It was lit by a string of paper lanterns that hung low overhead, just as it had been the night they'd met at the charity event.

"You didn't guess?"

"I wouldn't dare try to guess at the inner workings of your mind," she said, walking to the railing and resting her forearms on the top of it, leaning over, keeping her eyes fixed on the garden.

He moved so that he was standing next to her and pulled the ring box out of his pocket and placed it on the top of the stone railing. "I thought this was an ideal place to make our arrangement official."

She turned her head sharply, her eyes wide. Then she looked down at the ring box.

"Are you going to look at it?" he asked.

"I...so this is your proposal?" Her eyebrows winged halfway up her forehead, her expression one of pure incredulity.

"I think I proposed already," he said stiffly.

"Well, but...no, because now there's a ring." She didn't touch the ring box, she just looked at it.

"And most women at this point would be looking at the ring."

"Why all this?" she asked, ignoring his statement. "The museum and the lights?"

"Because I had to speak to quite a few people to arrange this romantic gesture."

She nodded slowly. "And they'll tell other people."

"Yes. Your social class is just small enough that word travels to everyone in it very quickly."

She frowned. "Right."

"I'm sorry, did you want something more public?"

She shrugged. "No."

Anger surged in him, anger and something else that he couldn't quite identify. "You're disappointed?"

"I'm not disappointed. That implies I had an expectation about this moment and, truly, for all I knew, you were going to courier me a ring at my office. But I did have expectations of this moment as far as my life goes."

"And this doesn't meet your standards?" he asked, his stomach tightening.

"Not really."

"You might want to look at the rock before you declare the effort subpar, *querida*," he said, conscious of the fact that his accent had thickened with his building anger.

He popped the top on the box and pushed it closer to her. She looked down and her eyes widened. Not a big surprise. Five carats would have that effect on someone like her.

"I hope that's fitting of a woman of your status."

Vanessa looked down at the ring, glittering beneath the lantern light. The large, square diamond set into a band of white gold with an intricate, antique-style weave was nestled in cream silk, looking as if it had been made just for her.

There was so much about the moment that seemed made just for her. An empty art museum, a gorgeous man and a marriage proposal. If it had been a real marriage proposal— real in the sense that there was love behind it and not just mercenary business dealings—he would have gotten down on one knee. They would have walked through the museum and talked about their future. They would have felt like the only two people in the world.

If they had never parted, if she had stopped him from leaving that night, maybe it would be real.

Her heart squeezed in her chest and she squelched the thought. It didn't matter. This was reality. And in reality, he'd shoved the ring in her direction and barely looked at her. He hadn't even asked the question, and it all just hung between them, awkward and unspoken. Painful. Because this was like some nightmare version of a fantasy she might have created for herself.

"It's lovely." She reached out and touched it, hesitant to pick it up, to put it on, because the ring made it all seem real. And final.

And because part of her wanted so badly to wear Lazaro's ring, so very badly. And that was embarrassing, humiliating. She didn't really want the Lazaro that had come back into her life with all the finesse of a jackhammer. She wanted the man she used to imagine he was. The man he never had been.

"Don't you like it, *querida?*" he asked.

"I love it. It's beautiful. Perfect."

"You seem giddy," he said, his expression flat.

"I love it," she said, teeth gritted.

"Put it on."

Anger surged through her, pummeling her tender heart. "That's your job, isn't it?"

She held her hand out, determined not to be the one to fasten her own diamond handcuffs. He took her hand in his, the heat of his skin on hers sending prickles of electricity through her body, making it nearly impossible for her to cling to the anger that was anchoring her to the balcony, reminding her that this was nothing more than a farce.

He took the ring out of the box and it caught the light. Such a beautiful sign of eternal bondage. She closed her eyes while he pushed it onto her fourth finger. It fit perfectly, and it was more disturbing than anything that it fit. That it somehow seemed right.

She pulled her hand back and brushed her palm down over her skirt, trying to ease the fiery, tingling sensation that was spreading from her fingertips to her wrist.

"How big is it?" Her own voice, the mercenary tone, cooled her off quickly. Reminded her that this was a transaction. Nothing more. Because she had to do something to stop her heart from pounding faster. To keep herself from thinking of all the what-ifs.

"Does it matter?" he asked, his voice as cold as the sick weight in her stomach.

"I've heard size matters."

A muscle in his jaw jumped. "Big enough to satisfy you."

She swallowed hard, the need to get the upper hand fueling her, choosing her words for her. "I'm not sure about that."

"The purebred could do better?"

She looked at the ring again. It was beautiful. Perfect. "Possibly." The lie stuck in her throat.

He jerked back, as though she'd struck him. He looked, just for a moment, like the boy he'd been the night she'd rejected him. Then any vulnerability was gone, replaced with an expression that was as hard as granite.

"I think," he said, "it's time we went and had a talk with your father."

CHAPTER SIX

"I've already heard your news, Vanessa. I've been down at the club this morning."

Vanessa fought the urge to hang her head and stare at the toes of her ruby-red shoes. Something happened to her when her father used that tone, that flat, disappointed tone that let her know she'd somehow made a mess of things. She felt like a child again. Small and desperately inadequate, trying to live up to an ideal that had been placed just out of her reach, an ideal she was falling so short of it was nearly laughable.

Michael Pickett wasn't a large man; he wasn't young anymore. His voice was thin now, wispy. He couldn't yell. He didn't need to. What he could do with a small hint of disapproval in his voice couldn't be underestimated.

Vanessa swallowed. "Well, it was…unexpected." She looked down at the rug, a floral-print rug, the same one that had been in place in her father's office since she could remember. Everything was the same at the Pickett estate. Nothing ever changed. The house was like a relic, surrounded by the modern world but not really a part of it. Like the owner of the estate himself.

"And what of your obligations to Craig Freeman? Do they mean nothing?"

"I want to marry Lazaro," she said. "I don't want to marry Craig." That, in the very strictest sense, was the truth. In spite

of the fact that things had been stilted between the two of
them since the previous night's engagement, he was still the
better option.

"Since when is life about what you want?" he said, his
voice soft, and deadlier for it.

"I…"

"Don't be stupid, Vanessa. This man is beneath you."

She could sense the moment Lazaro's control slipped its
leash. The moment he was no longer playing his part.

"You had better damn well watch what you say to my fiancée," Lazaro said, his voice hard, dangerous, each word
rougher, less civilized, as though a veneer was slowly being
stripped away, revealing the true man. Dangerous. Feral. As
far from the polished, old-money setting as it was possible
to be.

Lazaro had been silent for most of the meeting, letting
Vanessa do the talking. But the silence was broken now.
"Vanessa was handed a crippled corporation, and with the
remains that you gave to her she's fashioning something that
can survive the new market, the modern sensibility, something no one else on your staff, including you, had the cre-
ativity to do."

She waited for him to say exactly why they were getting
married. That he was the one saving the company from a
slow corporate death. But he didn't.

Her father curled his hands into fists. "I'm not taking orders from a man whose mother used to scrub my floors."

She felt Lazaro stiffen next to her. "But maybe you will
take orders from the man who is now the principal shareholder of Pickett Industries. Interesting thing about going
public, Mr. Pickett…the public can buy pieces of your company. And I've bought quite a few pieces for myself."

"Having money does not make you an equal with my family," her father said. "Money doesn't buy class."

"But money does buy stock."

"Vanessa." Her father leveled his cold gray eyes on her. "Did you know about this?"

"Yes." Vanessa cleared her throat and tilted her chin up, fighting the urge to look back down at the carpet. She wasn't going to look down anymore. "He's my fiancé. So it will still be all in the family, won't it?"

She felt a thrill of excitement race through her, a surge of adrenaline that chased away any intimidation or fear.

"You do not have my blessing on this." Michael Pickett stood from behind the desk, and suddenly Vanessa saw her father clearly for the first time. How he controlled her. How hard he tried to exert his will over her.

"I didn't come here to get your blessing." She bit out the words. "Just to tell you what was going to happen. What do you want?" she asked him. "Do you want the company to succeed? Because, trust me, right now we need Lazaro for that. Accept him, welcome him, and we stand a chance at some success."

"Are you threatening me?"

"No. I'm telling you how it is. This is reality." Her heart was pounding hard, blood roaring through her ears. She felt dizzy.

"We'll be in touch," Lazaro said, wrapping his arm around her waist and leading her from the room. He closed the heavy oak door behind them, the sound echoing in the expansive corridor of the old house.

"Thank you," Vanessa said quietly when they were back on the paved circular drive in front of her childhood home.

"For?"

"For saying that stuff. For making it sound like some of the good ideas were mine." She expelled the breath she didn't realize she'd been holding. "I don't think any of them were."

Lazaro opened the passenger door of his dark blue sports

car and she sank inside, letting the soft leather seats absorb some of her tension.

He rounded the car and slid into the driver's seat, putting the key into the ignition and turning the engine on.

When they were on the maple-lined highway, headed back into Boston, Lazaro flicked her a glance. "Why exactly do you work so hard to please him?"

"I..." She looked out the window and focused on the trees, watching them blur into a steady stream of color. "He's all I have. My mother died when I was four. And my brother died when I was thirteen. Thomas was going to take over the company. He was brilliant. He would have done an amazing job. But without him...there was only me." She turned to face him. "It's up to me, Lazaro. I can't be the one that fails."

"Do you love what you do?"

"Do you?"

He laughed. "I love the money that it brings in. And yes, I like solving problems. Fixing things. Making them run better."

"I don't love what I do. I have to take antacids when I get up in the morning," she said. She'd never said that out loud to anyone. She'd never even fully admitted to herself that she was unhappy, that she didn't like what she was doing. She was the CEO of a much-lauded company and saying she would rather do almost anything else seemed ridiculous. But it was true.

It was also too late. Her course had been set since she was thirteen. She knew there were plenty of people who would have walked away. People who would have pursued the life they wanted. But there was such a weight on her, a burden of responsibility. She couldn't turn her back on it.

If not for her father, then for Thomas's memory.

"And before you ask why I do it," she said, "I'll just tell you. Because how could I be the one to put an end to a legacy?

How could I let it be my fault? Because Pickett Industries has to keep going, for my eventual children as much as for my father and for the memory of my brother. I do it because it's the right thing to do."

She took her phone out of her pocket and fiddled with the touch screen, moving icons around with her thumb. "My father will accept the marriage because he has no other choice. But the bluster was kind of a necessity for him. It's how he is."

"I know," Lazaro said, his voice hard, his grip tight on the wheel.

Vanessa looked down at the ring on her finger and turned the phone camera on, snapping a picture of the diamond glittering in the late-afternoon sunlight.

"What would you do if you could do something else?" Lazaro asked.

She smiled. "I would take pictures."

"Of what?"

She leaned her head back against the seat and let the soft leather ease away some of her tension. "Everything."

"You might find the time to do that someday. Maybe not of everything, but...of some things."

She forced the corners of her mouth up into a smile. "Maybe. Maybe when all of this gets sorted out, and things settle down in the company I'll have time."

"You will."

"No one else knows that," she said, realizing it as she spoke the words.

"That can only be a good thing. Shouldn't a husband know things about his wife no one else knows?"

Heat made her skin prickle. "I suppose so." That made her think of sexy things. Erotic things. Things that made her lips tingle with the memory of his kiss. "But it isn't like we're going to have a real marriage."

"What will be unreal about it?" he asked.

Only the very core of the union. But of course, he didn't seem overly concerned with that detail. "Well, we don't love each other."

"No." Something about the way he said it, so matter of fact, so logical, made her chest ache. Maybe because there had been a time when she'd loved him, so much, with everything she had. It seemed like yesterday and another lifetime all at once.

She put her sunglasses on, all the better to avoid his eyes. "So that's the part that makes it seem…not real."

"You didn't love that purebred you were supposed to marry."

His choice of words made her snort. "No. I barely knew him. But I didn't really… I tried not to think about it."

"This is no different."

It was different. It was different because, with Lazaro, she wanted things. Things no other man had ever made her want. At sixteen, loving him had made her feel that the whole world was open to her. As if she could do anything. Be anyone. Not just Vanessa Pickett of the Picketts of Boston.

He made her feel like that now. It was dangerous and stupid.

"I suppose it's not."

She looked at his profile. Strong. Masculine. Angry. She'd said something wrong again and she had no idea what.

"Is there any way you can take time away from the office?" he asked, effectively changing the subject.

"For how long?"

"A week. I've been doing some consulting work with a corporation in Argentina and I have to make a physical appearance this week."

"And why do you want to take me?" she asked.

"What better way to celebrate our engagement?"

"I'm not just going to jump into bed with you. We already established that," she said, sounding prim even to herself.

"I remember. Vividly. Although you certainly do a good impression of a woman who wants to do some jumping when I kiss you."

"Kissing isn't sex," she said coldly. "You've always seemed to get the two confused."

"I assure you, Vanessa, I'm not confused about any part of sex. And a kiss is not sex, I'm well aware. Not even close."

"So don't equate one kiss with me being ready to sleep with you." He'd certainly made that assumption the first time she'd kissed him. "I'm not ready. I don't sleep with men I don't know. And if that's the point of the trip…"

"It will look nice if I take my fiancée on a celebratory vacation. If you're going to be a harpy you can stay here."

She thought of the two options for her week. Staring at the four walls of her office again, or escaping to Argentina for seven days. Even if it was with Lazaro, option two was the winner. She wanted to escape. Just go for a while. Leave reality behind.

"I'll go."

"*Bien.* You and I can…get to know each other."

Buenos Aires was electric. There was energy in everything, motion and lights and heat. Vanessa had never seen anything like it. She'd traveled quite a bit before she'd graduated from high school, but they'd been trips with her father, trips that had begun at airports in air-conditioned limousines and ended up at cloistered resort properties.

She'd never truly gotten to enjoy the culture of the country she'd been visiting. And she'd never realized how sad that was until now. Had never realized what she'd been missing.

She wished she could capture it forever. The curves of the buildings, the brick on the street, the sun-washed blue sky.

"You grew up here?" She turned to Lazaro, who was sitting next to her in the back seat of the limo, engrossed in something on his smartphone.

"We left when I was thirteen," he said, not bothering to spare her a glance.

"It's beautiful."

"Sure. If you don't go down to where I used to live. But every city has its slums."

Vanessa's stomach tightened. "And that's where you're from?"

"Does that bother you, *princesa*?"

"No. Yes. Only in the sense that I don't like to think of you…of anyone, living like that."

"It's reality," he said, his voice rough.

"I know." She did. But it was sort of a hollow, half-realized knowledge.

"It's where I'm from. I hope it doesn't cause you too much despair to have a husband who comes from nothing. As your father is so fond of saying, class can't be bought."

"I've never cared, Lazaro. Never."

"That isn't how I remember it."

"How do you remember it? Because I remember risking my father's wrath to speak to you whenever I got the chance, and I don't think I ever treated you like a second-class citizen. In fact, I pretty much remember my entire sixteen-year-old world revolving around you."

The limo pulled up the curb in front of a stretch of tall, white, connected buildings. "My penthouse is here," Lazaro said.

"Good."

"Good?"

"I like it," she said, opening her own door and getting out without waiting for Lazaro.

She liked it, and she was glad to be done with the conversation. She didn't want to talk about what an idiot she'd been for him back in her angsty teenage days. And she really didn't want him guessing just how close she was to being an idiot for him now.

Lazaro Marino was as hard as concrete and just as loving. The last thing she wanted was to cultivate feelings for him. She'd had her heart broken by him before. Granted, at sixteen, everything felt fatal, and she was sure that whatever it was she'd felt for him was more infatuation than anything else. But still, she had no desire to relive it.

This time, she did have Lazaro in her future. And a lifetime of living with him and loving him while he saw her as nothing more than a possession would be worse than a relationship with no emotions at all.

So she was aiming for cool and distant. She could do that. She had plenty of practice being treated with cool distance; she ought to be able to dish a little bit out.

Lazaro got out of the limo and opened the trunk, retrieving their bags without waiting for the driver or for aid from one of the apartment building's employees.

She couldn't help but admire the grace in his movements, the easy strength. Even angry—and he was angry with her, that much was obvious—he was the single most gorgeous man she'd ever seen. Deep bronze skin, square jaw—which he was clenching tightly. He always did that when he was annoyed with her.

"You're going to get TMJ," she blurted, following him into the building.

"Que?"

"TMJ. You can get it from grinding your teeth. There was a girl at school who had to wear a mouth guard to stop her from doing it."

A smile curved his lips and a ridiculous, happy, fluttering

sensation assaulted her. "Perhaps you should just endeavor to be less of a cause of stress."

She huffed out a laugh. "I stress *you* out, Lazaro? *Really?*"

He stopped walking and turned to face her, the look on his face intense. And for a second, she forgot that breathing was important. Because nothing seemed more important, more compelling, than what was happening between herself and Lazaro.

"Maybe *stress* is the wrong word."

Vanessa leaned back slightly and her shoulders connected with the wall. "It is?"

"But I am having trouble sleeping."

"Why is that?"

"Because every night since you came to me at the museum I have stayed awake. Wanting you. In my arms. In my bed."

The need to kiss him again was unbearable. It was hard to remember why she was fighting her attraction for him, especially when sleeping with him was inevitable.

A thrill shot through her system when she realized that fully, for the first time. It was a matter of *when*, not *if*, and having it suddenly seem real made the distance between Lazaro and herself seem that much smaller.

He released his hold on one of the bags and let it drop to the carpeted floor of the lobby area. He brushed his thumb over her lower lip, an action that was becoming familiar to her. Maybe *familiar* was the wrong word, because each time he touched her like that it made her knees weaken.

She flicked the tip of her tongue to his finger, curiosity and desire mixing together to create a potent temptation she couldn't resist. His body shuddered, the movement running through every strong inch of him. She leaned her head back against the wall, pulling away from him. But he was still close. So close it wouldn't take a very big action for him to close the distance between them and take her in his arms. To kiss her again as he'd done in her office. As he'd done in the guesthouse.

"Oh, yes, Vanessa, I very much look forward to getting to know you better this week." He picked up the suitcase again and turned away from her, the spell that had descended over her breaking.

He was playing with her. Teasing her. Proving that at any moment he could call up that desire in her that was so strong, so close to the surface.

If he kept behaving like that, it wouldn't be hard to keep her emotional distance from him. Not hard at all.

CHAPTER SEVEN

"What's this?"

Lazaro flicked her an uninterested look from his position at the sleek penthouse bar. "I had some things sent ahead for you."

A lot of things. Dresses, a swimsuit…the large armoire had been stocked with items, as had the freestanding vanity in the massive bathroom that was just off her expansive bedroom. But that wasn't what caught her eye. "This," she said again, picking up a black camera bag that was positioned in the middle of the sumptuous four-poster bed, almost afraid to open it.

She peered through the open door of her bedroom and out into the spacious living area.

Lazaro waved his hand in a dismissive manner. "You mentioned you liked taking pictures."

Her heart thundered hard in her head, and she felt dizzy. Overwhelmed. She ran her fingers along the edge of the bag. It was very high-quality heavy canvas sewn with thick nylon thread.

She grasped the zipper and pulled it open. Her hands shook as she pulled the camera out. It wasn't just a camera. It was lenses and filters and just about every other accessory she could think of. Much more than she would ever need to take pictures as a hobby.

She walked out of her room and into the living room, stepping up the marble steps into the bar area.

She felt short of breath as she turned the camera over in her hands, her fingers sliding over the slick black casing. Her body felt strange, hollow.

"Lazaro, why...why did you do this for me?"

He moved around to the other side of the bar, drink in hand. "Why not? You said you liked to take pictures. You were doing it with your phone and I thought you might want a real camera. Especially as I knew you would want pictures of Buenos Aires."

"I do... I was...I was so wishing I could capture it all forever while we were driving from the airport and...you knew."

He shrugged. "It isn't a big deal. Money is nothing to me."

"This is more than money."

"It's not," he said, his focus on the city skyline beyond the large window that extended the length of the living area.

"But I just don't understand why you went to the trouble to..."

"You're going to be my wife, Vanessa," he said, cutting her off. "I don't want you to be miserable. Do you think I mean to keep you as my captive and make you pay penance for the rest of your life? I have no interest in that."

"I hadn't really given it a lot of thought."

That he intended to make her happy was an entirely foreign concept. It wasn't that she'd imagined he wanted her to be miserable, it was just that she didn't think he'd cared one way or the other.

"Really?" he asked, his tone dry.

"I've just been trying to get through the day-to-day stuff. Not only since you decided to play a little game of Russian roulette with my life, before that too. I've just been trying to get by."

"I have a lot of experience in just trying to get by," he said slowly.

"It's not fun."

"No, it's not." He looked at her, his dark eyes veiling his emotions, but she felt that his eyes were able to see into her, to read her thoughts. "It begs the question, why do you choose to do it?"

"I don't. Not really."

"You do."

"Fine, maybe. I choose to do it because as I said before, it isn't just me. It's my family. It's the inheritance for all my— our children."

"You could take an inactive role."

"It's not the same."

"No, it would save you all that money you spend on ant-acids," he said, his voice flat.

"It doesn't come naturally to me, I'll admit that. I took all the classes, I got really good grades, in fact, but a classroom isn't the real world. I don't have that extra thing that takes someone from good to great."

He took a long sip of his drink and walked back to the bar, putting both of his hands flat on the marble surface. "You might not have it for business, but that doesn't mean you don't have it."

That was a revelation—but one she couldn't accept. One she'd been trained not to accept. "It doesn't really matter if I can't do the one thing that would matter."

"Is it all that matters?"

"You can ask me that? Does your success matter, Lazaro? And is it enough? Or are you still after more?"

"I think you know the answer to that."

"Exactly. You aren't happy because there's still that one thing. This is my thing, this is what I have to do. What I have to get right."

He nodded once. "Good for you. I wouldn't have thought you'd have this kind of determination."

That stung a little bit. "Because you knew me for a few weeks when I was sixteen?"

"It made an impression," he said dryly.

"Yay, me," she said, turning the camera over in her hands, suddenly fighting back a hot flood of tears. She cleared her throat. "Thank you for this. Really."

"You can bring it when we go out tonight."

"We're going out?"

"I thought you might want to see some of the city."

She nodded. "I do. I very much do."

"Great. I have to stop by Paolo Cruz's office and give him a rundown of what we're discussing at the board meeting tomorrow, but when I get back, we'll go and have dinner."

Dinner with Lazaro in Buenos Aires and a gift. A personal gift. Proof that he'd listened to her. That he wanted her to be happy.

The emotion thing kept getting trickier. Lucky her.

Vanessa on a normal day was enough to light his blood on fire and make his libido kick into high gear. Vanessa dressed to kill in a tight black dress with a low V-neckline and a slit in the skirt that revealed one toned, gorgeous thigh when she walked was almost too much.

Already, the past few days in Buenos Aires had tested him, his body now so hot that an ice-cold shower at night did nothing to cool the fire that raged beneath his skin. A fire only Vanessa could dampen.

But he had not gone to her. He would not let her see that she had that power over him. It was a power she had always had. He'd been bewitched by her body, her spirit, from the moment he'd met her. It galled him that she still had him under her spell.

After three days, no, more like twelve years of resisting, right now he ached to pull her into his arms, the need so strong he thought he couldn't resist it without the pain becoming crippling. His body throbbed with the need to have her. To feel those slim, perfect legs wrapped around his waist as he drowned himself in the pleasure only she could offer.

Tonight, she'd left her hair down, rich brown waves cascading over her shoulders, partially concealing the round swell of her breasts that the daring neckline of her dress did not.

She brought something out in him, something he didn't recognize. A need, a desire, a totally primal lust that defied anything he'd ever experienced before.

They'd shared a kiss. A simple kiss. Yet she'd burrowed her way inside him as no woman, not a long-term girlfriend or one-night lover, ever had. He wished this need was tied to vengeance. That he could explain. But it was separate from the issues with her father. Even if all of the events of the past sometimes tangled in his memory, the parts with Vanessa, the memories of her lips touching his, burned bright in his mind, washed everything else away. When he thought of her mouth, of her hands on his body, there was nothing else.

It was desire. That was all. Even if it was desire such as he'd never known. And he would have a lifetime to indulge that desire. To take the edge off it so that it no longer dominated his thoughts.

Her wicked red lips curved into a smile and all of his blood rushed south of his belt. "I didn't overdress, did I?"

She was absolutely overdressed. Anything covering those luscious curves was a crime as far as he was concerned. "Not at all," he said

"Are you ready then?"

"Si." Images of them together, limbs entwined, moans of pleasure issuing from those plump red lips had him hard and shaking. He didn't want dinner. He wanted her, wanted her

body pressed against his. He felt a smile curve his lips. "I think that, in honor of your dress, we need to go somewhere different than I originally had in mind."

Even at night the streets of Buenos Aires were alive. People were still walking around, laughing, talking, eating. Heat and moisture clung to the air, to Vanessa's skin, as they walked down the crowded sidewalk.

Lazaro was completely at ease in his surroundings. Passersby stopped and looked at him, and Vanessa couldn't blame them. In his black suit and open-collared shirt, he was absolute masculine perfection. He demanded to be stared at.

He didn't seem to notice, or care, that he drew attention from every woman they passed. He didn't return any of the hungry, open stares. His eyes were on her. And it was making her blood feel hot.

"Where are we going?" she asked. It was a long shot, but talking might break up some of the tension that was building inside her.

"Right here." He took her hand in his, lacing their fingers together, and led her into a small, narrow doorway. The outside of the building had seemed the same as every building they'd passed—white brick with rounded edges showing its age. But the interior didn't match the old-world feel of the streets outside.

Inside was open and clean, with pared-down, square furniture and a large bar area surrounded by plush seating. Pendant lighting hung low at different lengths, made to look like floating candles suspended in space.

There was plenty of room to move, but everything was arranged so that it felt close, intimate. There was a band playing, and couples were on the dance floors, wrapped around each other, dancing in a rhythm so sensual that it made Vanessa feel as though she was intruding on something by witnessing it.

"Would you like a drink?" Lazaro gestured to the bar.

"I… No." Her body already felt giddy, her thoughts light and fuzzy. She didn't want to add anything to her system that might encourage the feelings.

"Dance with me," he said, touching her hand, the sensation of his skin against hers lighting a fire that burned from her fingertips to her chest, settling around her heart. "And don't tell me you can't dance, because I'm sure a woman of your…status will have had dance lessons from the time she learned to walk."

"I don't dance like this," she said, flicking a glance back at the dance floor.

"This is how I dance," he said, taking her hand and drawing her to him. "And since I'm your future husband, you should learn to dance with me, don't you think?"

"We're going to tango at our wedding?" she asked, a short laugh escaping her lips as she imagined the seductive dance with the super-traditional Pickett estate serving as a backdrop.

"It would give people something to talk about."

"We already are something to talk about, Lazaro."

"I suppose we are," he said, dark eyes glittering in the dim light of the club. He looked different here. More dangerous. The polish of sophistication he'd cultivated seemed to have worn thin in the past few hours. This was the man she'd known twelve years ago.

Rough around the edges. Utterly deadly to her senses.

"Dance with me," he said again. Not a question, a demand. One she couldn't refuse.

She allowed him to lead her to the dance floor, her heart thundering so loudly she was certain people around her would be able to hear it, even over the steady beat of the music. But here, no one looked at them, not even at Lazaro. Every couple was totally enthralled with each other, with the movements of their partner.

Lazaro wrapped one arm around her waist and brought her up against his chest, his other hand clasping hers. "Follow my lead."

She knew she didn't look like the elegant women dancing around her, but with Lazaro leading, his movements strong and sure, she felt like one of them. She could feel his heart beating hard against her chest, strong and steady, and her steps began to match his, her body moving in rhythm with the beat of his heart.

The music closed in around them, making her feel as if they were alone, everyone else fading into murky, shadowy impressions. Nothing else mattered but Lazaro, the weight of his hand on her waist, the intensity in his eyes as he looked at her.

The strains of the violin wound through Vanessa's body, filled her, joined the arousal that had been building inside her since the moment she'd walked back into Lazaro's life, making her feel too full. But also more alive than she'd ever felt before.

Lazaro slid his hand down to the curve of her hip, down lower, edging beneath the daring split in the skirt of her dress. His hand connected with the very top of her stocking, the place where nylon ended and bare flesh began. He curled his fingers in and lifted her leg, curving it around his. It was part of the dance, nothing more sensual than anyone else was doing. And yet it made her feel dizzy with desire, held captive to it, waiting to see what he would do next. Where he would touch her next.

He pulled her closer to him and the hard length of his erection pressed against her stomach. She dug her fingers into his shoulder, bit down on her lip, trying to keep back the sound of pleasure that was trying to escape.

This was real. Sexual. Raw. It stirred primal hunger in her, a sense of feminine power.

He moved his hand from her thigh, back to her hip, his grip tightening. He pulled into his body and she melted against him. It was all part of the dance.

And yet it wasn't.

He pressed his face against hers, the stubble that had grown in since that morning abrading her cheek, the slight prickle of pain combining with her mounting arousal, making her feel as if she was drowning in sensation.

"Come with me," he whispered, his voice rough.

He was leading. She was following. This felt like part of the dance too.

And yet it wasn't.

He brought her into a small alcove just off the dance floor, partly secluded with swaths of fabric that cascaded from the ceiling to the floor.

"Lazaro…" She couldn't think of anything else to say. Not when he was looking at her as though she was the only thing he could see.

He leaned in slightly and braced himself on the wall behind her, his hand resting by her head, his other arm wrapped around her waist. She was effectively trapped, and she didn't mind at all.

She tilted her head slightly, hoping that he would take the hint and kiss her. Logic and self-preservation had no place in what was happening between them now. This was about feeling, desire, the kind of passion she'd tasted once twelve years ago and had been starving for every night since then.

He kissed her and she forgot everything—everything but the graze of rough stubble on her cheeks, the velvet slide of his tongue, the firm warmth of his lips. There was nothing else.

She kissed him back with everything she had, all of the pent-up desire that had lain dormant in her for so long. Desire for him.

He cupped her cheek for a moment before sliding his hand through her hair, weaving his fingers into the thick curls. He held her like that, anchored to him, his kiss giving and demanding at the same time. Too much and not enough.

She arched against him, needing to be closer to him, as close to him as she could possibly get. She needed his touch. His hands. Needed him.

He tilted his head and kissed the tender skin beneath her jaw, the curve of her neck, her shoulder. She shivered and he continued down, his tongue tracing the line of her collarbone. He lifted his hand and cupped her breast, teased her hardened nipple until she was panting, desperate, dying of the want that had taken over her body.

She gripped his shoulders, needing something to hold her to earth. He shifted his hand lower, palming her bottom, coupling it with a kiss to her collarbone. And then he was traveling down again, the tip of his tongue on the curve of her breast, exposed by the low neckline of her gown.

She opened her eyes for a moment and saw a flash of movement through the partly closed curtains. A reminder. Just enough to bring her back to reality.

"Lazaro, stop. We have to stop," she said, her tongue thick and clumsy, unable to form words effectively.

"No, *querida*," he whispered, kissing her throat. "Not yet."

"But…what…what will people think?"

Lazaro froze, all of the heat, the molten lust that had been roaring through his veins turning into ice.

What will people think?

He tightened his hold on her for a moment and then released her. "Don't worry, no one here will think anything, Vanessa. No one here knows that you are the Pickett heiress and I'm your housekeeper's bastard son." He spat the words from his mouth, vile words that reflected the clash of emotions raging inside him.

She shook her head and took a step toward him, her hand outstretched. "Lazaro..."

"How will you bear the humiliation of being married to a man like me?" He stepped away from her, his stomach tight with disgust. "Although my money is good enough for you. My ring—" he reached out and took her hand, lifting it so that the diamond caught the light "—seems to be good enough for you."

"Don't say that. That's not fair. I..."

"Don't say what, Vanessa? Don't tell you the truth? I'm good enough to marry, as long as I'm bailing you out and giving you a ring that ought to come with its own security detail? Good enough to screw around with in your father's guesthouse as long as no one sees you slumming it with the boy who cuts the grass?"

"Lazaro..."

"You need me," he said, his voice sounding like a growl, shocking even him. "Admit it."

"I..."

Pain tore through him, made him want retribution. "Say it."

"Or what? You'll walk away? You'll forget that *you* need *me*?" She pulled away from him. "Because no matter how much you pretend to disdain me, my father, society, you want your place at the top. And you need me to get it."

Angry brown eyes clashed with his, a tear, not one of sadness but of pure rage, spilled down her cheek. "I want to go now," she said, her voice low.

He inclined his head. "Of course, *princesa*," he said, the term not meant as one of endearment.

She turned, walking ahead of him, pushing the door open.

It was warmer outside than it was in the club, the night air heavy and clinging, weighing him down, along with what felt like a rock in his gut. She was acting as though she'd been deeply wronged—offended by his touch, most likely. Because he was so beneath her. At least in public.

He curled his hands into fists, holding them so tight the tendons in his wrists ached.

The penthouse was only a couple of blocks away and Vanessa maintained her stony silence the entire way there. Once they were inside the lobby she kept a few paces in front of him, clearly determined not to look at him or acknowledge his presence.

Anger roared to life in him, replacing the unsettling guilt that had momentarily crept in. She wouldn't have her way. Not now. He wasn't a boy anymore, at the mercy of her father's henchman. And she was no longer the princess in a tower, no longer so far above him she could dismiss him at will. She couldn't just walk away from him.

"You will have to get over your aversion to being seen with me in public, *mi amor*," he said.

She stopped mid-stride and turned to face him, her dark eyes shimmering with heat. "Do I also have to get over my aversion to being groped in public? Does it somehow offend you that I want to maintain some level of public decency?"

"You maintain a high level of private decency as well, since you do not allow me in your bed."

"You take it pretty personally when a woman says no to you. I remember that well."

"No, what I take personally is a woman thinking I'm good enough to tease, but not good enough to take to her bed."

She took a step toward him, her lips tightened into a line.

"Is that what you think that was? Me teasing you?" She shook her head. "I wasn't thinking. If I was thinking I would never have let you touch me."

"You think that's the basis for a happy marriage?"

"I think maybe the basis for a happy marriage is not pursuing the union for business purposes, but then, I'm not really an expert."

"That is a shame, as you have agreed to marry for the benefit of your company. And, as we've discussed, no one has forced you into this. And I will not be made a fool of. Not twice. Not by the same woman."

"You think I made a fool of you, Lazaro?" Her voice was barely raised above a whisper, the force of her emotions making her words tremble. "You weren't the one pressed up against the wall in a public place and…and you have the gall to be angry at me?"

He took a step toward her, softening his voice. "Is that what bothers you the most, Vanessa Pickett, that I make you lose all of that respectability that's so important to you and your family?"

"No, what bothers me is that you think nothing of…of… humiliating me like that in public. Treating me like a thing, your possession that you can put your hands on whenever you want to."

"Is that it? My touch humiliates you?"

Vanessa took a step toward him, her breasts rising and falling with each breath, her delicate hands curled into fists. Arousal and lust warred with anger for prime position inside him. His body still wanted her, was still craving her after that small taste he'd gotten back at the club.

It shamed him, how badly he wanted a woman who saw him as she did. And yet, he could not stop himself. He had been craving her for twelve years. There was nothing that could destroy the desire. Not years of separation, not other lovers, not even the anger that was rolling through him like a tidal wave.

He curved his arm around her waist and pulled her to him, his hand drifting down until it touched the rounded curve of her bottom. "I don't believe that. I think what you really hate, Vanessa, is that no matter what, no matter how much you wish you didn't, no matter how ashamed you are of it, you want me."

Her expression was tight, mutinous, her dark eyes blazing with heat and rage. She put her hands on his chest, curled her fingers around the fabric of his shirt and stretched up on her toes, her breasts brushing against him. She kissed him, her mouth hungry on his, the explosion between them making the kiss at the club seem tame, harmless.

Desire was a living entity between them, dark and dangerous, driving them, pushing them. It was like hurtling toward a cliff, knowing they would both go over the edge if they didn't stop. And yet, knowing that, neither of them stopped.

Lazaro doubted if he could.

She slipped her tongue between his lips, tasting him, teasing him, and a flood of pure lust spread through him, overtaking him. He slid his hand down and cupped her bottom, drew her hard up against his erection.

Vanessa's stomach contracted when she felt the evidence of his arousal. He still wanted her. And even though she was angry at him, she wanted him. Maybe even more because of that anger, all of her emotions mixing, the anger in her a lit match against flammable desire. She wanted him more than she wanted her next breath, and it didn't make any sense to her.

Sex, in her mind, had always been about love and roses and perfect moments. This was as far from a perfect moment as she'd ever imagined, and yet she wanted him. All of him. Every last muscular inch.

She slid her hand sideways and wedged her fingers into the gap of his buttoned-up shirt. He was all hot, hard flesh. She traced a line along his skin, the faint scrape of chest hair against her palm sending a shiver of excitement through her.

On the dance floor, she'd felt as if a part of herself had been unlocked, releasing a desire for more of life than she'd been living. It had been a taste of freedom, and now she was starving for it.

She always thought things through. She planned and rationalized and made sure she was making the right decisions for everyone involved, the right decision for her family name.

But now she wanted Lazaro. And it wasn't about the company, or the marriage or anything beyond the desire to find pleasure in the man who aroused her beyond words.

"Let's go upstairs," she said, her voice breathy and unfamiliar, her words echoing in the empty lobby.

He looked down at her, his jaw tight, a muscle ticking in his cheek. Every hard line of his body was locked and tense, and she could feel his heart raging beneath her palm. He wanted her every bit as much as she wanted him.

The knowledge sent a shot of pure giddiness through her, a kind of power she'd never fully understood before.

"I don't like to be teased," he said, his voice rough, his accent more pronounced.

"I'm not teasing." She held his gaze, tried to keep her hands, her legs, from trembling. Her voice at least was steady. She was deadly serious.

"Tell me what you want." He lowered his head, his lips hovering above hers.

"You," she whispered, the word torn from her.

"More," he ground out. "Tell me more."

Her heart thundered hard, her cheeks hot. "I want…" She swallowed. This wasn't the time to be timid. There was no room for lies, for self-protection. "I want you. Your hands, your mouth, your…" A shudder of desire racked her body. "I want to make love with you. Tonight."

CHAPTER EIGHT

FINALLY. Tonight she would be his. At last he would take the edge off of the burning desire that had plagued his sleep since the day he'd first seen Vanessa Pickett.

He growled low in his throat and pulled her to him, kissing her, tasting her, his body on fire with the need to push her up against the wall and take her then and there. It would be so easy to slide that dress up over her hips and have her that way, so easy and so tempting.

He pulled away from her and pushed the button on the wall to bring the elevator down. He wanted her, desperately. But he knew she didn't want a public display. And it mattered. Because when she'd spoken of humiliation, it had been genuine.

His stomach was a tight ball of pain. Her humiliation might simply be because it was him and not some purebred show boy her father had selected for her.

But then, Vanessa's relationships had never been news- or gossip-worthy, and he had a feeling she was simply private. The intense desire to protect that part of her, to protect *her*, shocked him.

Even if her humiliation was centered around being caught with him, he found he didn't want to make her feel that way.

The lift doors opened and he took her hand and led her

inside, hitting the button immediately, unwilling to wait any longer than absolutely necessary.

She looked at him, her cheeks flushed pink, her lips bright and swollen from kissing him. He cared about her not being humiliated because he wanted her filled with nothing but desire. He wanted her mind blank of everything but the need for him to be inside her, because when he was touching her, that was how he felt, and he wanted her to feel the same.

This moment wasn't about revenge. It was about satisfying a need that had gnawed at him for the past twelve years.

As soon as the elevator doors opened into the vast living area of the penthouse he took her in his arms again, and she came willingly, her soft, delicate hands sliding over his chest, his back. Her lips were hot and soft against his neck.

Vanessa didn't think. She just felt. Nothing else mattered. Nothing. She was determined not to let it matter.

She just wanted to feel. She wanted Lazaro. And she was going to have him. There were so many things in life she'd denied herself, so many things she'd wanted that she'd walked away from because of propriety. Lazaro was one of them.

Not now.

This was her moment. All hers. It was only about desire and want and satisfying the ache inside her, filling the cavernous void that had seemed to grow with each passing year.

She'd spent so long drifting. Walking down a path simply because she'd gone too far to turn back. But she didn't really feel alive. She felt heartburn and angst and stress. But there had to be more than that.

This was more. This was different. And it was hers.

He was hers.

She slid her hands up his chest, his muscles tightening beneath her palms, his chest rising sharply with his quick intake of breath. He'd accused her of teasing him. Maybe she had teased him, but no more than she'd teased herself. She was haunted by her memories of him, of what might have been.

No more what-ifs. No more teasing.

The first step was always the hardest. Her fingers trembled as she slid the top button on his shirt through the buttonhole. The next one was easier, desire taking over and banishing nerves and doubts.

She flattened her hands on his bare chest, felt his heartbeat, strong and fast. She pushed his shirt from his shoulders and let it fall to the floor. He didn't move, he only stood in front of her, a bronzed god of masculine perfection, each muscle perfectly cut and defined. The way the light worked with his physique, adding even more extreme definition to his body, made her want to capture it on film. Forever. For her.

Her fingertips skimmed down his torso, over his washboard-flat stomach and down to his belt buckle. She sucked in a breath and worked the belt loose, letting it fall open. She felt driven now to uncover him, to see him, all of him. She had wondered, for so many years she had wondered, and now she didn't think she could wait another second to see the body her mind had woven fantasies around since she was sixteen.

She pushed his pants and underwear down his hips in one jerky movement, and he kicked them to the side, his eyes never leaving hers. He made no move toward her, he simply stood, naked, completely aroused, in the middle of his living room.

His confidence boosted hers. He wanted this. He wanted her. For once, she wasn't going to worry about possible inadequacy.

She moved her hands down, not quite touching him intimately. He closed his eyes and put his hand over hers, guiding her toward his erection. Her stomach tightened, nerves making a guest appearance now.

She took a breath and placed her hand over his hard shaft. He was hot steel beneath her palm, the hard length of him speaking of his desire for her. She felt her internal muscles tighten as she explored him, nerves fleeing, unable to exist alongside the need that was filling her now.

She squeezed him gently, then again with more strength, increased boldness, when a raw sound of pleasure escaped his lips. His civility was all gone now. Lost in desire, his custom suit on the floor, he was just a man. And he called to everything feminine inside her, made her ache with the need to have him.

"You are overdressed now, I think, *querida*," he said, his voice raw.

She felt the slide of the zipper, a rush of cool air on her back, and then her dress was pooled at her feet. She was still wearing her high heels and a barely there bra and panty set. She should have felt silly, or embarrassed or something. But she didn't.

Because she saw the hunger in his eyes. Saw the need that reflected her own.

And she felt powerful. Powerful and turned on.

"Kiss me," she said, reaching for him.

"Un momento." He unclasped her bra and discarded it. "Beautiful."

He cupped her breast, sliding his thumb over her nipple. She sucked in a breath and watched his dark hand cover her pale flesh. He leaned in and kissed her neck, then lower still, drawing one tightened bud into his mouth, teasing it with the tip of his tongue.

"Laz…" She gripped his head and held him to her, hoping that he would keep her from sliding to the floor.

He lowered himself to his knees, his lips skimming over her ribs, her stomach. He pushed her panties down her legs, baring her to him. She closed her eyes then and just felt. He kissed her thigh, his hands moving down her legs, unfastening the buckle on one of her shoes. He moved his thumb over her ankle as he removed her high heel, the contact on a totally unerotic point on her body sending sparks of sensation skittering through her.

He did the same with her other shoe, tossing it to the side along with the rest of her clothes.

"Sit down," he said, his voice rough but steady.

She looked behind her and saw the plush velvet couch. She'd forgotten where she was for a moment. Everything had gone fuzzy around the edges, everything except for Lazaro.

She lowered herself to the couch, unsure why she was doing it, only knowing that, in this instance, obeying Lazaro was going to be the most rewarding course of action. She didn't know how she knew, only that she did.

"I have dreamed of this. Of you," he said, on his knees before her. "Of how you would look. Of how you would taste."

He pressed a kiss to her inner thigh, his hands moving to grip her hips and draw her to the edge of the couch.

Her entire body was trembling, inside and out, desire and curiosity defeating any of the embarrassment she should be feeling. Because this wasn't about propriety. This was about need. And she needed Lazaro.

She wove her fingers through his hair as he continued kissing her, higher, until he hit the spot that was aching for his touch. He slid his tongue over her, the friction sending heat and flame through her body.

She could feel something building in her, could feel the onset of her climax, so close. So close. He released his grip on her hips and pushed one finger inside her, the rhythm of his penetration working in time with the flick of his tongue over the bundle of nerves at the apex of her thighs.

The tension that had been building, low and tight, released, pleasure rolling through her in pulsing waves.

When she came back to herself, Lazaro had joined her on the couch, his hands moving over her curves, caressing every inch of her body. He leaned in and kissed her lips. "Good?" he asked.

She nodded, her voice lost to her.

He shifted positions so that he was over her, and she parted her thighs for him, making room. The head of his erection pressed against her and she held her breath for a moment, waiting, for pain or satisfaction or completion, whatever it would bring.

He cursed sharply and got up from the couch, crossing to his discarded pants.

"What?" she asked, feeling dizzy.

"Condom." He fished a packet from his wallet and tore it open, making quick work of rolling it on.

They'd stopped at the condom point once before. But she had no intention of stopping him now. She couldn't stop. She had to have him. All of him. For her. For him. Because they both needed it. She did.

She shook with her need to have him. Only him.

Her heart jolted when he moved to her, not from virginal nerves, but because she understood why there hadn't been another man. It had been so easy to blame it on circumstances. To believe it was because of the specter of her almost-fiancé.

It was because of Lazaro. Because she wanted him. Because she'd been waiting for him. So stupid. So dangerously foolish. But she'd had a taste of true passion in his arms, and no one else had ever aroused anything remotely as intense.

Why take less?

And tonight, Lazaro wasn't offering less than what she'd felt before. It was more. So much more than she remembered.

"Thank you," she said, her teeth chattering slightly as a wave of emotion washed through her, making her shake inside.

"For?"

"For remembering. The condom. I think I would have forgotten."

She was glad he'd thought of it, because she hadn't. There was so much happening and she couldn't think straight. Marriage or not, she wasn't ready for a baby. Not when everything at Pickett was so unstable.

She pushed that thought to the side and focused on Lazaro. Nothing else mattered. Not now.

She wrapped her arms around his neck and kissed him as he moved back into the position he'd been in, poised to take possession of her body. She kissed him as he thrust into her, focusing only on the pleasure he was giving her with the erotic glide of his tongue, ignoring the vague, tearing pain.

It passed quickly at least, her body adjusting to him, welcoming him. He put his hand on her thigh and urged her to wrap her leg around his, as she'd done on the dance floor. The move opened her up to him, made each of his thrusts stimulate her inside and out.

Pleasure built inside her again, lower, deeper, more intense. He kissed her neck, her collarbone, lowering his head so that he could take one of her nipples into his mouth, his thumb gliding over the other one.

She arched against him, meeting his thrusts, letting his hands, his body, his touch, block out everything. Everything but the climax she was working toward, everything but the pleasure that was threatening to overtake her, body and soul.

His thrusts came faster, harder, his control slipping. He moved his hands to her hips, his fingers digging into her skin. She slid her tongue over the line of his jaw and she felt every muscle in his body shake, then seize as a harsh groan escaped his lips. His pleasure—seeing it, feeling him pulse inside her—pushed her over the edge and she was lost in her own sensation, in the ecstasy that drowned out everything else, every thought, every worry.

She wrapped her arms around his neck, holding on to him, holding him to her. For the moment, nothing else mattered. It was only Vanessa and Lazaro, and everything else was just peripheral. For now, this was the reality, and everything else was the fantasy. Distant and fuzzy. Unimportant.

Lazaro shifted and extricated himself from her arms, standing and walking into the bathroom. She watched him walk the whole way, dazed, sated and enjoying the view.

Her eyes started to flutter closed, a drugging sleepiness overtaking her, making her limbs feel heavy, pleasantly numb.

Lazaro walked back in, his expression blank. "Vanessa..."

"Don't," she mumbled, sleep slurring her words. "I promise, we can fight in the morning, but right now, can we just... sleep?"

He returned to the couch, settling beside her and drawing her into his arms. She put her head on his chest, his heart thundering beneath her cheek. Tomorrow would be reality. For now, she was going to enjoy the fantasy.

Lazaro watched a shaft of pink sunlight catch one of the windows on a building outside, throwing its reflection into the living room of the penthouse, illuminating Vanessa's perfect body.

He had built fantasies around the idea of what her body might look like, of the way her face would look when he brought her to the peak of pleasure. Of what her silken flesh would feel like beneath his fingers.

He had convinced himself that there was no way she, any woman, could live up to what he had made Vanessa in his mind. A fantasy spun in the mind of an eighteen-year-old, left to grow, had to be beyond reality. Beyond what was possible.

But Vanessa had surpassed a mere fantasy last night. She had been perfection, a taste of heaven and light and a kind of soul-deep satiation he had never believed existed.

He could not have conjured up something more, something better.

She was complete female perfection. Every curve. Every dip and swell. Skin like cream; plump, pink-tipped breasts that made his stomach tighten with desire. Everything about her—touch, taste, sight and scent—satisfied him in a way that was utterly foreign.

But, incredibly, coupled with that bone-deep satisfaction was a need for more that made him ache.

She stirred against him, her nipples brushing his chest, the contact lighting a fire in his blood. He moved his hand over the curve of her hip and she made a soft sound of pleasure and arched into him.

He dropped a kiss onto her bare shoulder and her eyes popped open. She rolled slightly and slid off the couch onto the floor, cursing before standing, her cheeks bright pink.

"Where are my clothes?" she asked, her voice rusty from disuse.

"Around," he said, pushing himself into a sitting position.

"Could you not look at me for a second please?"

"I've seen it, Vanessa. More than seen."

"Please," she said again.

He looked out the window, all his concentration taken by the effort it took to pull his focus away from her perfect body.

"You act as though you haven't had a morning after before," he said.

The telling silence made his stomach tighten, and he couldn't keep himself from looking back at her. She was standing there, clutching her dress to her chest, biting her lip.

"You haven't?" he asked.

She huffed out a breath, shifted her weight to one side, one bare hip looking more rounded, more prominent. "How many women have you slept with?"

"Excuse me?"

Her dark eyebrows shot upward. "Rude question, isn't it?"

"Odd," he said. "And pointless."

"Then I don't suppose I have to answer either."

His heartbeat quickened. It really shouldn't matter, and yet, he found it did. Because he wanted her to be his. His alone. The idea that no other man had ever been with her like that sent a rush of pure, unenlightened testosterone through him. His. In every way possible.

"I don't know," he said, disgust filling him as he spoke the words.

"You don't know if I have to answer the question?"

"I don't know how many women I've slept with," he bit out.

She frowned. "Oh."

He hadn't anticipated this. That his vast experience could cause him shame. He didn't brag about his luck with women, but inevitably, if there was an article about him written anywhere, his reputation with the opposite sex was mentioned. It had always earned him a certain measure of respect.

It wasn't respect on Vanessa's face. It was disappointment. It passed quickly, her expression neutral again, her eyes focused on a spot just past him.

Even though it was a fleeting impression of disappointment, it left a hollow feeling in his chest.

"I answered," he said.

She met his eyes. "Then no, I haven't had a morning after before."

"How is that possible, Vanessa? I didn't pick you out as a virgin when you were sixteen."

"But I was. Well, obviously I was then, since last night I still was."

"Why?"

"Why don't you know how many women you've slept with?" she countered, clutching her clothes more tightly against her.

Because I was trying to forget you. He held back the stark, honest thought that filled his mind.

He shrugged and stood. "Because I'm a man, Vanessa. Once I made money, women were readily available and I took advantage."

She stood, her focus on an undefined spot on the carpet. He didn't like the look on her face. She sighed heavily and then lifted her face, meeting his eyes. "We're trading, are we?" He nodded in confirmation. "Because, in addition to the fact that my father is a professional at chasing men out of my life, I wanted…someone to want me. Not my father's money. Or my status. Or… I just hadn't found that." She averted her gaze.

"I didn't care about your money or your status."

"You just wanted sex?"

Her words bit into him. He shrugged. "I was eighteen. There isn't much more a horny teenage boy wants. Not only that, I was experienced, too much for my age. It's what we did. I think it was part of what made being so poor bearable. Taking advantage of those few moments of oblivion. It's how I related to women, so, yes, it was what I wanted."

"But it's not all you want now. Now you want my connections too."

"Things have changed."

She nodded slightly. "Can you turn around again? I don't want to have to back out of the room."

"Why did you decide to sleep with me last night?"

Her lips flattened into a line. "When I figure that out I'll get back to you."

Lazaro turned his back and faced the view, letting her walk out without an audience. He tried to ignore the odd, crushing weight that was pressing down on his chest.

CHAPTER NINE

"WHERE have you been?"

Vanessa walked back into the penthouse after a day spent in careful avoidance of Lazaro, exhausted, feet aching.

Lazaro was standing at the bar, palms rested flat on the black marble surface, his dark eyes filled with intensity. She'd spent the afternoon taking photographs of Buenos Aires, deliberately not thinking about the night before and generally having a very relaxing day.

Well, the relaxation was clearly about to end.

"Out," she said.

"Out where?" he said, his voice low, deadly.

"It's not really your business is it?" She felt compelled to put distance between them, to exert some kind of control in a situation where she really didn't have any.

"It is my business," he said.

"No, Lazaro, it's my business." She started to walk toward her bedroom.

"You're mine, Vanessa, that means I have a right to know how you spend your time."

She turned sharply. "I do not belong to you. And I never will. A marriage license isn't a deed of ownership."

He slammed his palm on the top of the bar. "That is not what I meant."

Anger fired through her. "It is, though, isn't it? You want

me to be this sparkly possession that you can show off. The proof of how far you've come. A chance to give the world the finger. Well, great. But you had to make sure that I had no other options open to get me to agree to marry you. I had no other choice. Don't forget that."

She walked straight ahead to the balcony, tears, hot and angry, blurring the lights of the city. She slammed the sliding door behind her and leaned against the railing, pressing her palms hard against her eyes, trying to stop herself from dissolving, trying to keep from making a total idiot of herself.

She couldn't let him affect her like this. Because he was dangerously close to being right in some ways. It wasn't that she truly believed he had any ownership of her, but power... she was letting him have all kinds of power over her emotions. And as long as she did, he would always be the one in control, because she didn't have a hold over him. He might like her body, but that was sex, and with nothing other than lust behind it, it would be temporary.

And what would happen then? She would be left behind, the faux-political wife committed to standing at her husband's side no matter what he'd done. No matter how broken she was inside.

And if she let him, he could destroy her.

She gritted her teeth. She didn't know why it was Lazaro. Why was he the only one who brought this out in her? She only knew that he was.

She closed her eyes and pictured a day twelve years earlier, the hot summer sun warming her skin, a boy with a smile that seemed to be meant only for her.

It hadn't been true then. Yet part of her still clung to the ridiculous fantasy. The part of her that had been waiting for him...

It was why she'd slept with him. She'd told him she didn't

know why, and that had been a lie. He was the only man she'd ever really wanted.

And part of her…part of her believed he had to feel the same way. She housed some serious delusion inside herself.

"I didn't force you into bed last night. It had nothing to do with our agreement or blackmail or the future of Pickett."

She turned around and saw Lazaro striding toward her, his expression cold with black fury.

"I didn't get in your bed. That was your couch," she said tightly.

"I didn't force you to have sex with me." he said. "You wanted it."

She couldn't deny it. She wished she could. Wished she were capable of lying on that level, to his face, without remorse. But she couldn't. She'd told him last night that she wanted him. She had directed the evening activities once they'd left the club.

"You want *me*," he said, his eyes never leaving hers, coal-black and intense, glittering in the dim light. "Say it."

She swallowed hard and turned away from him, her eyes focused on the skyline.

She felt him approach, her body responding to his, her breasts getting heavy, the pulse between her thighs pounding hard. The empty ache threatening to swallow her. She wanted him, again, during a fight. She didn't know herself. Didn't know what it was he did to her.

Only that he sparked a fire in her that no one else ever had. And it wasn't just about sex or lust or desire. It was so much more. He showed her how lacking her life was. Being with him, near him, seeing the steps he'd taken to change his life, made her so acutely aware of how little she'd done. Of how hollow all of her so-called achievements were. She'd had it all handed to her and she'd still messed up.

All her thoughts evaporated when Lazaro put his hand on

the curve of her waist, swept her hair to one side, exposing her neck to the warm night breeze. "Tell me you want me," he said, a raw note in his voice now, showing a crack in his iron control.

And she realized that he needed to hear it. That her words hadn't glanced off his thick armor, but that they'd struck a blow. She'd imagined that he was invincible—a man with so much power, the freedom to do what he wanted. A man who lived without restriction.

But he wasn't. She flashed back to that moment in the club and saw his anger for what it was. She had hurt him. She had rejected him.

He slid his hand up, cupped her breast, the thin barrier of her dress providing no protection from the sensual assault. He pinched her nipple lightly between his thumb and forefinger and tugged.

Her head fell back, and he took advantage, kissing her neck as he continued to tease her body.

"You want me, Vanessa," he said, not a question this time. "Me."

"Yes," she whispered.

"And it's not about money or what I can do for Pickett right now, is it?"

She shook her head, biting her lip to hold back the whimper of pleasure that was climbing her throat. She felt her dress give as he slid the zipper down, exposing her back. His hand drifted over the line of her spine, the light touch sending heavy waves of arousal through her.

She relaxed her shoulders and let her dress fall, the warm, heavy breeze kissing her bare skin, a completely foreign sensation. But no one would be able to see them. Even if someone might be able to, she wasn't certain she could bring herself to care.

Lazaro moved his hands over her stomach, his touch firm, warm, so sexy it made her knees weak.

"No, it's not about anything but…" She sucked in a sharp breath when he covered her breasts with one of his hands and pressed against her stomach with the other, drawing her more tightly against him, bringing his erection into firm contact with her bottom. "But how much I want you," she choked out.

He kissed her neck, her shoulder, and a tremor wracked her body, longing making her weak. But there was a fire smoldering in her stomach, a need for more. For more than simple lust. She'd confessed to wanting him, apart from their marriage arrangement and everything else.

She needed him to do the same.

She wiggled out of his grasp and turned to face him, her back against the balcony railing, her breasts pressed tightly against his chest. "Tell me you want me too."

He rocked against her, the hard length of him pressing into her stomach. "Doesn't it feel like I want you?"

"Tell me you want *me*, right now. Me. Not my status. Not my connections." She slid her hand down his chest, past his belt, pressing her palm over his erection. "Tell me," she said again.

His eyes were dark, nearly black with passion, his jaw locked tight, tension holding his body taut, every muscle rock-hard. "I want you."

"My name," she said, the words coming out broken. "I need you to say it."

"I want you, Vanessa."

She let out a gust of air. "Lazaro."

He captured her lips with his, his kiss hungry, devouring, and she returned it, sliding her tongue over his, taking his bottom lip lightly between her teeth and tugging. He growled and scooped her up in his arms.

"We're making it to bed this time," he said, striding into the penthouse and heading into his room.

She'd avoided his room since they'd arrived in Argentina, and not by accident. Just seeing that big bed pushed her desire up to another level. Of course, now her fantasies were strengthened by the memory of what it was like to be with him, to have him inside her, his steady rhythm taking her to the heights of ecstasy.

He set her down in the center of the bed and she shivered.

"Cold?"

She shook her head.

"Nervous?" he asked.

"I am, a little bit." It didn't seem like the place for self-preservation. In this moment at least, honesty seemed imperative.

He made quick work of the buttons on his shirt, shrugging it off and casting it to the floor. Vanessa could only stare at all the sculpted, masculine perfection before her. She'd been with him once, but it didn't mean it wasn't intimidating. He was perfect, experienced and fantastic in bed. She wasn't sure she was offering him an even trade.

"I just…" She got up on her knees and inched to the edge of the bed, putting her hand flat against his stomach, his muscles shifting beneath her palm. "I don't know if I can compete with the memory of…more women than you can remember."

He encircled her wrist with his hand and pulled her gently to him, kissing her on the lips. "There's a reason I don't remember. They didn't matter. They aren't here in bed with us. When I look at you, you're all I can see."

For now, she would accept his words. She wouldn't think too far into them. She refused to wonder if he'd felt the same about all of them at the time, only to have his desire for them fade as time went on, and to have memories of them fade completely later.

She pushed that thought aside because she didn't want to think of it now. Even if it was stupid and dangerous, she wanted to believe him.

He discarded the rest of his clothes and joined her on the bed, kissing her, putting his hand on the curve of her hip and dragging her panties down her legs. She kicked her shoes off and shoved them off the bed with her foot, anxious to have all of the barriers removed.

And when he took her in his arms, every inch of his body pressed against hers, she closed her eyes and inhaled his scent, tears forming in her eyes because he was everything she'd fantasized and more. He had been perfect the first night, but that had been frantic, and the main event had been so new it had been hard to focus on the finer points of what it meant to be intimate with a man. With Lazaro.

Her fingertips blazed a trail over his bicep, his skin smooth, hot, his muscles hard beneath. She skimmed her hands over his hair-roughened chest, flat abs, down to his hardened shaft. She kissed his mouth, catching the harsh sound of pleasure that rose in his throat as she explored his body.

He moved his hand down between her thighs and she stilled her movements then, luxuriating in the response he could call from her body. Orgasm built in her, quick and intense, ripples of sensation making her internal muscles tighten.

"I love watching your face when you come," he whispered.

She laughed, her throat tight with emotion. "I can't think of anything when you do that."

"Then I'm doing something right."

Yes, he was. It was something that reached down into her, something that surpassed her body and went straight for her soul.

He pulled away from her for a moment and opened the drawer to the bedside table, retrieving a condom.

And then he was in her, filling her, the friction so delicious it surpassed the climax she'd just experienced. She gave herself up to the sensation washing through her body, to the building pleasure that was blocking out everything else.

Her orgasm broke over her like a wave, spinning her in the tide, making her feel weightless. For a moment there was nothing more than her and Lazaro. Nothing more than what he was making her feel.

Dimly, she was aware of him coming with a harsh groan, his body braced hard against her as he kissed her fiercely.

Afterward, she lay with her hand on his chest, his fingers sifting through her hair, their legs tangled together.

Vanessa drew back and looked at him, running her fingers over his stubble-roughened jaw, tracing his brow, his high cheekbones. "You look different," she said, languor slurring her speech slightly. "But the same too."

"I do?"

"Mmm-hmm. You're older, in a good way, and your nose…" She touched the bump on the bridge of his nose. "What happened?"

"I broke it."

"I figured as much."

He rolled onto his back, away from her. "You said the other day that your father was very good at running interference when he doesn't approve of the men you're associating with. I carry permanent proof of that."

CHAPTER TEN

VANESSA felt as if all the air had been sucked out of her body. Because the meaning in Lazaro's words was stunningly, sickeningly clear.

She didn't know how it could be true, but she knew it was. Without knowing details, she knew. Because it explained everything. The animosity that rolled off Lazaro like a physical force when he spoke about her family, her father. She'd simply thought he was angry. Angry at life, angry in general.

That wasn't it. She'd been wrong. He was angry at her family. At her.

"What happened?" she asked.

She didn't want to know. She wanted to cover her ears and hide under the covers. But that wasn't an option. She had to know.

"Tell me, Vanessa. Did you ever question why I never came back to your father's estate? Why you never saw me again? Where my mother went?"

"I… Of course I did." And she'd made it all about herself. Because, of course, Lazaro had never come back because she'd refused to sleep with him. But she was a fool. A shallow idiot who had never been able to see past herself.

"What was your conclusion?" he asked, his voice soft.

"I thought you didn't want to see me anymore because I wouldn't put out," she said. She wished she could protect herself and lie, but in bed with Lazaro, nothing between them, there couldn't be any lies. No matter how much she wanted to lie to him. No matter how much she wished he'd lie to her.

"Amazing that it seems neither of us knew each other at all."

"What do you mean?"

"I thought you turned me down because I was good enough to play with, but not good enough to sleep with."

"That wasn't it at all. I was… You were my first kiss and I wasn't ready to go from first kiss to bed in five minutes time."

"I said things then that I should not have said," he said. "I thought you were playing a game with me."

"The same game you thought I was playing in the club?" She didn't need a hint of affirmation and she didn't get one. "It wasn't a game. I was worried about…what people would think if they saw me behaving that way."

"With me?"

"With anyone. But…you do make me lose control, Lazaro, and it scares me sometimes."

Silence settled between them and she knew it was up to her to ask again. Even though it had been derailed and she'd been given an out. There was no simple out. They had to wade through the mess of the past if they were ever going to go forward. It was that simple.

She took a shuddering breath. "What did my father do to you?"

"Not your father personally. He would never have gotten his hands dirty that way. He has people on hand to take care of life's more unsavory problems."

"You were an unsavory problem?"

"Of the worst sort. I had my sights set on his daughter's virtue." Vanessa felt every line in Lazaro's body tense, could sense the scarcely harnessed aggression that was flowing through him. She wanted to soothe him, and she honestly didn't know how.

"What did they do?"

"After I left the guesthouse that night I was upset. I went into town. I was followed. I don't know that you need details, but I woke up facedown in the alley and, at the time, a broken nose was the least of my problems."

"They beat you?" She scrambled out of the bed, her breath coming hard, fast. "My father had you beaten?"

"You didn't know, then," he said, his voice flat.

"No." She put her hand on her stomach, trying to quell the nausea that was rising in her. "You thought I knew? You thought that I..."

"Your father puts on a convincing front of civility, Vanessa. At the time I thought it was possible you did the same."

"I would never..."

"I know. I had let go of the idea of you being involved a long time ago."

She was relieved to hear him say that, even if that was selfish.

"I told you we were fired from the estate, but there was more," Lazaro continued. "Your father made sure no one else would hire us either. We were evicted from our apartment. Usually, we had a shelter to sleep in, but sometimes we ended up sleeping outside. My mother's health did not do well in those conditions."

For the third time since Lazaro had come back into her life, she felt the ground shift beneath her feet.

"I knew..." Her voice cracked. "I knew my father was a hard man, I knew he was controlling, but I didn't know...I didn't know he'd gone that far. I had a... There was a man I was interested in at Pickett when I was first hired on and my father was adamant about me not seeing him because he was just an employee. I did what he asked. I didn't want to be with anyone he didn't approve of. I just didn't imagine he would ever do something like… Something so horrible."

She felt like her world was falling away, shattering into tiny little pieces, fragile and in danger of being scattered by the wind.

She had protected her father's legacy at the expense of everything. Her dreams. She could hardly remember her dreams anymore because she'd shoved them to the side with ruthless efficiency when she was thirteen years old in order to fulfill the demands of the most important man in her life.

And that man was a coward. A criminal.

She believed Lazaro's words. She felt the truth of them all the way down to her soul. She was sick with the truth of it spreading through her like poison, undeniable and deadly.

"I survived, Vanessa," he said, his voice hard. "More than. And I don't want your wide-eyed pity."

"I don't pity you," she said.

She didn't. It was impossible to pity a man like Lazaro. He was too strong, the pride that radiated from him forbidding anything as debasing as pity.

But she felt betrayed. Betrayed by the man who shared her blood, the man whose legacy she had fought so hard to preserve. The man who had brought so much destruction into the lives of other people for the sake of his vision for the future.

It made her feel tainted. Made everything in her, her ambition, her *blood,* feel dirty. That blood that was supposed to be so important, that was supposed to define her…she hated it now.

"It is done, Vanessa. The only thing I regret is that my mother lived out her last days in discomfort, rather than in the lifestyle she deserved. But it was the defining moment in my life." The gleam in his eyes was deadly, cold and devoid of anything tender. "It was the moment when I realized that

I would stop at nothing to make it to the top where I could crush men like your father beneath my heel."

It was the venom in his voice, not aggressive or blatant, woven into every syllable, touching every word, that shocked her the most. The hatred that was there.

She had been a fool. She had imagined that Lazaro's quest was about vanity, but it was about something so much deeper. She had thought herself a trophy to him, but that was so far removed from the truth it was laughable.

She was his avenue to vengeance. He was using her, a fact she'd known from the beginning, but what she hadn't realized was exactly what she was being used for.

He would use her not only to bring him to the top, but to mock her father's efforts. To show him that he now owned everything that her father had tried to keep from him. That he, Lazaro, had won.

Even as the realization crashed through her, she could understand it, but she didn't want to be Lazaro's pawn. Or his queen, as the case may be.

And yet, she wasn't certain she had a choice because everything felt tangled now, complicated beyond fixing.

She couldn't feel nothing for this man who made love to her with such explosive, sweet passion. She couldn't shut off what she felt for her first lover, the man she had fallen for at sixteen. As clichéd as it was, she felt connected to him now. As though he were a part of her.

If she were really honest with herself, the connection wasn't new. Having their bodies joined was just a physical manifestation of what had been from the beginning. He'd been in her from the start.

It was why she had always kept an eye on his career when he'd started getting media attention. Why she'd silently cheered for his success even while she hurt inside over not sharing it with him.

It was why part of her wanted to cheer for his success now in this, his quest for vengeance and justice.

And part of her wanted to scream at him and ask him why he'd dragged her into everything. Or more to the point, why he'd made her care. Why he looked at her as though he wanted to devour her. Why he kissed her as though he were sampling some rare, exquisite wine. How he could make her feel this way when she knew he had to hate her.

Why couldn't he just be a jerk? Why couldn't she simply see him as he was: a man set on using her for his own ends?

But it wasn't so simple that it could be reduced to anything that easy to understand. There was nothing simple about it.

There was nothing simple about the massive knot of emotion that was filling her chest, making it hard to breathe. There was nothing easy about the thick tension that hung in the air. Sexual. Emotional.

"Come back to bed," Lazaro said, pulling back the covers.

"I should maybe go—"

"You're coming to bed. With me. You need to sleep, we're going to be flying out tomorrow."

And because she was exhausted, and because she ached to be in his arms, she climbed back into the bed.

He drew her close to his body, his hands moving over her curves, soothing her, making her brain fuzzy and her body sleepy.

Her last thought before drifting off was, how did a man with so much anger in him, a man who was only using her, make her feel more wanted, more desired, than anyone else in her life ever had?

Reality set in quickly back in Boston. Lazaro was busy, and Vanessa had a mountain of paperwork on her desk, thanks to the remaining fossils Pickett Industries had accounts with who had never heard of sending documents via email.

Her office was her home away from home again, and her personal life was back to being nonexistent. She doubted it had ever really existed. Lazaro was some unholy mash-up of her personal and professional life, not to mention her new-found sex life, which she was missing after a few nights alone in her big, cold bed.

She would see him tonight though. After work he was taking her to a big gala that was historically reserved for a very select group. The Pickett name was always on the list and, since word of their engagement had spread and Lazaro was now becoming a part of that legacy, he had secured an invitation too.

She was serving her purpose at least—bringing Lazaro into the hallowed institutions of the American aristocracy. Into a cornerstone of which she was about to put a big crack.

Her phone buzzed and she hit the intercom button. "Yes?"

"Ms. Pickett, your father is here to see you."

Vanessa swallowed hard. "Send him in."

Her father strode into the room, his expression dark. Dangerous. His gray eyebrows were locked together in a show of disapproval. "You've been on vacation?"

"I took some time off with my new fiancé," she said, striving to keep her tone light.

"Can you afford time off?"

"I have to do my part to ensure my marriage is successful."

"That isn't what you called me here to say though, is it, Vanessa?"

"No," she said slowly, standing from her chair, planting both palms firmly on her desk. She hoped the gesture conveyed confidence, because what she was really doing was trying to keep her knees from buckling. "I know what you did to Lazaro."

Her father didn't flinch. "I thought you might."

"You're a cold-blooded bastard," she said, through clenched teeth.

"I did it for you, Vanessa, so we could avoid a situation like this—you marrying so patently beneath your station."

"My station? Because Lazaro wasn't born into money he's somehow beneath me? Beneath you? Lazaro is a better man than you will ever be, and you have to keep men like him shut out because he has something you don't. He's brilliant, he solves problems. He even knows how to fix this disaster you and I are standing in."

Michael Pickett looked at her, his eyes—eyes she'd always imagined looking like her own—stared back at her, cold and dead. "Did you call me in here for the sole purpose of hearing your impassioned little speech or did you have a point?"

"I had a point," she said. "You will make sure Lazaro is welcomed into high society with your blessing. Because if you don't, I will let this place crumble. Hell, I'll tear it apart myself. Brick by brick."

"Insolent, ungrateful…"

"I don't think you understand the reality here. Lazaro and myself combined own the majority of this company. You don't have the power here. Not even close. Lazaro and some of our board members have close professional relationships and his influence carries a lot of weight."

"You would dismantle your family legacy? The one meant for your brother? The one he would have seen flourish?"

"For the man I love? In a heartbeat."

They were the truest words she'd ever spoken. She didn't realize it until she spoke them. She loved Lazaro. She would move heaven and earth for him. She would stand up to Michael Pickett for him. She *had* stood up to Michael Pickett. She would do it again, ten times over.

"Lazaro isn't a boy that you can have beaten and left for dead in an alley, not anymore." She took a breath. "And I'm not a little girl. I won't simply do as I'm told without looking into what's really going on. Lazaro isn't just going away," she said, watching her father's face for a hint of what he was thinking, whether he was going to explode.

Silence hung between them, the only sound Vanessa's thundering heart in her ears.

Her father's face remained set in stone. "Of course he will be welcomed," he said, his tone cold. "He's my future son-in-law."

"Yes," she said, over the blood roaring in her ears. "He is."

She watched her father leave and felt a pleasant numbness spread from the pain in her fingertips to the pain in her chest, blocking it out. She'd done what she had to do. She wouldn't allow her father to have any kind of victory, not in Lazaro's life, not in hers. Not now that she knew who he really was. Who she had been protecting, helping for so many years.

Her secretary buzzed her again. "Yes?" Her voice was shaking now, the adrenaline seeping from her system and leaving her weak, drained.

"Mr. Marino has sent a limo."

"And is Mr. Marino in said limo?"

"Not that I saw."

A spike of disappointment pierced the blessed numbness. A limo, but not the man himself. Well, that was life with rich, important men, she was well aware. As long as she served her purpose, things went smoothly. But she wouldn't be getting any excess attention.

"I'll be right down."

CHAPTER ELEVEN

Lazaro's heart squeezed tight when Vanessa walked into the main living area of his Beacon Hill penthouse.

She was dressed in her business clothes, wide-legged slacks and spiky heels combined with a dark fitted jacket and a brightly colored top underneath. Her dark hair was swept back into a low ponytail and the gloss on her lips was a sedate rose, perfect for board meetings. And, apparently, for making his blood pump hot and fast.

But then, there was never a time when his desire for Vanessa seemed to cool, no matter what she was wearing—or not wearing.

He had missed her over the past few days. He had hoped the separation might help him regain some of his control. But now that she was here, he was on fire with lust. A response that was as instant as it was beyond his control.

"I didn't bring my dress with me," she said, shifting her weight, her eyes scanning the room, careful not to land on him for too long. "I didn't realize you wanted me to meet you here."

"I bought you a dress."

Then she did look at him. "You bought me a dress? For tonight? I have one. I had what I was going to wear planned out."

"You won't need it," he said.

He'd seen the dress at a shop in Buenos Aires when they'd been there, and he'd instantly envisioned Vanessa wearing it. He'd contacted the designer and ordered the dress in a color and size he thought would suit Vanessa and had had it shipped back to Boston just for the gala.

It was the kind of thing she should have. Something made just for her. Something nice and expensive. She deserved everything he could give.

"But you didn't ask me."

"It was a surprise."

That earned him stony silence and a censorious look from her dark brown eyes. "Show me," she said, after a pause.

He led her through the main living area of the house and up the open staircase to the loft floor that overlooked the open kitchen, living- and dining-room portions of the penthouse. He opened the door to his bedroom and ushered her inside.

He noticed, for the first time, how Spartan everything was. How masculine. Vanessa looked so pale and delicate in these surroundings, out of place. The black-and-gray design scheme, the stark angled lines, didn't suit her at all.

That his room was a wholly masculine domain had never mattered before. He didn't bring women into his home. It was much too personal. Vanessa was the first woman he'd brought into his bedroom. And the first person he'd brought into the house for a very long time. Entertaining at home wasn't high on his agenda.

Vanessa walked over to the bed where the dress was draped across the black comforter, the red silk shocking against the dark background. There were gold shoes beside it, high heels with delicate ankle straps that he knew would draw attention to her slender legs.

She frowned as she examined the offering and his gut tightened.

"I don't know that it's a red sort of event," she said crisply.

He locked his teeth together, then loosened them, the stupid thing she'd said about TMJ ringing in his ears. "That's why you should wear it."

"So I'll stand out?"

"So everyone will look at us."

"And that's a good thing?"

Frustration boiled inside him. "Yes. I want everyone to see us there. To know I'm with you."

She frowned again. "I see."

"There's a wrap to wear over it. It will be cold tonight." As if that fixed his intent somehow.

"Okay."

Vanessa watched Lazaro stalk from the room, his annoyance with her a palpable presence that lingered long after he left.

She examined the dress spread out on his bed and the black cashmere wrap that was folded next to it. It was such an intimate thing, and yet he had presented it in a way that was anything but. The gesture spoke clearly of what she was to him, the part he expected her to play tonight. She was his accessory for the evening and he hadn't trusted her to dress accordingly. He had to go to extraordinary lengths to ensure that she was exactly as she should be. So that people would look at them.

So that he could use her as a status symbol.

Her stomach lurched.

Was he any different than her father?

Yes.

Yes, he was different. He would never have anyone harmed, would never do anything so reprehensible. But as far as his feelings for her? She was a thing. A possession.

You are mine.

His. His status symbol in red.

She picked the dress up by the spaghetti straps and held

it in front of her, the delicate fabric swishing as she lifted it. This was what she'd signed on for. Trophy wife, agreeable accessory who did as she was told in public, who put on a good front so that Lazaro could move freely in the upper levels of society.

It was what she'd signed on for, and now it seemed unbearable.

She didn't know if she had the strength to walk away, even if she wanted to. But she didn't know if she had the strength to stay, either. To stay and fulfill, in her husband's mind, the same thing that Beacon Hill property did. Nothing more than status.

She slowly took her clothes off, hands shaking as she folded her top and slacks and set them on the bed. She picked up the red dress and held it in front of her naked body, looking at herself in the mirror.

She picked the dress up and pulled it on, contorting her arm so that she could pull the zipper into place. It was daring, sexy in an overt way.

She picked the wrap up and draped it around her shoulders. It went a long way toward making the dress more respectable. She flung it back on the bed. If he wanted a show, she'd give the people a show. And if he didn't like it, that was too bad.

The gala was crowded with glittering men and women, the majority of them in black. Vanessa knew she stood out like a very vulgar sore thumb. For the first time in her life she wasn't dressed appropriately for the gathering. It wasn't a very good feeling.

But when she'd come out of the bedroom, Lazaro's eyes had lit with hungry flames, his expression telling her just how much he approved—until she'd told him she was going without the handy cover he'd given her. Since they'd arrived at the party he'd had his hand on her, on her back, her waist, his manner possessive.

She sighed and took a glass of champagne from a passing waiter. If his goal was to have them be the center of attention, his mission was well and truly accomplished. She was maybe being a little more obvious than he'd intended, but she hadn't been about to just cater to his wishes. If she'd had another dress at her disposal at his penthouse, she would have simply gone with that.

She tried to let the stares slide off her, tried not to worry about them.

Of course, it might not have been her the other guests were staring at. The women could just as easily be staring at Lazaro and not at her at all. In his custom-made black suit he looked a cut above every other man present. His olive skin was complemented perfectly by his red tie, and the suit showed the shape of his fabulous physique. It certainly made her want to undo every button and see the man beneath. She was sure she wasn't the only one with that thought.

Lazaro worked the room, his natural charisma on display tonight, charisma she had been pulled in by at the age of sixteen when he'd flashed her that killer smile of his for the first time.

She was so proud of him. Of all he had become. And she was merely his invitation to the event. She gripped the stem of her glass more tightly.

"Lazaro." A man Vanessa recognized from some gatherings at the Pickett estate stepped forward to shake Lazaro's hand. "I've been wanting to have a talk with you about some of the things going on at Garrison Limited."

"Have you?" Lazaro asked.

"Yes, I... Well, times being what they are, I thought you might want to come and give me a consultation on what I can do to keep up with the changing market."

"You can call my secretary and arrange an appointment."

"I will, I will. But…would you like to come and meet my business partner?"

Vanessa could sense Lazaro tensing beside her, could feel the annoyance radiating from him like a physical force.

"Of course," he said, ever the diplomat. "Hold this, please, Vanessa." He placed his champagne flute in her hand and walked away with the other man.

Vanessa's stomach sank into her toes as a similar scene flashed through her mind. The night at the art museum. Lazaro had been with a woman then. Vanessa had dubbed her a human cup-holder at the time.

She looked at her hand, at the full glass of champagne, the condensation running down the sides as the bubbles floated up to the surface. She set it down on the nearest table and leaned against the wall, dizzy with anger and hurt.

She wasn't different. She was the same as every other woman he'd ever been with.

No, even worse, she *was* different. He was stuck with her if he wanted to make it to the top, because of her name, her connections, things that were beyond her control. Things that couldn't be bought or negotiated for. If he could have done it any other way, he would have.

She was sure of that now.

It struck her now, just how foolish she was. That she'd imagined he could care for her when he carried so much anger toward her family, anger she couldn't even blame him for.

But, as sorry as she was for the sins of her father, they weren't her sins. They never had been. Her only crime had been loving him, wanting more from him than he could give. And she had committed it again twelve years on.

Because she loved him. And all she would ever be to him was status. A symbol of thoroughly meted-out vengeance. A trophy. He had never pretended otherwise. She was a fool.

He would never love her for who she was. Only for what she could do for him. And if she couldn't do anything for him anymore he would discard her without a backward glance. There was no doubt in her mind.

Could she handle another lifetime of that? Her father had only ever used her. He had held Thomas's memory, her love for her late brother, over her head to get her to do what she was told. He had played her like a master all of her life.

And Lazaro would have even more power. Because he had her heart.

"No," she whispered the word.

She had always defined herself by her last name. By the family legacy. But she had found more to herself in Buenos Aires. In Lazaro's arms. There was more to her than the preservation of a business. More to her than becoming a status symbol for her husband.

And she knew for a fact that she couldn't stay with him and take the crumbs of his affection. She deserved more. She deserved what everyone else had. Freedom. Choices.

Her heart expanded, even as it cracked inside her. She had the freedom to make choices, to follow the path she wanted to go down. She always had had.

She was making a choice now. For herself.

She looked at Lazaro, engrossed in his conversation, and then at the glass of champagne she'd set on the table.

Then she turned and walked out of the ballroom. Out of the building.

She called her driver. "I need to be picked up."

"Vanessa?" The voice on the other side of her door was frantic. Familiar.

She opened it and her heart jumped when she saw Lazaro, still dressed in his suit, his tie untied and draped over his shoulders, his jacket open, the top few buttons of his shirt undone.

"Where did you go?" he asked, his voice soft.

"I left."

"So I gathered, when I searched every last room in the building and didn't find you. I thought that something had happened to you."

The bleakness in his eyes, in his tone, spoke the truth of it.

Lazaro looked at her standing there, arms folded beneath her breasts, her dress, the dress she'd gone out of her way to tantalize him with, long discarded, and not by him as he'd fantasized. She was wearing blue pajama pants and a gray long-sleeved top, her makeup scrubbed off, leaving her face pink.

When he looked closer, he could tell it was not pink from being scrubbed. Her eyes were rimmed in red and there were shimmering tracks on her cheeks.

"Did something happen?" he asked, stepping into her home, not bothering to wait for an invitation. "Did someone hurt you?" He swore then and there that whoever it was would wish that Lazaro had been merciful and simply killed him. Because he would ruin the man. No one would ever harm Vanessa. Ever. She would want for nothing, not while she was his woman. His wife.

When he'd realized she wasn't at the gala, that she was gone…he'd imagined every horrible scenario possible, all of it flashing through his mind's eye at a rapid pace as panic flooded his body.

He'd stared into his future, one without her, black and empty, stretching before him. Blank nothing. The terror of it had been beyond anything he'd ever imagined.

But she was home in her pajamas. Safe.

"No. Yes."

"What happened?"

"I realized something."

"What was that?" he asked, his heart thundering, his body still high from the rush of adrenaline that had been propelling him since he'd realized she was gone.

Her brows locked together, her expression fierce and sad and completely stunning. "I can't marry you. More than that, I don't want to marry you."

The meaning of her words became clear slowly, and along with the meaning, a searing, tearing pain started deep in his chest, growing as her words resonated in him until it was a blinding, overwhelming ache that overtook him, immobilized his limbs, made his heart feel as if it had been removed and discarded.

"We have a deal." He managed to force the words out.

"We can work something else out. I don't want to do this," she said.

"Why is that, Vanessa? Because you didn't like the stares you were getting tonight, being with me? The man from the gutter? Or was it that the damn dress wasn't good enough for you? Do you need a bigger ring, is that it?"

"Lazaro…"

"Enough," he cut her off, unable to bear hearing her reasoning. Unable to be told how much he was wanting in her eyes. How beneath her he was. *Dios,* it choked him, made him feel as though his chest was caving in.

Desperation clawed at him, a black hole that threatened to take him down. He couldn't lose her. Not again. "You *will* marry me."

She shook her head. "I don't need to be in charge of Pickett anymore. I don't care about my father's legacy."

"And what about the employees? Their jobs?" If there was a problem, he would solve it. He always left himself the means to do so. If Vanessa thought otherwise, then she'd thoroughly underestimated him.

"Of course I care, but they'll still have jobs even if you replace me as CEO."

"Not if there is no more company."

She took a step back, her hands on her chest. "What are you saying?"

"I've bought more shares."

He'd never stopped acquiring them. When the opportunity presented, he had taken advantage. Leverage was valuable, and he had gone after all the leverage he could get himself. He was glad he had now. Because she was intent on backing out, and he couldn't allow it.

Her eyes widened, her lip curling into a snarl. "When?"

"I never stopped buying them. The company was going down, and there were people eager to get out and get what they could. I'm now the majority shareholder by a very large margin, and I'm sure that, given that the recovery of Pickett is still in its fledgling stage and not one-hundred-percent viable, the board would be open to the idea of liquidating and distributing assets."

"But all those people…some of them have been with Pickett for more than twenty years and there is no comparable place for them to work, not for all of them, or even half of them, not here."

"It's your choice, Vanessa. It's on your head if they lose their jobs." Lazaro turned and walked back out into the frigid night, his body wracked with pain, guilt spreading through him like a sickness.

He couldn't lose her. He needed time to think.

He *needed* her.

Vanessa moved to the door, her heart in her throat. Before, he might not have loved her, but now it looked as if he hated her. She put a hand to her stomach and tried to ease the nausea, tried to ease the pain that was flowing freely through her body.

She had thought, for a few fleeting moments, that she would sell her house and go somewhere else. Cut ties from her family. Be Vanessa, just Vanessa and not The Pickett Family with all of the expectations and baggage.

She could study photography, as she'd dreamed of doing when she was younger.

But the bottom had fallen out of that fantasy when she'd realized that when she pictured starting over, Lazaro was in the background, his warmth and encouragement spurring her on.

And then even that little fantasy had been crushed by the force of his anger when he'd shown up at her door tonight.

She thought of all the people who would lose their jobs. Hundreds of them. Family men and women, some of them with no other job experience.

Boiling anger churned in her stomach, anger that he would do this to so many people. That he could keep doing this to her. "Why can't you just leave me alone?" she whispered.

It would be so much simpler if he would. If she could excise him, her feelings for him, from her life. And yet, it seemed impossible. Twelve years apart hadn't managed to accomplish it.

She couldn't let him do it. Couldn't let him destroy the lives of her workers. The legacy that belonged to her family, her future children.

"Lazaro." She stepped outside, arms crossed over her chest as she jogged after him. "Lazaro."

He turned, his expression unreadable in the dim light provided by the street lamps. "I'll marry you," she said.

Lazaro studied her expression, the hard glitter in her dark eyes, the deep sadness peering out beneath her rage. He felt no triumph in that moment, no sense of victory. Only the need to hold her in his arms and the knowledge that, at the moment, she would not allow it.

"I'm going to get in touch with a wedding coordinator tomorrow," he said. "We'll have the wedding as soon as possible."

She nodded slowly. "I'll do whatever I have to."

He had her. She was his. She had agreed to marry him.

And he felt as if he had truly lost her.

CHAPTER TWELVE

"As soon as possible" turned out to be two weeks. And they had gone by in a blur of motion and anguish and tiny bouts of happiness that had given way to stark slaps from reality.

Vanessa sort of hated reality. She liked the cocoon of her fantasies. The ones that seemed to have been left behind in Buenos Aires.

The wedding day seemed too bright. The sun shone a little bit too much, the sound of birds and traffic was too loud. It was too clear. And she couldn't hide from it.

Vanessa shifted her bouquet from one hand to the other. Orchids. And they were gorgeous. So was her dress, a flowing, fitted white gown that skimmed her curves and flattered her figure. It was elegant, sophisticated and without an ounce of princess, which suited her perfectly.

It was all romantic and dreamy, at odds with the prenuptial agreement she'd signed earlier in the week that kept her assets and her future husband's firmly separated and had custody agreements for hypothetical children and punishments for infidelities. That had been one of the week's low points.

One of the high points was booking St. John's on short notice, a lovely, historic cathedral with stained glass and high arched ceilings. Everything was just how she would have wanted it if she'd had years to plan.

Well, had she had her choice her groom would have seen

her as a person and not a commodity. He would have loved her. As she loved him. Still. In spite of the ugliness that had passed between them. Lazaro Marino had a piece of her. He always had had.

It was because she saw the man beneath the trappings. She saw the boy he used to be. The boy with the easy smile. The boy who had had a straight nose before her father had sent his henchman to break him and to steal that perfection. To steal his smile.

If Lazaro was hard, full of anger, so much of it was on her father's shoulders.

That was just one of the many reasons she was walking down the aisle alone today. She already felt like a thing, an asset. She wasn't about to let her father "give her away" to Lazaro.

She sucked in a deep breath and walked through the double doors and into the sanctuary, her heart pounding hard in her chest.

She looked up at Lazaro's face, and, for a moment, everything, everyone receded. The clarity was gone, and things were fuzzy around the edges again. For a moment, she thought she saw something soften in him, thought she saw a return of the heat in his eyes—not just the heat, but something tender, an emotion she'd never seen on his face before. An emotion she would only ever see there in dreams.

And then it was gone, replaced with that hardened resolve, that flat, unreadable mask that Lazaro wore to keep her, and everyone else, out.

His voice was measured, controlled as he spoke vows she knew he didn't mean. Her voice cracked, wavered, because she meant every word. And she wished that she didn't.

The priest pronounced them man and wife, and gave them the invitation to kiss. She hadn't touched Lazaro in over two weeks, not any kind of contact. Her heart fluttered as she looked at him, and this time she knew, the heat wasn't imagined.

He swept her hair over her shoulder and cupped her cheek, his thumb brushing her skin gently as he studied her face.

And she realized he was waiting for her. It was her move. Her decision.

She angled her head and leaned into him, touching her lips to his tentatively. His hold on her tightened and he wrapped his arm around her waist, drawing her to him. She clutched his shoulders tightly, kissing him with every ounce of passion pent up inside of her, and all of the anger and the love and the sadness. Because if he was marrying her, he was getting all of it.

She wasn't just a passive thing to add to his collection. She was a woman. A person. She was Vanessa. He might be able to force her into marriage, but he couldn't change who she was.

He kissed her back, matching her emotion, her passion, making her dizzy with it.

When they parted, they were both breathing heavily. Vanessa felt her cheeks heat, because during that kiss, the crowd of people witnessing their sacred vows had very much faded away, and now they were in crystal clear focus.

Lazaro leaned in to the priest and said, loud enough for everyone to hear, "I'm a very lucky man."

That broke some of the tension and brought laughter from even their stuffiest witnesses. It made Vanessa's cheeks heat further. Made her body ache with the longing to have more of him. To do more. To make love with him.

Tonight was their wedding night, and it seemed as though that was what should happen. It was the only thing that felt right. They were back on civil footing, but after the way things had happened…she wasn't sure. She wasn't sure about anything.

As they walked back down the aisle, applause filling the sanctuary, Vanessa fought back tears and an overwhelming ache of loneliness she was afraid would never go away.

"I've had all of your things moved in already," Lazaro said when they reached his penthouse. "Your clothing and personal items are in the room next to mine."

"Oh. And my furniture?"

"Still at your home. We can hold on to your house as long as you like. Rent it out or keep it vacant. Although, we don't need two homes in the city."

"Right." She walked further into the main area of the house, feeling disoriented—a stranger in a strange land. And this was supposed to be her home. But there was nothing of her in it.

It was cold and clean, with sparse furnishings and a lot of brushed metal giving it a sterile, unlived-in feeling. It was top of the line, no question, everything in it of the highest quality money could buy. But it wasn't her.

Her town house was plush and luxurious, furnished with her father's money. But it still had a homey feel. It was a place she was glad to be in at the end of the day. A place that made her feel warm. Lazaro's penthouse felt like her office. And it kind of gave her heartburn, which made it even more like her office.

"I guess you did it, Lazaro," she said.

"I did what?"

"You have everything. You're rich, the richest man in Boston, possibly in the United States. You're the principal shareholder of Pickett Industries and you have me, your ticket into high society. I guess there's nothing left for you to go after."

He looked at her, his dark eyes assessing. "There's always something more, Vanessa."

"What?"

"There's always work to do," he said, shrugging.

"I see." That made it all even worse. She was just a means to one end. For Lazaro there would never be rest. Never be satisfaction with what he had.

"Speaking of, I have some work to do. We can have dinner later."

Vanessa nodded, more than ready to go to her room and sleep off the stress of the day. The stress of the past month.

She walked through the house, feeling a sense of disconnection so strong that she thought she might crumble beneath it. She'd cut ties with her father. She and Lazaro seemed to have lost whatever connection they had found in Buenos Aires.

She blinked and looked around again. No, her surroundings weren't really to her taste. And yes, she and Lazaro weren't engaged in the love affair of the century, not emotionally anyway. But they had passion. And she had options.

She had let other people make her decisions for far too long. She had seen herself as honorable, continuing her family's legacy, doing her duty, being the kind of daughter, the kind of person everyone should be. So self-sacrificing.

She laughed into the empty room. She wasn't any of that. She was a coward. Too afraid to make her own decisions and step out on her own. So she'd let other people do it for her. Her father. And then, following down that same path, Lazaro. And then, of course, if she was unhappy it was somehow down to someone else. And that made her what? A long-suffering martyr doing her duty?

No. She shook her head and sat down on the couch. She'd made this choice. And she'd hidden behind all kinds of reasons, but the fact remained that she'd made the choice. Just as she'd chosen to put aside her dreams and go to school for business. Just as she'd chosen to give up photography for a life behind a desk.

She had no one to blame. And no one to fix it for her now but herself.

Lazaro's housekeeper had decided that the newlyweds needed a nice, intimate dinner prepared for them before she went home for the evening. Which was how Vanessa found herself sitting opposite her stoic husband, searching for conversation so they weren't trapped in uncomfortable silence.

"I want to step down from my position at Pickett," she said. Those weren't the words she'd been searching for, but it was the truth. It was her heart. And it was too late to call them back now. "I want to keep my ownership, my stock, but I don't want an active role in the company."

"You want to take up lunching?" he asked, looking up from his dinner plate, one dark brow raised.

"Photography," she said. "I want to take some classes. I want to pursue it as a career."

"Then you should," he said. That simple. That easy.

"Really?"

"I told you in Buenos Aires, I want you to be happy."

"I thought all bets might be off on that."

"Why is that?"

"Since…you know. Since things haven't been overly amicable between us for the past couple of weeks," she said studying her plate of pasta.

"I want them to be."

"Well, you forced me to marry you, so…the odds of that are low."

This time she was certain what she saw in his eyes was hurt. A brief flash of it, a tiny glimpse past the stone wall he built over his emotions.

She lifted her glass of wine and touched it to her lips, then set it down without taking a drink. "I don't have to tell you how it happened. I'm sure you remember," she said, her voice cracking.

"I don't want you to be miserable, Vanessa."

"Am I supposed to be happy? You could have fooled me. Was any of this ever about happiness? Mine or yours?"

He didn't speak, he simply toyed with the stem of his wineglass, his dark eyes glittering in the candlelight. A nice touch from his housekeeper, meant to give them a romantic atmosphere. What a sad farce it was.

"This has always been about business," he said, taking his hand away from the glass and curling it into a fist.

"And revenge."

"Yes, that too. I had never planned on seeking revenge…"

"But the temptation was too great. I get that. I just don't think I like being in the middle of it. But I've told my father that he isn't to bar your entrance into the inner circles of society in any way. He's to roll out the red carpet for you."

"And how did you get him to agree to that?"

Vanessa looked down at her food again, unable to meet his searching gaze. "I threatened him. You would have been proud. I actually used the same threat you used on me. I told him we would dismantle Pickett Industries, brick by brick if necessary. Because what he did to you, what he's done to me all of my life, it's not right."

"How do you feel now that you've stood up to him?"

She sighed heavily and spun her glass in a slow circle on the table. "I felt free. For about ten minutes." She looked at Lazaro again, then down at the diamond engagement ring and the thick platinum band next to it. "I'm tired. I think I'll go to bed."

She stood from the table, expecting him to stop her, to kiss her, demand she join him in bed on their wedding night. He did none of those things. He hardly flicked her a glance.

"Good night."

Her throat tightened. "Good night."

Vanessa felt empty. The bed felt empty. Everything did. She rolled onto her back and stared at the unfamiliar ceiling. No tiles to count. It was smooth and glossy, just like the rest of the house.

She wondered if Lazaro was in bed. If he was asleep.

It was their wedding night and it didn't seem right for them to sleep separately. But then, they were married and it didn't seem right for there to be this…distance between them.

She was the one who'd tried to back out of the agreement. She was the one who'd created the distance between them—to protect herself because she was afraid of her feelings for Lazaro. They were so strong, woven through her being, like roots of one plant overtaking the roots of another beneath the surface of the ground. Impossible to extricate either without destroying the delicate flower involved.

She loved him. All he had been, all he had become. The man with so much determination and brilliance. The man who was still hurting beneath it all. She sensed that hurt, mostly because she kept coming close to the wounds. She had a knack for saying the wrong things, things that brought those little flashes of pain into his eyes.

He didn't feel like he was enough. She knew it now, recognized it, because it was what she felt about herself. Lazaro had married her for status, she had done it for Pickett. And none of it was that clean or simple now. Because if all of the external things were stripped away, Lazaro was the man she would want.

It was all the *things*, they were the deterrent now, not the draw.

She wanted just him. She wanted to forget. To let go of all

of the pain and just feel alive. Feel what only he could make her feel.

She slid out of bed and padded over to the door, and out onto the mezzanine floor that overlooked the living area, the windows that stretched from the floor to the ceiling showing the lights of Boston shining in the inky night.

The city, at least, was home, even if the house didn't feel like it.

She knocked on Lazaro's bedroom door.

"Vanessa?" She heard his accented voice, sleepy and muffled through the bedroom door.

She pushed open the door and crossed to his bed, standing at the side of it. "I couldn't sleep. And it's our wedding night, and frankly, I didn't imagine I would be spending my wedding night alone."

"You said you were tired, was I meant to break down your door and demand you make love with me?" He was lying in the bed, a blanket pulled up over his lap, revealing his bare chest.

She tried to keep her eyes on his face and not glued to his amazing body. But it was hard. "No. But I…I don't want to be alone."

"Neither do I." He drew back the covers and she slipped in beside him, her heart hammering.

She placed her hand delicately on his chest, excitement and arousal firing through her. "I missed you," she said. "I missed this."

This was the man she loved. Here, in bed, it brought him back. There was nothing else now. No revenge. No company. No status. It was everything he'd made her feel from the beginning, before so many things had gotten in the way.

"I did too," he said, brushing her hair away from her face, trailing his fingertips down over her shoulder to her hand. He lifted it to his lips and kissed the sensitive skin of her palm.

Her heart ached. It was tempting to wonder what might have been. Where they would be now if they had never parted. Maybe poor. In an apartment somewhere with him mowing lawns and her taking wedding pictures. With children. Without all of the anger and the trappings of life that they seemed so tangled up in.

With love.

She closed her eyes, fought the tears that were mounting. She wasn't living in a fantasy. Right now, this was her reality, and she meant to feel all of it.

He pressed his lips to hers, his kiss urgent, his hands roaming over her curves, slow and firm, his movements sure and expert. "I will never tire of this," he said against her lips. "Of you."

Her heart burned in her chest, pain lancing her. He *would* tire of her. She was a status symbol, the ultimate I-told-you-so. He had been told he couldn't have her, and Lazaro wasn't a man who liked to be told no. Beyond that, there was nothing unique about her. He'd wanted to select a society bride and she had been available, and had come with the added perk of vengeance.

She believed him when he said he hadn't been planning revenge for the entirety of the past twelve years, but she also knew that she served to satisfy a wrong that had been committed against him. And in his place, she wasn't entirely certain she wouldn't have done the same thing.

She blocked out the thoughts that were flooding her mind, increasing the flow of pain to her chest. She focused only on Lazaro's hands, his lips, all the amazing things he could make her body feel. She ignored the pain gushing from her heart with every beat.

"It's convenient that you don't wear pajamas to bed," she said, sliding her hand over his washboard-flat abs and down to where he was hard and ready for her.

He tilted his head back, and even in the dark, she could see his expression, one of pure pleasure. It filled her with feminine pride to know she had the power to make him feel that way.

"More than convenient," he said, his voice strained.

"I want to try something."

She moved down his body, flicked her tongue over the head of his erection.

Air hissed hard through his teeth and he wove his fingers through her hair, holding on to her tightly while she explored him, taking pleasure in giving him pleasure.

His thighs were tight beneath her hands, his muscles starting to shake as she took him fully into her mouth.

"Vanessa, someday we'll do it this way…but now…now I need you."

The words were broken, strained, and she understood exactly what he meant, because she needed him too. She'd been without him for too long, aching and lonely. To the outside world, she was only the part that she played. But Lazaro knew the woman beneath.

Having one person in the world who knew, truly knew, what she wanted, what made her happy, had made her wonder how she'd ever lived without that. And being without him had been so isolating. She'd felt cut off from everyone, even more than she normally did. She'd felt trapped inside of herself.

She'd been squeezed into a box all of her life, trying so hard to be who she was supposed to be. Not now. Not with him.

Here and now, she was free.

She pushed herself up and positioned herself over him, leaning in to kiss his lips, her palms on his chest, his heart raging beneath them. He was watching her, not giving instruction, just watching and waiting. And she knew that she was in control now.

She smiled and changed her position slightly, bringing the head of his erection against the entrance to her body, slick and so very ready for him. He helped her by guiding himself to the right place and she sank onto him slowly, sighing as he filled her completely.

She locked eyes with him as she moved over him, finding her rhythm slowly, awkwardly at first. Lazaro gripped her hips and urged her on, his words alternating between sweet and explicit, encouraging her.

She could feel her climax building within her, could feel it building with each thrust, could feel, as Lazaro's muscles tensed and shook, that he was close too.

He thrust up into her and pushed her over the edge, her orgasm moving through her like a crescendo, building as it flowed through her body.

"Lazaro." She gripped his shoulders hard, her nails digging into his skin.

He groaned harshly as he found his own pleasure and Vanessa collapsed against him, her cheek resting on his sweat-slicked chest, his heart pounding hard beneath her ear, evidence of what she'd done to him. To them.

She wished she knew what it had meant to him. What he felt. It was frightening, being connected with someone physically and feeling so blocked out emotionally. Feeling alone.

Her eyes filled with tears and one escaped, sliding down her nose and onto Lazaro's chest. He tightened his hold on her and kissed her hair.

Vanessa closed her eyes, trying to focus on the sweet languor that was making her limbs feel heavy, that was bringing her closer to sleep.

Anything to dull the ache in her chest.

CHAPTER THIRTEEN

LAZARO couldn't erase the impression of the tear on his chest; it was as though it had burned into his skin, through to his heart. He felt weighted down by it, by the unhappiness it represented. Vanessa's unhappiness.

In the days since, she'd spent every night in his bed, making love to him with an abandon that blew his mind each and every time. The passion between them was explosive, but afterwards she seemed to retreat, to fold in on herself and move away from him. He hadn't seen her tears since, but he wondered if they were still there.

He had never thought it possible, but he wanted to hold her after they made love. He wanted to ask what she was thinking. To tell her his thoughts, to pour himself out to her. He had never felt that need, had never understood it.

But he needed it with Vanessa. Needed to find some way to feel close to her. To make her happy. He could make her happy. He could give her everything she desired. He *would* make her happy.

He would do whatever it took. He would buy her her own studio, her own gallery to display her work. Take her to any location she wanted to photograph. Whatever she could possibly want to have, he could buy for her. Money was no object.

She'd been enjoying her classes, and had been cutting back

on hours at Pickett while the board worked on finding a replacement they could all agree upon. In some ways, she was
more relaxed than he'd seen her. But sometimes…sometimes
he saw a deep sadness in her eyes that tore at his gut. And
with that pain came a sense of helplessness. He had given her
everything he knew to give, and he didn't know another way
to make her happy.

He pushed the thought to the side and headed upstairs,
hoping he could entice Vanessa into bed for the afternoon.
Or, if not that, maybe entice a smile from her.

Her bedroom door was partway opened and he let himself
in. Vanessa was sitting at her computer, leaning in, examining images on the screen.

"Did you get some good shots?" he asked.

"I did." She turned to face him and he felt as if he'd been
punched in the chest. Her smile made him weak and as though
he could move the earth if he had to, all at once. "We're doing
a mini exhibition at the end of the class. A lot of the techni-
cal things I knew already, but I love the way the teacher talks
about melding art and technique. It's all so fascinating."

"You love it," he said, looking at the way her eyes caught
fire when she spoke. He would chase the happiness he saw in
her eyes now. Would give her whatever she needed to made
her smile like that.

"I really do." The light in her eyes turned impish. "Hey,
we're supposed to do live subjects this week."

"I have a friend who has a dog. He might be willing to
help."

The corners of her mouth turned up. "No, I want to take
your picture."

"Wanting and having are two very different things."

"Lazaro, please?" The look of sweet supplication on her
face undid him entirely. He couldn't say no to her, not when
the idea made her so…happy. She truly looked happy now,

not because she was smiling, but because of what he saw reflecting in her eyes. He hadn't seen her look that way since Buenos Aires.

"Where?" he asked, indulging her because there was nothing else he could do.

"The bed."

"No, Vanessa."

She walked to him and pressed a kiss to his cheek, her fingers working at the buttons on his shirt. The flood of desire was instant, unstoppable.

"I just want you to look relaxed," she said. "You always look relaxed in the morning, right when you wake up."

"There are other times I look relaxed."

She laughed. "No, there really aren't."

She gripped the lapels of his shirt and tugged and he went willingly, allowing her to bring him down onto the bed. He gripped her hips and held her to him, kissing her, tasting her. Just being with her. She was happy with him. She wasn't acting as though he was her jailer.

Aren't you?

He gritted his teeth and banished the thought, focusing instead on the slide of her tongue, the scent of her body, the way her hands moved over him.

She pulled away from him and got off the bed, going to her desk for her camera. She clicked off a succession of shots.

"What is it you want me to do?" A male model he was not.

"Just look at me."

How could he do anything else? With her glossy brown curls loose and mussed, her cheeks flushed with the same arousal that was pounding through him. Those lips, full and pink, and her body…so perfect. Made for him.

She stopped and lowered the camera, looking at the screen, her lips parting. "Wow. Can you…can you look away now?"

He did, tearing his focus from her one of the harder things

he'd ever attempted. He heard the click of the shutter and turned back to her.

"Come here," he said.

He didn't have to ask twice. She came willingly, camera in hand. He took it from her and used the viewfinder screen on the back, taking a picture of her. "Fair is fair," he said.

She smiled, one corner of her mouth turning up higher than the other. It made her look wicked and very, very tempting. He took the shot, capturing it forever. The look that spoke of her desire, and all the naughty things she was thinking of.

"I think you're done now," she said, kissing his neck.

"With the camera, yes. With you? Not nearly."

His heart pounded fiercely as he lifted her shirt over her head, exposing her breasts to his gaze. She was so beautiful, everything he had ever desired and so much more. Things he had never known to want.

He shrugged his shirt off the rest of the way and made quick work of the rest of his clothes. He always wanted to spend hours touching and tasting her, to lavish her with every sort of pleasure his mind could conjure up. But when he started uncovering her body, inch by delicious inch, impatience seemed to overtake him.

He tugged her jeans and her delicate, barely-there panties down her thighs and tossed them to the floor. "Now I'd like the camera back," he said.

Pink color suffused her cheeks. "No way."

"Someday."

She shook her head and he leaned in and captured her lips, pulling her up so that she was sitting on his lap, her thighs draped over his. He pressed a kiss to her throat, her breasts, his hands moving over her elegant curves, her waist, her hips.

"I want to capture this perfection forever," he said.

He urged her up, positioning himself at the entrance of her body, and she accepted, took him in on a sigh of pleasure.

He watched her face as she moved over him, the way her lips parted, the way a heavy flush of color spread over her skin as she neared her climax. How she squeezed her eyes tight, and grabbed his shoulders as her orgasm started to take her. Every detail seemed important. Every nuance of who she was and what gave her pleasure.

He wanted to give her everything, to be everything she needed.

And then he was too caught in the grip of his own pleasure to think of anything else. He let himself go over the edge, let his release steal everything from his mind, let it break through the walls surrounding his heart so that he felt everything, truly felt it.

Sex had always been something he'd enjoyed at a distance, pleasure he'd let his body take while his emotions stayed unaffected.

Not now. Not with Vanessa. Never with her. From the first moment she had put a crack in his defenses, and this time, the walls crumbled down. He felt raw, exposed, naked and vulnerable to the kind of pain that intense emotion promised to bring.

And yet, he couldn't stop the flow, wouldn't if he had the power.

He held her after, her silken hair spread over his chest, her breath hot against his neck as she slept off the post lovemaking lethargy.

He knew how to bring her pleasure. He could make her happy.

Except he would always be the man who'd had to buy her to make her his wife. Who'd had to threaten her down the aisle. She was here for what he had, not who he was. And he was a fool to have believed otherwise, even for a moment.

The pain he'd cleared a path for began to flood him. Overtake him.

She was growing now, changing what she did, who she was. And he had clipped her wings. He was everything he had always despised. A man who used people. A man who treated everyone like steps, there to be trod upon as he made his way to the top.

But she was his wife. He tightened his grip on her. She was his. He needed her, like air.

He loved her.

Vanessa noticed a change in Lazaro after their afternoon photo session. He seemed distant. Cold. The only time he warmed for her was in bed at night, and then he was on fire. The flames of their passion were enough to consume both of them for a moment, to make the reality of their situation fade away.

She was a bought bride, no more important than any of the other signs of status that were evident in Lazaro's home: a home with the right view in the right neighborhood, some high-end art on the wall and a wife with the right bloodline.

She was no more important than any of it. And it killed her. She wanted to be special to someone, and she truly never had been. Her father had seen her as a last-resort way to continue his dynasty, her ex-almost-fiancé had seen her as a great acquisition in a merger of families, and Lazaro…well, she was his ticket to the top. The checkmate to her father. Revenge and power in one move.

She didn't care about Craig Freeman's feelings—or lack thereof—for her, and there was no point in wishing her father would suddenly gain the ability to see people as anything other than pawns to be moved around at his every whim.

But Lazaro…she wanted him to love her. Her. Not what she could give him. Not as an addition to his almighty empire.

He was the only one who truly mattered, and every day

he slipped further and further away from her. He was closing himself off to her, his guard never slipping, his eyes never betraying what he was thinking or feeling.

And even though he held her every night while she slept, she felt alone.

She took a deep breath and walked out of her bedroom, fastening her earring and pushing her foot the rest of the way into her high-heeled shoe. She wasn't going to be passive anymore. She understood the things that were holding Lazaro back. At least, she hoped she did. She prayed she did.

Because if she was wrong, it would only end in devastation. Hers specifically.

She pulled her phone out of her pocket and dashed off a quick text to Lazaro. Specific instructions on where he was supposed to meet her tonight, because she wanted to show him and she knew it was going to take more than sweet words spoken in private to undo all of the hurt that was inside him. It might even take more than she had planned.

But she was willing to try.

She pressed Send and grabbed her coat, covering her daring dress with the sedate, gray wool outerwear.

Now she just had to hope her husband followed her instructions. She smiled slightly at the thought. If there was one thing Lazaro didn't do, it was follow orders.

She needed him to tonight though. Because tonight, she was going to reveal her heart to him. There was a time for self-protection, and this wasn't it. Lazaro had given her the strength to find out who she really was.

And he was going to have to deal with the consequences of that newfound strength.

Lazaro wasn't sure what to expect when he walked into the smoky, downtown club. A rare experience, although, with Vanessa rare experiences seemed to be getting more and more common. She surprised him. Challenged him. Turned him on and made his heart pound faster.

She was like no other woman, no other person he'd ever known.

He shut off his line of thinking and scanned the dense crowd for his wife. His wife. The thought still made his chest feel tight. Made his stomach ache with longing because while he had her, he would never truly have her.

She had not married him because of any great love for him. She didn't stay with him out of a desire to. He was making her stay.

Then he saw her, weaving through the tightly packed bodies. She was wearing a shockingly brief dress, black and tight, revealing the killer curves of her body. Possessiveness coursed through his veins. Possessiveness and pride. She was his wife, and she was the most beautiful woman in the room.

Not only that, she was the smartest, the bravest, the most artistic. She was everything.

She smiled at him and his heart began to pound, hard, heavy and fast in his chest. He sucked in a sharp breath and tried to regain control. He had let his defenses drop and he'd spent the better part of the past two weeks trying to rebuild them, trying to hold Vanessa at a distance when he knew it was a futile effort. She was in him. Entwined with him. In his blood, flowing through him, keeping his heart beating.

She wrapped her arms around his neck and kissed him in greeting, in front of everyone in the club, passionately and shamelessly.

When they parted, she smiled. "Dance with me." Not a request, but an order he didn't want to refuse.

"Like in Buenos Aires," she whispered when they were on the dance floor.

He pulled her to him, one hand clasping hers, the other planted firmly on her lower back. "Here? But people will see."

"I'm glad," she said. "I'm proud to be seen with you."

His heart expanded inside him, making everything in him feel tight, as though he might burst with the feelings that were taking over his body. He swallowed hard. "I feel the same way."

She didn't dance with precise skill, but she put everything into it, the freedom she'd found in life that he'd watched grow in her over the past weeks. When she smiled now it came from deep within her, a light that radiated from the inside out.

And yet the smile could not be for him. He had forced her into marriage, had treated her the same way her father had always done.

His heart seized in his chest. When the opportunity had presented itself, he had become so consumed with the undoing of Michael Pickett that, in the process, he'd become him. He had taken Vanessa, a vibrant force of life and beauty and tried to bend her to his will. To make her fulfill his needs, without thinking of hers.

And, just as she'd done with her father, she was doing her duty. Doing what she knew she had to do, the honorable thing. Bile rose in his throat when he thought of the soft sighs she made in bed, the way she gripped his shoulders. Was that duty to her? The only way to preserve the company she loved?

She leaned in, her lips grazing his ear. "I was doing research on some really interesting ways we can bring energy-efficient manufacturing techniques into Pickett. I was also thinking we might try and do something about the packaging? I know that you consulted for someone who makes boxes and containers out of recycled materials."

He pulled back from her, his heart thundering in his chest. "Is that why you asked me here?"

She moved her hands over his shoulders. "Of course not. But we haven't really talked in a few days and I had the idea earlier. I think with a little more money invested we can see some huge returns. You really did have a fantastic idea on how to resurrect the company."

Lazaro felt as though he'd been punched in the stomach. Every doubt that had ever gnawed at the back of his mind roared to the forefront. Of course this was about Pickett. She had married him to save it, to keep people she cared for employed. He had been a fool to think that any part of their relationship, their marriage, had been separate from that.

He had forced her into it. He had no right to stand in judgment of her. She hadn't lied to him. He was the one who'd asked her to be his wife, who'd wanted her in his bed. He had created the deception for the world, but he was the one who had fallen prey to it.

A sharp pain stabbed at him, ripped through his chest. It was real, physical pain unlike any he'd ever known. He pulled away from her, stumbling back a step before righting himself. He took a breath and concentrated on shielding himself, his emotions. He had lied to himself, pretending any part of what they shared had been real. It could not be. How could she ever care for a man like him? Why would she?

"Lazaro?"

He ignored her and turned, walking off the dance floor, away from the throbbing beat of the music and the heavy crush of people, out into the crisp air. He shook his head, trying to clear it, trying to find the man he'd been before Vanessa had walked back into his life. The man who thrived on emotionless dealings, success without any personal ties.

The man who had ruthlessly pursued what he wanted with single-minded determination. The man who had been willing to do whatever it took to reach his goals.

"Lazaro?"

He turned and saw Vanessa standing a foot away, her arms crossed in an attempt to keep warm. She'd left her coat inside, nothing but her insubstantial dress between her and the increasingly cold night.

"What was this, Vanessa?" he bit out. "Were you trying to make a fool of me? Trying to use your body to talk me into investing more money in Pickett?"

He wished she would say yes. That she would prove herself to be the woman he'd imagined her to be in the beginning. That she would do something to abolish the feelings he had for her.

Her eyes widened. "What?"

"Why did you want to go out tonight?"

"Because I...I wanted to dance with you." She looked at him, her eyes glistening in the moonlight. "Because I missed you."

"I've been with you every day."

She shook her head, dark hair swirling around her shoulders. "No, you haven't been. You've been gone. You've gone somewhere I can't reach you, and I want you back."

"I'm not quite sure what you mean, Vanessa. I've complied with my part of the deal, and I haven't made you unhappy. I'm paying for your photography courses." He shrugged, trying to look casual even as his throat tightened. "I can only assume you're upset about not having a chance to hit me up for more money for your company."

"You know what I mean. You aren't stupid, Lazaro. Don't pretend to be now."

"What exactly do you mean by that?"

"Don't pretend everything is fine when it isn't," she said.

"Everything is fine, Vanessa. As long as things continue going as we agreed. Pickett Industries will keep improving, and the employees will keep their jobs. And I'll have what I want.

"Status and some kind of sick sense of justice?"

His stomach churned and he had to force the next words out. "There was never anything else."

"Never?"

"No," he ground out, the lie acrid in his mouth.

He would not humble himself before her, would not admit that she had breached his heart, as no one else had ever done. He wouldn't confess his feelings to a woman who must hate him. A woman who had every right to.

And he couldn't be the man who held her captive anymore. He had forced her to marry him, and all his pretending it had been her choice was rubbish and he knew it. He knew her, he knew where her priorities lay, that she loved her employees. That she was too good, too loyal to let the company crumble if there was anything she could do to solve the problem.

He had practically forced her hand to sign the marriage license. He hated himself for it now.

You had to make sure that I had no other options open to get me to agree to marry you. I had no other choice. Don't forget that.

He hadn't. Not for a moment. It had been there, in the back of his mind while he had fooled himself into thinking that she could grow to care for him.

For the man who had forced her to the altar. Not likely.

"I have what I want now, Vanessa," he said, the words scraping his throat raw. "I've been invited to go to your father's country club. I have potential business connections made with several people who had never considered dealing with me prior to our marriage."

He watched the color drain from her face. "And?"

"And I think the marriage is unnecessary at this point in time."

She blinked rapidly. "Unnecessary?"

"I have what I want," he repeated, the lie bitter on his

tongue. "I see no point in continuing with the charade. I think we should divorce."

She stumbled back, her hand on her stomach, her dark eyebrows locked together, her eyes shimmering. "You…*you bastard*. You dragged me to the altar, you forced me into this farce of a marriage and for what? So you could divorce me less than a month later? Are you going to use this as an excuse to destroy my father's company too? Your last laugh against the Pickett family?"

Her words, the anger, only reinforced the rightness of what he was doing. She was too loyal to Pickett Industries to initiate it herself, but the simple truth was that she was more put out by what he'd put her through than the actual dissolution of the marriage.

And he couldn't force her to stay with him anymore. He had been wrong to do it. Selfish beyond measure. A man he hated.

"It would be poetic, no?"

"No." She shook head. "Lazaro, I love you."

He felt as though he'd been punched in the gut. She was offering him words of love, words he was so far from deserving. Words she could not mean. Words he *knew* she didn't mean. She was trying to protect Pickett. Because hadn't she already proved she would do anything to save her family's legacy? Hadn't she married him? Made love to him? Why not a little lie, three little words, words that might make him change his mind.

They could not be true. He was beyond the point of being a man anyone could love. Least of all Vanessa.

"Don't, Vanessa," he bit out.

"I do."

"No," he roared the words, not caring if they drew stares. "I do not want your love." He denied the need even as his heart wept. The desire to believe her was so strong it was nearly overpowering. He shook with it.

Worse than never hearing the words at all was having them used against him.

"And you don't want me," she said, her tone flat. "Was this your plan all along? To cast me aside and destroy my company? After you talked me into stepping down as CEO, of course."

"No," he said. "I'm not out to destroy Pickett, and I don't need you to try and manipulate me to get me to change my mind. You kept your end. I will keep mine," he said. "I will continue to be active in Pickett, in its improvement. But I do not see the marriage as a necessity at this point."

"So—" she swallowed and he saw the tendons in her throat working, as though it were hard for her to do "—you want a divorce?"

"I think we should," he said. But he didn't want a divorce. He wanted to cling to her forever, force her to stay with him. Make her want him. Failing that, he wanted things to go back to the way they were. He wanted the walls back up around his heart. He wanted anything but to be standing on the sidewalk in downtown Boston offering Vanessa her freedom while his heart was torn to pieces with each and every syllable out of his mouth.

He wanted to cling to her last, desperate lie. Her greatest attempt at saving Pickett. He wanted to claim it as truth and hold it inside him. He wanted to take her love and let it heal the raw wounds in him.

But those words weren't about feeling. And there was no way for him to be certain of the truth of them. Not as long as he held the fate of her beloved company over her head.

He wanted anything but a divorce. Anything but this moment. But he couldn't force her to be with him anymore. It was emptier than being without her.

"Okay," she said softly.

He had to grit his teeth to fight against the anguish that was tearing at him. "I knew you would be grateful for the out."

She nodded. "I'm going home."

"I don't think I will."

She shook her head. "My home. My town house."

His stomach tightened, tense with the strength it took to keep from crumbling under the agony that was overtaking every inch of his body. It was like death, worse than being beaten in an alley.

"I will have your things sent over in the morning."

"I won't be there."

He nodded curtly. "It's for the best."

She bit her bottom lip. "Goodbye, Lazaro."

He couldn't force a goodbye from his lips. He simply turned and walked away, wishing he could dull the pain by being angry with her, by making this her fault.

He couldn't. And the absence of anger only left him with a raw, searing pain that threatened to destroy him from the inside out.

Lazaro's penthouse was empty when he returned. As he had expected. Had he truly fantasized that Vanessa would have come back to him? He had destroyed any chance of that. He had made it swift and final.

He had been truthful though about one thing. He was guaranteed an in at her father's club, entry into that last exclusive grouping of people. Access to new clients. A kind of forced respect. It was all likely due to the fancy bit of threatening Vanessa had done on his behalf.

He poured himself three fingers of Scotch and walked out onto the balcony, letting the cool night air numb some of his pain, hoping the alcohol would take care of the rest.

The view he had was worth millions. It represented a physical manifestation of all of the work he'd done over the past decade. He was at the top now. He was the richest man in Boston, a world-famous consultant. There was nowhere else for him to go. Every door was open, everything he'd ever been barred from available to him now. The world was at his feet.

Suddenly, the emptiness of it all threatened to consume him.

There was no sense of triumph. No feeling of accomplishment. He had chased this moment for the entirety of his adult life—the moment when he would overlook the city, a man apart. The man at the top. The man no one could ever hold any power over, ever again. The man who had won.

He was there now, finally, after all the years of pushing for it. And there was nothing. Only a dark, blank void. The sweetness of victory turned to ash in his mouth.

In that moment, he would give it all away to be the boy who mowed the lawn, the boy who had earned a genuine smile from the one girl who held his heart. To grow into a man who deserved a woman like Vanessa.

But there was no going back. He had gained the entire world and lost the only thing that had ever had any meaning.

CHAPTER FOURTEEN

TRUE to his word, Lazaro had had all of her things delivered the day after he asked for the divorce. Vanessa left them packed, stepping over them when she came home from her photography class, digging through them when she needed something.

He had only ever wanted her for what she could give him, and then he'd gotten it, and he'd had no use for her. And she had done exactly what she'd promised herself she wouldn't do. She'd fallen deeply and irrevocably in love with him.

She felt bruised inside. It hurt to breathe. To eat. Just *being* hurt.

She wished that she could just turn her feelings off, quick and clean like shutting off a water main. But it wasn't that simple, not even close.

There was more to Lazaro than mindless acquisitions and status. She knew there was. She'd seen it. A man consumed only by a desire for *things* never would have cared that she had to take antacids to get through her day at work. He never would have encouraged her to work on her photography or bought her a camera.

He would never have made love to her as Lazaro did—with skill and tenderness, passion and heat. Always ensuring her pleasure came before his.

He had brought her out of her stagnant life. She felt as

though he'd opened her eyes to living. To feeling. He had given her so much—the strength to chase her own desires.

She wiped a tear off her cheek, frustrated that she was still crying four days after he'd rejected her love. Unsure if she would ever stop.

No one else had ever really seen *her* before. She was afraid no one else ever would.

But I see me now.

She took a deep breath. At least she knew what she wanted now. No more living behind the four walls of her office, no more pouring everything she had into something that she didn't love to do.

She'd found her own life. Her own path. And she'd lost her heart in the process.

But at least she was alive now. Truly living, making her own choices and living with the consequences, rather than hiding behind honor and duty. Cowering in fear of making choices and mistakes and playing the martyr instead of taking responsibility for things.

Still, right now, her newfound self was consumed with heartbreak that felt nearly fatal at the moment.

"This too shall pass. I hope," she said into her empty living room.

At least this time she'd told him she loved him. Back all those years ago in the guesthouse, the words had hovered on her lips, and she wondered if things would have changed if she had just spoken them. If he had said he loved her too, or if the honesty would have at least made them talk. Made them understand each other.

Yes, he had rejected her love. But she'd offered it. She'd tried.

There was a sharp knock on her front door, followed by a rich, familiar voice. "Vanessa?"

Her heart stopped beating for a moment before racing forward, tripping over itself. She swallowed hard and went to the door, opening it but keeping the shield of the wood between her and her soon-to-be-ex-husband. If there was nothing between them she might just cast her pride aside completely and fall into his arms.

"Lazaro…I…didn't expect you."

"I have something for you."

Her heart sank into her stomach and she opened the door wider, allowing him in. "Divorce papers? Do you want to sit down?" She gestured to her blue Victorian love seat.

"If you want them, and no."

"If I want them?"

"I brought divorce papers. But…that is not all."

She looked at him, really looked at him. He looked like she did. Tired, sick, tormented. His cheekbones looked sharper, the grooves that bracketed his mouth deeper. His black hair was disheveled, as though he'd been running his fingers through it.

"What else?" she asked, her throat tightening.

He cleared his throat, raising his hand and running it through his hair, just as she'd envisioned him doing. His hand shook as he lowered it. "I have to tell you this. I…I have spent every moment since that day I woke up facedown in the alley working my way up. I swore I would never stop until I reached the top. And I did. I reached it, Vanessa."

"I remember," she said, her voice cracking. "You asked for a divorce ten seconds after telling me this the first time."

"Yes, I found it, all I was looking for. And then I found out the big hole that's been inside me for all of my life was still there." His voice broke. "I fixed nothing. I accomplished nothing. Because I was at the top, and I was alone. I used you as a stepping stone. I *used* you. I forced you to marry me. It's unforgivable."

Vanessa watched Lazaro's expression contort, his eyes filled with bleak torment. "Laz…"

"Don't, Vanessa. Don't excuse me," he ground out. "I don't deserve it." He drew his hand over his face. "When I was eighteen I had more than I do at this moment, because you smiled at me as though I meant something to you, and now when you look at me…there is no light. And you left me."

"You asked me to."

"I was a fool. I wanted to run after you the moment you turned away from me, and I did not. I couldn't."

Vanessa felt her heart fold in. "I thought…I thought you only wanted to be with me because of what I could give you and then…and then you asked for a divorce when you had what you wanted…" Her voice broke. "I needed so much to have someone love me. Me and not my name, not what I could do for them. *Me.* And you didn't. You were just like everyone else." The words were torn from her, her pride be damned.

He took a step forward and extended his hand, his fingers trembling as he cupped her cheek, ran his thumb over her lower lip. He let his hand fall back to his side. "I'm sorry I made you feel that way. I'm sorry I was such a fool. I didn't realize, Vanessa. I thought I couldn't be whole until I had all the money, all the status. All the power. I thought that when I was certain I would never be weak or helpless again, everything would be perfect. But I had it all. I've had it all since the moment I put that ring on your finger, but I am not whole. I'm in pieces. More now than I ever have been. I became a man I despise to gain the power and wealth that I craved. But I lost my soul. I lost my heart."

He reached into the pocket of his jacket and took out a stack of papers. "I'm hoping that this will help me get it back." He took her hand in his and lifted it, then he put the documents in her upturned palm. "This is everything I own. All of the shares for Pickett. All of my money. The title to the penthouse…all of my houses. It's yours, Vanessa. Because it means nothing if I don't have you. Without you, I have nothing, I am nothing. This isn't just some empty gesture. If you want me to leave, I will. And I'll leave you with everything I've acquired in the past twelve years. This is what I hurt you for, all of the things that I have defined myself by, and I would trade it all to have you in my arms again."

Vanessa stared down at the papers in her hand. "There are no divorce papers?" she asked, the words sounding hollow, inane.

"They're in there too. Whatever you want. But if you take me, it is only me. You can have it all without me. Money, power. Pickett will be safe. I'll have no hold over you."

"But…this is everything you have."

He shook his head. "It's nothing. I thought it was everything, Vanessa, I truly believed it. Do you know how frightening it was? To achieve my goal and realize that it was nothing more than vain emptiness? That I was more unhappy than I had ever been?"

He moved to her, cupped her cheek. "I do love you for what you can give me. Happiness. Hope. Satisfaction. Things I have chased all my life and found nowhere. Nowhere but with you. I love you, Vanessa Pickett. Everything about you. I have from the first moment I saw you, in your bright pink bikini, and I will love you until I take my last breath."

He pressed his forehead against hers. "I come to you with nothing. I am just a man who loves you."

She put the stack of papers on her hall table and wrapped her arms around his neck, her cheeks wet with tears. "I love you too."

He pulled back, his dark eyes searching hers. "How?"

"Same as you. I always have. I always will."

"What I said the other night…I was afraid you were only telling me you loved me so that you could secure Pickett's future. I didn't want that. And I didn't want to hold you to an arrangement that I had forced you into."

"I meant it then, I mean it now. With everything or with nothing, sickness or in health, I love you, Lazaro Marino. You. Not your position or your bank balance. Everything you are, everything you will be." She kissed him, pouring all of her love into him. When they parted, they were both short of breath. "And I don't want anything from you but you," she said, looking down at the documents on the table. "I really, really don't want the divorce papers."

"I'm very glad to hear you say that," he whispered, his voice rough.

She touched his face. "It's easy to be angry for so many years lost. So many years when we could have been together."

"I don't know if I could have been the man you deserved then, Vanessa. I wasn't the man you deserved twenty-four hours ago. I'm not sure if I am now."

"You are. You're the man I need. You push me. You make me stronger. You've shown me who I am."

"That's what you've done for me, Vanessa. I'm stronger, better, because I have you." He kissed her lightly and she sighed, happiness filling her. "I've turned down your father's offer to join his club," he said, the corners of his mouth lifting.

"You don't have to do that."

"I do. I don't want to do business with men like that. It's not worth any amount of money or prestige." He looked at her, his eyes unveiled, the love in them clear and true. "I don't need it. I love you, Vanessa Pickett. Not for your last name, not for your connections. For all of my days."

She smiled, her heart so full she thought it might burst. All of the pain flooded from her, washed away by Lazaro's love, the love they shared, leaving everything in her feeling clean. New. Complete for the first time.

"I'm glad you aren't too attached to my last name," she said. "Because I'm going to have it changed. Vanessa Marino suits me better. You're my family now. I want everyone to know how proud I am to be your wife."

"Vanessa Marino," he repeated. "I am honored."

She touched his cheek. "The honor is all mine."

EPILOGUE

THE past three years had been the best of Vanessa's life. She felt as though all the time spent apart from Lazaro was slowly being restored, as though wounds were truly healing, the past no longer something filled with hurt and regret.

She took a deep breath and looked around the gallery, at the people looking at her photographs. It was her first real exhibition. She hadn't been confident enough in her skills to have one right away, and she'd wanted to earn the right to have one, not simply have it handed to her because of her maiden name or her husband's position in the community.

The picture that drew the biggest crowd was the one that was still her favorite. Lazaro, in their bed, looking at her with so much desire in his eyes that it made her burn to see it even now.

She walked over to the photo, drawn to it still.

"That's a man in love." It came from one of the women gazing at the print.

Vanessa smiled.

Lazaro came to stand beside her, his arm around her waist. "Yes, it is." He leaned in and kissed her neck. "I'm still in love with you, too."

"I know," she said.

"Sure of yourself," he said, smiling at her.

"Sure of you," she said.

He'd never given her reason to doubt. He showed her his love every day in a thousand different ways. He loved her as she was, in all her moods.

He kissed her again. "Have I mentioned how very proud I am of you?"

"About a hundred times, but tell me again."

"I'm proud of you," he whispered, pulling her close. "Of everything you've accomplished. Of everything you are."

Vanessa blinked back tears and leaned into his embrace, love filling her. "The feeling is one-hundred-percent mutual."

* * * * *

The Inherited Bride

MAISEY YATES

Mom, Dad, this one is for you.
Thank you for always believing in me.
If everyone had parents like you,
the world would be a better place.

CHAPTER ONE

HE WASN'T Room Service. That was for sure. Princess Isabella Rossi looked up, way up, at the tall, forbidding man who was standing in the doorway of her hotel room. His muscular frame was displayed to perfection by the tailored black suit he was wearing. But the suit was where any semblance of civilization ended.

His expression was inscrutable, his dark eyes blank, his lips flattened into a firm line. His squared jaw was clenched tight, the tension mirrored in his stance. His golden skin was marred with scars in some places; his cheek, the exposed part of his wrists.

She swallowed hard. "Unless you have my dinner stashed on a cart somewhere, I'm afraid I can't allow you to come in."

He uncrossed his arms and held his hands out, as if to show that they were empty. "Sorry."

"I was waiting for Room Service."

He tapped the top of the door with his open palm. "They make peepholes in these doors for a reason. It's always wise to check."

"Thank you. I'll remember that." She made a move to close the door, but it didn't budge. He was propping it open with his shoulder. She tried to close it again, this time putting more weight behind it. The door still didn't move, and neither did he. His expression did not betray even a hint of strain.

"You've caused a lot of big problems for quite a few people. Including your security detail, who now find themselves without jobs."

Her heart sank into her stomach. He knew who she was. She didn't know whether to be relieved or even more upset by that. Relieved he wasn't here to hurt her, but… but he was here to take her back. Either to Umarah or to Turan, and she didn't want to go to either country. Not now. Not when she'd fallen so short of everything she'd wanted to accomplish.

One night of freedom. That was all she'd gotten. A glimpse of the world as she would never know it.

"Do you work for my father?"

"No."

"You work for Hassan, then." That should have been obvious. Judging by the faint accent that tinged his deep voice, she should have guessed that Arabic was his native language. She should have known that he was in league with her fiancé.

"You're in breach of contract, *amira*. You should have known the Sheikh could not allow such a thing."

"I didn't imagine he would be thrilled about it, but…"

"You did a very foolish thing, Isabella. Your parents were concerned that you'd been kidnapped."

The guilt she'd been holding at bay for the past twenty-four hours made her stomach feel tight. But with that tightening came a strange fluttering sensation that seemed to grow stronger when she looked into those dark, fathomless eyes. She looked down. "I didn't mean to scare anyone."

"And what did you think would happen when you

disappeared? That everyone would go about their daily lives as if nothing had happened? You did not believe that your own parents would be frantic with worry?"

She shook her head mutely. In truth, she'd known her family would be upset, but she hadn't considered that they'd *worry* about her. Be angry, yes. She'd imagined they would be angry. That they might be afraid the sheikh would want to renege on their bargain if there was a chance she'd been out in the big bad world long enough to become *damaged goods*, or something.

"I...no. I didn't really think they would be worried."

He shifted his focus to the hallway, to a young couple standing a few doors down, kissing passionately against the wall. "I am not going to continue this discussion in the hallway."

She sneaked a glance at the passionate duo and her face began to burn with embarrassment. "Well, I can't let you in!"

He looked past her and into the simple room. "Slumming it?"

"No. This is a perfectly nice hotel. Anywhere too up-market and—"

"They would have known who you were. And they would have wondered."

She nodded mutely.

"I will be coming in," he continued. "With your permission or without it. One thing you'll learn about me very quickly, Princess. I don't take orders."

"There are two months and ten days until the wedding," she said, desperation clawing at her. "I need...I need this time."

"You should have considered that before you ran away."

"I didn't *run away*. That makes me sound like a naughty child."

"Then what would you call it?" He looked down the long corridor, back at the couple, whose activities had heated up in the past minute, and then back at her. "I'm waiting to be let in. I find I've been extremely patient."

She could tell from the fierce glint in his eyes that he absolutely would push his way into the room if she didn't allow him access. She could tell by all of the barely harnessed power of the body, the strength that was radiating from him, that he was only seconds away from doing it.

A sound that could only be described as ecstatic came from the couple in the hall, and Isabella jumped slightly, releasing her hold on the door.

"Wise decision." He stepped past her and into the small hotel room.

He stood rigid, his posture straight, his expression neutral. He was handsome. Extremely handsome. She realized that now. She'd been so struck by the immensity of his power, the energy that seemed just to radiate from him, that she hadn't had the time to really look at him. But she was looking now.

Now that his mouth was relaxed she noticed that his lips were full and well shaped, even with the small scar running through a corner of his mouth. He had the darkest eyes she'd ever seen. Nearly black, and so intensely focused that she felt as though he could see everything about her—as if he was looking into her. He was the sort of man who evoked a visceral reaction that was impossible to fight or ignore; one she didn't fully understand, and one she definitely didn't know what to do with.

"I wasn't letting you in. I was startled, that's all." she

said, hoping she sounded at least mildly imperious. She was a princess; she ought to be able to do imperious.

"I did tell you I was coming in regardless of whether you wanted me to or not."

She cleared her throat and focused on a spot just past him. Everything seemed to slow down a bit as she looked at him. Even the air felt thicker, making breathing a labored thing. He was just so… He was a force rather than a person. "Yes, well, now you're in."

"Yes. I am. And we're leaving."

She took one step backward. "I'm not going with you."

One black eyebrow shot up. "You think not?"

"Are you going to carry me out of here?"

He shrugged. "If I have to."

The thought of being touched, held closely by this man, this stranger, was entirely off-putting.

She took another step backward, trying to put some space between them. "I don't really think you would do that."

"Make no mistake, Princess, I would. You have a binding agreement with the High Sheikh of Umarah, and I have been charged with bringing you to him. That means you're coming with me one way or another. Even if I have to carry you kicking and screaming down the streets of Paris."

She stiffened, trying to look composed, trying to hide the nerves that were making her hands shake. "I don't think you would do that either."

He leveled that intense focus onto her. "Keep issuing challenges and we'll see just what I will and won't do."

He appraised her slowly, his gaze lingering on her curves. Something about the way he looked at her, the

way his eyes glittered in the dim light, made her feel like
she was exposed, like she was undressed.

Her heart rate sped up, something unfamiliar and hot
racing through her bloodstream, making her pulse soar.
Her heart was pounding so loud she was almost certain
that he must hear it. She sucked in a deep breath, trying
to calm herself, trying to slow her racing blood.

She looked away from him, trying to grab a shred
of sanity that might be lying around somewhere in the
corner of her mind. And her eyes locked onto the big
bed that was in the corner of the room. It made her think
of the lovers out in the hall. Blood roared into her face,
and she could feel her heart beating in her temples, her
cheeks so hot they burned.

Focus!

She had to get her thoughts together, had to figure out
a way to get rid of this man and get back to the business
of living her life before she had to sacrifice it all in the
name of duty. The heavy diamond on her finger, delivered
by courier six months ago, was a constant reminder of the
fact that there was a timer ticking against her freedom.
And this man was completely destroying her only hope
of actually living for herself.

For two short months she wanted a life that was her
own. It was a simple thing, and yet everyone seemed
hell-bent on making sure it didn't happen. When she'd
actually asked her father if she could have some time his
disdain for her request, his immediate refusal—as though
it didn't even bear considering—had been horrible. So she
had set out to make it happen on her own. She couldn't
go with him. Not now. Not when she was so close.

There had to be a way to get him on her side…a way
to turn the tide in her favor. But she didn't know anything
about men. Not really. The most exposure she'd had to

a man had come in the form of her older brother, Max. She *had* seen how her sister-in-law interacted with him, though—how she managed to appeal to Max's softer side when no one else could.

Although, she had her doubts that this man *had* a softer side. But she had to do something.

Taking a breath, she stepped forward and put her hand lightly on his arm. His eyes clashed with hers and a bolt of sensation shot to her stomach. She pulled back quickly, the heat from his skin lingering on her fingertips.

"I'm not ready to go back yet. I have two months until the wedding, and I really want to take this time to…to myself."

Adham al bin Sudar fought down the flash of anger that rose in him. The little vixen was trying to tempt him, to use seduction to get her way. The soft touch against his sleeve hadn't been an innocent action, but a calculated maneuver. One designed to stir a man's blood, make it pump hotter, faster. And when the woman doing the touching looked like Isabella Rossi, how could it not?

He thought, not for the first time, that his brother was an extremely lucky man to have her as his future bride. Although Adham would have been happy enough to take her as a temporary mistress, rather than a wife.

The woman was beautiful, with full, tempting curves and a face that was flawlessly lovely. Her beauty was not subjective, but universal. Her high, classic cheekbones, small upturned nose, and perfectly formed lips were designed to turn heads wherever she went. Even with a total absence of make-up her beauty was enough to rival that of any of the world's great beauties.

She didn't have the fashionable, streamlined look of a supermodel, but he had always preferred his women to look like women. And Isabella Rossi certainly had the shape of a woman. He allowed his eyes to linger on that shape for a while, to appreciate the full, rounded curve of her breasts. Breasts that would lead even the most disciplined of men into sin.

Immediate disgust filled him as he realized what he was doing, blocking out the flood of desire that was making his body harden and his heart race. She was his brother's fiancée. Forbidden in every way. Even looking was not permitted.

Adham's brother had asked him to bring her back for the wedding—had begged him to bring him his future bride so that his honor would not be compromised. That was what he was here to do—though he was beginning to doubt her suitability. A selfish, spoiled child with no sense of duty would not make an appropriate sheikha for his country. But Isabella Rossi came with the allegiance of an entire country—a trade and military alliance that would not come from any other bride. That made her essential, irreplaceable.

"Going off on your own was extremely foolish," he bit out, calling on all his willpower to squash the desire that had risen up in him. "Anything could have happened to you."

"I was safe," she said. "I'll continue to be safe. I'll—"

"You will do nothing but come with me, *amira*. Do you honestly think I would leave you to yourself just because you put on a pretty smile and ask nicely?"

Her lush lips parted in shock. "I…I had hoped that—"

"That you would not be held to your word? If the people of Umarah were to find out that their sheikh's bride has deserted him his honor would be compromised. He would be shamed in the eyes of his people. You might be deemed an unsuitable choice. And if that were to happen, what would become of the alliance? Jobs, money, security, all meant to benefit our people, gone."

She bit down hard on her lower lip, her blue eyes glistening. Annoyance surged through him—a welcome replacement for the sudden physical attraction that had hit him the first moment he'd seen her. He didn't have the patience to deal with emotional women. Emotion in general was useless to him. Although he had a feeling Isabella was employing it as a manipulation technique.

She would soon learn that he was the wrong man to try to soften with tears. Tears meant nothing to him.

"I wasn't going to run out on the wedding. I just wanted some time."

He noticed the way she turned the large solitaire diamond ring around on her slender finger as she spoke. She was still wearing the ring Hassan had sent her—a possible sign that she was telling the truth.

"Time's up, I'm afraid."

The devastation in her eyes would have affected most people. He felt nothing. Nothing but contempt. He'd seen far too much of the world to be swayed by the tears of a poor little rich girl, bemoaning her marriage to an extremely wealthy royal.

"I didn't get to see the Eiffel Tower," she said quietly.

"What?"

"I didn't get to see the Eiffel Tower. I took the train from Italy, and I just arrived here this evening. I wasn't going to go out by myself at night. I didn't see anything of Paris that I wanted to."

"You've never seen the Eiffel Tower?"

She blushed, her sun-kissed cheeks turning a deep rose. "I've *seen* it. But seeing it from a moving motorcade and actually going to it, getting out and experiencing it, are two very different things."

"This isn't a holiday, and I'm not here to give you a guided tour. I'm taking you back to Umarah as soon as possible."

"Please—just let me go to the Eiffel Tower."

It was a simple request. One that could be easily accommodated. And, while he wasn't moved by her drama, he wasn't cruel. It would also make it much easier to remove her from the hotel if she came of her own free will. He wouldn't hesitate to remove her by force, but it was not his preference.

"In the morning. I give you my word I will let you stop there on the way to the airport. But you have to come with me now, and not kicking and screaming."

"And you'll keep your word?"

"Another thing you will learn about me, Princess: I'm not a nice man, and I'm not particularly good company, but I do keep my word. Always. It is a matter of honor."

"And honor is important to you?"

"It's the one thing no one can take from you."

"I'll take that as a yes," she said. He inclined his head in agreement. "And if I don't go with you…?"

"You're going with me. Kicking and screaming optional—as is sightseeing."

"Then I suppose that means my choices are limited." She chewed her bottom lip.

"That's understating it; your choice is singular. The method, however, is up to you."

She blinked furiously, her shoulders sagging in defeat, her eyes averted as if she didn't want him seeing the depth of her pain. Although he was certain that in truth she wanted nothing more than for him to witness just how distressed she was.

"My bags will have to be packed. I've just gotten all of my things put away." She didn't make a move toward the closet, she simply stood rooted to the spot, looking very sad and very young.

"I'm not doing it *for* you," he said sardonically.

Her eyes widened and her cheeks flushed a delicate rose. "I'm sorry. You work for Sheikh Hassan, and I assumed…"

"That I was a servant?"

She mumbled something he thought might have been a curse in Italian, and stalked over to the closet, sliding the lightweight white doors open.

"I don't know how you meant to survive in the real world when you still expect someone else to deal with your clothes for you, Princess."

Her shoulders stiffened, her back going rigid. "Don't call me that anymore," she said without turning.

"It's what you are, Isabella. It's *who* you are."

A hollow laugh escaped her lips. "Who knows who I am? I don't."

He let the comment pass. It wasn't his job to stand around and psychoanalyze his brother's future wife. His duty was to return her unharmed, untouched, and he intended to do that as soon as possible.

He had other matters to attend to. He had geochemists actively searching for the best place to install a new rig, looking for more oil out in the middle of the Umarahn desert. He liked to be there on site when they were making final decisions about location. He didn't micromanage his team, he hired the best. But during major events he liked to be on hand in case there was a problem.

Facilitating the growing Umarahn economy was only half of his job. Protecting his brother, and their people, was his utmost concern. He would give his life for his brother without hesitation. So when Hassan had informed him that his bride had gone missing Adham had offered to ensure she was found. He was now regretting that offer.

She whipped around to face him, a pile of clothing, still on hangers, draped over her arms. "You could help me."

He shook his head slightly, watching as she began to awkwardly fold the clothing and place it in her bag. By the third or fourth article she seemed to develop some sort of method, even if it was unconventional.

"Who packed for you in the first place?"

She shrugged, the color in her cheeks deepening. "One of my brother's servants. I was supposed to leave his home this morning. I just left a few hours earlier."

"And went to an undisclosed location?"

She narrowed her eyes, her lips pursed in a haughty expression. "What did you say your name was?"

"According to the report I read on you, you're a very smart woman. Perfect marks in school. I think you know perfectly well that I didn't offer you my name."

Her delicate brow creased. "I think that, considering you know everything about me from my marks in school and I shudder to think what else, I should at least know your name."

"Adham." He left out his surname, and in so doing his relationship to Hassan.

"Nice to meet you," she said, folding a silk blouse and sticking it in the bottom of a pink suitcase. She paused mid-motion. "Actually, it isn't, really. I don't know why I said that. Habit. Good manners." She sighed. "Because it's what I was *trained* to do." She said it despairingly, her luscious mouth pulled down at the corners.

"You resent it?"

"Yes," she said slowly, firmly. "Yes, I do." She took a breath. "It's *not* nice to meet you, Adham. I wish you would go away."

"We don't always get what we wish for."

"And some of us never do."

"You'll have the Eiffel Tower. That has to be enough."

CHAPTER TWO

ADHAM's penthouse apartment in Paris's seventh district wasn't at all what she'd expected from a man who worked for the High Sheikh. It was patently obvious that he had money of his own, and likely the status to go with it. He was probably a titled man—another sheikh or something. No wonder he'd looked at her as if she was crazy when she'd expected him to collect her things.

That had been mortifying. She hadn't meant to be rude. It was just that she was used to being served. She'd always devoted the majority of her time to studying, reading, cultivating the kinds of skills her parents deemed necessary for a young woman of fine breeding. None of those skills had included folding her own clothes. Or, in fact, any sort of household labor.

She'd always considered herself an intelligent person; her tutors and her grades had always reinforced that belief. But the realization of what a huge deficit she had in her knowledge made her feel…it made her feel she didn't know anything worth knowing. Who cared if you knew the maximum depth of the Thames if you didn't know how to fold your own clothes?

The penthouse didn't provide her with any more clues about the man who was essentially her captor. Unless he really was as sparse and uncompromising as the surrounding décor. Cold as brushed steel, hard as granite. Arid, like the desert of his homeland. That seemed possible.

She looked around the room, searching for any kind of personal markers. There were no family photographs. The art on the walls was modern, generic—like something you might find in a hotel room. There was no touch of personality, no indication as to who he might be, what he liked. That just reinforced her first theory.

"Are you hungry?" he asked, without turning his focus to her.

"Can I get something besides bread and water?"

"Is that what you think, Isabella? That you're my captive?"

She swallowed hard, trying to move the knot that had formed in her throat. "Aren't I?"

Wasn't she everyone's captive? A puppet created by her parents and trained to respond to whoever was pulling the strings.

"It depends on how you look at it. If you try to walk out the door I can't let you. But if you don't make another escape attempt we can exist together nicely."

"I believe that makes me a prisoner."

Her words made no difference to him. It was as though he took a hostage every day of the week. The only change in his facial expression was the compression of his mouth. The scar that ran through his top lip lightened slightly at the pull of his skin, the small flaw in his handsome face only reinforcing the warrior image her mind had created for him.

"Prisoner or not, I was wondering if you might like some dinner. I believe I took you from the hotel before you had a chance to have yours."

Her stomach rumbled, reminding her that she'd been

hungry for a couple of hours now. "I *would* like some dinner."

"There is a restaurant nearby. I have them deliver food whenever I'm here. I assume that will be all right for you?"

"I…" *Now's the time to do it…get what you want now or you'll never have the chance.* "Actually, I'd like to have a hamburger."

His eyebrows lifted. "A hamburger."

She nodded curtly. "Yes. I've never had one. And I'd also like chips. Fries. Whatever you call them. And a soft drink."

"Seems a simple request for a last meal. I think I can accommodate my captive." She thought she might have heard a hint of humor in his voice, but it seemed unlikely. He pulled out his cell phone and dialed, then spoke to whoever was on the other end in polished French.

"You speak French?"

He shrugged. "I keep a residence here. It's practical."

"Do you speak Italian?" she asked, moving to a sleek black sofa that looked about as soft as marble and sitting gingerly on the edge.

"Only a little. I'm fluent in Arabic, French, English and Mandarin."

"Mandarin?"

His lips curved slightly in what she assumed might be an attempt at a smile as he settled in the chair across from her. "That's a long story."

"I speak Italian, and Latin as well, French, Arabic—obviously English."

"You're quite well-educated."

"I've had a lot of time to devote to it." Books had been her constant companion, either at the family home, or for those brief years she'd gone to an all-girl school in Switzerland. Her imagination had been her respite from the demands that her parents had placed on her. From their constant micro-managing of her actions. In her mind at least she'd been free.

But it hadn't been enough lately. She'd needed more. An escape. A reality apart from the life she'd led behind the palace walls. Especially if she was expected to go and live behind more walls, to be shut away again. Set apart. Isolated even when surrounded by hundreds of people.

She shivered, cold loneliness filling her chest, her lungs, making her feel as if she was drowning.

"It's nice to know all those languages when you move in the type of circles my family do. I've gotten to practice them with various diplomats and world leaders." During their frequent trips to Italy they'd always met with politicians, wealthy socialites. The same kind of person, the same sort of conversation. Always supervised. She clenched her fists. "So, what have you used your linguistic skills for?"

Probably for seducing women all over the world...

"They have been a matter of survival for me. In my line of work, understanding the words of the enemy can be a matter of life and death."

A chill settled over her, goosebumps rising on her arms. "You...that's happened to you?"

He gave her a hard look, one void of expression, but conveying an intense amount of annoyance over having to carry on this extended conversation with her. "Yes. I am in the service of my country. My king. It's my job to protect him, and now to protect you."

The fierce loyalty in Adham's voice shocked her. She didn't know if there was anything in the world she felt so much passion for. She'd lived her life by the rules until recently, but she hadn't followed the rules out of any great love for them. She had just done it. Existed. Her future, her marriage, was a given—her duty to her people. But there was no fire of conviction there.

"Is that why you're here? To protect me?"

"He trusts you with me. He would not send just any man to search for his fiancée. He was concerned for your safety. And I will protect you. I will bring you back to him."

"Why is it that everyone seems to think I can't walk from room to room without someone holding my hand?" Frustration pulled at her, making her feel she might explode.

His jaw tightened. "Because you present yourself in such a way that suggests it."

"That isn't fair. I've never been given a chance to make my own decisions. It's assumed I'm incapable."

"If you show as much maturity in the rest of your life as you have with your decision to run from your duty, I can see why."

"I'm not running from my duty. I understand what's expected of me. I even understand why. But I realized something a few weeks ago. I've never been alone. *Ever.* Not really. I've always had a security detail following my every move, chaperones making sure I never put a toe out of line, dressers telling me what to wear, teachers telling me what to think—all leading up to a future that was predestined for me and that I have no control over." Her throat tightened. "I just wanted time. Time to find out who I am."

A buzzing sound echoed in the room, signaling the arrival of their food. Adham stood and walked to the door, punching in a security code that she assumed allowed the delivery man access. In a few moments Adham returned, holding two bags that looked as if they were packed full of food.

She tried to find some of the optimism she'd felt earlier, when she'd first boarded the train from Italy. She only had this one night of freedom, and a very limited amount tomorrow. There would be a lot of time for her to cry later. And she would. For now she was seizing the moment. She was going to enjoy her dinner. A dinner *she* had chosen—not the palace dietician.

Adham set the bags on a glass coffee table and opened them. The smell that filled the room made Isabella's stomach growl more insistently. She lost focus on that, though, as she watched Adham remove the tightly wrapped food from the bag, her eyes transfixed on his hands. They were so masculine, so different from her own. Wide and square, with deep scars marring the golden skin of his knuckles.

What kind of man was he? What had he done to earn so many marks of pain on his body? He'd said he'd been in life-or-death situations. It was clear that he was still alive. Not so clear what had happened to his opponents. Not for the first time she wondered if she should be afraid of him. But she wasn't. He unsettled her. Made her feel a strange sort of jumpiness, as though she'd had one too many shots of espresso—one of the only vices her parents allowed her.

One thing she knew for certain was that she wanted to be rid of the man. No one had babysat her brother while he'd gone out and had his taste of freedom. No one had doubted he would return to do his duty. She would do what she was meant to do. She'd always known that a love match wasn't in her future, even before Hassan had been chosen for her. But that didn't mean she wanted to be kept under lock and key her entire life. A few short weeks was all she'd asked for. A small concession when a lifetime of what amounted to servitude was in her future.

She wasn't going to think about it now. All she was going to do was enjoy her dinner.

She took the first bite of her burger and closed her eyes, sighing with absolute pleasure. It was much better than she'd even imagined. A literal taste of freedom. She chewed slowly, savoring the experience and everything it represented for her.

Her last meal, he'd called it. He'd been joking, but it was true enough to her. Her first and last night on her own, making her own choices. Except she wasn't really. *He* was here.

She blinked back the tears that were forming in her eyes and took another bite. She sighed again, relishing the flavor. Relishing freedom. All she would ever have was a taste, before she was shipped off to marry a man she didn't know. A man she didn't love or even have a special attraction to. And she was prepared to do that— had been her entire life. Was prepared to face her duty for the sake of her country. But she'd wanted time out from it all first. She hadn't thought it was too much to hope for. Apparently it had been.

Now the food felt dry in her mouth and heavy in her stomach.

"Isabella?"

She looked up, and her eyes locked with Adham's. Being the subject of his intense focus made her insides feel jittery. She didn't like being on the receiving end of that dark, knowing gaze. It was as if he could see into her, into every private thought and feeling she'd ever had.

She lowered her eyes, staring hard at her food. Anything to keep from showing him just how much he unnerved her. She was used to being at an advantage, used to being royalty and feeling like it. But it didn't seem to matter to this man at all. There was no deference towards her position, not even the semblance of respect she was used to receiving from strangers by virtue of her status.

"You are thinking hard, Isabella."

She looked up at him. He flexed his hand, curled it into a fist as if he'd been seized by sudden tension.

"Your emotions are easy to read," he said finally.

"There are two months until the wedding," she said, trying to cultivate her best vulnerable expression, trying to appeal to him in some way. If her emotions were easy to read, she would use everything she had. "Two months and ten days. I haven't gotten to do anything I planned to do. I've never been to the cinema, or to a restaurant. I just want…I want something of life—my own life— before I…I get married." She watched his face, hoping to see some expression of sympathy, a sign he was at least hearing her words. She got nothing but that coal-black impenetrable stare. She could feel the wall between them, feel the distance he'd placed so efficiently between them.

She pressed on, her heart beating faster. "Could you…? Why couldn't I do some of the things I planned, only *with* you?"

This at least earned her a small response, in the form of a fractional lift of his eyebrow. "I am not a babysitter, *amira*." The Arabic word for princess was tinged with mockery.

"And I'm not a baby."

"I am here to bring you to your fiancé, and that is where our association begins and ends. After you've been to see the Eiffel Tower tomorrow we will fly back to

Umarah. You will go to the palace there, and then I will leave you in the capable hands of the High Sheikh."

"But…" She was stalled by the look on his face, the blank hardness that conveyed both disinterest and contempt with ruthless efficiency. She took another bite of her hamburger and tried not to cry. Not in front of him. She wasn't going to confirm what he thought—that she was some silly child who didn't know what was best for her own life.

Although that was half true. She *didn't* know. She realized that. How could she possibly know what was best for herself if she had no idea who she really was? She didn't know her own likes, her own dislikes, her own moral code. She only knew what she'd been *told* she liked. What she'd been *told* was best for her. How could she go to a strange country, with customs entirely different from any she was familiar with, marry a man she didn't know, if she still didn't know herself? What would be left of her when she was stripped away from everything she knew?

When her surroundings changed, when the people who chose her clothing, dictated her actions changed, she was terrified she might lose herself completely. That was just one reason she needed some time to find out more about herself on her own terms.

Her throat felt tighter. It felt as if everything was closing in on her. The room, her family's expectations. This was why she'd left in the first place. It was why she couldn't stay now.

She took a deep breath and made an effort to smile. She had a limited amount of time to form a plan, and she couldn't sacrifice her head start by tipping him off to what she was thinking.

"I'm tired," she said. It was true. She was so tired she

felt heavy with it. But she didn't have the luxury of collapsing yet.

"You can sleep in the guest bedroom." He gestured to a doorway that was situated across the open living room. She put her half-eaten dinner back on the wax paper, sad that she hadn't been able to enjoy it more, and stood, making a move to grab her pink suitcase.

Adham reached over and put his hand on the suitcase. Over hers. The heat singed her, blazed through her body. It shocked her that his touch could be so hot.

"I'll get it," he said, standing. He kept his hand on hers, though and the warm weight was comforting and disturbing at the same time. "That's called chivalry, not servitude."

Her face felt warm, and it seemed as if her pulse was beating in her head. "I didn't know you considered yourself chivalrous."

His dark eyes clashed with hers. She pulled her hand away, shocked at the steady burn that continued even without his touch.

"Generally speaking, I don't. Would you like to call your parents? Let them know you have not been kidnapped?"

"No." She felt mildly guilty for not wanting to speak to them. But she also felt angry. She wasn't certain she could even speak to her father without everything—all the repressed frustration she felt—flooding out of her. He could have let her have this time—realized how important it was. But he hadn't.

The slight hitch of his eyebrow let her know that he disapproved. Well, fine. He could handle *his* parents the way he wanted, and she would handle hers her way.

Adham set the suitcase down just inside the door of the guest bedroom, not placing a foot inside. "I will call

them, then. There's a bathroom just through that door.
If you need anything, I will see that you are provided
for."

She tried to force a smile. "When does the jailer make
the rounds?"

His dark eyes narrowed. "You think you suffer,
Isabella? You're here in this penthouse and you think
yourself in prison? You are to go from being Princess
of Turan to Sheikha of Umarah and that seems lacking
to you? You are nothing more than a selfish child."

His words pounded in her head as he turned and
walked away. How was it selfish to want some time for
herself before she gave it all up for king and country?
Sheikh and country? Why was it so wrong for her to want
something—anything beyond what had been given to her
by her well-meaning handlers? Because that was what
it felt like. As though everyone in her life was directing
her, guiding her. Forcing her. She knew her place. But
she didn't have to like it. And she was not going to let
Adham bring guilt on her head for seizing what little
time was available to her.

It was after midnight when Isabella was certain Adham
was no longer awake. Waiting had been nearly impossible. She'd been lying in the plush bed, the only thing
in the penthouse that wasn't hard and modern, trying not
to give in to the extreme exhaustion she felt. It had been
twenty-four hours since she'd last slept, but the high of
her escape from her brother's Italian villa, coupled with
her first day of freedom, had been enough to keep her
from sleeping on the train and then when she'd gotten
into the hotel room.

He had to be asleep by now—and she had to go now,

or she wouldn't have a chance to get far enough ahead of him. Sleep, for her, would have to wait.

She got out from under the covers, still fully dressed down to her shoes, and walked as quietly as she could across the room. She picked her suitcase up and took a deep breath. No point in wasting time. The faster she got out, the better.

She cracked open the bedroom door and scanned the darkened living room. She didn't see him, and across the way there was no light coming from under his door. She said a quick, silent prayer before making her way to the front door, turning the deadbolts and letting herself out. She closed it silently behind her, and took a moment to catch her breath to calm her raging heartbeat.

Her second escape attempt in as many days.

The hallway suddenly seemed endless, the world extremely open. Her options were timed, but with that time she would grab hold of what freedom she could. And maybe she could find a way to satisfy that yearning ache inside her—that relentless thing that ate at her, made her so conscious of all of the emptiness that just seemed to sit there inside of her.

Other people had their whole lives to figure out what to do about it; their futures stretching wide before them, the unknown an exciting and beautiful thing. She had two months. Her future ended abruptly on Umarahn soil, with a title, expectations, and a husband who would be a total stranger. But she would have her time until then, and it would be her own. Not Hassan's. Not Adham's.

Her determination renewed, she walked to the elevator and pressed the button for the ground floor. In just a few moments she was down on the boulevard, dodging raindrops. Streetlamps reflected off the pooling water. Despite the late hour there were still people milling around, sitting at café tables, standing beneath awnings, talking, laughing, kissing.

It was the real world. And it was finally within reach— along with the keys to her identity.

She began to scan the darkened streets for a taxi. She wasn't sure where she would take it when she found one, but she had quite a bit of cash on hand, so she imagined she could cover a lot of ground in the space of a few hours.

A hand clamped onto her arm, fingers biting into her flesh like a vice as she was pulled into an alleyway be- tween the penthouse and the *boulangerie* next to it. She opened her mouth to scream, but one of her attacker's arms locked like a steel bar across her chest, bringing her tight against a hard, warm body. Her assailant's other hand clamped over her mouth and stopped her shriek before any sound could emerge.

She looked around wildly, trying to see if any of the people who lingered on the street had seen. No one had. She struggled impotently. The strong body behind her didn't even move as she kicked and thrashed, spraying muddy water from the puddles into the air, throwing all her weight into her attempt to gain freedom. She might as well have been struggling against solid stone.

"Your manners leave a lot to be desired." The sound of Adham's familiar, faintly accented voice made her sag with relief. For a moment.

She swore violently in Italian—very colorful and inap- propriate words she'd learned from her brother, muffled by Adham's hold.

"Will you keep quiet if I remove my hand?" His tone had an edge to it—anger, extreme annoyance, and some- thing else that she couldn't place.

She nodded, and he let his hand fall away from her mouth but kept his arms around her.

He held her tightly against his solid body. She tried to wiggle out of his hold and his arms tightened, making her extremely conscious of all the hardened muscle of his body. All that finely honed masculinity. For a moment she could only be fascinated by the feel of him, by each and every minute difference between the male and female body.

Her breasts felt heavier, and she could feel her nipples tightening against the silken fabric of her bra. Her pulse beat heavily. In her neck, her head, down to the apex of her thighs.

"Do you have any idea what you're asking for?" he asked, his voice rough.

No. She truly didn't. Her body was asking for, craving, more of his touch. But she didn't have a clue as to why. Why she wanted to lean into his strength rather than struggle against it. Why she wanted his arms to stay locked around her. Why she wanted more of the sweet languor that was spreading through her.

"You're asking to be *killed*," he growled. Clearly he was letting the subject of their mutual attraction drop. "I could have been anyone. You're walking around out here in the middle of the night with designer luggage. You *look* as wealthy as you are. Worse, you look as ridiculously naive as you are. You're asking to be robbed. Or worse."

"I didn't…I didn't think of that." Logically, she knew crime rates in urban areas were much higher than in the small island nation she was from. But the thought had never crossed her mind. Her only thought had been escaping Adham. She'd set out to prove a point about her ability to look out for herself, and she'd done a spectacular job of not thinking it through.

He turned her so that she was facing him, her arms still pinned tightly to her sides. His hands held her steady, preventing her from running.

"What do you think you're going to do with all this freedom you seek, Isabella? You have no job, no skills. You are so naive you shouldn't be allowed to cross the street on your own!"

His words hurt. They hurt because, as much as she hated to acknowledge the truth in them, it was there. He was right. She'd never had a job. She didn't know how to go about getting one. Or an apartment. She didn't know how to drive. She had a lot of knowledge, but all that had come from books. She had never had to apply the things she'd learned to anything real or practical.

"I can find something to do," she said, pushing her reservations to one side.

"With a body like that there will be many men willing to help. For a price." His eyes raked over her, hot, glittering. There was nothing passive in those black depths—not now. There was only fire.

She struggled against him. "Let go of me." She needed to get away from him. It wasn't about the broader scope, the two months of freedom. Now it was all zeroed in on getting out of his hold—away from him and the strange electric feelings that were zinging through her system.

A man who was walking by the alley turned toward them. His expression, barely visible in the light of the lamp he stood under, was concerned.

Adham backed her up a few steps, so that she rested against the brick wall of the *boulangerie*, and before she could protest his mouth was covering hers, his tongue sliding against the seam of her lips, requesting entry. She gave it.

Her mind was blank of everything but the feeling of his lips on hers. His hands roaming from her hips to her waist, to the swell of her breasts. She gripped his shoulders, steadying herself, grateful for the wall of the building behind her and the wall of his body in front. If not for those things she would have melted into one of the rain puddles at his feet.

He pulled away suddenly, his breathing harsh in the stillness of the night air. Isabella touched her lips, confirming that they were as swollen as they felt.

"What...?" she breathed, unable to speak any more coherently than that.

"It's Paris," he bit out. "No one is going to interrupt lovers. Even if they are having a disagreement."

He took her arm and led her out of the shadows and back toward the main door of his building. Her rage mingled with something else—something hot and dangerous and completely unsettling. She put a hand to her mouth again, to confirm she hadn't hallucinated the entire event.

When they were back in the building he propelled her into the lift, the doors shut behind them. She couldn't believe he had done that. Kissed her as though he had every right to touch her, as though he...he had some *claim* on her. And only to shut her up. Her first kiss had been a diversion.

Worse than all of that, she couldn't believe the restless ache that was building in her body. The curiosity. The need to know what it would be like to kiss him again. Only this time longer and gentler, slowly so she had time to process it, to learn the texture of his lips, the rhythm of his movements.

She shut that traitorous part of her brain down. He'd had no right to do that. She wore another man's ring. Even in her wildest fantasies of escape she had never imagined betraying her fiancé in that way. She didn't know the man. She certainly didn't love him. But they had a signed agreement, and she had no intention of violating it.

He'd done it to shut her up. That stung her pride. Much more than it should.

"I can't believe you did that," she said icily.

He looked at her, his dark eyes unreadable, his lips—lips that had just claimed hers with what had felt like hunger—now pressed into a flat, immovable line. There was no passion there. He was unaffected. A man made of cold, unyielding stone.

"If you learn one thing about me learn this, and learn it quickly," he said, his voice hard. "I will do whatever it takes to ensure my objective is met. I intend to take you back to Sheikh Hassan, and I will do it."

She believed him. Her scarred captor with the fathomless eyes was most certainly capable of getting his way. Of seeing that she didn't get hers. She felt as if she'd stepped into water, expecting a wading pool, only to find she had swum out into the middle of an ocean. Out of her depth didn't begin to describe it.

She walked from the lift back into the penthouse, and tried not to imagine a barred cell door swinging shut when Adham closed the door behind them.

"How did you know? How did you get down there so fast?"

"I was expecting it. I deal with masterminds, Isabella, one naive princess is not going to pull one over on me. There's an alarm on the door that's linked to my mobile phone, and the stairs are faster than the elevator."

She closed her eyes against mounting anguish, tried

to fight the tears that were threatening. She didn't want to dissolve in front of him. Didn't want him to see how defeated she felt. How could a man who was allowed to do whatever he wanted, a man who roamed the world, lived by his own rules, possibly understand the preciousness of two months and ten days worth of freedom?

She looked at his hardened face, the scars. Appealing to him for a show of kindness would be like attempting to squeeze water from a rock. It was impossible. You couldn't extract what wasn't there.

"Go to bed, Isabella." His voice was as hard as everything else about him.

She felt as if she was going to break, but she wouldn't do it in front of him.

She nodded jerkily and stumbled into her bedroom, closing the door behind her with a click.

Adham stalked across the room and retrieved his phone from the coffee table, hitting the speed dial for his brother, not caring what time it was in their home country.

"*Salaam*, brother," Adham said curtly.

"*Salaam,*" Hassan returned the greeting, his tone questioning. "You've found Isabella?"

"I have found your wayward fiancée, as requested."

"And she is well?"

"She is uninjured, if that's what you mean. But she did make another escape attempt."

"She's unhappy?" His brother sounded genuinely concerned.

"She is a spoiled child. She has no reason to be so discontent. She wants for nothing."

Hassan sighed heavily into the phone. "I regret that she is reluctant about the marriage. But it's a much needed alliance, and marriage is the best way to seal such bargains. It is necessary insurance in something so critical."

"I understand the reason for your union. But I find her childish."

"You do not think she will make a suitable bride?"

"I will gladly hand her over to you and see that she becomes your problem as quickly as possible."

Hassan laughed. "You make me eager for her to arrive." He paused for a moment. "Is there nothing that can be done to make her happy? A gift, perhaps? A ring that is more to her liking?"

"She wants to see the Eiffel Tower," Adham bit out in response.

"Simple enough."

"She has some idea that she is lacking in life experience. She intends to go and find herself some *experience*."

There was another pause on the other end of the line. "The wedding is not for two more months, Adham. If that is what she wants, I see no reason why you can't accommodate her—so long as the experience she seeks is not in a man's bed."

There was something different in his brother's tone. A desperation he had not heard before. Adham had the feeling that his request had little to do with Isabella, but he would not ask.

"I am not a babysitter." He repeated his earlier words. "Have one of your other men come and watch over her while she tries to play at living her spoiled princess fantasy of what real life is."

"I don't have that kind of trust in anyone else. Another man would be too tempted by her. I'm certain that you've noticed she's an incredibly beautiful woman."

He'd noticed. It was difficult not to. She had the sort

of beauty that no red-blooded man could ignore. And he didn't want to spend any more time with her than was necessary.

"You will keep her safe?" Hassan pressed.

"You have my word. On my honor, I will keep her from harm. I will keep her untouched." His vow was from the heart. He served Hassan always. Gladly. Hassan was his only family, and there was no bond stronger than that forged in blood.

"I have absolute faith in you, Adham," his brother continued. "You will keep her safe and make her happy. It will ease my conscience."

"As you will it," Adham ground out, before ending the call.

He tossed the phone onto the couch and tried to calm his raging pulse. At the moment he felt like a fox that had just been asked to guard the henhouse.

Kissing her had been a miscalculation on his part. He had not anticipated his body's reaction to such a simple thing. He had far too much experience for a mere kiss to fire his blood.

And yet kissing Isabella had done just that. His body was still hard, and a dark, physical need was gripping him. There was no denying that in a physical sense he desired her. And she was the one woman he was forbidden to touch.

But it was a simple matter of control. And once he had made his decision he would not deviate from it. He never did.

CHAPTER THREE

ISABELLA surfaced quietly the next morning, creeping out of the sparsely furnished bedroom and into the main living area. Her eyes were puffy from crying and from lack of sleep. But the moments of indulgence had been worth it in a way. And now she was done with feeling sorry for herself.

She pulled her thick hair up into a ponytail and walked through the expansive living room and into the kitchen. She took an apple out of a fruit bowl on the counter and sat down at the small dining table.

Adham strode into the room a moment later, his crisp white shirt open at the collar, revealing a V of golden muscular chest. His black hair was wet and curling around the neck of his shirt. He smelled fresh, clean and wholly male, his natural scent spiked with a hint of sandalwood—exotic, spicy, and completely erotic. She couldn't remember ever noticing the scent of a man before. Her father's cologne, her brother's aftershave, but never the scent that was beneath the product. She noticed it now. It made her lungs feel tight, as if she couldn't bring in enough air.

She placed the apple on the table. "Good morning."

He gave her a skeptical look, one that told her he quite plainly disagreed, and jerked the refrigerator door open, turning his attention to hunting for food. "Have you eaten?"

She shook her head mutely, before realizing that he couldn't see her. "No. I just got up."

"Late nights prowling the street do tend to make one tired."

She gritted her teeth to bite back all the angry words that were swirling in her head, all the justification and excuses. None of it would matter to him. As far as he was concerned she was simply a package for him to deliver. "So I'm discovering."

He closed the fridge abruptly and straightened, training his dark, impenetrable gaze on her. "Never endanger yourself like that again, Isabella. You do not understand how dangerous the world is. How can you?"

"I live surrounded by bodyguards. I understand that life is dangerous."

"Do you? Because you did not seem like a woman who understood that last night."

"I didn't really imagine that the neighborhood around your upscale penthouse would pose a danger."

"Danger can be anywhere. Even in the most luxurious surroundings. Especially there."

The dark note in his voice told her he spoke from an experience she couldn't begin to understand. His scars ran deep. Those on the surface were only a glimpse of what was beneath. But it didn't repel her. It only made her curious about the man who was the Sheikh's most trusted employee. The man who seemed to have no fear for himself, yet feared for her safety.

He took her apple from its spot on the table and placed it back in the fruit bowl. "Let's go to a café. You can see more of the city."

Wariness along with a small surge of hope flared to life inside her. "I thought you didn't babysit."

"I don't. Consider this your guided tour of life."

"What changed your mind?" she asked, apprehension combining with excitement now, and her stomach tightening with anticipation.

"It has nothing to do with me. It's what Hassan wants. If it were up to me you would be on a plane to Umarah right now and would no longer be my problem. But your future husband has seen fit to allow you to have your *life experiences*. Within reason, of course."

She imagined it was what prisoners might feel like when they found out that their execution date had been pushed back. It was a reprieve, but the execution still loomed. And she would be living her remaining days with her jailer as her constant companion. But she wouldn't let herself think of what would happen after her time in Paris. This was about her. She deserved it. Deserved to have some time devoted to things that interested her. Some time devoted to discovering what things interested her.

"Thank you," she choked out, the lump in her throat keeping her from speaking more. She closed the distance between them, wrapped her arms around his neck.

Adham stood rigid, his arms pinned tightly to his sides. He was unwilling to do so much as breathe, for fear his control would slip even more and he would give in to the ache of arousal that was pounding heavily through his body.

He could not remember the last time a woman, or anyone for that matter, had hugged him. Clung to him, kissed him, rubbed her body against him in invitation— sure. But just a hug—a show of warmth, of affection, an innocent gesture… He didn't know if he had ever experienced that. He had been so long without his family, so long without frequent, human contact, that he could not remember any more what it had been like. Since the death of his parents it had only been Hassan and himself, and neither of them were given to overt displays of affection.

"I do not want your gratitude," he said, pulling away from her hold, ignoring the tightness in his body. Ignoring what it meant. "This was not my doing."

Her eyes widened, and hurt evident in their blue depths—as though she was a child responding to being scolded. Such a contradiction. She was a woman, not a child, but she seemed to switch roles with ease. A woman when it suited her to be enticing. A sweet innocent when she wanted sympathy. It was a façade, an act, and though it was effective it would not work on him.

She bit her lip and looked down, the crease between her dark, perfectly shaped brows deepening, as if to show contrition. "I'm sorry. But this is the only chance I'll have to…to figure out who I am. I don't know if someone like you could understand."

"Someone like me?" he asked, mildly amused that she'd clearly taken him to be nothing more than a bodyguard.

"Someone who's had freedom his whole life. Someone who's had the ability to make his own decisions. I haven't had that chance. It's…it's more than that. I don't know if I can fully explain it. I just know that I need to be able to have some experiences of my own."

He crossed his arms over his chest, unmoved by her speech. "And what is at the top of this list of yours?"

She raised her eyes again, a glimmer of excitement there now. "I want to do things I haven't done before. Go to the movies. A club, maybe?"

"Not a club," he said flatly.

If she went to a club every heterosexual male in the area would be all over her. Given her sheltered upbringing, she likely had no clue what kind of effect a body like hers had on men. She'd played at flirting with him, but playing was all it had been. In that sort of environment she would be like a lamb that had wandered into a wolf pack.

"Okay, not a club," she said, not looking at all dented by his refusal. "But definitely the Eiffel Tower, the Champs-Élysées, a restaurant. And *definitely* shopping."

"Get dressed. I'll take you to breakfast."

Isabella took a long sip of her espresso and followed it up with a bite of pastry. She closed her eyes and moaned.

The burn that hit him hot and hard in his stomach, along with the slow flood of blood that went south of his belt, made him tense.

He hadn't noticed before what a sensual person Isabella was. Watching her eat a pastry and drink coffee, listening to the sounds she made—small kitten moans in the back of her throat—watching the way she closed her eyes as if she was in ecstasy, seeing her lick each remaining crumb from her full lips, was erotic torture.

The only thing that matched the arousal racing through his system was the growing disgust that had settled in his gut. She was his brother's woman. She was forbidden. He should not want her, should not touch her, should not look at her as a man looked at a woman. And yet he found himself looking. Wanting. But he would never touch her. *Not again.* That time in the alley, when his lips had met hers, it had been necessary. It was a moment that would never be repeated.

He would not betray his brother in such a manner.

The loyalty that existed between them was not something that could be thrown aside for a mere woman. The bond between himself and his brother had always been strong, but after the death of their parents that link between them had been strengthened. Hassan had devoted his life to ruling Umarah, guiding their people, forging diplomatic alliances and handling the delicate matters of state. Adham's life was devoted to protecting Hassan, to guarding their people. They were a right and a left hand. Hassan had been the public ruler from the time their parents had died, but they functioned as a team, working with their strengths for the betterment of their people.

There would be no compromising that.

"This place is amazing. Like a fantasy."

She inhaled deeply, and his eyes were drawn to the shape of her rounded breasts pushing against her top.

Clearly her fantasies were different from his. But then, that was to be expected. Another reminder of why she was not the sort of woman who should arouse his libido. Even if his brother weren't a factor. She was an innocent. A virgin. He had never touched a virgin and never would as he didn't ever intend to take a wife.

"Paris can hardly be beaten for atmosphere, although I'm partial to the desert. I like the heat, the open space, the solitude."

Her smooth forehead creased. "I've never been to the desert. I can't really imagine it being beautiful. Whenever I envision the desert I see cactuses and bleached bones."

"It's not an easy beauty to see. Not like the architecture here in Paris, and not like the green mountains in Turan. It's fierce and barren—just the sand and the sky. It asks a lot of a man, but if the man can rise to the challenge, if he can learn to exist in such a place, he can't help but love it."

Her blue eyes glittered, the sudden humor there unexpected. "And you've risen to the challenge and defeated the desert?"

Her mischievous smile pulled a reluctant laugh from him. "I haven't beaten it. It's impossible to tame the desert. There are fierce sandstorms, unforgiving temperatures, and poisonous reptiles. The best you can hope is that she'll allow you a peaceful existence."

She offered him a sweet half-smile that just barely curved the edges of her full lips. "And the desert is a woman?"

"Of course she is. Only a woman could be such a fierce mistress."

"I can't imagine the kind of freedom the desert must offer," she said, after a long moment of silence.

"It's a freedom that demands responsibility. You have to respect where you are at all times. You have to keep the rules and mind the boundaries."

"And uphold duty and honor?"

"What is there in life without those things, Isabella? If men discard such notions, what keeps the world moving?"

Isabella hated how right he was. Hated that what he said made so much sense. She understood the importance of her alliance with Hassan, High Sheikh of Umarah. It was good for the economy, good for building a strong bond between nations in case of any sort of crisis. And if it weren't her life, if she were only a casual observer like Adham, who wasn't the one being forced to marry a stranger, she would have felt as he did.

But it was her life. Not some vague idea of honor and duty. She was the sacrificial lamb for the masses. Easy for him to speak that way when in the end he got to ride off into the sunset and be with whom he wished, doing whatever he wished.

"I have accepted the path I have to take, Adham," she said, trying to keep her voice from wobbling. "I only wanted to take a small detour."

"And where would you like your detour to take you now, Princess?" His voice was hard. Condescending. A sharp contrast to the small moment of near camaraderie they'd just shared.

Well, fine. She didn't much care for him either.

"I thought we could walk. See the sights."

He nodded in what she assumed was acquiescence. He had a way of making her feel as though he disapproved with nothing more than the slightest movement. Even though he'd agreed, the tension in his body told her he'd rather do anything else. Not the most accommodating man, her keeper.

He turned and began to walk up the boulevard, not getting too far ahead of her, but not exactly waiting for her either. She knew that no matter what it seemed like his focus was still on her. She knew it because her skin felt too tight and her stomach was queasy with knots.

She quickened her pace, taking two steps to his one, her much shorter legs making her work harder to gain the distance he was managing. She looked around at the tourists pouring from buses that lined the sidewalks. They were in groups. Pairs. Holding hands. Why did it suddenly seem as though it would be natural to be linked to Adham in that way? To hold his hand while they strolled through Paris together?

She fell into step beside him and her hand brushed his. Her heart leapt to her throat at the contact. He didn't even look at her. Didn't give her any indication that he had noticed her touch, let alone been affected by it.

Except she noticed him curling his hand tightly into a fist, the tendons shifting, the scars on his skin lightening as he squeezed tightly before relaxing it again. She rubbed the back of her own hand idly, her skin still hot from his touch. Maybe his skin was hot from the brush of her hand too?

She looked at him again, at his hard, immobile face, so perfect it seemed to be etched in stone. The marks on his skin were evidence of time and living rather than a detraction to his masculine beauty. An addition to the form the artist had wrought, showing the character of the man, of all he had endured.

No. It was impossible that she'd manage to have any effect on a man like him. He was quite incredibly out of her league, in more ways than she could count. She didn't know how old he was, but she was certain he was quite a bit older than her own twenty-one. Add his experience and living to that, and it seemed they were from different worlds.

That realization made an uncomfortable weight settle in her stomach. He probably didn't take her any more seriously than if she were a child whining for an ice cream cone.

She shook her head. It didn't matter what Adham thought of her. He didn't have to live her life. *She did*. She looked over the tops of the tour buses, past the neatly shorn trees that were carefully crafted into tall hedges, at the top of the Eiffel Tower, visible above all of it.

They reached the end of the row of foliage and the full tower came into view. People were everywhere, snapping photographs of the intricate scaffolding and of each other.

She wondered how she and her stoic companion must look to them.

She noticed very quickly that women were all but giving themselves whiplash with extreme head-turns when Adham walked by. Pride warred with another more uncomfortable emotion. Pride because he was the best looking man even in this densely populated spot, and he was with *her*. But the other feeling, the one that made her stomach ache, was not welcome.

"Would you take my picture?" she asked, fishing for the small digital camera she'd tucked into her purse before leaving her brother's home and holding it out to him. She wanted memories. Reminders of the time when she'd been free to make her own choices.

He raised his dark eyebrow at her, clearly less than pleased to be playing tourist.

Another feeling roiled in her stomach, and this one she knew for sure. Anger. "Please. Just take my picture and stop acting like you're here under sufferance."

She caught a small, barely detectable curving of his lips. "I *am* here under sufferance." But he took the camera from her outstretched hand.

She positioned herself in front of the lawn and smiled wide. Suddenly she wished she were taking *his* picture. His face would be compelling on film. His masculine bone structure, his scarred golden skin. Maybe if she had a photo she could look at his dark eyes long enough to read his secrets.

He snapped the picture and she jumped, realizing she'd been somewhere else entirely. That wasn't right. She needed to be living in the moment. She was at the Eiffel Tower, in Paris. No looking ahead, no looking back, and no looking into Adham's eyes. He was just an unfortunate accessory to her trip, nothing more.

"Did it turn out okay?" she asked.

He looked at the small screen, his expression tight. "It's fine." He walked to her and thrust the camera back into her hand, his manner abrupt. Nothing new there. Was there any way to penetrate that wall he had up? Was there a woman, one he loved, that those dark eyes softened for?

The thought made her feel nauseous. She didn't want to think about the woman who got to see past his defenses. But if she were to try and imagine that woman she pictured her being older, sophisticated—not just in the sense of having an affluent upbringing, but savvy in the ways of the world. Knowledgeable of things Isabella was hardly aware of.

She would certainly be the opposite of Isabella, since the only thing she seemed to arouse in Adham was extreme annoyance.

"Ready?" he asked, his voice clipped.

No, she wasn't ready. But she doubted it really mattered. "Sure."

Her pique was forgotten as they walked through the city, past beautiful stone architecture and historic sites. She lingered in one of the narrow streets, taking photographs of a rustic wooden door painted a rich, saturated blue. She wanted to capture it forever, to remember the simple moment of unexpected beauty and color amidst the monochromatic grays.

"It's a door, Isabella." Adham's bored voice sent a shiver of irritation and tension through her.

"Yes, it is, Adham. A blue one. Glad your gift of observation is so well-honed. It's little wonder you're such an indispensable member of the Umarahn guard."

He captured her arm, gently but firmly, and turned

her so that she was facing him. "I am not a member of the Umarahn guard. I *am* the Umarahn guard."

He was so close. Like he'd been in the alley. It was so easy to imagine him pulling her to him, capturing her lips again.

She moved away. "They're lucky to have you."

She walked ahead of him this time, keeping her eyes locked in front of her. She didn't know why his comment had bothered her so much. Maybe because she'd seen beauty in that simple thing and it had meant something to her to try and capture that. Something that had felt important. And he hadn't seen it at all. Not that it should matter.

The alleyway spilled out onto a busier street, lined with shops and cafés, and further down the massive Printemps department store.

She felt a renewed flaring of excitement. "Can we go shopping?"

"Shopping? Does that rate as an important, life-altering experience for you?"

Mild irritation gave way to seething anger. "I don't know. Maybe it does. I haven't really been before. At least not without the aid of my mother's personal shopper, telling me what is and isn't appropriate. But you wouldn't understand that. You take for granted your God-given free will because no one's stolen it from you."

"And you think these shallow experiences will teach you something of life? It shows how little you know, Isabella. You see only what's been denied you, not what you've been protected from." His dark eyes burned into her, making her feel exposed, as though all her inadequacies were revealed to him. "Not all experiences are good."

She swallowed hard. "You speak as a man who has never been a prisoner."

He took a step toward her and she stepped back, dodging a pedestrian. "I *have* been a prisoner. A prisoner of war. Where do you think these came from?" He indicated the marks etched into his cheek. "You are nothing more than a foolish child. You know nothing of the world. Be grateful for that."

CHAPTER FOUR

ISABELLA flicked her eyes up and focused on Adham's cool expression, reflected in the dressing room mirror. "You don't like it?"

He shrugged, his expression one of cool disinterest. "Buy what *you* like."

She fixed her gaze back on her reflection. Yes. She was going to buy what *she* liked. It didn't matter what he thought, or what her mother's personal shopper would say. The only thing that mattered was how she felt about the outfit. The crisp white button-up top hugged her breasts and nipped in at the waist, accentuating her hourglass shape, while the brown satin shorts showed off more of her golden legs than she was accustomed to. But she thought she looked nice. She was reasonably certain she looked nice.

She looked back at Adham. "Is it unflattering?"

His coal-dark eyes raked over her, and it made her want to tug on the wide cuff of the shorts so that she could get some more coverage. "It's very flattering."

Isabella was suddenly conscious of the fact that they were alone in the dressing area. Her skin felt sensitized. She could feel the air touching her, closing in on her. She could feel Adham's heat across the small space.

"Th-thank you." Her heart was beating harder now,

her palms damp. She needed…she needed distance. She didn't want to be closed in with Adham anymore, didn't want to share the air with him. Air that suddenly seemed thicker, harder to breathe. "So…so you like it, then?" She despised the hopeful tone in her voice.

His Adam's apple bobbed; his eyes flickering over her curves. "I like it."

She noticed that he tightened his hands into fists again, then released them, flexing his long, masculine fingers.

He was the most infuriating man. He'd all but crushed her before they'd gone into Printemps, making her feel like a silly child, and now, only half an hour later, he was making her more conscious of the fact that she was a woman than she'd ever been before.

"I'm finished," she said tightly, disappearing into the dressing room and putting on her own clothes as quickly as possible, before exiting with her carefully chosen outfits.

She added the packages to the shoes she'd purchased already, which included a pair of very sexy, strappy high-heeled sandals and tall butter-soft brown leather boots. Definitely not things her mother's personal shopper would have chosen.

They meandered through the massive department store, and Isabella did her best to simply block out everything but the moment she was living in. She loved being surrounded by the crowd of people, by the low hum of conversation. She was *with* people rather than above them—a part of things rather than held back, kept separate from everyone.

Although Adham seemed content to hold himself separate on purpose. From her, from everyone. Though he wore designer jeans and a T-shirt with ease, he seemed out of place in their urban surroundings. He stood out—his height, his breadth, his handsome features, his scars all drawing attention to him. But it was more than just his looks. He seemed too exotic, too wild for something as prosaic as a department store.

He was so completely unaffected. By the sights, by the crowds, by her. And he was making her feel edgy and restless and…nervous. He was definitely affecting her, no matter how much she was trying to pretend otherwise.

With a spark of defiance she checked the map of the large store that she was carrying with her and headed to the lingerie floor. That was another part of her wardrobe that needed dragging into the contemporary era. She had lovely underwear, it was true. The highest quality. But the styles gave no concession to a woman's sexuality—which had always been fine with her, since she hadn't given much thought to hers. But this was about self-discovery, and she was not changing dictators without discovering what her personal preference in undergarments was. If she wanted ultra-sexy panties she was going to get them.

And Adham was coming with her. Like it or not. He was doing a decent job of making her uncomfortable. She might as well return the favor.

Of course her boldness nearly deserted her when they reached the lingerie floor. She looked at Adham out of the corner of her eye and noticed him clenching his fist again. He did that a lot. She was convinced it meant that he was uncomfortable. Good. He deserved some discomfort. His presence was one big giant discomfort in her behind, so a little turnabout seemed like fair play to her.

"I'd like to look around here for a while," she said, trying to keep her expression as neutral as possible.

Adham's eyes darkened, his jaw clenched tight along with his fist. "If you wish."

"You could wait in one of the cafés." But she knew he wouldn't.

"I don't think that would be wise."

She took a deep breath and tried to look casual—tried to look as if having a man with her while she looked at intimate items of clothing was both normal and no big deal at all. "All right."

She moved to one of the display tables and began to pick out the smallest, filmiest panties she could find, and thongs—something her mother never would have allowed her even to look at. She would think they were the sort of undergarments only suited to women of questionable moral character. A surge of power coursed through Isabella as she selected one thong in each pattern and color available, every one briefer, more revealing than the last.

It didn't matter if her mother would have disapproved of them. It was her decision to make. The very fact that there were people in her life who controlled what she wore beneath her clothing was sad beyond belief. But that would change. Even when she went to Umarah she would not allow that to be dictated to her. Not anymore.

Of course she would want to wear them only in her own chambers. She couldn't possibly imagine wearing them for her future husband. She didn't even know the man.

That thought made her want to throw all the revealing items down and run out of the store. But she wouldn't do that. This was about her. About what she wanted. Not what anyone else wanted or didn't want.

She finally sneaked a glance at Adham, who had fallen quite a bit behind her. She noticed his dark eyes were

burning with intensity, his hands locked so tightly that
the scars were bright white against a backdrop of golden
skin.

She was getting to him. Pleasure uncurled in her
belly, winding through her. Pride that she might hold
enough appeal for him that she was capable of making
him uneasy.

With a sudden surge of confidence she sauntered to the
negligees. The selection was phenomenal—silks, sheers,
pale pinks and electric blues. And every style was sexier
than anything she'd ever seen, let alone been permitted
to own. She didn't see why she should be confined to
floor-length nightgowns. She was twenty-one, for heav-
en's sake, and she still had nightwear in the same style
she'd worn at the all-girls boarding school she'd attended
seven years ago.

She picked up a gauzy peach babydoll-style nightie that
would barely cover the tops of her thighs. The Grecian
pleating over the cups wouldn't be sufficient to cover her
breasts—not when the fabric was nearly see-through.
The glass beads sewn beneath the bustline looked sinful,
somehow. Decadent. She loved it.

A wicked impulse seized her and she turned to face
Adham, holding the negligee up so he could get a good
look at it. "How about this? Do you think it would be
flattering?"

Adham's face remained as coolly impassive as ever,
a slight tightening of his jaw the only indication that
he'd heard her. He began to walk toward her, the heat in
his eyes causing an answering fire to ignite low in her
belly.

He was so close, too close, his masculine scent teasing
her, making her heart pound heavily. She tried to swallow, but her throat felt as if it was coated in sandpaper.

He extended his hand and ran his fingers along the edge of the nightie's neckline, his callused fingers abrading the delicate fabric, the sound sending a faint shiver through her. His eyes were locked with hers, the dark intensity in them robbing her of the ability to breathe.

He slid his fingers down over the negligee, his thumb caressing the part that would have been covering her breasts had she been wearing it.

It was far too easy to imagine those rough fingers moving over her body, imagine how his fingers would feel against her soft, tender skin. Evidence of his strength, his hard work, his character.

Her breasts suddenly felt heavy, her nipples stinging as they tightened into hard points. She was absolutely, completely disturbed by what he was making her feel. But she was also captive to it, spellbound by the power he had over her body. He could make her feel more than any fantasy or real-life person ever had without even touching her.

Her breath was caught in her throat, every nerve, every cell in her body waiting to see what he would do next.

"I don't know that it's your color," he said, his eyes never leaving hers. "You should try for something more daring."

For a moment—one heady, wonderful moment—she thought he was going to lean in and capture her lips again. He was so close. It would have been the easiest thing to close the distance between them, for her to touch her lips to his.

"A brighter shade, I think," he said, his voice rough. "Sheikh Hassan prefers women who wear vivid colors."

He stepped away from her then, his eyes flat, all the heat gone. She couldn't have been more shocked if he'd dumped a bucket of ice water over her. He'd had her spellbound, unconscious of where she was, who she was. It was a shock to find out that she was still standing in Printemps, beneath the bright lights, with other shoppers milling around them as though they weren't there.

And she was still wearing Hassan's ring.

"I like this one," she said, trying to inject authority into her voice. Difficult when she could hardly catch her breath.

She held the negligee tightly to her chest and clutched the panties in a bundled-up knot of fabric as she headed to the register to pay for her lingerie. He had been trying to put her off, but she wasn't going to let him.

She imagined he'd also been trying to show her that *he* was in control, that she was out of her depth. And that he had succeeded in, she hated to admit.

She'd felt confident enough in her knowledge of men and sex to tease him, torment him a bit as he'd been doing to her. She'd gleaned enough knowledge from her time away at school, from late-night chatting sessions with her friends, and then, more recently, from her sister-in-law Alison. But with one searing look, with the effect he'd had on her body, Adham had proved to her that she knew nothing. Nothing real, anyway.

Romance novels and jokes with friends were one thing, but actual sexual attraction, need, desire was quite another. She'd never really realized just how different the two were until she'd watched him stroke his fingers over the silken material of the nightgown. As she'd imagined him touching her in the same manner.

The thought made her hot all over.

She handed the clerk her credit card—no point being discreet now that she'd been found—and waited while her sexy new nothings were packaged into two neat little boxes with satin ribbon handles. She added those to her other shopping bags, a small feeling of accomplishment swelling in her chest.

Maybe Adham thought shopping was stupid, but she felt as if she'd claimed some small portion of her life for herself, and there was nothing stupid about that.

"Are you ready to go?" he asked, his voice rougher than normal, his accent thicker.

"I am getting hungry. But we could just eat here…"

"I have my limits on shopping," he said, his lip curled slightly. "Normally I hand women my credit card and send them on their way."

He started to walk toward the exit doors and she followed him quickly. "What? Women you date?"

He turned and looked at her for a brief moment, his dark eyebrows drawn together. "I don't know that I would call it that."

Of course not. Men like him probably had affairs. He'd probably had lots of rich lovers who reveled in having such a tough, macho man for a bedmate. Except he really didn't seem like the sort of man who would be content to be a woman's plaything. And, as he'd said, he was the one handing out credit cards.

She looked at him, her heart stuttering as she took in that broad, muscled back, his tapered waist and slim hips. Oh, no, Adham wouldn't be any woman's plaything. He was too much a man for that. He would want the upper hand in every way. He would be dominant in every situation.

Not for the first time she thought he seemed nothing like the staff at the Turani palace. He didn't defer to her. Ever. He acted like a man who was used to being in control, used to having his orders unchallenged, used to having his way. But then, he'd been in the military— likely as a leader—so it could be true.

"What would you call it, then?" she asked, curiosity demanding more than speculation.

"I don't know that I'm ever in one place long enough to date. I have arrangements."

That hot emotion stirred her stomach again, and this time she recognized it. Jealousy. Not really directed at the women, but because it was such a casual thing to him. He had *arrangements*. No one dictated to him whether or not he could have them, who he could have them with, how he conducted them.

Isabella was reasonably certain that even if she'd been given carte blanche to have relationships with men they wouldn't have been casual *arrangements*, but having the freedom would have been nice. Learning her own moral code, her own limits—that would have been nice too.

It would be nice to know her parents had that kind of trust in her.

Of course relationships hadn't been feasible, because an arranged marriage had always been a foregone conclusion. She'd been ten when it had been decided that Hassan al bin Sudar would be the man. There would never have been any point to her dating anyone. Even so, she was jealous of Adham's freedom, of the casual way he spoke of it.

"I've never had a relationship," she said, closing her eyes as they exited the store, as the cool air hit her face, the slight breeze ruffling her hair.

"You're engaged. Most people would count that as a relationship," he said, his voice tight.

"Well, most people who are engaged have met their fiancé, or at the very least selected him."

"It's different for royalty, Isabella. You know that."

"Of course I do."

Adham halted mid-stride and turned, taking her bags from her hands, his fingers brushing hers, sending a shock of heat straight to her toes. Then he turned and started walking again, as though the world hadn't just tilted a little. Although she supposed the world had remained upright as ever to him.

"What about you?" she asked, suddenly wanting to know more about her scarred guardian. "Do you ever plan to marry?"

"No."

"Just…no?"

"My life isn't suited to marriage and family. It is full. And I have no desire for a wife."

"Well, it's a good thing you aren't the High Sheikh, or you would be required to marry me."

He paused slightly, his shoulders tensing. It was a small reaction—one she would have missed if she weren't so tuned into him. "If it were required of me, I would do it."

"That's it? If it were required of you, you would change all of your expectations to fulfill your duty?"

"I would."

He said it with such certainty that she didn't doubt him. But it was easy for him. He didn't have dreams of love and romance. Even knowing she'd had an arranged marriage, part of her had always harbored fantasies of love. It was normal for women—for most people, really. Everyone wanted to be loved.

Except Adham, apparently. *He* only needed lovers. A thought that was much more intriguing than it should be. Because her thoughts had no place wandering down that road—not with Adham. Not with any man other than her chosen fiancé.

Even knowing that, when they rounded a corner and

she closed her eyes against the harsh shaft of afternoon light that shone between the tightly packed buildings, it was an imprint of Adham's face that she saw.

CHAPTER FIVE

ADHAM was taking her to the cinema, and she was unac-
countably nervous. It felt like…like a date—even though
the very idea was completely ridiculous. He'd all but
ignored her for the past few days—conducting business
in his office, checking on his oil field, making contact
with other security officers, and leaving her to fend for
herself.

But that morning she'd brought up the subject of the
movie theater, and he'd agreed.

She'd been trying to decide on an outfit for nearly
forty minutes. Which was ridiculous, because it shouldn't
matter what she wore so long as *she* was happy with it.
But she kept picturing Adham's face, his reaction to her,
wondering if any of that smoldering heat would flare in
his eyes when he saw her, and what article of clothing
might help her accomplish that.

It was not a productive line of thinking. But she was
wandering down the rabbit trail anyway.

She rifled through her new things and finally decided
to put on the sexy crimson wrap sweater she'd purchased
on their shopping excursion. The soft, clingy material
hugged her curves and had a neckline that dipped low,
showing just the right amount of cleavage. She decided
to pair it with dark-wash jeans and some strappy heels

that would no doubt make her feet ache after a few hours. But they would be worth it.

The underwear was almost as big a decision for her—which was more ridiculous than being so indecisive over the outerwear. But it mattered. Adham had seen them, had watched her purchase them. She didn't think a man had ever seen her underwear before, even when she wasn't wearing it. Knowing he would know what they looked like…the thought that he might try and guess which ones she was wearing…well, that made her feel wicked. And edgy. And just a tiny bit guilty.

She selected an ivory-colored bra, made from web-fine netting. Intricate flowers added provocative detail, framing her dusky nipples, which were clearly visible through the sheer fabric. The panties were no better—framing rather than concealing.

She looked at herself for a moment, stunned by the fact that she could look so…provocative. She'd almost entirely ignored her own sexuality because it had always seemed inextricably linked to her unknown, pre-selected future husband. But now, despite the fact that Hassan's ring was on her finger, that part of her so long denied was becoming tethered to the man who was out in the living area.

The attraction had been instantaneous. But she had been confident that once she'd spent some time with him it would diminish. It seemed as though she'd have to become accustomed to his sex appeal after all. But his appeal hadn't diminished. And her attraction was growing. Being stuck with him certainly didn't help.

She looked down at her breasts, at her nipples pushing against the gauzy fabric. She couldn't even think about him without having an actual physical reaction.

She huffed out a disgusted sound and pulled her jeans,

top and shoes on quickly. Anything to disguise that sensual image she made, standing there in her underwear. Underwear that was definitely meant to be seen.

Her mouth dropped open with shock and a mild amount of pleasure as she took in her fully dressed reflection. She'd never looked so...so outright sexy in her entire life. She turned and admired the view from the back in the mirror. Yes, she looked totally sexy. But... more than that...she looked like herself. She was different, but totally familiar. It was as if that other version of herself—the one who'd been wearing khaki slacks and a matching jacket—had been the stranger. And this was Isabella.

She stepped up to the mirror and looked at the woman staring back at her. Her make-up was lighter than the way her personal servant did it, and her hair was left natural. Loose curls tumbled past her shoulders.

For the first time she felt as though she matched her reflection. This wasn't the glossed-up princess, made to look so much older and more sophisticated than she was. This was the woman that she was inside.

She took a deep breath and got ready to go back into the main part of the penthouse. She was nervous, she realized. Because she'd only just seen herself for the first time, and now Adham would see her too—with no façade to hide behind.

She turned the handle and opened the door. Adham was sitting on the couch when she came into the main living area. His eyes were closed, his hands clasped behind his head, and his black T-shirt stretched tightly across the hard muscles of his broad chest. The sight of his tanned, toned arms made her stomach knot.

Once again she was very conscious of the fact that

he'd seen her underwear. Which was stupid. It wasn't as if he'd seen her *in* it. Or as if he'd want to.

Except when he opened his eyes and looked at her, his dark gaze taking a slow tour of her body, there was heat there. Unmistakable, undeniable heat, that burned down to her toes and every interesting spot in between.

"I'm ready," she said, aware that her voice sounded husky, affected.

The heat in his eyes intensified, and she realized her words could be interpreted to mean something different. She also realized that part of her meant them in that way.

That was wrong. Even if she wasn't happy about her engagement to Hassan, she was committed to it. The expectation was that she would go to her marriage bed a virgin—something she'd tried decently hard not to think about, if only because it was frightening to think of sharing such a momentous thing with a man she didn't love or even know.

But now it seemed…it seemed worse, somehow. Maybe because when she thought of kissing she could still feel Adham's lips moving against hers, still feel the hard press of his chest, the way it had felt to be in his strong arms. As though she were something exquisitely special and fragile. He'd held her firmly enough to keep hold of her, gently enough that she wouldn't break.

It was *him* she wanted to touch again. Not just a random man—even if that man had given her a ring. Hassan still seemed random to her. A stranger. While Adham…she felt as if she was starting to know him. To care about him in spite of his hardened nature. Or maybe because of it.

She wanted to reach him, to find out if there was anything soft behind the hardened wall he placed between himself and the world. She wanted to find the root of his scars—not only those he bore physically, but the ones that ran far beneath the surface of his skin. She wanted to soothe his pain.

She looked at him again. The heat had been extinguished, his eyes now cool, flat and black. Perhaps she was imagining everything. The heat and the softness. Maybe he was all rock. But she didn't really believe that.

"Do you want to walk or drive?" he asked, pulling her coat from the peg and handing it to her, his fingers brushing hers. The sweet, unexpected contact giving her body a jolt.

"Always walk. I love taking in the sights."

The evening air was crisp, and she enjoyed the bite of it on her skin—especially with Adham's solid warmth so close to her. It was easy to pretend that it was a date.

Now, dating she'd dreamed of—and often. She'd shut out thoughts of sex, because in a lot of ways it was too challenging, since she knew she would only ever experience it with one man—a man selected by her family for his status, not for any other reason. But dating...

Just being with a man—the companionship, the romance. She'd thought about that so often late at night. Wondered what sort of man she would pick for herself. What it would be like to hold hands, to have her first kiss.

Well, kissing accomplished—even if it hadn't been anything like she'd imagined—but no hand-holding. That seemed a bit backward. But she was certain Adham wouldn't be looking to remedy it.

She forgot about hand-holding—well, she didn't forget, but she shuffled it to one side—when she saw the cinema.

It was everything she'd imagined, with neon lighting and brightly lit posters that reflected off the pools of rainwater on the sidewalks, adding a dim glow to the darkening streets.

"Wow. It's gorgeous," she said, then felt embarrassed—because it was such a typical thing for most people, yet it was amazing to her in that moment.

"You want to take a picture, don't you?"

"It's only a movie theater, Adham," she said pragmatically, arching her eyebrow.

"Yes, but you still want a photo. Just like you needed to take a picture of your blue door." He said it now as though he understood, and that made her heart ache with a need that frightened her. It was intangible, something she hardly understood, but so raw, so real, she thought she might double over with the intensity of it.

She couldn't speak past the lump in her throat as she pulled her camera from her purse and clicked off a dozen pictures of the posters, the lights, the curve of the architecture. She would always remember how she'd felt as she'd stood and looked at this theater. Every time she saw the photos she would remember. Adham's warmth. His unexpected understanding. The pain in her chest.

She looked at the screen on the camera, at the pictures she'd taken. He positioned himself behind her, studying the photos. His fingers bruised the tender hollow of her neck as he brushed her hair back. "You see beauty in so many places. So many things," he said, his voice husky.

Her heart thundered heavily in her chest. "Sometimes people miss beauty because it's buried in everyday objects. But none of this exploration is everyday to me."

He laughed softly, his breath hot against her cheek. "There is certainly nothing everyday about you."

She turned to face him then, and she caught the barest hint of warmth in his expression before the hardened mask returned and he stepped away, his body tensing.

"We should go in, or we'll miss our showing," he said, moving away from her and opening the door to the theater, allowing her to go in first.

It didn't escape her notice when he paid for her ticket. That made it feel even more like a date. He bought her popcorn too—greasy and over-salted, and one of the best things she'd ever tasted.

She was excited about the film—until the lights went down and she suddenly realized how close and intimate it seemed to be seated next to Adham, so close, in the dark.

She shifted and her arm grazed his. Her heart jumped into her throat. She sneaked a glance at Adham out of the corner of her eye. He sat, rock-solid, his expression betraying nothing, the planes and angles of his face stoic. His features were sharper, more defined in the flickering light of the movie screen, his scars deeper, more exaggerated.

Thinking of someone harming him, of him being forced into a life or death situation, made her feel physically ill. She felt sorry for the woman who loved him. He said he didn't want to get married, but her brother hadn't wanted to get married again, and all it had taken was the right woman. The right woman would find Adham, but *her* life would be a misery of worry. She could picture Adham's wife, curled up in bed alone, wondering if that night was the night her husband would never return.

Isabella's heart lurched into her throat. When the picture in her mind had sharpened, the woman she'd seen sitting in bed in the dark, her knees drawn up to her chest, had been *her*.

She blinked and turned her focus back to the movie, back to the story unfolding in front of them, and for a while she was carried away by the beautiful classic romance.

But when the hero finally kissed the heroine she was reminded of what it had felt like when Adham's lips had moved over hers, his tongue sliding against hers, the friction making her nipples tighten and her breasts ache. Like they were doing right at that moment.

She took a piece of popcorn from the tub and his fingers brushed hers. A short gasp escaped her lips, and she shot him another quick look to make sure he hadn't heard. If he had, he certainly wasn't showing it.

Why did he have to appeal to her so much? Why couldn't her chaperon be short, fat and completely horrible? Why did he have to be this enigma of a man who called to everything feminine inside her?

Adham had opened up a new world of fantasies and desires—made her ache for things she'd never wanted before.

It was pointless and cruel. She didn't even have the hope of a brief romance with him, let alone a happily ever after.

She looked at his hands, curled around the shared armrest that sat between them. She examined those scars again. She doubted a brief, light romance with a man like him would even be possible. He was the sort of man who would give nothing or everything. There wouldn't be much in between. And she…she would only be able to give everything. And she would want everything in return. An impossible situation even without the ring on her finger.

His hand brushed hers again and she nearly jumped out of her skin. Attraction, she was discovering, was about a lot more than butterflies in your stomach. It could be all-consuming, a need as elemental and necessary as food or drink. It was quickly becoming that way for her.

Curiosity. That was all it was. It had to be. After all, she'd never really felt drawn to a man like this before. All of the men she'd met at galas and balls and parties had been…insipid. Especially when she compared them to Adham.

Maybe if she were to meet another man like Adham she would feel the same way. Maybe she simply had a type. Except there wasn't another man to equal him. She was certain of that.

When the credits finally rolled on the movie she let out a gust of breath she hadn't been aware she'd been holding. She needed distance, or she was afraid she might crawl out of her skin.

Adham's swift exhalation of breath shocked her. It was almost as though he'd been experiencing the same thing she had. As if he were held in the thrall of this attraction, just as she was.

Once again realism compelled her to ask why on earth a man of Adham's experience would be interested in a virgin princess who didn't even know proper kissing technique.

"Did you enjoy the movie?" he asked as they exited the theater, his voice clipped, his manner detached.

"Yes. I did." Hopefully he didn't want a summary, because all she would be able to give him was a recap of how many times his arm had accidentally brushed hers.

"I'm glad." He didn't sound glad. He sounded detached. Bored. That irritated her. She felt edgy and… and turned on. And he was *bored*.

She couldn't stand next to him anymore—not feeling as if every nerve ending was on fire, as if the light touch of the breeze was going to tip her over the edge into the dark depths of arousal. Discomfiting to a woman who had scarcely experienced arousal in her life—at least not in such a personal sense.

She walked ahead of him, her steps quick and staccato, her heels clacking loudly on the pavement. He was infuriating. Yes, it would really be pointless for him to feel the same way, because neither of them could act on it, but it would have gone a long way toward satisfying her if she knew that he was at least half as uncomfortable as she was.

He kept pace behind her, obviously unconcerned with her pique, which just made her feel more irritated. No wonder women in romantic movies acted so strange sometimes. Men were infuriating. No two ways about it.

"Isabella." His deep voice startled her, and she wobbled on her high heel, her ankle rolling as she pitched to the side.

A strong hand clamped tightly around her arm and kept her from crashing to the cement. She found herself drawn tightly against his firm, muscled chest, his heart pounding heavily beneath her cheek.

"Be careful," he bit out, still holding her.

"It's the shoes," she said, unable to catch her breath, her hands shaking from the adrenaline surge of her near fall—and from his hold on her arm.

"And the fact that you were stomping off like an indignant teenager."

She drew herself back so that she could look at him, conscious that the action pushed her breasts against him. "I was not acting like an indignant teenager."

"Yes, you were."

"I was not!" She looked at his face, at his maddeningly flat, controlled expression. "Does anything *ever* get to you?"

"No."

"Well, it does to me. It seems like I feel everything and you feel nothing." She had only intended to reference the way she felt about shopping and blue doors, but she knew that it hadn't sounded that way. Knew that she had meant much more than that. She wanted to call the words back as soon as she'd spoken them. She'd all but broadcasted her attraction to him, and he was just staring at her, controlled as always.

"You don't think I feel anything, Isabella?" he said, his voice soft, as tightly reined as the rest of him.

He drew his finger over the line of her jaw, his dark eyes intent on hers, and then she felt it—the first crack in his façade. A slight tremor in his hand, unveiled heat in his eyes. Her heart-rate ratcheted up several beats per minute.

"I feel. Things I have no business feeling. I want things that are not mine to covet."

He moved slightly, drawing her back away from the glaring streetlight and turning her, pressing her against the side of one of the buildings. The chill from the brick seeped through her sweater. But Adham was still holding her, and his heat was more than enough to keep her warm, to make her feel as if she might be incinerated where she stood, reduced to a pile of ash at his feet.

"What do you think I felt watching you flaunt all that sexy lingerie? Watching you tease me?"

She opened her mouth to protest at his words.

"Yes, Isabella, you *were* teasing me."

"Yes," she said, her throat almost too tight to allow the word passage.

"And tonight? Sitting with you in the dark? You think I felt nothing? With your soft body so close to mine? Your sweet scent enticing me?" His tone was rough now, his hold on her tightening.

And her body was responding.

"You...you're always controlled."

"Not always." He pressed into her, the hardness of his erection evident against her thigh. "Not always."

And then he was kissing her, his mouth rough at first, demanding, as it had been the first time they'd kissed. She whimpered, wiggled so that she could put her arms around his neck and hold him closer, angling her head so that she could part her lips and kiss him back.

Then something happened. His hold gentled, his lips softened, and the slide of his tongue against hers slowed, became almost leisurely, as though he were savoring the taste of her. The thought sent a sensual shiver through her body, made her moan and arch against him.

He moved his hands down, sliding over her curves, cupping her breasts. She gasped. No man had ever touched her like this before. And he was almost reverent in his exploration of her, as though she were a masterpiece.

"Oh, yes..." She tilted her head back, her breath broken, her words a half-sob.

He rocked against her, his hardness teasing her, tantalizing her, igniting passions she'd never dreamed imaginable. He moved his mouth away from hers, pressing his lips against her neck, biting her gently and then lapping the sting away with his tongue before taking her mouth again.

"Adham..." she sighed against his lips

He abandoned her mouth, breaking contact with her

abruptly. The sudden rush of air against her body was a shock to her system. He pushed himself away from her, using the wall as leverage, his chest rising and falling sharply, his breath visible in the cool night air.

Embarrassment mingled with unquenched desire, making her feel nauseous, making her knees weak. Now, with only the chill of the brick against her back, and none of Adham's solid warmth, she shivered.

"Adham?" She reached out her hand to touch his forearm, and he jerked back with a harsh intake of breath.

"No."

"But..."

He took her hand then, held it up beneath the streetlamp until the engagement ring on her finger glittered in the yellow light. "No."

She snatched her hand back, her head swimming, her body shaking. She had forgotten for a moment—about Hassan, about Adham's position working for her fiancé, about her own position in life. There had only been Adham. His arms, his lips, the hardness of his body.

But now reality was back with a vengeance.

She was engaged to be married.

But she wanted another man with a ferocity so strong that it made her feel as though her heart was being torn in two.

Adham paced the length of his office, his body raging at him, his blood pounding hard through his system. He was still hard. He wanted her with a need that defied anything he had known before, a desire that rocked all the control he had so carefully built up over the years.

He and Hassan had been thrust into adulthood, into power, in their early teens. Hassan, the oldest by two years, had assumed the throne; Adham had taken control of the military, of national security. Both of them had been required to put away childish things and embrace manhood, embrace control. Sacrifice, duty and honor.

But this…girl…this virginal princess, with the face of an angel and a body that could make a man lose every last shred of sanity, had cracked it—had made him do something he had sworn he would not.

He'd left the little temptress sitting in the living room, her black hair tumbled wildly over her shoulders, her eyes bright with desire and embarrassment. He didn't trust himself to be in the same room with her—didn't trust that he would not press her back into the soft couch, settle between her thighs so that she could feel his hardness against the place he knew ached for him. He wanted to cup those luscious breasts again, then tease her nipples, explore them more thoroughly. He'd felt their aroused peaks against his palms and he longed to see them—the shape of them, the color—to taste them with his tongue, suck them into his mouth…

He swore violently and picked his mobile phone up from the desk, dialing his brother's number. There was no answer. Little wonder. Hassan was a busy man, and difficult to access at times. At the moment Adham knew he was steeped in diplomatic negotiations, and the delicate process of changing and signing new laws. Just another reason Adham was grateful that the ultimate leadership of his country had not passed to him.

He was a man who needed action, needed to physically see and ensure that Hassan and his people were safe from harm. It was why he had been glad of a military position rather than assuming a diplomatic role.

And now action was needed—with or without Hassan's blessing. He could not stay with Isabella any longer. Not with his control so dangerously cracked. Even now it had not returned to him. Even now he longed to take her, fill her, possess her, make her his woman.

The last few days had been hell. She had paraded her sexy little body for him at the department store, had teased him with the thought of her in that brief lingerie.

It had been far too long since he'd had sex. He needed to get rid of his charge and contact one of his ex-mistresses as quickly as possible, so that he could soothe his raging libido.

He opened the office door and saw that Isabella remained where he had left her, knees drawn up to her chest, her dark hair spilling over her shoulders in a shiny curtain. She straightened when he came out of the office, her expression wary, her cheeks flushed.

"We're leaving," he said tightly.

"What? Where?"

"We're going to Umarah. To the palace. To Hassan."

"But…why?"

"Why?" he said roughly. "I shall tell you why, *amira*. Because back on the street I was thirty seconds away from stripping you of your jeans and taking your carefully guarded virginity against a wall." The words were torn from him, his voice raw. "*You* may be able to betray your word to the High Sheikh in such a way, but I will not."

"I…" Her pretty mouth dropped open, her blue eyes wide.

Good. She was shocked—as he had intended. He had been intentionally crude in order to show her who she was dealing with, show her the disparity between them.

"I don't want to leave," she said quietly, those wide eyes filling with tears.

"I do not care what you want," he said coldly, the roaring of his blood making the words harsh. "We are leaving. *Now.*"

CHAPTER SIX

ADHAM's private plane touched down in the Umarahn capital of Maljadeed just before dark. Even with the sun disappearing behind the flat, rock-hewn mountains on the outskirts of the city, it was the hottest weather Isabella could ever remember experiencing.

The limo that was waiting for them at the airport was air-conditioned, providing immediate relief from the thick, stifling air. The road system was clearly new and expensive—a sign of a thriving infrastructure. It wound through the city, which was still alive with movement despite the late hour. The marketplace was bustling with people selling their wares. The smell of street food and spices mingled together. Crumbling buildings were backed by high-rises, supermarkets next to craft stalls, mixing the old world and the new in a way Isabella had never seen before.

It was a strange place, void of anything familiar. And it was to be her home.

It was a frightening thought—and much more real than it ever had been before. She'd known that she was going to marry Hassan, known that Umarah was destined to be her home, since she was ten years old. But facing it now…seeing how different the city was, how different the road systems were, how strange and foreign the marketplace and the clothing on the people milling around…it was difficult to imagine her life here—what it would be like not only to change homes, to be married, but to change cultures, languages.

She swallowed, longing to draw strength from Adham, to lean against him and have him shield her. But she couldn't. He had made it plain that contact between them was impossible, and he was right. She knew he was. She was engaged to Hassan and she had always planned to honor that—had never even contemplated betraying him.

It was because Adham was a known entity in a land of unknowns. That was all. Nothing more. There couldn't be more.

The palace came into view, set in the middle of everything and shrouded partially by a high stone wall. The dim light made the palace glow purple, the domed roof a pale yellow. She imagined that during the fiery heat of the day it was an intense sight.

Her stomach bottomed out, her heart twisting in her chest. She was about to come face to face with the man she was to marry. About to meet the Sheikh who had gifted her with his ring. The man she did not want. While she stood next to the man she'd grown to desire. The man who was slowly winding his way around her heart with his hardened demeanor and his battle scars.

Adham opened her door for her and she got out of the limo, trying to avoid brushing against his hard body. She was too weak for that. She couldn't touch him without betraying how much she wanted him, how much she ached. And she did—her stomach, her heart and her head hurt.

Suddenly the thought of being separated from Adham made her want to sink to her knees and weep, made her want to cling to him in desperation. She had no idea what it meant, only that it seemed like life or death.

She kept her arms tightly at her sides to discourage him from placing his hand on her. If he touched her, even by accident, she would shatter. She noticed he was holding himself rigid too, his jaw tense, his entire body locked tight, his muscles strained as though he were engaged in a physical war.

But that horrible, flat look in his eyes made it impossible to read what he was truly thinking. Only the tension in his body made her aware that there was anything behind the stony mask he wore. She hated it. Hated that she couldn't read him. Hated that what she needed more than anything was comfort. From him. Comfort she was certain he wouldn't—couldn't—give to her.

She gripped her arms, trying to stop her teeth from chattering. Nerves swept over her. She swallowed convulsively, trying to keep from crying. She felt ridiculously weak, and she also felt like her life was ending.

They walked up a long walkway lined with ash trees that were immaculately trimmed, as was the bright green lawn. The greenery was a show of the High Sheikh's wealth, Isabella assumed. Water in a desert nation was likely worth more than gold or oil.

The double doors to the palace were opened by two armed guards who stood still, faces stoic, as she and Adham passed them and walked into the outer chamber.

The palace in Turan was beautiful, but it was comprised of hand carved stone and antique, woven tapestries, sedate next to the inlaid marble that covered the domed walls and ceiling in the entryway of the Umarahn palace. The floors were black high-gloss tile, the walls a deep green and blue, with fine gold filigree separating the different stones. There was so much color—color that was designed to show the riches of its owner.

"So," she said, exhaling, "this is my palace?"

A short laugh escaped Adham's lips. "Indeed it is, *Principessa*." The Italian version of his usual name for her made her heart trip. His accent was more pronounced when he spoke Italian—a language he was obviously less comfortable with than English. She found it very sexy, his heavy Arabic accent putting a unique stamp on her native language.

She turned her face away from him sharply. There was no point in lingering over all the things about Adham she found attractive. Not when she was about to meet her future husband.

She gritted her teeth, fighting the sting of tears again.

A man dressed in flowing robes came sweeping into the room, and Isabella's heart sank. But as he walked closer she could see that it was not her fiancé. She'd only seen a couple pictures of Hassan, but she remembered his face.

"Numair." Adham inclined his head.

"Sheikh Adham," the other man returned.

So she'd been right. He was nobility of some kind, an important man. Not simply a bodyguard.

"I am here to see High Sheikh Hassan. I bring him his bride." Adham's words were clipped, his manner formal.

Numair looked to the side, as though he were reluctant to look at Adham directly. "Hassan is not here. He is on retreat."

Adham stiffened. "And how long will he be gone?"

This time Numair turned shifty eyes to her. "He is to be…delayed until the wedding, I'm afraid."

"I see. Please bring someone to show the Princess to her room."

Relief washed through her. She didn't have to face Hassan. Not today. Not for another two months. But she was still to be confined to the walls of the palace. Would Adham leave her here alone? The idea made her stomach churn with nerves.

"You will not accompany me?" she asked, hating the obvious fear that edged her voice.

"It would not be appropriate," he said tightly, not looking at her, his eyes fixed ahead, his hands locked behind his back. "Hadiya will show you to your chambers."

A small girl with glossy dark hair and a sweet smile came into the room as if on cue. *"Salaam,"* she said, inclining her head, and Isabella returned the greeting.

Isabella followed Hadiya, but she was powerless to stop herself from looking back at Adham. His eyes were fixed on her, intensity blazing from them. She felt the heat burn through her, her stomach contracting sharply. She whipped her head back around and turned her focus to where she was headed, her heart thundering madly.

"These are the women's quarters," Hadiya said. "Men are not allowed." A slight sparkle lit her dark eyes. "Of course they do not always follow the rules."

Would Adham? He was a man who seemed to live to enforce rules, to ensure that honor was upheld. Which probably excluded visits to the women's quarters. She wasn't sure how to handle that. It felt as though he was her lifeline.

Isabella could only offer a weak smile.

"The High Sheikh had this room prepared for you months ago—for after the wedding."

Isabella nearly sighed with relief. She would have her own room. In her own wing of the house. That way, at least, she would have some space from her husband. The word made her stomach clench.

Hadiya opened a massive door and revealed a spacious room draped in swathes of fabric in rich, saturated colors. They hung from the ceiling, and were draped so that they gathered around the bed like an extravagant canopy. There were doors that led out to what looked like a walled garden. So this was her cage. It was gilded nicely. She would say that for it.

"Thank you, Hadiya," she said.

The girl inclined her head. "I'll bring your things in later."

"Thank you," Isabella repeated, somewhat inanely.

When Hadiya left Isabella fought the urge to give in to her grief. Instead she walked across the high-gloss jade floor and went to stand at the window, pulling the heavy blue drapes back. The garden was lovely—an oasis with man-made waterfalls and flowering trees and bushes. There was a carved stone bench in the middle of all of it.

It was clear that real effort had been put into the space, although it hadn't been tailored to her likes and dislikes specifically. It was simply an elaborate space designed to please any woman. And she *did* like it, so it would be childish to find fault with it simply on principle.

She pressed her forehead against the glass, felt the heat from outside, and hoped that it might warm the chill that was spreading through her.

"Isabella."

Adham's husky voice made her pulse jump. She turned and her heart stopped. He was standing there, her bags in his hands.

"I thought men weren't allowed here," she said.

"We aren't." He set her bags down at the foot of the sumptuous bed.

"You're breaking the rules. Doesn't that violate your code of honor?"

"I'll risk it."

"Are you leaving?" she asked.

He nodded curtly, and she hoped that the devastation she felt wasn't evident on her face. "I have other business to deal with."

"Babysitting another princess?"

A small smile curved his lips. "You're the only one."

"Good." And she meant it. She didn't want to think of him with another woman. Although just because he wasn't princess-sitting it didn't mean he wasn't going to find a woman. One of the women he had an *arrangement* with.

"We're installing a new rig in our oil fields. I like to be on site for major events like that."

"You do so much, Adham," she said. "What have *I* done?"

"You've seen the Eiffel Tower. You have a picture."

"Yes." Now it really did feel as if tears were imminent. Her throat was aching with the effort of holding them back. "I don't have a picture of you, though."

"Bella…" he said, the name so soft and sweet on his lips that her body shuddered.

"Just one." She reached for her purse and pulled out her camera, aiming it at him. His facial expression didn't change.

"Didn't anyone teach you that you need to smile for pictures?" she asked.

Then he smiled, and she felt a tear escape as she captured the moment she'd so longed to see. "You should smile more," she said softly, touching the screen, the image of Adham.

"I don't smile?"

She shook her head. "Not enough."

"I used to."

"What happened?"

A shadow passed over his handsome face, his dark eyebrows locking together. "I had to grow up much faster than I should have. That life experience we've talked about. I know you feel you've been overprotected, but trust me, Bella, it is better than seeing what I have seen."

His hand flexed as he lifted his arm, as if he meant to touch her, but then he dropped it, clenching his hand tightly into a fist. "I'll see you again at the wedding."

He turned and left there, alone, feeling as though something inside her had broken.

"Where are you?" When Hassan finally answered his phone, Adham was on the point of losing his temper with his older brother.

"I'm at the summer palace."

Adham tamped down a surge of annoyance. His brother was at their recreational home—a place they had gone as children for vacations. Before they had lost their parents.

"Well, I am here in Maljadeed, with your bride, only to discover that you are not."

"You were supposed to entertain her in France." His brother actually sounded angry—a rarity.

Adham's pulse quickened at the thought of how he might have kept Isabella entertained had they stayed in Paris. She had become too great a temptation. Hassan was the most important person in his life, the last remaining member of his family and his king. Betraying him was unthinkable. Isabella was only a woman, a beautiful woman, but beautiful women were plentiful. He would be able to find another one now, to help take the ravenous edge off his libido.

"She wished to come here." A lie, but in the circumstances he felt it a well-justified one.

"I cannot come back just yet."

"And I cannot stay here, if that is what you have in mind."

"Adham, please stay with her. I would not ask this of you if it were not so important."

"What is so pressing that your bride becomes my responsibility?"

There was a long stretch of silence before Hassan spoke again. "I am with Jamilah."

"Jamilah"

"She is… I am in love with her, Adham. And soon I must marry Isabella. Jamilah will not have me then. She has told me. She will not be my mistress—and, believe me, I have begged her to change her mind. But what can I do? The contract is signed. I need these last moments. I cannot leave her now."

His gut response to his brother's pronouncement was anger. Anger at the thought of Isabella being betrayed, that his brother was willing to be unfaithful to Isabella once he had made vows to her. He shut it off, ignored it. His loyalty lay with Hassan, not Isabella.

"And you intend me to stay here with your fiancée while you toy with your girlfriend?"

"I am not toying with her," Hassan said, his voice rough. "I have only these two months; do not ask me to sacrifice them."

"I would not," Adham said, clipped.

"Then stay with Isabella, so she does not feel abandoned. I cannot imagine she would wish to be left there at the palace with no one but staff to keep her company."

"Of course not."

"You could take her to see some of the city. Show Isabella her new home. I'll bet she would enjoy seeing the oasis at *Adalia*."

She would enjoy it. She would want to take pictures.

"I will owe you for this, Adham," his brother said, his voice pleading.

Adham gritted his teeth, his grip on the phone tightening. "Yes, you will."

"I'll be indebted to you for this. Gladly."

Adham gave his brother a curt farewell and snapped his phone shut. He had thought to escape the hell of unsatisfied longing he'd been living in back in Paris. He had thought that he would be getting away from his future sister-in-law, gaining distance, plus time with another woman, so that when he saw her again on the day she was to become his brother's wife he would feel nothing.

She is only a woman.

There was no reason that she should tempt him. Yes, she was beautiful—sexy beyond belief. But she was nothing more than an innocent virgin. Virgins held no appeal to him. He enjoyed women with experience. Women who excelled in coy flirtation and sexual games. Women who kept their emotions in control at all times, who were as hardened and cynical as he was. Not women with eyes that were unguarded windows to their souls.

Isabella was not meant for a man like him. He would only tarnish her. He could not give her what she deserved, and neither did he want to. She needed someone who could treat her with softness, possibly offer love—which he had no doubt, given a couple of years to forget his woman, Hassan could do.

Adham had lost the ability to love when he'd watched his mother fall to the ground at his feet, her life snuffed out by an assassin's bullet. His father had met with the same end. Only he and Hassan had remained. Adham had been able to keep Hassan barred from the room—had spared him the sight, spared him the injury.

But *he* had seen. He had watched his parents die in front of him. It was only by a twist of fate the bullet he had taken hadn't killed him too.

Years in military service and protecting his country had helped the wounds created on that day to scar over, to harden completely. There had been times when he had been forced to choose between his own life or the life of his enemy. The fact that he lived was testament to the choices he'd made.

He could not offer a woman love. Did not know how to be a husband or a father. His hands—hands that had taken life—could never cradle a child.

Even if Hassan were not in the picture, he would not touch Isabella.

There would be no taking the edge off tonight. Yes, there were women who worked in the palace who would be willing to come to his bed, but he would not take advantage of them in such a way. And, no matter what his plans had been, he would not sleep with one woman while picturing the face of another.

He stalked into the bathroom that connected to his chambers. The only way he would be able to relax tonight would be with the aid of a cold shower.

When Isabella emerged from her room the next morning to find some breakfast, Adham was sitting at the dining table, with nothing but a mug of coffee placed in front of him.

"I thought you would have left." She hoped the surge of happiness that had just rocked her wasn't totally obvious in her tone. It disturbed her, the intensity of the joy that overtook her when she saw that he was still there, when she saw he hadn't abandoned her.

"Hassan is detained, and shall be until the wedding. He has asked that I stay with you so that you are more comfortable." There was no warmth in his voice. It was clear by how he spoke that he didn't want to be with her.

"Did he order you to stay?"

"No. But I would not feel right about leaving you here by yourself."

"I would be fine." Three servants came into the room, one carrying a carafe filled with coffee, one with a platter of fruit, the other with two bowls of some kind of hot grain cereal. "And I would hardly be alone," she said, as one of the bowls was set in front of her.

"Should there be a security issue, I would feel better being here."

"Is that a possibility?"

"It's always a possibility. When Hassan is here it will fall to him to protect you, but as he is not I will ensure that you're safe."

"Thank you," she said stiffly.

She was glad he was staying. In fact she was much happier about it than she should be. And that made her wish he had left. What was the point of nurturing her feelings for him? Feelings that were growing along with her attraction to him, despite her best efforts.

"If you wish to explore I could take you to see *Adalia*. It's an oasis about two hours from here that the royal family has used for centuries. In times of war, or imminent threat, they would escape to the desert and wait until the danger had passed."

The idea of escaping the confines of the palace made her feel as though a band that had been slowly tightening across her chest had loosened, enabling her to breathe again.

"Yes, I would like that."

"You will have to change into suitable clothes. Hadiya can help you with that."

Suddenly she was brimming with excitement again. She wasn't simply going to be locked in the palace until the wedding. She was going to be with Adham.

And, as foolish as it was, she felt that if she was with Adham the most important piece of her life was in place.

CHAPTER SEVEN

ISABELLA could tell they were getting closer to the oasis when the sparse scrub brush that lined the road began to grow taller, the color deepening, giving way to a line of cypress trees that reached to the faded blue sky.

"You were right," she said softly, her eyes trained on the horizon, on the flat topped rocks that looked as though they had been set right on top of the red sand, "it is beautiful."

"And dangerous."

"Life is dangerous, though, isn't it, Adham?"

She noticed his knuckles whiten as he gripped the steering wheel of the off-road vehicle more tightly. "It can be."

"You know that more than most people, don't you?"

"Why do you ask that?"

"Because you're always telling me how much life experience can take from you. I imagine you must have personal experience with that."

"I was in the military," he said, his voice clipped. "You see things...do things that are not always easy. But it was to protect my country and I cannot regret it."

"But you do." She looked out of the window, at the fruit trees that were starting to appear with increasing frequency. "Have you ever been shot?" She didn't really want to hear the answer—didn't want to imagine him in so much pain.

"Yes. I have also had to use my weapon against others." He paused, and the full meaning of his words gripped her, took root. "No matter the reasoning, taking another man's life is not something to find pride in."

She shook her head. "You wouldn't. I know you wouldn't. You would have had to have good reason." She believed it. Absolutely and implicitly. She knew Adham would never harm someone unless it was to save his own life, or the life of an innocent party.

"You know this for sure?"

"You're a good man, Adham. Even when you irritate me I don't doubt that."

"I irritate you?" he asked.

"Sometimes. But I know that I irritate you as well."

"Sometimes," he agreed easily.

She was glad to hear some humor in his voice. Especially after the bleakness she'd heard when he'd spoken of his time in military service.

"Is this man-made?" she asked, staring at the rock crag that seemed to have grown straight out of the desert sands, arcing over them slightly, providing very heavy cover from the midday sun and making shade for trees and animals beneath its bulk.

"No. This is God's provision. Even in the desert there is life, if you know where to look."

They drove around the curved rock and stopped in front of a large pool of water. It was surrounded by rock, a solid stone basin, with plants and palms growing thick and green all around the perimeter. And beyond that, set into the unexpected jungle, was a large tent, barely visible behind the thick fronds of the trees.

"This is certainly a good refuge," Isabella said, opening the car door and stepping out into the warm air. It was dry, and still very hot, but the rocks, water and plant life absorbed some of the heat, making it warm, but not scorching as it was out on the sands.

Adham got out of the vehicle and surveyed their surroundings. He looked as though he was a part of the landscape, as if he belonged. As though he alone could tame this wild beauty.

She was suddenly very aware of how alone they were. They had no servants with them, no chaperons. Because Adham was her chaperon. The High Sheikh's most trusted man.

But he had violated that trust in Paris. He had kissed her. Had wanted her. And she couldn't forget that. Her body wouldn't let her. She wondered if he was as plagued by it as she was, or if she was just one woman he'd desired in a long line of many.

"The tent is designed to house staff and all the members of the royal family in total comfort. There is plenty of privacy available," he said, answering some of the questions that had been rattling around in her head.

He hoisted her bag from the back seat of the Jeep and slung it over his broad shoulder with ease, the muscles in his back shifting beneath his button-up safari-style shirt. She followed him as he moved toward the tent, her footsteps awkward and heavy in the work boots she wore, which came halfway up her shins and made walking stiff.

"Why are we wearing boots?"

"Snakes," he said carelessly.

She sped up then, walking alongside him. "Snakes?"

"It's the desert, *amira.*"

"I know that. And I know that there are several species of snake native to the area. I just didn't think you would take me anywhere there might be serious danger from them."

"There isn't serious danger from them, but there is a possibility of running into them. They like to keep cool, and they need water. This is a very attractive place for wildlife."

"Well, it is beautiful." She jumped to the side slightly, after hearing a rattle in the dry brush, but managed not to shriek or do anything horribly embarrassing. "Are there a lot of oases in Umarah?"

"A few. Several along the most common trade routes. But this one has been a well-guarded secret for many generations. So you might run into snakes, but not other people."

"I love that there's a way for even the hottest desert to be habitable. It doesn't seem possible for all this life to be hiding in the middle of the sand…but it is."

He turned and offered a smile. Her heart stuttered, and she wished she had her camera at hand. "I told you that there is beauty for those who are willing to look."

It was there in Adham as well. She knew it. He tried to keep people out—at least he tried to keep *her* out—but she could see there, underneath all the layers of rock, what a good man he was. Strong, but also compassionate—firm, but understanding. He would make a wonderful leader. It was a shame *he* wasn't the ruler of Umarah. A shame he couldn't be the man she was meant to marry.

He doesn't even want to get married.

Still, she was thinking that being Adham's unwanted bride would be better than belonging to a man she didn't love while she longed for another. And how had that happened? She had been determined to be faithful to her fiancé, to be true to their arrangement. She doubted if this raging attraction, combined with the increasingly tender feelings she had for Adham, landed beneath that heading.

The tent was more like a permanent dwelling than the sort of thing she'd been imagining. There were hand-woven rugs on the floor, providing a plush surface for tired feet if the inhabitants had been traveling. Lanterns hung low from the support beams, well away from the canvas that made up the tent.

There were big blocks of canvas hanging from the sides, dividing rooms, creating privacy. The living area was large and open, with divans and plush couches placed around in a wide half-circle, perfect for a big gathering. She could imagine it filled with people, laughter.

"I really love it."

"I'm glad," he said, setting her bag on the floor. "It's a special place for the al bin Sudar family."

"I wonder if Hassan will want to take vacations here," she said idly, running her hands along the rich velvet of a red divan. Even her own father had taken them on vacations. They had homes on the outlying islands near Turan, and in Italy. Those times, away from palace life and some of the protocol, were her very favorite memories.

She and Hassan would have children, if all went according to plan. It would stand to reason that he might want to come here with them someday. The thought caused a stab of pain to pierce her chest.

It didn't seem right, thinking of having Hassan's children. She didn't even know the man…and the only man she could imagine having children with was Adham. Why? When had that happened? Why was her heart so tied to this hard man who showed less emotion than granite at times?

Hassan was a handsome man. She remembered that from his picture. Being married to him wouldn't be a terrible thing. She had never been repulsed by the thought, though it hadn't exactly made her jump for joy either. But now...now it seemed so wrong. Adham was the man she desired, the man she.... *No.* She wouldn't go there. She could not. There was no point in it.

Adham watched Isabella run her fingers lightly over the furniture. His body tightened as he imagined those delicate hands on his body, even as his stomach churned with rage at the thought of her vacationing with Hassan, the thought of her bearing Hassan's children.

It was a betrayal—of his brother, his country—to despise the thoughts and yet he did. He could not abide the thought of another man touching her—even if that man were his brother, a man who, according to the contract signed by Isabella's father and by Hassan, had every right to her.

He had brought her here at Hassan's suggestion, and also to prove to himself that he could master his desire for her. And he could. There was no other option. It didn't matter that she appealed to him more than any woman in his memory. She was to be a member of his family, a part of his existence, a woman he was sworn to protect for the rest of his life. He had to master his body's response to her, not simply sublimate it.

It was simply his denied libido reminding him that it had been six long months since he'd had a woman in his bed. A swim in the cold water later would take care of it. Isabella was much happier here than she'd been at the palace. He'd seen the life leech from her when they'd entered the palace at Maljadeed, but here...it seemed returned to her. It made the trip more than worth it. Even if there was a small amount of torture he would have to endure.

He could understand how she'd felt in the confines of

the walled palace. It was a difficult place for him as well. It was where his family had been killed. It represented the darkest moments of his life. It was one reason he had always been grateful he'd come into the world two years after Hassan. He had no desire to rule, to care for matters of State. To be trapped in the palace where he had lost his family.

He always felt most free in the desert—less shackled to the bonds his position demanded of him, less tied to the things of the past. In the desert his mind had to be in the present. Watching the weather for torrential downpours and sandstorms, keeping an eye out for dangerous wildlife.

He would welcome the respite from Maljadeed.

Adham cleared his throat. "Hassan is not a big fan of being out in the desert. He prefers the luxury provided by our palaces. There are several in different parts of the country. One on the coast. You will enjoy that one. It might remind you of your home."

"It's funny…I find I haven't really missed my home… Turan. I've felt more at home away from my family than I ever have in my life. I think it's because I was finally able to be myself. I was away from everyone's expectations of me." She looked at him then, a small smile tugging her lips. "Well, not everyone's. But you…I've actually enjoyed being with you."

His chest suddenly felt tight.

"Are you hungry?" he asked, knowing it was abrupt, realizing it was the question he always asked when he wanted to divert her.

"Yes." It always worked.

"Hassan ordered some staff members to come here ahead of us and stock the fridge."

"There's a fridge?"

"There are windmills nearby, and they provide a small amount of power. That way, if there's a need to charge a satellite phone, or if we need to keep food cold, it's available. For lights we still use the lanterns."

"Very efficient."

"We believe in using the resources the desert provides us with." A movement Adham had spearheaded. He'd begun drilling in the middle of the uninhabitable places in the desert, had started programs that employed harnessing solar and wind power to provide the people with electricity even in remote places.

"I like that. You'll have to talk to my brother about all of this. He'll be very interested in bringing this kind of thinking to Turan."

Adham moved through the room to the small refrigerator that was in the corner. He pulled out a platter with fresh fruit, stuffed dates and meats and cheeses. His gut clenched. His brother had planned his fiancée's seduction for him. He could not have given him better tools—unless there was also champagne in an ice bucket somewhere. Which, given his surroundings, he would not discount.

"Lovely!" Isabella said, her eyes bright.

Seeing all that excitement on her beautiful face, an excitement that seemed to be aroused by things he hardly noticed, caused a strange tightness in his entire being. She seemed to revel in everything—the taste of foods he took for granted, views he had seen thousands of times. They were all things that brightened her face, things that brought about her unbridled joy.

He lived his life with his emotions kept carefully in check, yet Isabella wore hers boldly. She had said back in Paris, just before he had made the mistake of kissing her, that she felt everything. It seemed that she did.

She sat on the divan, her legs tucked under her, eyes

bright with happiness, her dark hair tumbled over her shoulders. The sight made him ache. Blood pulsed, hot and hard, down to his groin. He wanted her. *Her.* Not a nameless, faceless woman to take the edge off his desire.

He wanted Isabella Rossi—his brother's fiancée. But that was a line he refused to cross. He would not abandon everything of importance in his life to find physical satisfaction in the arms of a woman. Even if it was a woman who called to him, body and soul, more than anyone ever had.

Isabella couldn't sleep. It was comfortable in the tent; the night air of the desert was cool. She could hear thick drops of rain hitting the canvas roof, beating on it mercilessly. She knew that sudden downpours, along with flash flooding, were common in this region. But it wasn't fear that kept her awake.

No. She was so hot inside. Burning. Emotions were at war with desire—a desire that was growing quickly into a need as powerful as her need for food. Water. Breath.

She didn't know what it was she felt for Adham. She wasn't certain she wanted to know. It was nothing she had planned. She'd wanted to get to know herself better. To find out if she liked blue because she liked it, or because her mother had told her it flattered her coloring. She'd found a lot more than that, and with it she'd started a battle inside herself.

She swung her legs over the side of the bed and stood, padding out into the living area. Adham was there, reclining on a divan, his eyes closed, his muscles tensed, sleep obviously eluding him.

"You can't sleep either?" She pulled her robe tightly around herself. Beneath the robe she was wearing the peach negligee, but she felt reasonably secure with thick terrycloth covering her curves.

"I don't sleep very often." He opened his eyes and straightened.

She noticed his jaw tighten, noticed the muscles in his forearms tensing as he looked at her. A rush of feminine satisfaction rocked her. Never had she felt more beautiful than in that moment—barefoot, in a robe, and making Adham very uncomfortable.

"It's hard for you to rest and it's hard for you to smile," she said, feeling sad for him. He really was an example of life experience being a bad thing. She wished she could shield him from it. Offer him some comfort. She wished it with everything she had.

The ring on her left hand suddenly felt very heavy. Because it was holding her back, keeping her from what she desired most. She had thought it was freedom that she wanted, but freedom seemed like an empty, elusive thing now. Something that didn't matter—not if she had it alone, not if she didn't have Adham.

"But everything else is so easy for me," he said, dark humor lacing his voice.

"That is true. I won't challenge you there." She pulled a downy blanket from one of the sofas and sat on the soft floor, wrapping the blanket around her shoulders. "Duty and honor—that seems to come easily to you. You *want* to do it. I…I'm just sort of going along with it. It seems meaningless. But you…it means something to you."

"Because I have seen what happens when men turn from it. If I do not protect the High Sheikh, who will? If I do not put my all into protecting my people, where does that leave them? I cannot turn away from it. I cannot resent it."

"I resent my lot in life plenty." She dipped her head

forward and her hair slid over her face, making a shield between Adham and herself.

Suddenly she felt warmth. Adham's warmth. He was kneeling on the floor, his knee nearly touching hers. He brushed her hair back over her shoulder. "Your duty costs you. I understand why you felt the need to escape it. Even for a while."

"You didn't think that at first. What changed your mind?"

"Knowing you. Knowing that you are not a spoiled child, but a woman who simply wishes to make her own decisions."

Tears formed in her eyes, thick and hot, and as she blinked they fell, sliding down her cheeks. Adham brushed them away, his thumbs rough, comforting against her skin.

"Your duty has cost you too," she said, looking at the scars that marred his perfect skin, at the slashing line that started at his collar and disappeared beneath his shirt.

"These scars are nothing," he said, shrugging. "I live. My family does not."

"Your *family*?" Horror stole through her, chilling her, making her shiver.

"My mother, my father…they were killed in front of me. I could not stop it from happening."

"Adham.…" His name escaped her lips on a sigh of anguish. She ached to hold him, but she was certain he wouldn't allow it, so she kept still, kept her hands in her lap.

"That was when I got this." He pulled the collar of his shirt to the side, exposed a light-colored patch of skin that was raised up from his undamaged skin. "I was shot as well. They thought I was dead. That is the only reason I'm alive today. That is why I welcome my duty. I will protect my people, my High Sheikh, from men like that. Men who would kill for money, power, land. Men who would take life for things that mean nothing."

She let her fingertips brush the scar, whispered a prayer of thanks that he was still here, still living, even when his parents were not. Unbidden, her fingers moved to the first button of his shirt, and she pushed the button through the hole, revealing a wider wedge of bronzed skin, revealing more livid scars that marred the landscape of his perfect body.

Without pausing to think she reached out and touched the raised skin. She felt him tense beneath her fingertips, felt his body go rigid with tension. She began to release each button, all the way down, exposing a slim strip of flesh from his chest all the way down to his washboard-flat belly, bared for her inspection. She swallowed, her mouth dry, her heart hammering in her chest, another tear sliding down her cheek.

She moved the edges of his shirt aside, baring a ridge of scars that ran along his ribcage. With the tip of her finger she traced a slashing line that rose up from the waistband of his trousers and extended up through the indentation of his navel. The scars were lighter, ridges of flesh that were hard and smooth.

The body surrounding the damaged skin was perfect. Deep bronze and well muscled, without an ounce of spare flesh to hide his superb definition from her hungry gaze. His chest was sprinkled with just the right amount of dark hair. She let her fingers drift over his muscles, let them slide over the hard-cut edges, the rough hair tickling her fingertips, teasing her senses.

He inhaled deeply, his chest expanding under her hands as she continued to touch him, explore him.

Adham stiffened, pulling away from her hot touch.

His heart was hammering in his chest, his muscles so tight they ached. His whole body ached for her—for her to flatten her palm against his skin, to continue her exploration into more intimate territory. He should stop her. Should have stopped her the moment she placed her hand on him. Yet he had been held—a captive of what she was doing to him, of what she made him feel.

It had started out as an innocent, comforting gesture. Because Isabella *was* an innocent. A virgin. A woman he had no business touching.

Some of the fractured light from the overhead lanterns danced over her hand, made the ring on her finger glitter brightly. He gripped her wrist and pushed her away.

"Bella," he said roughly, "do you know what you're doing to me?"

She moved closer to him, her eyes glistening with hurt and a heartbreaking undertone of confusion. "I hope it's close to what you're doing to me. I hope I'm not the only one that feels this."

She licked her lips and leaned in, pressing a kiss to the first scar. His muscle, his body, jumped beneath her lips. She slid her hand up to his pectoral.

"I've never touched a man like this before," she said softly.

Arousal pounded through him. Unneeded. Unwanted. And hotter than anything he'd ever experienced before in all his thirty-one years. That an innocent could appeal to him like this—could tempt him to betray the man he protected above all others, the brother he had always loved more than his own life, made him feel as though he were bewitched. He wanted to break the spell, and yet he was caught in its thrall. And part of him was so unbelievably tempted to see what would happen if he gave in.

If a simple touch could arouse him so easily, so intensely, what would happen when he eased inside her slick, tight body? If he made her his.

His.

His heart pounded heavily, his blood flowing hot, thick.

"That night in the alley...I'd never been kissed before that."

She began to move her hand over his chest again, heading to his stomach, and a shock of desire so strong, so overpowering that it nearly undid him, shot through him. He captured her wrist again and pushed her away with more force than he'd intended. She wobbled in her spot on the floor, but caught herself with her hand, her eyes huge, the pain in them clear.

"Bella." Remorse filled him. "Are you hurt?"

"I...no." She shook her head.

He inhaled deeply, trying to clear his head. But he only succeeded in filling himself with her essence. "You must not touch me like that," he said roughly. "Ever."

"Adham, I...I want you so much," she choked. "I want you so much I hurt with it."

He closed his eyes, tried to block out the vision of perfect temptation that she created, with her black hair loose and wild, her full lips reddened with arousal, her cheeks flushed.

A tear slipped down her cheek and he was powerless to stay where he was—powerless to deny the need to comfort her. He drew her to him, wrapped his arms around her, inhaling her scent—uniquely Isabella, and more affecting than any form of torture he'd yet been subjected to.

He slid his hand over the silky black curls, giving himself permission to touch her, if only for a moment. For just one moment he would forget. Forget that this burning ache was forbidden, that she was meant for someone else.

She wrapped her arms around his neck, her moist lips brushing his neck. He closed his eyes, tried to fight against the rising tide of desire that was threatening to overtake him.

"Adham." She lifted her head, her blue eyes intent on his. She leaned in and pressed her lips lightly to his— only for a moment, her movements shy, her inexperience evident.

He held himself still, kept his fists clenched. Because if he allowed himself any sort of free rein he would tunnel his fingers through her hair and devour her mouth, as he had longed to do since the first moment he'd seen her.

She pulled back, the hurt in her eyes almost too much for him to bear. "Don't you want me? I thought…I thought you did."

He ground his teeth tightly together, trying to fight the urge to pull her to him, to take what she was offering. Everything she was offering and more. His heart was pounding, sweat beading on his forehead. He swallowed thickly, the motion almost painful to his hypersensitive body. Everything in him ached for her. And he couldn't take her. *He couldn't.*

She was looking at him, those expressive blue eyes trained on him, wanting answers he shouldn't give.

"I do want you," he bit out, the words torn from him. "But wanting is not the same as taking."

His pulse pounded. His muscles ached. It was taking every ounce of his strength, every bit of his physical and mental willpower, to keep himself from leaning in and tasting her lips. But his control was slipping, the pain of resistance so acute he wasn't certain if he could hold on any longer.

She looked down. "You said…you said I'm an independent woman who makes her own decisions. I've decided that I want you."

Sweet, innocent Isabella, with the words of a temptress rolling off her lips, but without any of the practiced ease he was used to hearing from a woman, undid him completely. The fire that had been burning hot in his stomach exploded into an inferno, igniting his veins, taking over everything.

Life asked too much of him. He had never resented it before. Had never longed to escape his duty until this very moment. But faced with Isabella—beautiful, hungry for him, and with a need that also burned in him like a flame—he wished that he could be a different man.

Then she moved her hands. Her soft palms slid up his chest, over the place where his heart raged inside him. She kissed his jaw. He closed his eyes, everything, every thought, deserting him. There was nothing but this. Nothing but her. Nothing but the need to make her his, wholly and completely, in the most primitive way possible. His body shook with the force of his need, his mind blank of everything. Everything except for her.

Isabella gasped as Adham tightened his hold on her, pulling her onto his lap, bringing her into contact with the hardened length of his erection—the evidence she needed to know that he desired her as she desired him.

Excitement, fear and need slammed into her. Her entire body was shaking with it. Then he leaned in, taking her mouth with a ferocity she hadn't expected, his lips firm, insistent, his tongue hot as it slid between her lips. She moaned, all the fear deserting her. This was *Adham*. The man she desired above all else.

She could have lived her entire life without having her picture taken in front of the Eiffel Tower. She would have been fine if she'd never been to a cinema. But this…she could not have lived never knowing what it was to make love with Adham.

She pushed his shirt from his shoulders, letting it fall to the floor. The sight of him in the flickering lantern light was enough to push her arousal to unbearable heights. She moved her hands over his shoulders, across his back, loving the play of muscles beneath her fingertips, the smoothness of his skin, the heat that radiated from him.

And then she was on her back, his movement so quick and practiced that she hardly realized what was happening until she was flat out, looking at the swags of canvas and the spangled light from the punched-tin lanterns that were lit overhead.

He kissed her jaw, her neck, her collarbone, and she arched into him, running her fingers through his thick dark hair, holding him to her so that he would never stop giving her body attention with that amazing mouth.

His hands were quick at the belt of her robe, loosening the knot and parting the edges slowly, revealing most of her body, barely concealed in the filmy peach negligee. She wasn't embarrassed for him to see her, for her body to be bare to him. She was thrilled beyond words. So excited to have him touching her, to be touching him. She wanted him so much. Beyond reason, beyond anything rational or sane or right. If she could just have him—just once. If he could be the man to show her what it really meant for a man and a woman to be joined… It wouldn't be a lifetime, but maybe…maybe it could be enough.

"I thought of you in this," he said, his voice rough, strained. "And I thought of you out of it." The way he looked at her, the tone of his voice, spoke of how much he desired her. The fact that his need seemed to match hers awed her completely.

He pushed the robe from her shoulders, then slid one of the tiny straps down. His eyes, so dark they were coal-black in the dim light, roamed over her, his breath harsh, fast and shallow.

He put his hand on her breast and moved his thumb over her nipple. It tightened for him, caused exquisite pleasure to shoot through her veins, made the dull ache at the apex of her thighs increase until it was a hollow pain.

She hooked her leg over his calf, pulled him against her, rubbed herself against the thick ridge of his arousal, evident through his jeans, in an attempt to assuage her need.

He tugged the top of the negligee down all the way, revealing her breasts, revealing her nipples, tight with need for him. He groaned and lowered his head, pressed his face to the valley between her breasts, inhaled deeply, slowly. Something about it seemed reverent, as though he were memorizing the moment, her scent, *her*. It made fresh tears spring to her eyes.

Then he rasped his tongue over one tightened bud before sucking it gently into his mouth. His body shuddered and hers matched him, shaking beneath the sensual assault. She dug her fingernails into his back, almost unable to handle the intensity of the pleasure that was rioting through her system.

He turned his attention to her other breast, nipping, licking, sucking until she was trembling beneath him, her body poised on the brink of something monumental, the tension in her belly so tight it had to unravel or she feared she might break.

"Adham," she said, her voice shaky. "Please."

It was all he needed. He stripped his jeans off, kicking them to the side, then pushed her negligee up and pulled the sheer matching panties down in one swift motion.

He touched her, sliding his finger through her slick folds, slipping it inside her. She let her legs fall apart, opened to him, trying to ease some of the tightness she felt. He added a second finger, slowly, gently stretching her, preparing her for him.

Then he moved, replacing his fingers with the blunt head of his erection, pressing his mouth against hers as he eased into her tight body. She gripped his shoulders, digging her nails into his back as she held back a cry of pain. He was big—bigger than she'd expected—and she hadn't realized that it would hurt.

It made her even gladder that it was Adham. How could she trust this moment to anyone else?

She wrapped her legs around his, making more room between her thighs, helping some of the discomfort abate. And then the pain was gone, and waves of pleasure were slowly returning as her body adjusted to his, expanded to accommodate him. It seemed as though she were made for him, and he for her—as though he fit her perfectly, as though they would never be separate again.

And when he began to move inside her the star shapes cast by the lantern light seemed to rain down on her, brilliant flashes of light swirling around her. She felt that tension rising in her again—so tight she could barely move, think or breathe. Then she shattered, as Adham did, her muscles contracting around him as he spilled himself inside her, his muscles quivering, a harsh groan escaping his lips, mingling with her cry of completion.

They lay together, joined still, their breath, harsh and

uneven, the only sound other than the rain that was still pounding against the canvas.

Adham rolled to one side, his arm over his face, his body tense. She reached out and touched his forearm and he flinched, moved away from her. "Get dressed, Bella."

She sat up, tugged her negligee and robe back into place, her heart thundering, her hands shaking. She ached between her thighs, both from pleasure and pain.

"Adham…"

"We are leaving." He stood, taking his jeans from the floor and tugging them on, his movements quick and precise, his face flat, his jaw clenched tight.

She didn't have to ask why. All she had to do was look at her left hand, at the diamond that rested there. The ring that had been given to her by Hassan—by the man he was sworn to protect. She felt sick.

You said I was an independent woman.

Her own selfishness was staggering. She had asked him, pleaded with him to ignore everything that was important to him. But the consequences of this, no matter what they were for her, would be so much worse for Adham.

She loved Adham. She knew that now—understood what had been growing in her from the first moment she'd seen him. Her love for him had made the price worth it to her. But she knew, looking at him now, that it had not been worth it for him. She had been a part of causing him to violate the very core of who he was. There was no love in that. What she had done had been an act of selfishness. And she didn't know if he could ever forgive her for it. She didn't know if she could forgive herself.

CHAPTER EIGHT

ADHAM ignored the pounding rain that was battering the windshield of the military helicopter he was maneuvering through the night sky. Staying at *Adalia* with her was not an option. He had already proven he could not trust himself with her, and he would not prolong a test of his strength that he was destined to fail.

The betrayal that he had committed burned in him—along with an intense, churning arousal that refused to be satisfied.

Half of him was crippled by shame, while the other half was replaying those heady moments of being inside Isabella over and over again. Reliving the tightness of her body, the unquestionable evidence that he was the only man to have joined himself to her, the rush of his orgasm as he'd spilled inside her. It had been heaven. And for that small glimpse of it he had earned himself the hottest spot in hell.

He had shamed himself, betrayed his only family. All for his own pleasure. There was no redeeming his actions.

Yes, Isabella had tempted him, enticed him, but he had acted of his own free will. He alone was responsible for what had transpired between them. His weakness had been the cause.

And now it could not be undone. Her innocence was lost. Innocence he was certain his brother was entitled to per the contract he had signed. Innocence that any traditional Umarahn man would expect of his bride on their wedding night.

Adham had never touched a virgin. And now he had not only taken a woman's virginity, when he hadn't the ability or the intention of offering her marriage, but he had taken the virginity of his brother's woman. His brother's future bride. A greater sin to have added to his already lengthy list he could not think of.

"I won't tell him it was you." Isabella's soft, choked voice brought him out of his thoughts. "I'll let him think it was some boy when I was at boarding school—or a man I met at a ball or something. I won't ever tell him that you were the one I was…with…the first time. Because he'll know, won't he?"

She sounded sick. As sick as he felt at the thought of his brother, of any man, putting his hands on her, joining his body to hers. Everything elemental in him rejected the idea. His body was convinced that Isabella was his, even if his mind knew it was not possible. Even if Hassan's ring hadn't rested on her finger it would be an impossibility.

He was not the man for a woman who saw beauty, excitement in everything. What could he offer her but darkness? His memories of watching his parents die before his eyes? He had seen how painful just hearing him speak of it had been for her. And now her bright world view would forever be tainted with a black spot. Because of *him*.

"Yes. He will know. There was no mistaking it."

She lowered her head, her cheeks turning a deep rose

visible thanks to the bright lights on the dash. "Oh. Was it…did you find it…distasteful?"

Lust and regret swamped him in equal measure, his body burning with both. "There is no good answer to that question, Isabella."

"Maybe not."

He maneuvered the helicopter through the night sky, bringing it in for a smooth landing despite the raging storm.

Isabella finally loosened her grip on the handle above the door, her heart still pounding hard—from nerves and from her proximity with Adham.

He had acted totally unaffected by the weather, and by her—which was much more than she'd been able to manage on both counts. Her entire being still ached with need for Adham. Sex with him had been like a sudden immersion into a new world. She had been so innocent, so much more out of touch with the reality of lovemaking than she'd imagined herself to be. And now she felt as if a veil had been torn from her eyes—as though she could see things clearly, feel things more fully than she ever had before. Unfortunately that included the intense pain that invaded her chest whenever she thought of the reality she now found herself in.

She was promised to another man. And she loved Adham more than she could stand. He had just shown her what it was like to be loved by a man, even if it had only been physical love. And now she had to give it up. Give herself to another man. Even if she didn't she still couldn't have Adham, because he wouldn't want her. And her people, her family, would suffer greatly if she did not honor the contract.

It was her duty. A duty she should have cared for more before she'd compromised everything the way she had.

A tear rolled down her cheek and she wiped it away absently. She would marry Hassan. She would do the one thing that would redeem her in Adham's eyes, even if it meant he would be lost to her forever.

"Do you intend for me to meet with Hassan tonight?"

"I intend to drag him out of bed if I have to," Adham said, his voice cold, uncompromising. A match for his manner.

All the warmth and any semblance of a relationship they had built over the course of the past week together meant nothing to him anymore. And why should it? He was disgusted. With her. With himself. She could read it in him clearly.

She sat in her seat until Adham got out and came around to her side, wrenching the door open and offering her his hand. She looked at it, unable to bring herself to touch him.

"Bella," he said roughly.

She took his hand and allowed him to help her from the helicopter. Water splashed up her legs when she made contact with the wet cement of the helipad.

His hand was warm and firm on hers, his touch almost more temptation that she could bear. The strong flare of desire momentarily immobilized her, rooting her to the middle of the puddle she was ankle-deep in.

His eyes blazed, his chest rose and fell sharply, and the glow from the windows of the summer palace played with the shadows, highlighting Adham's features, his muscular frame and his angular jaw. Her heart hammered hard in her chest. She knew that look—knew it and responded to it. Her blood flowed hotter, faster, her nipples tightened. Her body was readying itself for Adham, for his possession.

"Come," he said sharply, turning and heading down the exterior stairs that led to the heavily guarded second-floor entrance to the massive palace.

It had a more modern look than the palace at Maljadeed—the hallways less cavernous, the displays of wealth much less obvious. Despite the size, it had a look of home, rather than a look of grandeur.

There was a sitting room rather than a formal throne room, and Adham ushered her inside quickly, gesturing for her to sit on one of the divans that lined the wall. A servant girl came rushing in, her expression flustered.

Adham cut off whatever she was about to say. "Go and get to the High Sheikh, tell him I will not be put off."

Isabella's heart was hammering so hard she was certain it was audible. She had told Adham that she wouldn't reveal it was he who had taken her innocence, but she had no idea of what he planned on saying to Hassan when the time came. He might intend to confess her sins for her.

Would Hassan break the agreement? Would he want her imprisoned or exiled? It shamed her now to admit that, while she knew a great many facts about Umarah, she didn't know as much as she should about that aspect of society. One thing she knew for certain was that if Adham's sense of honor was born of Umarahn beliefs, then that wouldn't be an issue. So that concern was eased.

Her heart pounded harder, desperation pouring through her, her palms slick with sweat. "Adham..." She whispered his name. She knew that this was it. She would never touch him again. He was no longer her ally in any way.

But he never had been. Not really. She had fooled herself, and she had done a world-class job.

Then, so lightly she might have imagined it, he swept

his finger along her jaw. One last touch. Barely there. But a connection she needed more than she needed her next intake of air.

"Adham? Has something happened?"

The deep voice entered the room before the man, but when the man followed she knew exactly who he was. His regal bearing gave him away immediately, and then there was his face, which she recognized from his picture. But as he got closer, as she observed the way his long strides carried him over the high-gloss floor, her heart caught. He looked so much like Adham—not precisely in features, but in manner—that she could hardly believe it.

"Everything is fine," Adham responded, his voice even, not a hint of emotion evident.

Hassan's eyes widened when he saw her, his body tensing. *"Principessa,"* he said, his Italian even less polished than Adham's.

She inclined her head, her throat tightening, words deserting her.

"Adham, I need to speak with you in private."

Hassan's words echoed the refrain playing in her own mind. *She* wanted to talk to Adham without anyone else in the room, to ask him who he really was. To ask him why he looked so much like her fiancé that they *had* to be related by blood.

Adham shifted, trying to calm the rush of adrenaline that was still racing through him. He turned and looked at Isabella. Her eyes were narrowed, glittering. She was naive, that was true, but she was smart, and she hadn't missed the fact that Hassan so closely resembled him. In a picture it would be easy to miss, but when they were together it was impossible for anyone to ignore the way their mannerisms were so closely matched. The way they stood, the way they walked, the inflection in their voices. It had been pointed out on many occasions how alike they were.

One of Hassan's servants came into the room as if summoned, which Adham had a feeling she had been. His brother, no matter how careless he might seem at times, never did anything without a plan.

Adham put his hand on Isabella's back. Her heat seared him even as she jumped beneath his touch, but he kept his outward appearance neutral. "Isabella, go to your room and wait there."

He could tell she wanted to argue, but instead she swallowed hard, nodded once, and followed the young girl out. He noticed how stiffly Isabella held her shoulders. He was powerless to ignore the sway of her hips, the way her waist dented in, so narrow, and then gave way to the curve of her round, lush bottom.

"You are familiar with her," Hassan commented, when the doors had closed behind Isabella, blocking her from his view.

Adham swallowed. "I have been with her for over a week—at your bidding, I might add."

"You do no one's bidding but your own, Adham."

It was said goodnaturedly, as a joke. And Adham would have taken it as such even yesterday. But now he could only agree. He had betrayed his brother, and while part of him wanted to confess it, another part of him wished to protect Isabella from the cost of such an admission. Yes, Hassan might know that she was not a virgin after they married, but Adham did not want to expose her.

And, in brutal honesty, he did not want to expose his own lack of control. What had happened with Isabella had been beyond anything in his experience. The way need, desire, lust, had melded together and taken hold of him, gripped him so tightly that he had nearly choked with it, had been completely outside of anything in his reality. He had always considered himself a man with supreme control. He'd always had to be. But Isabella had stripped him of it, unmanned him, and yet at the same time made him feel more of a man, more of a conqueror than he had ever felt he was on any battlefield.

But, as in war, the end result was total devastation.

"I am sorry about your situation with Jamilah, but I cannot be your babysitter any longer. You need to accept responsibility—reality." His chest tightened, as though the words were meant for himself. "Isabella is your fiancée. She deserves to be treated with some level of respect. That means no more running around with your mistress while you use me to keep her busy."

Hassan rubbed his hand over his forehead, suddenly looking much older than he was. Adham had never seen his brother look so torn, so broken. And they had been through the death of their parents together.

A long silence filled the room. Hassan's eyes fixed on the wall behind Adham. Finally he spoke.

"I can't do it, Adham. I know you think I am weak. You have always faced your duty—even when it took you into the middle of a war zone. You have protected our people, sacrificed so much of yourself, while I cannot bring myself to marry the woman who has been given to me. Compared to you, I *am* weak. But I want Jamilah. I *need* her."

Anger shot through Adham—instant and powerful. "It is not a matter of what you want, but what must be done. The alliance with Turan is a necessity. Our people need it. Their people need it. We need the loyalty of their military, an ease in trading, the increase in jobs it will provide. And you would cast that aside?" Even as he spoke Adham knew he was a hypocrite—knew that if anyone had compromised the future of their countries it was him. That if, of the two of them, one was weak, he was the one. And yet that knowledge only fanned the flame of his rage.

"What else am I to do, Adham? Sacrifice myself, Jamilah…our child?" On the last word Hassan's voice cracked. "All for duty and honor? It would make me the better man to many, but it would make me a villain to those who matter most."

"She's pregnant?" As Adham spoke the words he realized it was possible that he had made Isabella pregnant. He hadn't thought of protecting her. He had thought of nothing. He had simply embraced the need that had been pounding through him. He hadn't thought of the consequences, and that included conceiving a child. It seemed a stunning reality when faced with Hassan's inadvertent admission.

"Yes. Would you have me abandon my son or daughter? Should I allow them to become the royal bastard, hiding in hallways, living with the servants, a part of nothing and ridiculed quietly by everyone?"

Adham could suddenly easily imagine Isabella being pregnant. The child being his. He had never wanted children, still didn't, and yet he knew he would never be able to deny that child his birthright. He would never be able to let another man raise that child in his place either.

He tried to force himself to consider his brother's problems and not his own. "Then what do you propose, Hassan?"

Hassan looked away again. "I would not ask this of you, Adham, if it were only for me."

Everything in Adham's body tensed. Always the possibility of his assuming the throne had existed, yet he had never truly imagined it coming to pass. Had never wanted it. He craved action. The physical act of protecting his country. Not signing documents and crafting laws. When he saw a need—like the need for more oil rigs in the desert—he brought it to Hassan, who worked out the finer points of it while Adham set to work on making it a reality in the physical sense.

He disliked the idea of being a figurehead. Hassan was more than that, was a man gifted at creating relationships with world leaders and bringing people around to his way of thinking, but Adham had never envied him the job.

And a part of him—the selfish part, the part that had been in command tonight when he had made love to Isabella—rebelled. Had he not given enough? How much more blood did he have to spill on the sand for the sake of his country? How much more could be taken from him? He didn't want to rule. He didn't want that sort of… confinement. But if not him, who else? There was truly no other choice.

"You want to abdicate." Not a question, for he already knew what his brother intended.

"I don't want to. I find myself in an impossible situation, and I…I feel it is what I have to do."

"What of Isabella?" Adham asked.

"You will marry her," he said, as though it were that simple. As though she could be simply handed from one man to another. "The contract will not be violated, and the alliance between our countries will go forward."

And Isabella would be his.

For a moment he allowed his body to revel in that victory. But then he let his mind take over. Yes, physically he desired Isabella, but he did not wish to marry her. As miserable as she thought she would be with Hassan, she would be even more so with him. He had nothing to offer her. Hassan, at least, would have grown to love her in time. Adham had lost the ability for such fine emotions.

His heart was too scarred.

As he'd watched the life drain from his mother he had vowed he would not let men like those who had killed his parents, men with a lust for money and power—commit such an act on Umarahn soil again, and he had set about making sure it was so. Personally, ruthlessly, until every last one of the dissident factions had been rooted out and destroyed.

The price for that had been his soul, in many ways, and yet he would not have changed it. But it left nothing for a wife—especially for a woman like Isabella.

"I am not suited to her," he said roughly.

"You do not desire her? She's a beautiful woman."

"Yes," Adham bit out. "She is a beautiful woman. Desire is not the issue."

"But you have no desire to marry?" Hassan said, his voice quiet.

No. He didn't want to marry—more for the sake of whoever his bride might be than for himself. He didn't want to rule. But it didn't matter. What he wanted, what he desired, had never mattered.

"What I want is not the issue. You are right. You cannot marry another woman when Jamilah is carrying your child. You are too good a man to let your son or daughter go without recognition. But the contract cannot be broken. You do what must be done, brother, and I will see that everything else is taken care of. I will assume your position as High Sheikh. I will marry Isabella."

Isabella had been putting her personal items away ever since they had been brought to her by one of Hassan's young servants. She had waved off the girl's request to let her see to it. Isabella needed to stay busy—needed to keep her hands occupied.

Adham hadn't told her he was related to Hassan, but she saw it clearly now. That meant she would see him often during her marriage to Hassan.

Hassan. He was a handsome man, but she felt no fire when she saw him. He did not move her. He seemed like a good man—a man who would smile easily, a man who could sleep at night without all of his demons haunting him. But he did not call to her heart. How much easier life would be if he did.

How she felt about him didn't matter, though. What mattered was honoring the contract, doing the best thing for her people, for Adham's people. She had already made a mess of things, but she would not compound her sins by turning her back on her duty.

The door to her bedroom opened. Horror stole over her as she turned, half expecting to find Hassan standing there, wanting to stake some sort of claim on his fiancée. There was no way she could do that. No way she could be with him like that now.

Of course she would have to be with him in that way someday. But not now. *Oh, not now.* Not when Adham's touch still burned on her skin. In her body.

But it wasn't Hassan. It was Adham, his body still, backlit in the doorway, his broad frame highlighted to perfection. Her stomach tightened with need, desire, want, regret—all swirling together, making her dizzy.

When he walked into the room, his face hard, immovable like stone, a chill emanating from him, she felt her heart drop. He was a stranger now, this man who had touched her, taught her what it was to be a woman. The man she loved. In his place was a man guarded by stone—a man even more unknowable than the Adham she had first seen standing at her hotel room door, all hell and fire and determined to bring her back to Umarah if he had to do it by force.

"What are you doing here?" she asked, gripping her elbows, trying to keep from shivering, to keep herself from betraying just how much he did to her by merely walking into a room.

"Hassan and I have spoken."

She noticed his use of the High Sheikh's first name, not his title. "What did you speak to him about?" Part of her hoped he'd confessed their sins, while another part of her had no idea what to want. What had happened between her and Adham had changed her forever, and yet in the real world it changed nothing. She still had to marry Hassan.

In a strange way her journey of self-discovery was responsible for cementing that in her. Being an adult, being her own person, meant nothing if she didn't do all she could for her people. Yes, she had been born into royalty—no choice about it—but, like Adham, she was determined to fulfill her purpose, to serve where she was required to serve. She had great power, great influence, and if she didn't do all that she could with it, it served no purpose.

"Hassan does not wish to marry you."

Her thoughts stalled completely, her brain refusing to function. "I... He doesn't... But he had you... What about the contract?" Then her thoughts started again, her mind racing at top speed. "What does this mean for the military alliance? For the trade routes and oil prices? My country is counting on it. My people. Your people. The wedding *has* to go forward." She said it, and she believed it with a burning conviction even while her emotions, her heart, her very soul, rejoiced at the thought of not having to marry Hassan.

"You will still marry the ruler of Umarah. But Hassan has decided to step down. He is in love with his mistress and she is carrying his child. Under those circumstances, he has decided he must do what is best for his growing family."

Heat prickled her arms, the back of her neck. "Who is the new ruler of Umarah? Who am I meant to marry now?"

"You will marry me, *amira*. I am the new High Sheikh of Umarah."

CHAPTER NINE

THERE was no triumph in his voice. No warmth. Nothing to signal that the news he was delivering was positive or negative in any way. It simply was. But that was Adham's way. If something needed to be done, he did it. He picked up the slack when others failed. He came through when others fell short. It was who he was.

"So now might be a good time to explain your relationship to Hassan, then," she said, her throat tight and dry like sandpaper.

"He is my brother. Older by two years."

"I thought your family had been killed."

"All but Hassan and myself. He is the only family I have left."

The knife of guilt that had been sticking sharply into her ribs twisted again. He was not simply Adham's friend, he was his brother. That made those stolen moments at the oasis seem even worse.

"Why didn't you just tell me?" There were a lot of other questions she needed to ask, a lot of other bases to cover, but she had to know that first.

"That I was Hassan's brother? Because I wanted to gain your trust, and I knew that would not happen if you knew of my relationship to him."

"So you lied to me?"

"And we both cheated."

She knew instinctively that it didn't matter if she was no longer marrying Hassan. What had happened between them was still an aberration in Adham's eyes. The sin had been committed, and it was not forgiven. And she knew that he would never forget her part in it, or his.

"Yes. We can't take it back, though."

"No. But we will move forward."

"And you're intent on marrying me in order to honor the contract?"

"I said that I would."

She remembered the conversation they'd had on the street in Paris—a conversation that seemed as though it had taken place in another lifetime. He'd said he didn't want to marry, but that if he had to, if others were dependent on him doing so, he would. She had become to him what Hassan had been to her. It made her feel sick.

"Yes. You did."

"The country is going to be shaken by this. Hassan is a beloved leader, and though I have served Umarah all my life the people don't know me well. That is by design. It is easiest for me to conduct my duty if I'm not high-profile. But that will make this transition difficult."

Isabella took a breath. "I'll do what I can to help it go smoothly."

"Our marriage will help. The Umarahn people were expecting you as their Sheikha."

"There isn't a better man to rule than you, Adham. I'm certain of that. You have given everything for your country, for your people…"

"I think I have proven that I am as capable of weakness as anyone else."

She could tell it physically hurt him to say it—that the words scraped raw as they left his throat.

"You're not weak, Adham," she whispered.

"I never will be again."

There was finality in his tone—a coldness that chilled her straight to the bone.

"Hassan and Jamilah are leaving tomorrow. We will stay here while we prepare a formal announcement of the passing on of leadership and our wedding," he said.

"We won't go back to the city?"

"Not yet. We will marry in the city, but until then we will stay here. We will be closer to some of the Bedouin encampments, and it would be best if we were to go and visit them. Too often they feel as though they are on the fringe, and yet they're very much a part of our country. I would have them feel as important as they are."

Isabella's heart swelled. Pride, she realized. Because, whether or not this was what Adham had envisioned for himself, he was born to lead. And she would have to find her place. Figure out where she fit, what she could do to help him.

Although she had a feeling he would rather her place were far away from him. The gulf between them had only widened since they'd made love. That moment of closeness—that brief, burning instant that she'd spent in the center of the sun—had been an illusion. And she was paying the price for it. She had lost any real link she'd had with Adham.

He turned to go, and without thinking she put her hand on him, desperate to find some sort of connection with him. "You aren't staying?"

He turned, his eyebrows locked together, his jaw tense, the muscle of his forearm beneath her hand tight. "I have my own quarters. You will stay in yours."

His words—harsh, final—were like a physical slap.

"And after the wedding?" she asked, despising herself for the hopeful note in her voice.

"That will depend on whether or not you are pregnant. We didn't take any precautions."

She nodded, feeling sick to her core. Now that she had given herself to him he didn't want her at all. Now that she would be forced to marry him, live with him for the rest of her life, he despised her. Living with Hassan while loving Adham would have been less torturous than having Adham while his heart was locked tightly away from her—being his wife while he didn't desire her at all.

When he left, closing the door behind him, she sat on the bed, her eyes dry and stinging, her pain too acute for tears. She felt brittle, as though the life was being drained from her.

It was one thing to be denied a life with Adham. But to be given a life with him and have him withhold himself from her…she did not know how she could live with that.

Adham swept a shaking hand over his forehead, disgusted with himself for how hard it was to deny Isabella. Even now he wanted her, after having possessed her only a few short hours ago.

Everything in his life had suddenly changed. All the things he had never desired—a wife, family, becoming High Sheikh—were thrust upon him, and still his most pressing need seemed to be for Isabella's ripe body.

He despised the weakness in himself. Despised that she had such control over him—a control he could not seem to regain.

Until he could, he would not allow himself to touch her. He had a country to think of. His duty extended beyond simply protecting borders and rooting out threats. He was now responsible for everything. And he would do it—would do the best thing possible for his people, as he had done during his years of military service.

He would marry Isabella. But he would not allow her to lead him around by vulnerable body parts. He had never given a woman such power over him. Women were women—easy to find and interchangeable. Sex, no matter how much he enjoyed it, was only sex. It was an easy thing for a man of wealth and power to get, should he want it.

Though he knew he would not find another woman. Not now that he was going to marry Isabella. He would be faithful to her, as he would demand faithfulness of her.

But first he had to gain control of the wild heat that seemed to overcome him when he was in her presence.

The next morning Adham sat at the head of the breakfast table, preparing a formal announcement, while Hassan and his mistress sat in the middle, the woman's eyes downcast, Hassan avoiding Isabella's gaze. Isabella was seated at the end, with aides and servants buzzing around her, the conversation in rapid Arabic moving too quickly for her to follow.

She put her head down and concentrated on eating her hot cereal. She couldn't imagine a more awkward moment. And she'd never felt more like a commodity than she did right then, with Hassan sitting next to the woman of his choice, caressing her tenderly, making sure she was well. And there *she* was, sitting leagues away from her new fiancé—the fiancé who didn't want her, who wouldn't even look at her. Who had inherited her as part of a package deal with his new kingdom.

Her ears perked up, picking up the word *wedding* when spoken by Adham's deep voice. "I see no reason it should not take place as planned."

Hassan nodded. "It will give the people a sense of security."

Oh, good. She was a security blanket for the people.

She sighed. It seemed ridiculous that she had been prepared for this with Hassan, but that now it was Adham it seemed…worse. Worse because she actually wanted Adham, because she loved him, and because she knew he was now stuck in a life, a position, he had not wanted. And she was a part of that.

She loved the man, and seeing him now, seated at the head of the table, going through massive stacks of paperwork, was like watching a tiger that had been caged. Adham would be a wonderful king. The best. And yet it was not what he had wanted for himself. And hadn't he given enough?

She was just another sacrifice he was being forced to make.

"Isabella, where is your ring?" Adham spoke directly to her for the first time since she'd sat down at the table.

She flexed her fingers. "Oh… I thought that…" She looked at Hassan, then back to Adham. "It seemed inappropriate."

"The ring was designed specifically for you by the palace jeweler."

Designed for her? By whose standards? Her mother's? Her father's? The ring was a brilliant solitaire, beautiful in its perfection, but it had nothing whatsoever to do with her as a person. And it had been Hassan's ring. She wanted Adham's. More than that she wanted his heart. He didn't seem prepared to give her either, or even understand why it might be important.

For the first time Jamilah spoke. "You can't expect Isabella to wear a ring that was given to her by another man."

"Actually," Isabella said crisply, "it was delivered to me by courier. So I suppose it's impersonal enough that it should not matter."

"But it does," Jamilah insisted. "Men are foolish when it comes to such matters."

On that she could wholeheartedly agree with her. And, since Jamilah was to be her sister-in-law, she was glad that she and the other woman had something other than a fiancé in common.

Hassan cleared his throat. "Yes, men are foolish. It takes us extra time to see what we truly need sometimes."

Isabella felt her heart squeeze tight, seeing the love that passed between Hassan and Jamilah. Isabella blinked back hot tears and cleared her throat. Seeing Hassan in love, seeing the way he looked at Jamilah…it brought to light just how far she was from that place with Adham.

She stood, pushing her bowl back, tired of the pretense of enjoying breakfast while life swirled around her, out of her control. "I'm finished. Nice to meet you, Jamilah."

She turned and walked from the room, unable to say anything to Adham for fear she might break down entirely. Everything should feel perfect now. She was marrying the man she loved. But it wasn't perfect. It was a mockery of her feelings. The man she loved was being forced into a union with her, and being a part of his unhappiness was worse than not having him at all.

A gentle touch on her shoulder stopped her. "Isabella." It was Jamilah, her liquid dark eyes full of concern. "I hope that you are all right, Isabella. I know what it's like to lose the man you love…or to think you will. I would hate it if you were heartbroken over this."

She let out a watery laugh. "I'm not. I'm very happy for both of you," she said, choked. "I would have hated to be the cause of your separation."

Jamilah looked down. "I resented you, Isabella. How could I not? You were going to marry the man I loved, the father of my child, and I had no argument against it. I still don't. Now Adham has had to give up his life too, and you have been shuffled around like a commodity…"

"Don't feel guilty. Adham and I… I would rather be with Adham."

A smile lit Jamilah's beautiful face. "Then this is a *good* thing for you! For both of you."

Isabella laughed, the sound hollow and brittle in the empty corridor. "I don't know if it's good for both of us but…I care for him."

"It's a good start," the other woman offered.

"I suppose." She left out the fact that Adham resented her, that he felt she was responsible for revealing some sort of weakness in him. She didn't need a big loud confrontation with him to know that.

With Adham, the silences were the worst. That icy, indifferent expression that he was so good at projecting was more cutting than angry words could ever be. It was in the small things, like the ring, that he showed just how little she mattered.

"Hassan and I are leaving the country for a while. Until everything dies down. He's concerned for my health…the health of the baby."

What must it be like to have a man care like that? Adham had always protected her, but he had protected her because it was the right thing to do. In that sense duty was entirely inadequate. Just as it was a wholly awful reason for the man you loved to marry you.

The door to the dining room swung open and Adham and Hassan came into the corridor. Adham's eyes locked with hers, the dark fire there igniting a heat that burned slowly in her. Desire, need, and a longing so intense it made her want to weep with it. It wasn't just a physical need, a physical desire. She wanted his love. She wanted it so badly that it hurt.

But the man standing in front of her, the man with scars that ran deep, with roots buried in his heart, would never love her.

He did come to her side and take her arm, the gesture traditional, proprietary and devoid of anything personal. It hurt worse than the distance.

"We will see you when you return for the wedding," Adham said, gripping his brother's hand.

"Thank you for this, Adham. And you, Isabella."

She didn't know what to say to that. So she only nodded, pressure building in her chest until she was certain the dam would burst and her tears would flood the massive palace.

Hassan put his arm around Jamilah's waist and led her down the corridor, away from Adham and herself.

"I am happy for them," she said quietly as they moved out of sight.

"It is the right thing for Hassan to do. When a child is involved… Consideration has to be given to that."

"What about to him and Jamilah? To the fact that they love each other?"

"What does love matter, Isabella? The kind of love between men and women, lust, that fades with time? It is easily broken, abandoned for a thousand insignificant reasons every day. But a marriage that serves a purpose, that is bigger than the two people involved, *that* marriage has a chance."

"So you don't believe that Hassan and Jamilah will stay together?"

"They have their child. I believe that will bond them."

"But not their feelings for each other?"

"It doesn't matter."

"It does matter. Are you saying you don't believe in love?"

His expression calmed, his eyes suddenly looking beyond her. "You remember, Isabella, we talked about life experience. I have had my share. I have seen much of people—of what the human heart is capable of. Immense greed, unimaginable cruelty. Those things choke love out, kill it where it grows. I have not seen that elusive emotion conquer anything, but I have seen it used against people. I believe love has the power to weaken."

"That's terribly sad, Adham."

"You're young, Bella. You see life as full of wonderful possibilities because you have been given protection by your family—protection from the ugliness in life. But love did not save my parents, Isabella. Do you know, the men that killed my parents…they did not see my mother hiding in the garden, not at first. They used my father to draw her out. Used her love for him, exploited it."

"Adham…" Her voice cracked.

"She could have survived if she had used her mind instead of her heart. No matter what, they were not going to free my father. There was nothing she could have done, and in the end they were both killed."

She saw now where Adham's rigid control, his seeming absence of emotion, came from. He felt it necessary for survival—for the survival of others. And he had honed those defenses, made them so solid, so impenetrable, that she had no hope of breaching them.

"What if it were Hassan? Wouldn't you try to save him?"

"It is different. It is my duty to protect Hassan. I am trained to do so."

She wanted so badly to go to him, to wrap her arms around him and offer him the comfort of her body, offer him whatever he needed. But she stayed still, rooted to the spot, unable to face the rejection that would come if she made a move toward him.

"There is an event this evening," he said, changing the subject suddenly. "Other sheikhs, leaders of some of the larger tribal groups, are coming to the palace. I am to hear their concerns for their communities, listen to their needs, You will attend, of course."

"Of course," she said dryly.

"You will find suitable clothing laid out for you on your bed." He did not look at her when he said that.

Anger flashed through her. "So you're going to choose my clothing now?"

"Clothing that fits the event, your position, the customs of your new country. You may wear what you like in other circumstances."

It was a small concession, but one that meant something to her.

"Thank you."

"I'm not a tyrant, Isabella."

"I know that."

"Then don't look at me as though you expect me to be."

"Do you want honesty, Adham? I don't know what to think. I don't know where we stand, or how you will want your wife to behave. I don't know what you want from me."

He looked at her, his gaze assessing. "I'll give you honesty, since you gave it to me. I don't want a wife. But I do want to do what is best for my people, for your people. That is as far as my expectations of you will go. Otherwise you're free to do as you like."

She had a feeling he looked on that as a gift of some kind, as though he had handed her freedom. But it was impossible. Hearing that he didn't want her hurt worse than she had imagined it would. She hadn't thought that the verbal confirmation would be more difficult to handle than the physical signs, but it was. Much worse.

"I know you'll do what's best for everyone, Adham," she said tightly. "You always do."

"Not always."

"Well, that's done now. We can't go back. And there's no point in dwelling on it now."

"I don't intend to repeat my mistakes."

He strode away, and she stood, rooted to the spot. She was a mistake? Even now that they were going to be married she was nothing more than a mistake?

He had said they would see if she was pregnant or not. Did that mean he only intended to sleep with her to ensure that she produced an heir? When she'd faced marriage to Hassan she would have welcomed that, but with Adham…the thought of him coming to her bed out of duty…

She dashed away the tears that were falling down her cheeks and went to her room. She had to pick one of her pre-selected outfits so that she would be ready to present herself as a proper sheikha. Present herself as a woman her fiancé might be proud to have on his arm.

* * *

Adham disliked state functions. Diplomacy was not his strong point, as he had been told more than once since childhood. He shifted, trying to ignore the discomfort he always experienced when wearing the traditional Umarahn robes. He preferred Western-style clothing to the billowing garb of his ancestors, but meeting with tribal leaders required him to observe tradition in a way he was not accustomed to.

One thing he did discover was that he enjoyed talking to the people. Enjoyed finding out what their needs were, and knowing that he could help them with those needs in an immediate fashion. Being the High Sheikh would have many rewards, but the sacrifices were great. Already he chafed for the freedom of the desert. But that way of living was past.

His future bride was late—a fact he was grateful for. He had not found any more control over his libido since leaving her earlier that day. He still ached for her.

He turned his attention to the Sheikh of one of the larger nomadic groups, who was talking about a need for traveling schools, finding better ways to transport water. That was when he spotted a flash of red out of the corner of his eye and looked up.

Isabella was standing in the doorway of the throne room, her exquisite body draped in rich silk, her dark hair left loose, strands of silver chain woven through it, adding an ethereal shimmer to her glossy black locks. Her eyes were darkened with black kohl, her lips red to match her gown. The style was traditional and modest, yet on her... She looked like the essence of temptation, a call to sin that any man would be hard pressed to resist.

As she moved across the room the heads of every tribal leader turned sharply, their eyes fixed on her womanly form as she walked toward him. Her hips swayed, an enticing rhythm, and her eyes were full of sensual promise.

And she was his.

Mine.

She didn't offer him a smile as she came to join him. Her expression was neutral, much more guarded than he was used to seeing. He had hurt her earlier, with his admission that he did not want a wife. But she had to understand that he would not be the sort of husband to her that Hassan would have been.

He would be faithful, and he would give her children. But he did not know how to give the love of a husband. The love of a father. She and her children deserved both, and it galled him to know that he could not give it. Had it been up to him he would have spared her, but the need for their marriage remained. Which meant that she had to sacrifice more than she might have.

But hurting her in that way…it had made him ache to see her eyes so full of pain.

He put his hand on her lower back and felt her stiffen beneath his touch. She had not done that in a long while. She had grown to enjoy his touch, and now she recoiled from it. His body took it as a challenge when it should be pleased. He needed distance, needed time for whatever enchantment she had woven around him to wear off before he went to her bed again.

He raised his hand and the room fell silent, awaiting his word. "This is my future bride—your future Sheikha. Principessa Isabella Rossi. The union between she and I will bring about an alliance with Turan that will benefit both countries." He continued, outlining all that each nation stood to gain from the marriage, while the sheikhs looked on, nodding their heads in approval.

Isabella offered the onlookers a wide smile—one he

suddenly wished were directed at him. Then she did something no other sheikha would have done. "I am honored to be in your service," she said. "Umarah is a wonderful country, and I look forward to learning all that I can about my new home. Thank you for welcoming me."

He did not know what the response would be to a woman speaking, but the men only nodded, clapping and laughing at the end of her speech.

Afterward, they spoke to Isabella as well as to him, telling her specifically about the needs of the women and children in their groups.

When they sat down to dinner Isabella took her place at his side. "You should smile more," she whispered—the first words she'd spoken to him all evening.

"I should?"

"I've told you that before." Conversation and music swirled, loud and boisterous around them, as food was placed on the table.

"I don't know that the people expect their High Sheikh to smile."

"It's always better to talk to someone who smiles than someone who simply glares at you."

"I don't glare."

"Yes, Adham, you do."

"Do I glare at you?"

"All the time." A smile tugged the corner of her gorgeous red mouth. He was glad to see it—glad to see her smile again instead of that blank, serious expression. Perhaps that was what she felt when he smiled. A sense of pride, as though she had accomplished something.

"I will try not to."

She reached her hand up and touched his forehead,

as though she were smoothing out the lines. "I think it's permanent."

He gripped her hand, moved it to his cheek, held it there. The look in her eyes changed, her pupils expanding, the pulse in her wrist fluttering fast beneath his fingers. An answering pulse pounded in his groin, his body hardening for her.

He dropped her hand, disgusted with himself. That he could get an erection in a room full of people, at an important political event, only told him just how badly he was failing at regaining his control. Never before had a woman distracted him from the task at hand. But Isabella near…her skin so soft, her scent tantalizingly sweet, that lush body that he knew was so tight, that fit him so perfectly, close enough for him to touch, to taste…was a temptation he was not able to combat.

He turned his attention to the man next to him and began discussing mundane tax laws—anything to tone down his body's reaction to his future Sheikha.

Isabella had every man in the room eating out of the palm of her hand by the end of the evening, and as the men filed out they all bowed—a show of reverence and submission rarely given to women—offering her hospitality should she ever be traveling near their encampments.

She was a valuable political asset—something he had not fully appreciated about her when he had first met her. He had assumed she was immature, had thought her youthful enthusiasm would be a drawback, and yet he saw now that that wasn't the case. She was naive, yes, but that only added to her charm, made her seem disarming and sweet, and her enthusiasm, her ready smile, made people want to be with her, talk to her.

No matter who she was conversing with she gave them

all of her focus, all of her attention, and she did it with such an air of interest that whoever she was speaking to felt at the center of her universe. She was an asset that most politicians would dream of.

She leaned against the doorframe, exhaustion evident on her face. She looked so beautiful there, the light from the palace making a halo around her dark hair from behind, the moon casting a silver glow on her golden skin. There was still a lingering warmth in the night air, the scent of sun on sand not yet faded.

"Where did you learn to work a room like that?" he asked.

She shrugged, not looking at him, keeping her eyes fixed on a distant point out in the desert; that unusual reserve that she seemed to be showing only to him was back. "We held many diplomatic events in Turan, and traveled to several outside of the country. I told you, I speak many languages and I often conversed with dignitaries in attendance. I was trained to be a royal wife."

"And you were trained well."

"Yes. I was. I enjoy that part of it, really. I like people. I like hearing about their lives, their dreams and struggles. One thing I've found is that people usually want the same things, no matter how different they are."

"I have never spent a lot of time getting to know people," he said, realizing how true it was.

Other than Hassan, he didn't count anyone as his friend. He'd had affairs with women over the years—nothing permanent, nothing serious. And he hadn't wanted those connections. Hadn't wanted to be close to anyone. Yet Isabella seemed to want to know anyone and everyone. She was so open, so exposed to anyone who might try and hurt her.

"I don't know that I've really gotten to know very

many people. Being royalty, it seems like you're always…
separate. But I've gotten to be a small part of a lot of
people's lives. I like that."

"I thought you were very selfish when we first met,"
he said, remembering how he had assumed she was a
spoiled little rich girl, whining about moving from one
palace to the next. "But that was the only moment in your
life you've ever spared for yourself, wasn't it?"

She laughed softly, a small amount of warmth returning to her face. "I did sneak out shopping with my sister-
in-law once. She didn't know we were sneaking, poor
thing. That turned out to be a bad idea too."

"You think now that your time in Paris was a bad
idea?"

"I don't know, Adham. I learned to want a lot more
than I did before I left. Different things than I thought I
wanted."

"Freedom from the an arranged marriage?"

She pushed away from the doorframe, her eyes, which
had been avoiding him, locked onto him now. "No. I
learned to want things I had ignored—things I had never
thought I would truly desire. How could I when my husband had been chosen for me? There was never a reason
to look at another man, never a reason to want to know
about…sex."

She touched his arm, the brush of her skin sending
a shock of kinetic energy through him, straight to his
groin, making him totally hard in an instant.

"Being with you…that was when I learned what it
was to want." She licked her lips and lust kicked him.
Hard. "That was the other moment in my life when I was
selfish," she finished on a whisper.

He gripped her wrist, backed her against the door, his
mouth finding the sensitive curve of her neck, pressing

a kiss to her flesh, damp from the heat, tasting the salt of her skin, the essence of Isabella. His Bella. *His.*

A small moan escaped her lips and he caught it with his mouth, kissing her hard, devouring her. And she met him, her tongue thrusting into his mouth, her body moving against him, the restrictive fit of her red gown keeping her movements slight.

She tried to spread her legs wider, tried to move that sensitive part of her body against his hardened erection, to give them both the release they so desperately craved. Desire burned in him, wild, uncontrolled.

He gripped her hip, running his hand around to the curve of her bottom and down to her thigh, taking hold of the intricate beaded design on the gossamer fabric and tugging hard, tearing the material so that she was able to move with more freedom. She bent her knee and he lifted her leg, wrapping it around his calf as she leaned back against the doorframe, moving her body sensually against him.

He was ready to come then and there—from her delighted moans of pleasure, from the slick of her tongue against his, from the heat that radiated at the apex of her thighs, a heat that he knew signaled her readiness for him. One more decisive tear of that demure dress and he could sweep it aside and thrust into her...

"Apologies..." A nervous voice brought him out of his sensual haze and he moved away from Isabella, turning to see a young man standing in the corridor, his eyes downcast. "Sheikh Hassan is on the phone and wishes to speak to you."

He looked at Isabella, who had pressed herself tightly to the doorframe, her eyes squeezed shut, her cheeks flushed pink, her breasts rising and falling with each heavy breath she took. Her dress was torn from her thigh down past her knee, revealing smooth golden skin—skin he'd had his hands on only moments ago, that he wanted to have his hands on again. Even now, with a servant standing there looking on, he wanted to finish what they had started. What they had started in a public place in the palace while they were still unmarried.

The Umarahn people would expect a certain code of conduct from their High Sheikh and his Sheikha, and while most of the modern people would assume they were not abstaining, they would still find it distasteful to know that he had nearly taken Isabella against the palace wall, with doors opened to the desert.

No more distasteful than they would find it that he had taken her virginity on the floor of a tent in the middle of the desert while she'd been engaged to their beloved Hassan.

"Goodnight, Isabella," he said, turning away from her.

He heard a sharp catch in her breathing, knew she was holding back a sob, but he kept walking. He could not afford to let her control him—could not afford to let his need for her get so out of hand that he forgot everything for the pursuit of the pleasure he could find in her body. He could not afford to lose focus even for a moment.

He had seen the damage it could cause. And he wanted no part of something that could be that destructive.

CHAPTER TEN

"AGAIN you do not have your ring on." Adham's deep voice was full of censure.

Isabella looked away from the scenery, flying by in a red blur out the window of the Hummer, and down at her bare hand. "What does it matter?"

"It matters a great deal. You are my fiancée. It is expected for you to wear my ring."

She took a deep breath, pain lancing her. "But it isn't your ring. It's Hassan's. And it isn't *my* ring. There's nothing about it that has any personal meaning or value to me."

"You're being petulant."

"Maybe." She wasn't, though. He was just being too obtuse to see it. Because the engagement meant nothing to him. It meant nothing to him that her ring had been a part of an entirely different engagement, that it had been given to her by a delivery man.

It mattered to her, though. It would matter to any woman. It wasn't as though Adham hadn't had relationships before. He should know enough about women to figure that out. Or maybe his affairs had been so detached that he really didn't have a clue what something like a ring could really mean to a woman.

That thought made her feel both relief and heartrending sadness. Relief because she didn't like the idea of Adham's heart having belonged to any other woman, but sadness because the thought of him involving himself in such a soulless, purely physical affair made her almost sick. He was worth so much more than that.

He took one hand off the steering wheel and gripped her wrist, holding her arm up as if he was examining it. "You aren't putting it on."

"I left it back at the palace. I took it off when things were ended with Hassan."

"The engagement, the original arrangement, is still in place."

"Only the fiancé has changed. An incidental, I guess?"

He didn't respond to that. He set her hand gently in her lap, the touch sending a shockwave through her as it always did, and turned his focus back to the road.

"The people at the Bedouin encampment might wonder," he said tightly.

"Then they can wonder. I think it's safe to say that everyone in Umarah knows we have an unusual situation. They know I was promised to Hassan, and they know he's now chosen someone else and that I am marrying his brother. I highly doubt anyone expects our relationship to appear conventional."

"The faster we can erase the scandal from the minds of the people, the better. I see no point in drawing it out. It will all be forgotten eventually. The more we are seen together, the more natural all of this will seem. Then there will be the wedding, and children. None of this will matter."

"So we're putting on a show for the nation? Hoping they'll forget the truth?"

"What does it benefit our people to see tension between

us? We're building an alliance between nations through our marriage. Our union must appear strong, so that they will believe the alliance is strong."

"Much easier that it appear strong than actually have it *be* strong," she muttered, turning her focus back to the arid desert.

"The situation is what it is, Bella. It is not ideal, but we must make the best of it."

Pain shot through her. Not ideal. Well, maybe that was true for him. She *knew* it was true for him. But what did he think it was like for her? Did he really think she would rather be with Hassan? Did he believe that she had given herself to him that night in the desert out of rebellion? How could he be dense enough to miss how much she felt for him?

It came back to the way he saw relationships. The way he saw sex. Sex was recreation for him, affairs a simple diversion in between assignments or work in the oil fields. While for her…it had been life-altering. Being with him like that. Even now it sent a thrill through her body and caused tears to form in her eyes.

Shimmering waves of heat parted in the distance, and Isabella could see oil rigs against the backdrop of the faded blue sky.

Adham gestured to the right, to a mountainous stretch beyond the flat portion where the rigs were stationed. "The encampment is back there. Many of the men work on the fields, adding new joints, checking core samples, measuring depth."

"And the drilling projects were your doing?"

"We were already drilling, but I made the move to invest more in the operation. It's provided good jobs for our people, and a very valuable export. The benefits for the economy have been exponential."

"Really, Adham, is there anything you can't do?"

She turned to look at him, saw his jaw clench, his shoulders roll forward slightly as he tightened his grip on the steering wheel. "I don't know that I have you figured out."

It was such an honest, frustrated admission, one that shocked her. "I can't wear Hassan's ring," she blurted.

"You don't like it?"

"It's a beautiful ring. It's not my style, but it *is* beautiful. I can't wear it because I'm not marrying Hassan. It's linked to him, not to you, and as long as I wear it I feel…I feel like I'm still engaged to him."

"Why couldn't you just say that?" He sounded even more exasperated now.

"Because if I say it, it doesn't mean as much as if you just…figure it out."

"That's ridiculous."

"It isn't," she insisted. "It's like having to ask for flowers."

"Which isn't good either?"

"No. You want the other person to think of it, otherwise it has no meaning."

They were getting close to the rigs now. The sound of drilling filled the air, overpowering the sound of the car's motor, the scent of the crude oil coming through the air vents. The road they were on wound around the rigs, taking them behind the mountains, which did a good job of absorbing the bulk of the noise.

"Life would be simpler if you would just ask for things," he muttered.

"That's very male of you," she said stiffly. The pragmatic side of him reminded her of her brother, and her brother's pragmatic side irritated her.

"Well, *amira*, I am very male." That last comment hung between them as silence filled up the car.

She swallowed, her throat dry. "Yes." She knew that. She knew that so very well.

That one time together, though…had it only been two days ago?…hadn't been enough. She hadn't gotten to see enough of his body, hadn't had enough opportunity to simply admire his physique, to enjoy the feel of his hot skin against hers.

Her face flamed.

It was strange to think she'd actually slept with him. She'd imagined, when she'd even let herself think about it, that sex would bring people closer together, not make everything so…complicated.

Maybe it wasn't really complicated. She knew how she felt about him, and he'd made it clear how he felt about her. So it was just sad, then.

A row of low, dark tents came into view, and Isabella could see smoke rising from campfires, children running around with their mothers close behind them. Out here in the middle of the desert, with all of the sand so still, there was life.

"I can't believe they live out here. There's nothing for so many miles."

"It's their way of life. They've lived this way for centuries. We do the best we can to provide mobile medical service."

"What about emergencies?" she asked, looking at the children.

"We do the best we can. Many of the Bedouin encampments have satellite phones and generators now that enable them to call, and we can have helicopters sent if necessary."

"And schools?"

"Something that hasn't been handled to my satisfaction yet," he said, bringing the car to a halt on the outskirts of the camp.

She unbuckled quickly and let herself out of the vehicle, meeting him halfway around the other side. "Do you have any ideas?"

"Not any that are feasible at the moment, but it's something that Hassan was working on, and I'm happy to continue that work and see it through."

"Definitely. Education is so important."

"I didn't know you were so passionate about it."

"I am. Without the schooling I had…" She tried to think of a way to explain it. "It was my escape. I learned about what I couldn't do, places I couldn't go. It added so much to my life. Every child…every person…should have that."

Adham looked at Isabella, at the passion in her blue eyes as she spoke, and his respect for her grew. She was much more complex than he'd given her credit for when he'd first met her. He'd thought she was simply spoiled and immature, but that wasn't it. She was naive, but she was smart. Innocent in the ways of the world, but savvy in social situations.

And having *his* ring meant something to her. That was an intriguing thing. He hadn't imagined it would matter to her. It was still an arranged marriage—a marriage she didn't want but was willing to go through with for the sake of her country, just as he was.

Now that he knew, he wanted to ensure she had a ring she would love. A ring that fit her. He had no idea why it suddenly mattered, except that it mattered to *her*. Isabella should have some happiness, should have something she wanted.

The wind blowing through the camp was hot, and they

got a blast of it when they moved away from the car and began walking toward the camp. Isabella licked her lips, and he felt the impact of it hard in his gut. He wanted her—wanted her with a ferocity that nearly drove him to grab her and haul her back to the Hummer, so he could take her in the back seat, feel the tight, wet heat of her body around him again.

His hands shook with his need. This…this desire that was so all-consuming it was like a weed. It had taken root, and now it had gone so deep he couldn't extract it.

No. He would. She was to be his wife, and wanting her was expected—welcome. But he could not allow it to control him.

The leader of the Bedouin tribe walked out to greet them, children clustering around him, their eyes round with awe over meeting such a powerful man. Isabella imagined they had no real idea that Adham was the king, but they didn't really need to. Adham projected power effortlessly. In a group, he would be the one others would turn to for guidance automatically, even without a title connected to him.

A rush of pride filled her as she watched him—the man she loved, the man she was going to marry—walk with the other man over to the fire and sit with all the men, talking with them, treating them like equals, listening to their concerns. She knew Adham hadn't been comfortable at the big, formal event that had been held at the palace, but here he was in his element. Connected to his people.

One of the women ushered her into the tent where they were sitting, talking and laughing, sewing in the lantern light. She loved talking to them, finding out about their customs, hearing stories about their children.

They had so little, and yet they had so much love. It was how Isabella wanted to treat her children—the children she would have with Adham. She wanted them to have more than nannies and tutors. She wanted them to have this. Love. Acceptance. For them to know she was proud of them. She wanted them to have everything her parents had denied her.

When Adham came into the tent a couple of hours later Isabella's heart leapt into her throat at the sight of him. He made sure he greeted all the women, even taking time to ask for each of their names.

Then he turned to her. "It is time for us to go, Isabella."

She nodded and stood, and he placed his hand on the small of her back. The gesture was intended as a casual maneuver, and she knew that, but it still sent reckless heat blazing through her, made her feel as though she was on fire with her desire for him. Even in front of people it was like that. And he, as always, was a statue, never betraying a moment's discomfort, not affected in the least.

When they were back in the car, Isabella leaned toward the passenger door, trying to put some distance between the two of them.

"Did you enjoy making conversation with the women?" he asked.

She nodded. "Yes. We had some time to discuss the difficulties with schooling out here..." She hesitated. "I think...I think I have an idea."

"Do you?" He didn't sound condescending, as her father would have, he actually sounded interested. That bolstered her confidence.

"Yes. I was thinking that we could do a simple 'six weeks on, six weeks off' schedule and bring teachers in on rotation. That way the children would get the education they need, but a teacher who isn't accustomed to living out here won't burn out from living in the desert for so long at a time."

"That's a good idea."

"You think so?"

"Yes. We had thought of boarding schools, but the more traditional people want their children home, so that they can also educate them according to their customs. But having the teachers here, on a schedule that would allow them breaks, would probably be the best solution. I'll talk to the teachers we have out in the field and work at tailoring a schedule with them."

Isabella couldn't hold back her smile. She liked that she had been able to at least offer one solution to Adham. Especially since she was the cause of so many of his problems.

That thought made her smile fade again.

"We have more tribal leaders coming to the palace tomorrow. They are less…modern than some of the men we've met so far. They will not wish you to be present when we meet."

"Oh." She didn't know what else to say to that.

"I have always been proud of my father's legacy, of Hassan's, of what they have done to champion women's rights in our country, but these people…they live in the heart of the desert, untouched by technology or many other things from the modern world."

"I see." It hurt her feelings to be told she wasn't wanted. Of course it did. Even if it was silly. It wasn't as though Adham had said *he* didn't want her around.

But he didn't. That was why it bothered her. Because she felt as if he was using the wishes of the tribal leaders to get rid of her.

It would help if she could tell what he was thinking. But she couldn't. She never could.

"I wish I could read your mind," she said, not really intending to say it out loud, but not sorry she had.

"No," he said, his voice rough suddenly. "You don't wish that."

"Yes. I do. You said to ask for what I wanted. I wish I could understand you. We're going to get married. I think it would be helpful if we at least reached some sort of understanding."

He applied the brakes, stopping the car in the middle of the desert road and turning to her, his eyes glittering in the dim light. "If you could read my thoughts you would be scandalized."

"Maybe I'd like to be scandalized."

"I think you and I have caused enough scandal."

"We can't dwell on that forever. What happened that night happened. There's nothing that can be done about it now."

He extended his hand, cupped her cheek, and she realized that he was shaking. His eyes were intense on hers, his mouth set into a hard line, his jaw locked tight. He stroked the line of her jaw with his thumb.

When he kissed her, it was hot and hard, fierce but short, his lips burning her, searing her soul.

Adham reveled in the touch of her soft lips, enjoyed the velvet feel of the inside of her mouth against his tongue, her taste, her smell, everything uniquely and wholly Isabella. His heart was slamming hard against his chest, all of his blood rushing south of his belt, making him hard, making him ache.

He wanted her—wanted to peel her modest dress off and reveal her breasts to his gaze, to taste those hardened tips, suck them between his lips. He wanted to see all of her, touch all of her, sink into her tight body and lose himself in her, give up the battle he was waging against his own desire.

He wrenched his mouth away from hers, his hands unsteady, his stomach tight, his heart beating in a chest that felt too small to accommodate it.

This was a madness that could not be endured. If he were another man—a man with less responsibility, a man who didn't have two nations of people depending on him—he would take Isabella away and spend however long it took—weeks, months—exorcising her from his system. As it was, he didn't have that time. He was a man who could not afford to have any weakness in him, a man who needed to be strong, who needed to have dominion over his every fleshly need.

And that meant he couldn't afford to give in. Not to any desire that had the power to control him, that had the power to overshadow his good sense. That had the power to make him forget his loyalty to his brother, the only family he had left. Family he had betrayed so easily.

If he could break those bonds of loyalty with his brother, what would prevent him from breaking his vows to Isabella? Breaking the vows of service he'd made to his country?

He had to find his strength again. Find his control.

"This will not happen again until after the wedding," he ground out, satisfied that he had made a decree, that he had set a timeline. One he would follow. One she would follow.

She settled back into her seat, her head tilted back, exposing the smooth line of her elegant throat. Lust gripped him hard, challenged him. He squashed it ruthlessly, shutting off all feeling, all thoughts of anything except for the passing desert.

He was the High Sheikh of Umarah. Ultimate control belonged to him. He would not give in to temptation. She was only a woman—one in a long line of many. He would not allow her to get beneath his defenses again.

CHAPTER ELEVEN

ADHAM was a cold stranger the next morning at breakfast, although the servants and aides were still moving around, talking. It would die down, she supposed. It wasn't so chaotic at the Turani palace, but then, unless it was a formal occasion her father didn't often eat meals with the family. Perhaps if he had there would have been more activity in the dining room.

She wondered if Adham would always take meals in here, with her. With their children. She could be pregnant. It was unlikely, but possible. She wanted Adham's child, but she hoped she hadn't conceived yet. They had way too many issues to work through before adding a child into the mix.

Adham was either hot or cold with her. That was an understatement; he was either blazing or completely frozen. As he was this morning.

When the staff left, only the two of them remained. She hated the awkwardness. At least they'd had some sort of relationship before all of this. It had been tense at times, and they'd often been working toward opposing goals, with the undercurrent of attraction always there, making things difficult, but it hadn't been like this.

He was so closed off, all of his defenses up, his walls

thick around his soul. Keeping her out. Keeping every-one out.

"Do you want children?" she asked, blurting it out before she had a chance to censor herself.

"I need children. An heir."

"But do you *want* them?"

"Do you?"

She thought about it—really thought about it for the first time—about what she would choose if there was no one involved but herself and the man she loved. What it would be like to hold a child in her arms, a baby. The only baby she'd ever held was her niece. She was so perfect, a little mix of Max and Alison. Would their baby be the same? A mix of the two of them? It made her heart tighten, made tears well up in her eyes.

"Yes," she said, knowing it was true. "I had always taken it for granted before that I would but…yes, I do. Even if I weren't in the position I'm in, I would want them."

He didn't respond, he only lowered his eyes to the documents that were in front of him.

"You wouldn't, would you?" she asked, feeling a heavy sickness settle in her stomach.

"I do not want a wife. Why would I want a child?" His voice was hard, cold.

"So if we do have a baby…you won't love him?"

"I will give what I have, Isabella. No child of mine will be neglected."

"Of course," she said slowly, hearing the bitterness creeping into her tone. "You would do your duty. As you always do."

"At least I will do that. Many men do not."

"But is it enough if your relationship with your father is

only there because he feels he has to give it to you?" She knew it wasn't enough from a fiancé, from a husband.

"You're borrowing trouble. There is no child yet."

"But there will be, Adham. We're going to have a family together, and I have a right to know how you see that family in your mind."

He said nothing for a long moment, clenching his fists tightly, like he did when he was grappling with his control. "I wish that I could offer you more."

"You could."

"No, Isabella. I lost that ability long ago. That's what life experience can do to you. It hardens you. You simply haven't been through enough to know that yet."

"You're doing a wonderful job of making sure I reach that point," she said acidly, rising from her chair and exiting the room, her heart pounding in her chest.

She wanted to scream, wanted to run into the solitude of the desert and hurl obscenities at the sky. Why did there have to be such a painful distance between herself and the man she was supposed to marry? The man she loved.

It seemed cruel that in a room full of strangers she could connect, could laugh with them, talk with them, and yet the one man she could not reach was Adham. There was a war raging inside him. She felt it—felt the struggle, the tension in his body whenever they were near each other. She didn't know what he was fighting, and she had even less of an idea of who would win.

But if she could have nothing else she would find a connection with him again. She couldn't stand him being a stranger anymore. She couldn't stand that moment of connection, that moment when he'd been inside her, been one with her, to be nothing more than a distant memory.

She needed more than that. From her marriage. From life. There were choices in her life that had been made for her, things that were out of her control, but she would not let her relationship with her future husband be one of them.

The household was still when Isabella crept from her room that night. The staff had left long ago, the guards that were standing sentry outside silent and out of sight.

She had managed to get directions to Adham's chambers from one of the maids—which had been embarrassing, since the other woman had clearly been shocked that Isabella didn't already know the location of her fiancé's bedroom.

She wrapped her robe more tightly around her body, holding it against her skin like a shield. She was mostly bare beneath it, the only covering under the terrycloth the sheerest bra and panties set she'd bought while she was in Paris.

Pushing the bedroom door open, she walked in and took a deep breath, clenching her hands tight, trying to stop the shaking. The only thing she really feared was his rejection.

"Adham."

That voice—husky and sensual, so sexy—called out to him in his sleep, penetrated his dreams. Adham rolled over and froze. She was there, standing by the door, the pale moonlight bathing her body in a silver glow. Her white robe was bright in the light, and he could see clearly as she unfastened the belt and then shrugged it off her shoulders, letting it fall to the floor, pooling at her feet, leaving herself nearly naked to his gaze.

Even in the dim light he could see the faint shadow

of lacy lingerie, and beneath that the darker shade of her nipples and the curls that covered her feminine mound.

His heart-rate increased. His body was instantly, painfully hard. When she moved forward, those hips swaying, her perfect body moving with such feminine elegance, his whole body burned with a need so acute his teeth ached.

"Bella," he grated.

"Adham," she said again, her voice enough to make his shaft jump. "I need you."

He needed *her*. He had no idea how it had become so. Yes, he needed her in a physical sense, but suddenly it felt like more. It was almost impossible to keep himself in the bed, to keep from getting up and taking her in his arms, holding her to him.

"What happened between us…I know it was wrong. I know why you haven't touched me since. I do understand what a betrayal it was for you. The fault was with me." Her voice sounded thicker now. "But that's behind us now. It has to be. We're getting married. We're the ones who are trying to make a better future for our people. We can't have that night standing between us."

She reached behind her back and her bra straps slid down her shoulders, down her arms, revealing her full breasts. He gripped the sheets, willing himself to stay where he was. He wanted to watch her, wanted to let her lead. A first for him, but he was captivated by her, held captive by his desire for her.

"So, I want us to start again." She gripped the sides of her thong and shimmied out of it, dropping it onto the floor with her bra. And she was naked in front of him, her body, so lush and womanly, the most perfect sight he could imagine.

She put her knee on the bed, then brought her other

leg up so that she was kneeling before him, still out of his reach, but close enough that he could smell her scent. Floral and female, uniquely Isabella.

She gripped the edge of the sheet, pulled it toward her until it slid away from his body, revealing just how much he desired her. Her eyes rounded, her lips parting.

"I didn't get to see you the first time. Not really." She moved forward, her movements more awkward now, but he found that just as sexy.

She wrapped her hand around his erection, a small sound escaping her lips. He couldn't hold back the groan that rumbled in his chest. Her hands were so soft, and she looked so wicked and tempting that he was afraid he might not be able to hold back, that he might end things then and there.

She moved her thumb along his shaft, the motion unpracticed but even more erotic because of it.

"I want…" she began, but her voice deserted her for a moment. "I want to be in control this time."

She leaned forward, flicking her tongue lightly over the head of his penis. He gripped the sheets tighter, the breath hissing through his teeth. He should stop her. He would. *Soon.*

"I've been wanting to do that," she whispered.

Leaning in again, she continued to give him attention with her mouth, her exploration growing bolder as she continued, her noises of pleasure mingling with his.

"Bella," he ground out, feeling the first shiver of orgasm rack his body. "Stop. Now. I can't hold back."

She didn't stop, and he didn't possess enough willpower to make her. He could only wind his fingers through her hair as she continued, taking him deep into her mouth, the moist heat surrounding him, pushing him over into the abyss, waves of pleasure coursing through him, sending molten heat through his veins.

Isabella raised her head, situating herself so that her head rested on his stomach, her glossy black hair spilling over his chest as she moved her hand idly over the ridges of his abdominal muscles, over the hard, smooth flesh, scarred in places, but still so beautiful to her. So alive.

She could feel his heart raging, could tell by the fine sheen of sweat on his body how intensely he had been affected by what had just passed between them. She felt as if she had just won a small victory. For a few moments she had held the control, had made him shake with need, had pushed him over into that place where there was nothing but pleasure, nothing but the moment.

"Come here," he said, his voice husky.

She levered herself up so that her face was even with his, and he cupped her chin, kissed her deeply on the lips before reversing their position so that she was on her back, vulnerable to him now.

His eyes were hot, his pulse beating rapidly at the base of his neck, and she could feel his body hardening again.

Her eyes widened. "You can't be ready again already. I took biology classes, so I do know some things."

He chuckled, a wicked grin spreading across his face. He looked younger, more carefree than she'd ever seen him look, and, even as aroused as she was, she felt tears gather in her eyes.

"Give me a few more minutes," he said, "I'm not quite there yet."

"Then what...? *Oh!*" She let her head fall back onto the pillow as he closed his lips over the tip of her breast, sucking it hard into his mouth.

He pulled away, blowing lightly on her damp skin,

making her nipple harden painfully, before moving down, kissing the rounded curve of her breast, her ribs, her stomach, the tender spot just beneath her belly button.

His teeth grazed her hipbone lightly, the tiny sting of pain mingled with the pleasure roaring through her body was so erotic that she felt the first wave of orgasm begin to rise up, her internal muscles pulsing, ready for his possession.

"Adham," she breathed, reaching for his shoulders, trying to bring him up so that she could kiss him, so that she could have him inside her.

"Not yet, *amira*," he said, parting her legs, pressing a hot kiss to her inner thigh.

She shivered, her body anticipating the touch of his mouth to her most sensitive spot even before he made the move.

When the heat of his tongue did touch her there, sweeping over her clitoris, she arched beneath him, a sharp cry escaping her lips. Was this what he'd felt when she'd done it to him? So helpless and shaky? Desperate for release and feeling as if she was standing on the edge of a cliff?

He pleasured her that way until her entire body was rocking with wave after wave of pleasure, crashing through her, leaving her spent and breathless.

"Was it that good for you?" she asked, her words labored as she tried to catch her breath.

"Better."

"That's impossible."

She was rewarded with another dark chuckle as he moved to take her lips in a searing kiss.

"Now," she pleaded, another climax building inside of her. "Please."

He wrapped his arms around her waist and brought

her down so that she was on top of him, straddling him. He gripped her buttocks with his big hands as he moved her into position, so that his hardness was nudging the entrance of her body.

She sighed as he stretched her, filled her. There was no pain this time, only pleasure so deep, so intense, it seemed impossible for her body to accommodate it.

They moved together, their breathing building in a staccato rhythm, their sighs of ecstasy filling the air, and when they reached the summit this time they went over together.

"I love you." The words fell from her lips with ease, straight from her heart. And even though she hadn't intended to say them she wouldn't call them back. She did love him. With everything she had. He had made her who she was. He had helped her become a woman—not because he'd taken her virginity, but because he had shown her the importance of putting others before herself, the importance of living for more than her own happiness.

He had made her complete. And if he never loved her in return, she would survive. She could never be sorry that she loved him. He was good, strong, the most wonderful man she'd ever known.

Isabella rested her head on his chest, her cheek pressed against the place where his heart was beating, fast and ragged. Her body was satisfied, but her heart wanted to weep with the need to feel as though it had mattered to him, affected him, put a crack in those walls that surrounded him.

She looked at him, at his face, and saw his expression unguarded for the first time. Raw. Confused. And if he had been any other man she might have thought she saw fear there too.

She put her hand on his cheek, moved in to kiss him, but he derailed her, drawing her to him, wrapping her in his embrace and bringing her to rest again on his chest. It was a caring gesture…or at least it appeared to be. But she knew it was his way of regaining control. Of avoiding conversation.

So she let him. And he didn't seem to notice the warm tears that fell from her cheeks onto his bare skin.

His arms were tight around her, but as close as he held her, her breasts crushed to his bare chest, she felt there was a gulf between them. A gulf that was there by his design.

Desperate to find some closeness, a connection, she pressed a kiss to the scar that bisected his pectoral, the light dusting of hair tickling her lips. He stiffened, his muscles locking tight.

"I think it would be best if you went back to your own room, *amira*."

She looked up at him, at his face, closed off and cold. It seemed to come so easily to him. How did he do it? She was rocked to her core, her entire world tilted off of its axis, and he was detached.

Maybe he was right. Maybe he couldn't love. But she had a hard time believing that. He was the best man she had ever known. A man who put others before himself constantly. He had sacrificed his life for his country, continued to do so even now that he was the High Sheikh.

But for all of the goodness in him he was so hard, so damaged, she feared she would never reach his heart. She wanted to. She wanted to tear away those barriers if she had to do it with her bare hands, if she had to dig until her fingers bled. She wanted to reach him. Wanted to find the man beneath all the protective layers.

She wanted to heal him, but he didn't even realize that he was wounded.

"Did I do something wrong?" she asked, sitting up, not bothering to cover her breasts. It was pointless now. She'd already given him so much more than her body that her nudity was the least of her concerns.

"I do not want any of the staff to find you here."

"I don't care."

"Maybe honor and tradition mean nothing to you—"

"That isn't fair, Adham." She climbed out of the bed, unable to be close to him when she felt so angry. "I wasn't alone that night."

"I didn't mention that night."

"But that's what this is about. That's what all of it is about."

"You were the one who said you wanted it put behind us. Yet you bring it up now, when that it suits you to fight."

She wanted to scream in frustration. "Well, maybe I don't know how to handle this. *Any* of this. I'm so...I'm confused. And we just...we just shared that incredible experience and you want me to *leave*!"

His jaw tightened, and there was a dangerous glint in his dark eyes. "Just go, Isabella."

"You can't order me around. I thought you'd learned that by now."

He stood from the bed too, not bothering to cover his body either. His naked physique was enough to make her feel hot, even as angry as she was.

"You are still so young," he said. "You take everything personally, make it about you. I am guarding your reputation. A virgin princess is expected, required by the more traditional citizens of my country, and I will not bring shame to them with ugly rumors of their Sheikha.

Staff are only so loyal when money is offered to give up salacious secrets."

"But we're getting married. It isn't as though—"

"As though we slept together while you were engaged to marry my brother? Do not think we have escaped those sorts of rumors. It is one reason we have stayed here rather than returning to Maljadeed. The press in the city is rabid, and gossip is flying everywhere. Hassan has been open about his desire to marry for love, but our relationship is a source of great interest. I mean to protect your reputation."

"Maybe I don't need you to protect my reputation," she flung out carelessly.

"You feel too much, Bella, with too much passion," he grated.

"And you feel nothing."

He turned away from her, his high cheekbones, the square shape of his jaw highlighted by the moon filtering through the window. "It is better that way."

"I don't think it is."

She swooped down and picked her robe up from the floor, embarrassment hitting as she tugged it on. Somehow dressing in front of him and making the walk of shame out of his bedroom felt much more shameful than disrobing for him had.

But to her it had been an act of love, and to him it had been nothing but satisfying his libido.

It was a strange thing how after sharing that kind of closeness with him she seemed to feel more disconnected in the aftermath.

"That's just more evidence of how naive you are," he said, his voice hard, unyielding.

"I'm not naive, Adham," she said, her voice shaking.

"You've done a very good job of ensuring that I didn't remain that way."

She turned and stalked from the room and Adham watched her go, his heart tight in his chest. She was right. He was ensuring she was no longer naive. He was taking everything that was beautiful in her and destroying it. Poisoning it with the ugliness that tainted his life.

And yet there was no other course of action he could take but to keep her with him. She was to be the Sheikha of Umarah—his wife. She had already proven more effective than him at matters of diplomacy. And it would cost her.

That realization sent a shaft of burning pain through his chest more severe than he could ever remember feeling before. He had been numb there for so long he hadn't imagined himself capable of experiencing that level of feeling. Not anymore.

But Isabella…she made him feel.

I love you.

It was easy to dismiss her declaration. She was young. He was her first lover. And yet, as easy as it would be to use those things to discredit her, the passion, the conviction in her voice, had hit him square in the chest.

He had been shot. Multiple times. Her words had held no less impact than a bullet. They even burned the same.

He didn't want it to burn. He didn't want to feel anything.

Emotions couldn't be trusted. His people needed a leader—someone who led with his head, not his heart.

He had watched his mother lead with her heart, had watched her lose her life because of it. And he had lost her. He would not allow something to hold such sway over him that he would act so recklessly—not when other people needed him. As he and Hassan had needed her.

His chest ached. He ignored it. He could not afford this weakness. Not now. Not ever.

CHAPTER TWELVE

THERE were always reasons for Adham to avoid her in the weeks leading up to the wedding. He had many matters of state to handle, many press conferences and meetings with world leaders. And she was kept busy as well.

Being a sheikha was different than being a princess. In Turan she had done very little in the way of public service, but here there was an endless supply of things to do. She visited hospitals and listened to their needs, then met with the budget committee to discuss providing mobile medical units for the people who lived and worked out in the desert.

She was able to sit in on meetings with the education council and talk about the needs and concerns of the tribe she had met, was able to make it personal. She was making the most of her destiny even if her forced groom didn't seem to want to be around her.

And now the wedding was tomorrow, and the entire capital city was gearing up for a massive celebration.

They had arrived back in Maljadeed that morning. Adham had been on the phone the entire flight over, avoiding her as best he could in the luxurious cabin of the private plane.

Would he continue to be like this even after the wedding? She hoped not. They did have an heir to conceive after all. She'd found out weeks ago that neither of their times together had gotten her pregnant. But she wanted more than his child, anyway.

She ached for him, body and spirit, missed him with an intensity that took her breath away. But he was so guarded, so closed off, it seemed there was no way to reach him.

She looked down out of the window of her bedroom. Lanterns were being strung in the garden, cords woven together to create a tapestry of light over the lush landscape. It was beautiful, exotic. It was actually the wedding she would have chosen for herself.

Not simply because of the décor, because of the man. For a while she would put aside the knowledge that Adham did not love or want her and simply picture the man of her dreams standing at the head of the aisle, waiting for her, waiting for them to be joined as man and wife. For now reality could take care of itself, and she would hold onto that one image.

There was a sharp knock on the door of her room and she turned quickly. "Come in."

Her heart descended into her stomach when Adham walked through the door. She had seen him so rarely that the sight of him now sent her pulse racing. Although she knew that even if she had spent all of her time in the past two months with him she would still feel that way each time she saw him. She would never grow tired of him. Of that perfect scarred face that spoke of his bravery, his honor.

In that moment she loved him so much her whole being ached with it.

"I wasn't expecting to see you until tomorrow," she said, feeling her throat tighten, her breasts grow heavy with need.

"I have something for you." He lifted his hand and revealed a small blue box with a round brass pull on top. It reminded her of the door in Paris—the one she'd taken the picture of. She frowned and lifted the lid, her mouth dropping open when she saw the ring that was nestled in ivory silk.

She pulled the ring out and held it up, letting the late afternoon sun play across the jewels. "This is perfect," she breathed.

Tears stung her eyes as she examined the exquisitely designed piece. The lattice pattern of the platinum mirrored the Eiffel Tower, while the blue gems that were set next to the pear-shaped diamond were the same shade as the box, and her door. It was more than a ring. It was a small piece of her time with Adham. A bit of their history. This really was for her, really from him.

She held it out to him, her hand unsteady.

"Try it on," he said, his voice hard. "See if it fits as it should."

She frowned. She had expected him to put it on for her. She hadn't thought he would get on his knees—not a man like Adham, not for a marriage like theirs—but she had thought he would at least slide it onto her finger for her.

But he didn't. He only stood there, looking at her with no emotion evident in his dark eyes.

She put it on quickly, relieved when it went on easily. "Perfect," she said again, her smile forced now.

"There is a wedding band that had been made to go with it, but you will get that tomorrow."

She nodded, biting her lower lip. "Yes, okay."

It was his turn to frown. "I still haven't made you happy."

She tried harder to force the smile. "You have. I love it."

"You're crying."

She touched her cheek and her hand came away wet. "I…" There was nothing she could say. Not without sounding like a contrary female. And, truthfully, she *felt* like a contrary female. She had made such an issue over the ring, but now the ring wasn't enough. What she wanted was his love, and she didn't have it.

For one moment, seeing the ring, seeing everything that had gone into it, she had hoped. But then she'd seen his face, and her hope had dried up like water in the desert.

"Because it's so beautiful," she said, lying. He had his protection in place. She needed some too.

"I'm glad you're happy."

"Are you?"

"I am pleased that we are doing such a positive thing for our countries."

As romantic words went, they wouldn't win any awards.

I love you.

She wanted to say it. Wanted so badly to tell him how much he meant to her. But she couldn't. She had already said it once. Already faced his absolute indifference to it. He hadn't been angry, hadn't responded in kind, he had simply ignored her declaration. She couldn't face that again.

"I'll see you tomorrow," she said softly, needing him to go now. She couldn't be with him and not want to be in his arms. She couldn't stay with him like this and not tell him how much he meant to her. How she loved him more than anything.

He nodded. "Tomorrow."

She almost said it again. And if he hadn't looked like a man who was headed toward his execution she would have. Instead she waited until the door closed behind him and more tears spilled down her cheeks.

"I love you."

The last of the wedding guests were spilling out into the streets, the celebration continuing even as the palace staff began to clean up after the reception dinner.

The country was happy with its new High Sheikh, and just as happy with his new Sheikha.

Isabella's family had come. It had been wonderful to see Maximo and Alison, and their beautiful daughter. Her relationship with her brother and his wife was always easy. It had been her parents she'd been dreading. But they had been pleasant—happy, even. Likely because the deal was sealed, the contract fulfilled. Not even *she* could mess it up now.

Of course she wouldn't leave. She loved her new country, her new people. Her new husband. Her heart was here, as well as her duty.

Adham had been so handsome, the best looking groom she'd ever seen, in his loose white tunic and linen pants—a compromise between Eastern and Western fashion, as had been her cream wedding gown, with its intricate copper beading and loose, draping fabric that complemented her curves without clinging too much to them.

She had been involved in the design of her dress, which she had appreciated. She wondered if Adham had seen to that.

She closed her eyes, remembering the moment when she had walked down the aisle, when she had seen him and he had seen her for the first time. She had seen it again. That heat, the desire that had been absent from his eyes lately. He had not been able to hide it from her, not then. And when he had taken her hand in his their eyes had met, and she'd been shocked that neither of them were singed by the crack of electricity that had raced through them.

She had been filled with certainty in that moment. Now...now it had faded.

Now that she was in her room again, waiting for her husband. Waiting for her wedding night. She wasn't even certain he would come. He had been stoic at the wedding, and thanks to Umarahn customs, which did not call for the bride and groom to dance together, hadn't spent any time with her at the reception.

She wished not for the first time that she could simply read his mind. That she could know everything that went on behind that mask he put up, that wall he kept between himself and the world.

Maybe he was right and there was nothing but more rock beyond it. But maybe there was more. She believed it. She had to.

She sat on the bed, her wedding dress spread out around her. She hadn't changed because he'd seemed to like the gown so much, but now she was getting hot and itchy after hours wearing the intricate creation.

Another hour went by before she realized Adham wasn't coming to her.

She wanted to curl up and sob her heart out, to release all of her tears in the privacy of her room so that no one, especially not Adham, would ever know how much anguish she felt in that moment.

Life is simpler if you just ask for what you want.

He'd said that. And he was right. She could stay here and dissolve, give in to her tears, or she could go and get what she wanted. The Isabella who had run away from her brother's villa would have stayed in her room and wept. She might even have run away again.

But the woman she was now wouldn't do either of those things. And he was a part of making her who she was now, so he would just have to deal with it.

She opened the door to her room and walked down the hall, her bare feet not making any sound on the cold marble. She had done this before, snuck into his room at night, and then he had taken her body but ignored her love. He wouldn't ignore it tonight. She wouldn't let him.

She opened the door without knocking. Adham was standing by the window, his chest bare, the linen pants he'd worn at the wedding slung low on his hips, revealing his perfect body, his chiseled abs, trim waist and lean hips. Her heart bumped against her chest and her body ached with desire.

She shook her head. Later. There would be time for that later.

"Hi," she said, not knowing what else to say. And as greetings went it was harmless enough.

A breeze came in through the open window, ruffling his dark hair, and her heart clenched tight. She loved him so much.

Earlier, her only thought had been protecting herself, but now she realized something, watching him, looking at the guarded expression on his handsome face. She couldn't protect herself anymore. Not if she wanted him to open up to her. She had to be willing to lay herself bare to him, to put her own heart on the line, if she wanted him to be able to do the same someday.

"Adham...I love you."

He jerked back as though she'd struck him. "Bella..."

"No. Don't. Don't tell me I don't, or that I can't, because I do."

"Bella, this isn't what I want from you."

"It doesn't matter. It's the truth. I love you. Because you are the most honorable man I have ever known. Because you taught me what was important in life. Because you took me to Printemps, and took my picture in front of the Eiffel Tower."

"You don't know me," he said roughly. "Not really."

"I do."

He turned to her, his expression fierce. He walked toward her, stopping when he was close enough for her to reach out and touch. "Do not make me into some romantic paragon. I've killed men, Isabella. It doesn't matter what the reason was. There is blood on my hands."

She reached out, took his hand in hers, ran her fingers over his palm. "I don't see it."

"I do," he ground out.

She raised his hand and pressed a kiss to it. "I know that your hands have been gentle with me."

He pulled away then, the pain in his eyes apparent for a brief moment before he brought the shutters down again. "Stop," he said, his voice strangled.

"I'm being honest with you because I think it's important. I love you, Adham."

"Then I will be honest with you," he said. "I don't want you to love me."

She hadn't expected that. Not in all of the scenarios she'd played out in her mind had she expected that.

"I don't believe that. What about this?" She held her hand out to him, showed him her precious ring, the one that had been designed and crafted with such care. "This means something. I know it does."

He shook his head, his throat moving up and down. "It is just a ring."

"Not to me. I love you. You can't kill the love that I have for you. You can't make it so I don't feel it." Strength, love, desire, pain, all rolled through her body. Her heart was pounding fast and hard. "You taught me to be strong. You taught me about the importance of duty. And, I know you didn't mean to, but you've also taught me about love, about desire. So you have to deal with who I am because you were a part of making me. And I'm not backing down. I know you hate it, Adham, but you can't control the way I feel about you."

"Go, Isabella."

"What?"

"Get out. I don't want your love. I don't want you."

Her heart squeezed tight, and her lungs felt caved in, as though she couldn't breathe. "I…"

And that was when she was sure she saw fear in Adham al bin Sudar's eyes. Her warrior husband was genuinely afraid. Of her. Of her feelings. Of what they might mean to him, do to him. She remembered what he'd said about his mother—how her love for his father had made her act recklessly, how it had stolen her from him. And she knew he saw anything that had the power to control a person as a weakness.

"You're afraid, Adham. You're afraid of what you can't control, and you know that you can't tame an emotion as strong as love. You think it makes you weak, but it doesn't. I'm stronger because I love you. I'm stronger than you are because I'm not afraid, even though it hurts."

She inclined her head and turned, walking away from him, her heart feeling as though it was slowly cracking, breaking into thousands of tiny pieces.

"Where are you going?" he asked, when she reached the door.

"If you don't want me here, Adham, I won't stay." And she closed the door behind her and went back to her own room.

Adham's feet pounded on the desert sand. The night air was cold and dry in his lungs as he tried to force himself into a state of exhaustion that was strong enough to erase the last few moments of his life.

She had said he could not stop her from loving him, but he was certain that he had. The look in her eyes before she'd turned away from him had been so bleak, so desolate, he had felt the pain—her pain—reach into him and grab his heart from his chest.

She had taken it with her. But then, he suspected that Isabella had had his heart long before tonight.

And he had hurt her. He had told her the ring meant nothing. The ring…it was everything. The act of creating the design, of working with the jeweler to come up with the perfect thing for her… He had wanted so badly to remain distant from it, but it had been impossible. So he had poured everything into that design, had hoped it would get those memories, those feelings, out of him.

If anything, they had grown stronger.

He stopped and leaned forward, gripping his shins, trying to catch his breath. He didn't know how far he'd run, only that he had been desperate to drive every rational thought from his mind. It was impossible, though. No matter how hard he tried, he could only see Isabella.

She was in him. A part of him. What he felt for her was more powerful than anything he could ever remember feeling in his life. And she was right. It did terrify him. To his core.

He had faced down men holding guns, had been forced to make split-second decisions to save his life, had endured torture, and this was more frightening than any of that. To let someone mean so much to him...

Losing his parents—his mother, especially—had been so altering, so destructive to him. If not for Hassan, if not for the fact that he'd been able to pour all of his anger into protecting his brother, his country, he did not know that he would have survived it.

What would happen if he lost Isabella? Did he even know how to give her love? He had spent so many years traveling, working, burying himself in his sense of duty and honor so he didn't have to deal with real relationships. He didn't know if he would have any idea of how to open himself up now—not when he'd spent so long shutting himself down.

And she didn't deserve that. She deserved better than him. She deserved a man who had never been forced to choose between his life and the life of another man. She deserved someone who had not been so scarred by tragedy, both inside and out. Life hadn't touched her. She was beautiful. Pure and perfect. And being with him... he was afraid he might damage her in some way.

He heard the pounding of rotor blades as a helicopter flew overhead, away from the palace toward the city.

Bella.

What if she had gone? He had told her to go. He had not meant for her to leave, but he had said it. And he had hurt her. But if she left...if she left him...

He let out a fierce growl of desperation and turned back to the palace, running as though the very devil was at his heels, her name pounding in his mind in time with his footfalls.

He could not lose her. He needed her.

His heart thundered in his chest as he ran, each beat putting a crack in the protective stone until it fell away completely, leaving him raw and exposed, vulnerable. And he could feel. He could feel everything. There was no protection, no numbness, no buffer against himself and his emotions.

The pain was intense, the feeling of loss so over-whelming it stole his already shortened breath. And with that there was something else—an emotion that made him feel as though his heart might burst straight from his chest because he didn't think it could be contained inside him. It was too big, too much.

When he reached the wall of the palace he pressed in the key code and went in through the back door, hurrying quickly inside and moving around through the garden so that he could access one of the entrances near the bedchambers.

He slipped inside into Isabella's room. It was empty. The bed pristine, untouched. He saw a small dark shape on the center of the bed and he bent down to look at it. It was the ring box. And in it was the ring, along with the wedding band.

Despair gripped him. He had driven her away. He had finally done it. All of the times he had tried to rid himself of her, if not physically then emotionally, and now that he knew he needed her he had finally succeeded.

He needed her. His lovely Bella. His wife. She had shown him so many things, had taught him to see the world with new eyes. With her, things were beautiful again, fresh. He saw hope, goodness, where before he had seen nothing but the evil of the world.

She had said he had helped her become the person she was, that he had helped her grow up. But she had fixed him. Had helped him find redemption. Had pulled him from the mire he had been stuck in, from that dark hopelessness he had grown so accustomed to. He had not even realized how much he needed to be saved.

And still, in the end, he had lost her.

He picked up the box and walked outside, into the gardens. The sun was rising now; golden light shining over the palace walls, mist rising off the small pond that helped provide a cool respite from the midday heat.

He walked along the edge of it, aimless, directionless for the first time in his memory. The pain in his chest was blinding, agonizing. But he felt it.

Then he saw her. Sitting there in the midst of the garden on one of the benches, her hands folded in her lap, her cheeks wet with tears, her shoulders shaking as she sobbed.

The rose-gold light was shining on her, creating a halo around her dark hair, casting an angelic glow on her beautiful face. His wife. His love.

He loved her.

The realization staggered him. Was enough to bring him to his knees.

He walked toward her, and then he did go down on his knees, placing the ring box on the stone bench, taking her small, soft hands in his rough, scarred ones.

"Bella," he said, feeling his throat tighten, "I thought you'd left me."

She bit her lip to hold back a sob and shook her head. "No. I told you I wouldn't."

"But I said… I should not have said I didn't want you, Bella. It was a lie." He brought her hands up to his lips, pressed them against his mouth before speaking again. "And you were right. I was afraid. I was afraid of what loving you would do to me. I was afraid of what touching you would do to me. I thought it was a weakness in me that made me unable to control myself with you. But you are right. Love is not weak. Love is strong. My mother was brave. She did what she felt she had to do. I didn't see it before. I didn't understand. I do now. What she felt was beyond rational thought, beyond duty. Love is above any of those things. You helped me see that. Your strength humbles me, Bella. You're stronger than I am."

She let out a watery laugh. "No, I'm not. I'm a mess."

"Your strength inspires me," he said, raising his hand so that he could cup her cheek. "I feel as though I'm alive again for the first time since my parents died. I hadn't realized how much of myself I let die with them. Now it's like…like seeing in color when I had no clue I'd only been seeing in black and white. I love you, Sheikha Isabella Rossi al bin Sudar."

She laughed, and a tear spilled down her cheek. "That's a mouthful."

"Yes, it is, but I love saying it."

"I love *you*, Adham. I love you so much. I'm so glad I didn't check the peephole when you knocked on my hotel room door."

A hoarse chuckle escaped his lips. "I am too." He leaned in and pressed a kiss to her lips, and when he pulled away she reached forward and brushed her fingers over his cheek, wiping away moisture he hadn't realized was there.

"I love you," he whispered again. Now that he could say it, now that he knew it was true, he would never stop telling her. "I want you to know that if there was no marriage contract you would still be the woman I chose. I am not whole without you. You are my other half. I realize now that I could never have let you marry another man."

Her eyes widened. "Not even if it violated your duty?"

"Not even if it did. There is nothing greater than my love for you."

Marriage Made on Paper

MAISEY YATES

CHAPTER ONE

LILY FORD wasn't thrilled to see Gage Forrester standing in her office, leaning over her desk, his large masculine hands clasping the edge, his scent teasing her, making her heart beat at an accelerated pace. *She* wasn't thrilled to see Gage, the man who had turned her down, but her body seemed to be on a different wavelength.

"I heard that Jeff Campbell hired your company," he said, leaning in a little more, his shoulder muscles rolling forward. He certainly didn't spend all of his time behind a desk in a corporate office. A physique like that didn't happen by accident. She knew that from personal experience.

It took her four evenings a week in the gym to combat the effects of her mostly sedentary job. But it was important. Image counted for a lot, and it was her job to keep the images of her clients sparkling clean in the public eye. She felt that if her own image wasn't up to par she would lose her credibility.

"You heard correctly," she said, leaning back in her chair, trying to put some distance between them. Trying to feel as if she had some measure of control. It was her office, darn it. He had no call coming in here and trying to assume authority.

But then, men like Gage operated that way. They came, they saw, they conquered the female.

Not this female.

"So, are you here to offer me congratulations?" she asked sweetly.

"No, I'm here to offer you a contract."

That successfully shocked her into silence, which was a rare thing. "You rejected my offer to represent your company, Mr. Forrester."

"And now I'm extending you an offer."

She pursed her lips. "Does this have anything to do with the fact that Jeff Campbell is your biggest competitor?"

"I don't consider him a competitor." Gage smiled, but in his eyes she could see the glint of steel, the hardness that made him a legend in his industry. You didn't reach greatness by being soft. She knew it, she respected it. But she didn't necessarily care for Gage, or his business practices. Generally speaking, she thought that he was somewhat morally bankrupt. But an account with Forrestation Inc. would be a huge boon for her company. The biggest account she'd ever had.

"Like it or not, he is your competitor. And he's quite good at what he does. He doesn't leave half the mess for me to clean up that you would."

"Which is why he isn't really my competition. He's too politically correct, too concerned with his public image."

"It wouldn't hurt you to be more concerned with it. The endless stream of actresses and supermodels on your arm doesn't exactly give off an aura of stability. Plus you've had a series of very unpopular builds lately."

"Is this a free consultation?"

"No. I'm charging you by the half hour."

"If I remember correctly your services aren't cheap."

"They aren't. If you want cheap, you have to suffer incompetence."

He sat down on the edge of her desk and effectively threw half of her office supplies out of alignment. Annoyance coursed through her, along with the desire to reach out and straighten her stapler, which was nearly as strong as the need she suddenly felt to touch his thigh, so close to her hand now, and find out if it was as hard and muscular as it looked.

She grimaced at her own line of thinking, her train of thought irritating and confusing her. She didn't indulge in fantasies about men, she just didn't.

"That's one thing I liked about you when I interviewed you, Lily. You're confident in your skills."

"What was it you didn't like about me, Mr. Forrester? Because as you and I both know, you hired Synergy to represent your company, not me."

"I make it a practice not to hire women under a certain age. Particularly if they're attractive."

She felt her mouth fall open in shock, and she knew she looked like some sort of gasping guppy, but there was nothing she could do combat it. "That's sexist."

"Maybe. But I haven't had to deal with unwanted affections from my male personal assistant, unlike my previous PA, who fell hopelessly in love with me."

"Maybe you were imagining things. Or maybe you encouraged her." Privately, she had to admit that Gage was an attractive man, but that didn't mean that every woman under a certain age was immediately going to fall in love at first sight with him. Yet he probably believed it. Power did that to people, men especially. They started thinking of everyone as their property, like they were entitled to the slavish devotion of everyone around them.

Some men didn't even need wealth. They just needed someone weaker than they were.

She shook off the memories that were creeping in.

"I wasn't imagining it, trust me. And I never encouraged her," Gage said. "I was never interested in her. Business is business, sex is sex."

"Never the twain shall meet?"

"Exactly. To compound the matter, when I fired her she made a huge scene."

"Why did you fire her?"

One dark eyebrow shot up. "I came into the office one morning to find her perched naked on my desk in a pose that would make a centerfold blush."

Lily's mouth dropped open. "Are you serious?"

"Unfortunately, yes. But since then, I haven't hired women to work closely with me, and since then, I haven't had any other issues." He regarded her closely. "You aren't engaged or expecting a baby anytime soon, are you?"

She almost laughed. "No worries there, Mr. Forrester. I have no plans for wedding or baby in the near, or distant, future. My career is my focus."

"I've heard that said by more than one woman, more than once. But then the woman meets a man who makes her hear wedding bells, and I end up having wasted my time training someone who never intended to stay on with the company."

"If I ever hear wedding bells, Mr. Forrester, you have my guarantee that I will run in the opposite direction."

"Good."

"I still think you're sexist. Assuming that just because a woman is a…a woman…she's going to fall madly in love with you the moment she looks into your eyes, or that the moment she gets a job she's going to run off and get married and abandon everything she's worked for."

"I'm not sexist. It's called covering your bases. I don't make the same mistake twice. But I've seen the press releases you've prepared for Campbell. I've also watched his stocks go up."

"Yours have been going up, too," she added.

"That may be, but his were on their way down. The only thing that's changed is his hiring you."

She held a hand out, pretending to examine her merlot-colored nails, hoping he didn't notice the slight tremor in her fingers. "So, now you want me to go back on my contract with Mr. Campbell? It would have to be a pretty sweet offer, Mr. Forrester."

"It is." He named a figure that made her heart slam into her ribs.

She'd been working so hard, struggling to keep things going with her small public relations firm for so long the thought of all that money made her feel light-headed.

And money was only part of it. There was the notoriety, good and bad, that would come from working for Forrestation. Gage had a reputation as being a bit of a rogue, which was both appealing and frightening to investors. He took risks, sometimes at the expense of popularity, and they paid off.

Some of his larger building projects had been unpopular with a vocal minority, and while the hotel properties had been resounding successes once completed, he'd had protestors lining the streets in front of his San

Diego office building on more than one occasion. A lot of the protests were simply against any new building being built, but some of the issues had seemed understandable to Lily.

As controversial as Gage might be, he was a billionaire for a reason. And even if, sometimes, she had sympathized with the protesters, she couldn't argue with the numbers.

"Say I was interested," she said, feigning a lot more absorption in her manicure than she felt. "There's an early termination fee on my contract with Mr. Campbell."

"I'll cover it."

She blinked. "And I need an expense account."

He leaned in slightly, his scent—she was noticing it again for the second time in ten minutes—making her heart beat faster. "Done, as long as you don't consider manicures a business expense." He reached out and took her hand in his for a moment.

His hands were rough. Rougher than she imagined a man with a desk job's hands would be. It was just the right amount, though. Not too rough that having him touch her was uncomfortable. Although his skin was hot, and it made a rash of heat flare through her body, raising her core temperature at a rate that didn't seem physically possible.

She tugged her hand back, trying to seem as though his casual touch hadn't just flustered her like that. Nothing flustered her. Ever. She didn't *do* flustered. Especially not during business hours.

She cleared her throat. "I don't. Although I consider image to be an extremely important part of my job. I always present myself in a professional, polished manner. Your presentation and my presentation matter to each other. Our success is linked, which makes our business relationship very important."

"Is that your standard speech?"

She felt her cheeks heat slightly. "Yes."

"I can tell. It's very well-rehearsed. And I think I heard it during your interview."

She tightened her lips, trying to hold her temper in check. Something about Gage made her feel very shaky and almost…unpredictable. He brought her emotions very close to the surface. Emotions she was usually very good at holding down.

"Well, rehearsed or not," she said, eyes narrowed, "it's true. The better I look, the better I make you look, the more money you make. And the better you behave, the better you follow my advice, the more money you make, the more success I'll have."

"So, is this lecture your form of consent?"

"Yes," she said, not missing a beat.

"I want you to work with me personally. I don't want anyone else on your team involved with my account. It has to be you."

"I wouldn't have it any other way."

"The building project in Thailand is already controversial, which has my shareholders clutching their wallets in terror."

"And what about the Thailand project is controversial?"

"The fear that by building more resorts we're distorting local culture. That such a Westernized focus doesn't show people the real Thailand. That we're giving tourists a theme park rather than reality."

"And are you?"

He shrugged. "Does it matter to you?"

"I don't have to like you, Mr. Forrester, I just have to make sure everyone else does."

"So, even if you did have a personal problem with the project?"

"Like the wedding bells, not an issue. This is business. My business is presenting your best to the public and to your shareholders."

"I need to get the details hammered out as quickly as possible." He leaned over and picked his briefcase up from the floor, opened it and pulled out a thick stack of papers. "This is the contract. If you need anything changed, let me know and we'll discuss it. And you need to terminate your dealings with Jeff Campbell. One thing I require is that your firm no longer represent him in any capacity. Conflict of interest."

"Of course."

He looked at her, and reached across her desk, picking up her cell phone and holding it out to her.

"What? You want me to call now?"

"Time is money, or so I've heard."

She snatched the phone from his hand and dialed Jeff's number, her palms slick with sweat. She hated that he had the ability to make her lose her cool. It didn't help that Jeff Campbell had definitely been giving her the "let's make this business into pleasure" vibe. Which made terminating the contract sting just a little bit less, as the last thing she wanted to deal with was working with a man with sex on his brain.

The phone rang once before Jeff answered. "Hi, it's Lily."

Gage raised his eyebrows but didn't comment.

"I know." Jeff sounded far too pleased about it for her peace of mind, his tone of voice almost intimate. It made her skin crawl.

"I'm really sorry to have to tell you this, but I've been offered a better contract and I feel I can't afford to turn it down."

She listened while Jeff expressed his disappointment, in a very nice fashion, considering she was breaking a contract they'd drawn up a week ago. He was probably still hoping to get a date. Which was confirmed when he asked if they could meet over dinner to discuss it further.

"Sorry. I'm going to be really busy with…work. Because of the contract. The new one." Gage's blue eyes were locked on her and it was making her nervous, which she hated. Men never upset her personal balance. She never let them close enough to do that.

"There's a monetary penalty for terminating the contract," Jeff said, his voice icy now.

"I know. I was there when the addition was made and I read the contract thoroughly before I signed it." She looked at Gage, trying to judge his reaction. "But this is a business move that I feel I have to make. It's the best thing for my company."

"So ethics, fulfilling your commitments, aren't as important as money?"

Ouch. She took a breath. "It's business, Jeff. In my position you would do the same. Business is business," she said, unconsciously echoing Gage's earlier statement.

"You certainly never treated it like it was only a business arrangement." The inference and the venom in his tone shocked her. Though she knew it shouldn't. Men seemed to think a polite greeting meant she wanted to hop into bed with them. And that was their problem, not hers.

"Sorry to have given you the wrong impression," she

bit out, conscious of Gage's close study of her. "But as far as I'm concerned, yes, it was only a business arrangement. And now, it's a defunct business arrangement."

Gage took the phone from her hand, his expression far too satisfied for her liking. "Just wanted to affirm that Lily is working for me now."

And now Lily felt like a treat being fought over by two dogs, and it was not pretty. She didn't like that she was in the middle of some kind of alpha war. And the feeling was only magnified by the fact that Jeff had, apparently, assumed she was interested in him as more than just a source of income.

She could hear the tone, not the words, to Jeff's curt reply before Gage snapped her phone shut and set it back on the desk.

She stood up and rounded the desk, reckless anger coursing through her. "This is my office, Mr. Forrester. I might be working for you but I expect you to remember that."

"You're working for me, Ms. Ford, that's the bottom line, whether we're in your office or mine." His blue eyes held that steel that made him so successful.

On the outside he might seem like the kind of man who didn't take life seriously. The endless succession of models and actresses on his arms saw that he featured in the tabloids regularly, and he'd garnered a reputation as a playboy. But she knew that he hadn't reached the level of success he had without an edge of ruthlessness. He didn't often put it on show, but then, he wouldn't have to. The man radiated power. And beneath that she sensed that he had the soul of a predator. The fact that he was in her office now was proof of that.

At one time that would have intimidated her. *He* would have intimidated her. But not anymore. She was an up-and-coming player in the business world, and she wasn't going to reach her destination by backing down.

But she hadn't gotten where she was by being stupid, either, and even if she was angry beyond reason that Gage was usurping her authority in her own office, she wasn't about to spar with her brand-new boss.

"I apologize," she said, lowering the register of her voice, trying to project a calmer demeanor than she currently felt capable of projecting. "But I have to confess I'm a little bit controlling and I can be very territorial."

Gage tried to ignore the tightening in his gut. The woman practically purred when she spoke. And when she stood from her desk, she sauntered around to the other side, her walk as slinky and liquid as a cat's, her curves enough to remind him why it was so good to be a man.

She was stunning, not like the women he usually dated with their breezy West Coast manner, and their fake-and-bake tans. She was more like a museum display. Refined, elegant and partitioned off with thick velvet rope. She had Do Not Touch signs all over her, and yet, like a museum display, that made her all the more tempting.

She tilted her head and put one perfectly manicured hand on her shapely hip. Her skirt-and-jacket combo was expertly tailored to skim her curves, revealing her figure, but not in an obvious way. Her dark brown hair was twisted into a neat bun and her pale, flawless skin, rare in the sun-obsessed state of California, had just the right amount of makeup to look a bit more perfect than nature allowed.

"What are your terms?" she asked.

"My terms?"

"What do you expect from me so that I may be worthy of the somewhat exorbitant sum you're offering me?"

She had attitude, but that was a good thing. She would be dealing with the media on his behalf, and in order to do that, she was going to need a backbone of steel. She seemed eager to prove that it was firmly in place.

"If you really think the sum is exorbitant I could always offer you less."

"I could never turn down your generosity, it would be rude."

He chuckled. "Well, in the interest of good manners, by all means, accept it. As for the rest, I expect you to be on call twenty-four hours a day, seven days a week. I have projects happening all over the world in several different time zones, that means it's always business hours. That means if something happens and I need my PR specialist, you have to be available. I can't afford for you be off on a hot date."

"Your chauvinistic nature is showing again, but I assure you that nothing takes priority over my job. Not even hot dates." She quirked a dark eyebrow, her brown eyes glittering. She liked this, challenging him, he could tell. And he took it as a good sign. His last public relations specialist had cracked under the pressure in less than a year. It was a hard business, even harder in his industry and with his level of visibility in the media. The fact that Lily seemed to enjoy a little bit of friction was a good sign.

"In that case why don't you get down to the business of signing your life away to me?" he said.

A faint smile curved her berry-painted lips and she

turned to face her desk, grabbed a pen out of the holder and bent over slightly so that she could sign the contract. It was a pose she had to know was provocative. Her fitted pencil skirt cupped the round curve of her butt so snugly he couldn't help but admire the flawless shape. And she had to know that. Women always knew. No wonder Jeff Campbell had assumed she'd been making a play for him. Deluded idiot. Lily wasn't making an offer, she was out to intimidate. And on most men, he could see how it might work. But not on him.

She straightened and turned, her jaw set, her expression one of satisfied determination. She extended her hand and he took it. She shook it firmly, her dark eyes shining with triumph.

"I look forward to doing business with you, Mr. Forrester."

He laughed. "You say that now, Ms. Ford, but you haven't started the job yet."

CHAPTER TWO

THE fact that the very first thing she felt when Gage's deep, masculine voice pulled her out of the deep sleep she'd been in was a shiver of excitement, and not a pang of annoyance, was disturbing on a lot of levels, all of which she was too tired to analyze in that moment.

"It's one in the morning, Gage." Lily blinked against the blinding light radiating from the screen of her smartphone. After four months in his employ, she should know better than to be surprised by a midnight phone call.

"It's nine a.m. in England."

"And we have a crisis on our hands?" She rolled over and brushed her hair out of her face, the cool sheets from the side of the bed that had been unoccupied chilling her slightly.

"The sky isn't falling, if that's what you mean, but we have protesters lining the streets at our newest building site and I need a press release that will help cool things down."

"Now?"

"Preferably before the mob tears down the foundation of our new hotel," he bit out.

Lily sat up and swung her legs over the side of the bed, pushing the button for speakerphone and bringing up the specs of the project up on the screen. "What's the issue?"

"Environmental impact."

She studied the report. "It's a green build. Recycled materials are being used for as much of the hotel as possible, anything that isn't is being purchased locally and it's helping to stimulate local economy."

"Good. Put all of that in a press release and get it sent."

"Just a second. I was in bed. Asleep. Like a normal person," she said, sleep depravation making her grumpy.

She stood and made her way to her desk, which she had moved a mere foot away from her bed just for such occasions. Her laptop was still fired up, so she sat down, dashed off all of the necessary info and emailed it to Gage. "How's that?"

"Good," he responded a few moments later. "What do you suggest? Written or verbal?"

"Both. Call down there and see if you can speak to someone on the phone. I'll contact the local news station. Then we'll work on getting it into online editions of the papers today and print for tomorrow. That ought to defuse things, as much as possible anyway. They still might not be happy about the build in general, but if you show that you're conscientious it should go a long way in smoothing things over, at least with the general public, which is really the best you can hope for."

"You really are good," he said, that voice sending a little frisson of…something…through her again. She'd thought she would get used to him in the months since he'd walked into her office and hired her. In a lot of ways she had, but he still had the ability to throw her off balance if she wasn't prepared for him.

"I'm the best, Gage," she said sharply, "don't forget it."

"How can I? You never let me."

"I hope you mean in deed rather than word," she said archly.

"Take your pick."

"All right. I'm going to call some televisions stations and then I'm going back to bed."

"Fine, but I need you in the office by five."

She bit back a groan. "Of course." It was likely he was already at the office. Between work and dalliances with supermodels she wasn't sure if Gage Forrester ever slept.

She hung up the phone and proceeded to make her phone calls before falling back into bed. She could get two good hours before she had to be in the office.

And why did Gage's voice seem to be echoing in her mind while she tried to drift off?

She walked into Gage's office at 4:59 a.m. with two industrial-sized cups of coffee. "Thought you might need a hit," she said, setting the cup down in front of him.

He looked up from his computer screen. Annoyingly, despite the five-o'clock shadow he was sporting he looked fresh and well-rested, while she knew she had puffy eyes that were just barely made to look normal by gobs of under-eye cream.

"I definitely need a hit," he said, picking up the cup and bringing it to his lips. She couldn't help but watch him, the way his lips moved to cover the opening of the lid, the slight view of his tongue. His mouth fascinated her. Like the effect his voice seemed to have on her, she was certain she didn't want to know why his mouth fascinated her.

Well, she knew why. It was the same reason an endless stream of beautiful women were constantly on his arm. The same reason she did as much talking to the press about his personal life as she did about his professional life. Gage Forrester was one sexy man. Even she could admit that.

In theory, she liked sexy men, at least from a distance. When said sexy man was her boss, it made life a bit more complicated. It didn't really matter, though. Business was business and she had no intention of crossing any lines with him. She wasn't his type anyway. He liked party girls. The shallower, and the shorter the skirt, the better. And he definitely wasn't her type. Of course, she wasn't entirely certain what her type was as far as practical application went. Judging by her recent string of failed dates she didn't really have a type.

"How many shots?" he asked, lowering the cup.

"Quad," she answered, trying to bring her mind back into the present and away, far, far away, from his lips.

"Good. It's going to be a long day."

She sat down in the chair by his desk, pulled her notebook out of her briefcase and sat poised with a pen in her hand.

"Why do you do that?" he asked.

"Do what?"

"Take physical notes on paper. You have a million little gadgets for that kind of thing. I know because most of them were purchased with your expense account."

"This helps me commit it to memory. I always log it electronically later."

A small smile curved his lips, lips she was staring at again. She looked down at her notebook.

"The England site, how do you feel about the damage control that's been done there?"

"Great," she said. "You have a satellite interview scheduled with one of the news outlets very late tonight. Also, the written release is set to run in major newspapers tomorrow, and you spoke to the organizer of the protests personally, right?"

"Yes. Nice woman. Didn't like me very much. I think she called me a…capitalist pig."

She looked up and her heart jumped a bit. She looked back down at the lined paper of her notebook. "You kind of are."

"A rich one."

"Touché."

"I was able to explain to her the process by which we're building the hotel. I also explained, very nicely, how it would help the economy, and that, in addition to the construction workers who have work now, it would provide at least a hundred permanent positions. And the fact that it's being built on the site of what was essentially a crumbling wreck of an old manor, and not on any farmland, went over well."

"All very good," Lily said, scribbling on her notebook before reaching over to grab her coffee cup off of Gage's desk and taking a sip.

In the beginning it had seemed strange, coming in early when no one else was in the building, sitting in Gage's luxurious office, watching the sunrise, glinting off the bay, and the hundreds of boats moored in the San Diego harbor. It had almost seemed…intimate in some ways. Half the time he hadn't shaved yet when she arrived, and he would go into his private bathroom that adjoined his office and take care of it before the other staff arrived, but he didn't bother for her.

She'd never shared her mornings with a man before, so the insight into the masculine prep-for-the-day routine was an interesting one.

Then at eight his PA would arrive and Gage would brief him on the schedule for the day and Lily would go to her office. Her new office in Gage's building. She and her small crew had relocated once she'd realized the constant crosstown commute wasn't conducive to keeping tabs on her account with Forrestation, and they were essentially the only account she handled personally. Gage kept her too busy to do anything else.

"The build in Thailand is going well," he commented.

"Good."

"You've certainly managed to keep the public, and in turn, the shareholders, placated with that one."

"You're providing so many jobs for the area and the wages you pay are more than fair. It's only going to be good for the economic growth of the region. And you've certainly taken great care to keep environmental impact at a minimum. And the fact that you bought several hundred acres and had it set aside as a wildlife preserve is helpful. If you would let me announce it."

He shrugged his broad shoulders and his shirt pulled tight across his muscular chest, exposing the outline of his pectoral muscles. She looked away. "It doesn't matter to me what the vocal minority thinks. No matter how many protesters show up at a construction site, the general public still patronizes my hotels and I can still sleep at night. Anything else is an incidental. It wouldn't matter at all if weren't for the shareholders. The curse of going public."

"Why did you choose to go public then? You don't

strike me as the sort of man who likes to be account-
able to anyone."

He leaned back in his chair and pushed his dark hair
off of his forehead. "You noticed."

"Hard not to."

"I went public because it's a great way to increase
visibility. And at the time I had debts to pay off from the
start-up of the company. It helped increase my capital
immensely, and enabled me to pay off the business loans
I'd taken out."

Gage was from a fairly affluent family, that was
general knowledge. It surprised her that he'd had to
take out loans to start up his company. She'd imagined
him having full family support, both financially and
emotionally. The fact that he started the same as she
had, by herself, with nothing and no one standing by
to bail her out, made her stomach tighten.

"But now you have to play the diplomacy game," she
said.

"I would anyway. I develop resort and hotel properties, the public has to have a favorable view of me."

"That's true."

For the most part, the public *did* have a favorable
view of him. He was charismatic and charming and
dated the most eligible women in Hollywood, which
put him on the front cover of a lot of magazines and
made him very high-profile for a businessman.

He was also a slave-driving taskmaster, but only
his employees knew that. And in fairness, he never
expected anything from her that he didn't expect from
himself. In fact, he seemed to expect more from himself. Which was why, even when her phone rang at
3:00 a.m., she managed to resist hurling obscenities
at him.

"Anything else on the agenda?" she asked.

"I need a date for an event tomorrow. Fundraiser. Art gala."

"And you've misplaced your little black book?"

"No, it's in a safe somewhere so that no one can ever get their hands on it and use it for evil."

"*You* use it for evil," she said.

"On occasion. But the real issue is that none of my black book entries are suitable."

"Well that sounds like an issue of taste to me," she said. It bothered her sometimes—okay, all the time— that a man with his drive to succeed dated women who were such bubbleheads. But then, she didn't imagine he was interested in the contents of their minds.

"No, it's an issue of venue. I want you to go with me."

"What?"

"But you need something else to wear."

She narrowed her eyes. "What?"

"You're intelligent. You know how to make conversation."

"So do most women. You just tend to date women who can't talk and walk at the same time without injuring themselves."

"I didn't know you had an opinion on my choice of companion."

She gritted her teeth. "Doesn't matter, what matters is that I shield the public from the full horror of it. And what's wrong with the way I dress?"

She spent an obscene amount of money buying good quality clothing and having it tailored. She always, always, looked polished and ready for a press conference. Always. It was essential to her job and she took it very seriously.

"Nothing. If you have a business meeting. But you look more like a politician's wife than a woman I would take to a fundraiser."

"Politicians' wives go to fundraisers."

"But I'm not a politician."

"And I'm not for hire."

His dark brows locked together. "No. You're not, because I already hired you. You work for me, and if I need you I expect you to make yourself available. You signed a contract agreeing to it."

"To be your PR specialist at all hours, which is quite enough, thank you very much, not to hang on your arm at art galas."

"This is PR. I could skip the fundraiser and look like a capitalist pig with no conscience, or I could go with Shan Carter. She gave me her number the other night."

An image of the spoiled blonde heiress in her thigh-high boots and cling-wrap dress flashed before Lily's eyes.

"You can't do that," she said, all of her PR training recoiling in horror at the thought.

"I know. I didn't even need you to tell me."

"Fine. I'll go. But you're not picking my dress."

His icy gaze swept her up and down. "*You're* not."

"Why not? You've never seen me in date clothes. You don't know what my date clothes look like." She didn't own date clothes, but he didn't have to know that. She had confidence in her taste in clothes. She knew what she looked good in and she really didn't need some wafer-thin personal shopper to try and tell her what she already knew.

"All right, but no tweed."

"I don't wear tweed. Well, I have a jacket that's

tweed, but it's chic. Lycra isn't the official fabric of fashion, you know. Though I know you couldn't prove it by your dates."

He shrugged in that casual manner of his, that shrug that seemed especially designed to provoke her. "I like to have fun. I work hard. My obligations are met. I see no issue with conducting my personal life in the way I see fit."

He had a point, as much as she hated to admit it. Although she couldn't imagine why any woman in her right mind would date him. Well, that was a lie, it was obvious visually why a woman would want to date him. He was tall, broad-shouldered and perfectly built. But on a personal level, while he was smart and fun to banter with, he was also totally uncompromising when it came down to it, and she knew she could never deal with a man like that. She'd seen the kind of toll a man like that could take on a woman's life. And she'd vowed she wouldn't become like that. She wasn't letting anyone have control over her life.

Although, obviously Gage had some modicum of control over her life since he was her boss, but that was different. When a woman gave a man her body he owned a piece of her. She thought the whole thing was just entirely too unsettling. And no matter how gorgeous Gage was, it wasn't enough to erase the memories that she carried with her. Warnings. Her mother's mistakes had to count for something, otherwise they really would be a complete tragedy, and as contentious as her relationship with her mother was, she didn't want that.

"If you expect me to buy new clothes you have to give me time to shop."

"You can have the afternoon off."

She shook her head, her tight bun staying firmly in place. "Morning and afternoon. I need sleep."

"Morning to lunch hour," he countered.

"Deal."

"No black. No beige."

"It's an art gala, most of the women will be in black."

"I know, and that's exactly why I want you to wear something else."

She frowned. "I'm not in the habit of allowing men to dictate what I wear. I can choose for myself."

He stood from his desk, and she was distracted, as she always was when he surprised her like that, by the superb shape of his body. Narrow waist, broad chest. And she knew, though she was ashamed to admit it, that he also had the best butt she'd ever seen. Although she hadn't taken notice of very many men in that way before, so she didn't have much to compare to.

He raised an eyebrow. "So if your lover had a preference for lingerie you wouldn't consider that, either?"

She bit the inside of her cheek and tried to will herself not to blush. She never let men rattle her. She'd been on the receiving end of pick-up lines from cheesy to crude since she began to develop at the age of thirteen, and then, after she'd moved and started her new life, men had naturally assumed she was ready to bed-hop her way to the top of the corporate ladder. As a result, she'd assumed she'd lost the ability to blush a long time ago. Apparently not. She felt her face get hot.

She'd never worried about her lack of sexual experience. It was a choice she'd made. In the environment she'd been raised in it had been a fight to hold on to any sort of innocence, physical or psychological, and she'd been determined that no one would take it from her.

But in that moment she knew she would rather walk across broken glass than admit that no man had ever had cause to have an opinion about her lingerie.

"I have impeccable taste," she said instead, lifting her chin, trying to keep her expression smooth. Cool. Not completely flustered. "No one has ever had reason to complain." She picked her briefcase up from the floor and stood. "And neither will you." She turned on her heel and stalked out of the office, trying to ignore the thundering of her heart.

CHAPTER THREE

GAGE had never seen Lily look less than perfect. She always looked beautiful, even when she rushed into the office at two in the morning to handle some sort of media crisis. But in a dark navy blue gown with ruffled sleeves, a demure neckline and a back that dipped so low it ought to be illegal, she was stunning.

Her hair was pinned to the side so that her curls cascaded over one shoulder, and didn't cover any of the skin that was on display in the back of the gown. Her makeup was more dramatic than she usually wore to the office and her legs were bare, and on glorious show, the dress barely skimming her knees. And they were amazing legs.

Gage's libido kicked into gear, a reminder that he hadn't had sex in a very long time. But business had been intense and when he hadn't been focused on his various building projects he'd been handling Madeline's big move into her new, off-campus apartment. An apartment she hadn't wanted, because she couldn't afford it herself. But there was no way he was letting his little sister live in a dangerous part of town, not when he could afford to buy her any home she might want. But she was stubborn, and while he appreciated that aspect of her personality, it could also be a major pain. It was also time-consuming and detrimental to his sex life.

But that was why he was now standing in the foyer of the San Diego Aquarium eyeing his PR specialist's legs.

He put his hand on the curve of her bare back and he felt her jump beneath his touch. A slow smile curved his lips. He leaned in and her sweet feminine scent teased his sense. "You wore navy blue because I told you not to wear black, didn't you?"

She pursed her lips and looked to the side, her expression defiant and sexy at the same time. "Maybe."

"Because you like to challenge me without defying me outright," he said, his lips brushing her ear. He felt the small tremor that shook her body. Interesting. She wasn't as icy as she wanted him, and people in general, to believe.

"I don't want to get fired," she whispered, her dark eyes warning him to back up or lose a limb.

He frowned. He liked the feisty edge that Lily had, but she was his employee and he had no right to touch her simply because he felt an attraction. She was a good employee, and everything that made her so great to work with, made her the kind of woman he never wanted to get involved with.

He dropped his hand and studied her flawless face. She looked different out of her work suits, with her brown curls shimmering over her shoulder. Softer. Touchable.

His hands itched to do just that. To touch her petal-soft skin, to run his fingers through her hair. His body tightened in response to the thought, even as his mind rejected it.

"As if I would fire you," he said, putting distance between them. "You know too much."

"I think I might get that matted and framed. High praise indeed."

They walked into the main section of the art exhibit, which was being held in the kelp forest. The entire room was cast in a bluish glow, compliments of the massive, three-story cylindrical aquarium that made up the structure of the space. Water plants grew to impossible heights and fish wove through them. Art was placed on easels around the room, with a place to write down and submit bids next to each one of them.

Gage walked over to one of the displays and, without even glancing at the artwork, took a form and wrote an astronomical sum on it before dropping it in the box.

"You really should be less discreet when you do things like that, and when you do things like create wildlife preserves near your resort sites," she said.

"Why is that?"

"It would help your image. And you need it. 'Property developer' is kind of a tough profession to sell to the public. You could make my job easier by trumpeting charitable contributions."

He frowned. "You were a witness. Trumpet it."

"You don't want me to, though."

His jaw tensed. "Giving for the sake of your reputation is just paying for good publicity."

"Most people don't have a problem with that."

"And what's your opinion on it, Lily? And don't give me your 'my opinion doesn't matter as long as the public likes you' speech."

She bit her lip. This side of Gage always confused Lily. In some ways he seemed more uncomfortable having people know anything good about him. He didn't seem to mind the negative press that came when he dated one supermodel, then switched to an actress the next night. But he didn't seem to want to let anyone know about his good behavior. And there was something about that that made her almost like him sometimes, and that made all the other physical things he made her feel intensify.

"It's…okay, events like this are definitely a little bit fake. It's see and be seen. Most people are flashing their bids all over the place." She jerked her head toward the glittering celebrities and debutantes gathered around different pieces of art, waving their bids around while they talked.

"I don't play the game," he said. "It doesn't appeal."

"You have to play the game a little bit, Gage. It's good for business."

"What's it like for you, doing a job that's so at odds with who you are?"

The question was so strange and unexpected, she turned sharply, her mouth dropping open. "I…how is it at odds with who I am?" She knew better than most how important image was.

The Lily Ford from a Kansas trailer park, who had pulled her way from poverty and put her past far, far behind her, was not going to get anywhere in the field of public relations. She knew, she'd tried that. But the Lily Ford who knew how to present herself with icy cool dignity, the Lily who wore tailored, designer clothing and always had her hair done perfectly, *that* Lily was a success. And it had all been a matter of image.

Who she was underneath didn't matter to clients or to the public when she was making a statement. All that mattered was what they saw. That philosophy was how she made her living, and she believed it, lived it, more than anyone she'd ever come into contact with.

"You seem to value some sort of integrity. And you believe that these sorts of shows of wealth and generosity are false. But you wish I would engage in them."

She shrugged. "If the world were different, maybe these things wouldn't matter. But we're in a media-obsessed culture. That means making a good face to present to the media, and through that, the public."

"I don't like to pander to the public."

"I know you don't, but you do like to make money. And that means keeping your image favorable. Again, easier said than done for a capitalist pig like yourself."

He shot her a deadly look that she ignored.

They continued to walk through the room. She noticed how, though Gage greeted people casually, he seemed separate from them, too. He didn't really engage with people. She made her money partly by reading people, she had to have a good idea of who her clients were and what made them tick. But after four months, in a lot of ways, Gage remained a question mark. She spent nearly every day with him, but even with that, she knew very little about him personally.

The conversation they'd just had was probably the most revealing one she'd ever had with him. Otherwise it was confined to business.

Gage knew how to play the game. He said the right things to the right people, but there was nothing personal in the way he spoke to anyone. It was the first time she'd realized that even she had never seen past Gage's public persona.

A thin blonde socialite with cleavage spilling over the top of her dress grabbed Gage by the arm and beamed up at him, seemingly oblivious to the fact that Lily was standing on the other side of him.

"Gage," the blonde said breathlessly. "I'm so glad I saw you here. There's dancing out in the courtyard," she added.

She noticed that Gage didn't bother with his signature smile. "Thank you. I'll be sure to dance with my date." He hooked his arm around her waist and slid his fingers over her hip, the light touch sending heat ripping through her body. When he brought her close to his side her legs felt as if they might buckle.

She'd never in her life been affected by a man's touch like that. Of course, that could be because she rarely let men touch her. She'd watched her mother go through an endless succession of men. Men who had asked her mother to uproot them and move from one town to another, men who had berated and belittled both of them, men who had always held the control over both of their lives. Lily had never wanted that. By the time she was thirteen she'd decided that from what she'd seen of relationships she wanted nothing to do with them.

She'd finally left home at seventeen and moved to California. Ten years later she had her own business, a beautiful apartment, complete control over her own life, and still no man. She had never regretted it. Some of her friends thought she was crazy, and insisted she was missing out on one of life's fundamental experiences. But every time she agreed to go on a date with some guy her friends promised would be perfect for her, she found herself dissecting his behavior, imagined how the possessive hand on the curve of her back would change to a fist intent on controlling her once the newness of the relationship wore off. She didn't have second dates.

It was fine for her friends. Fine for other women who

hadn't seen the steady digression of a relationship over and over again.

But Gage's touch didn't make her think of being controlled. She couldn't think of anything. All she could feel was the gentle sweep of his fingers over the curve of her hip.

"Care to dance?" he asked, his lips close to her ear, her body responding so eagerly she felt certain he would be able to see just how much he was affecting her. Her breasts felt heavy and she was thankful for her moment of near-defiance in purchasing the navy blue. Hopefully it would help conceal her tightened nipples.

The blonde was giving her a glare that had the potential to turn a lesser woman to stone, and her pride only left her with one answer to give Gage. "Of course," she said.

In a moment of total madness, she reached up and touched his face, the dark stubble there scraping her palm. Her heart hammered hard, her throat suddenly dry. She dropped her hand back to her side. She'd thought about touching his face before. Fleeting moments that had invaded her thoughts while she fought for sleep at night, fantasies that had now bled over into reality. Her palm still burned.

She followed him through the hallway lined with more aquariums and out into one of the outdoor courtyards where a band was playing.

He took her hand, lacing his fingers through hers and drawing her into his body, his expression intense. Her heart was thundering in her chest now, and there was no pretending that what she felt wasn't attraction. The most acute, real, dangerous attraction she'd ever felt in her life.

"This is inappropriate," she said, horribly conscious

of the fact that her voice felt as shaky and jittery as her whole body felt.

"Would you rather I danced with Cookie?"

She snorted a laugh, then covered her mouth with the hand that had been resting on his shoulder. She lowered it when she caught her breath, not sure whether or not she should put it back on him. "That's not really her name is it?"

"It might be a nickname, I'm not sure."

"You never asked?"

"It wasn't important at the time."

That spoke volumes about the way Gage treated relationships. He avoided commitment with flings. She avoided relationships by not having romantic contact with men altogether. But they were both avoidance tactics. In that, at least, they obviously saw eye-to-eye. Relationships were overrated.

Gage put his hand on the small of her back, on her bare skin, and he felt a small shiver go through her whole body. She was feeling every bit of the attraction he was. Strange, because he had only ever seen her in her buttoned-up professional mode, now suddenly she was unbuttoned and very, very hot. Although, she'd always been hot. He'd thought more than once about uncoiling her tightly wound hair and watching the dark curls tumble down.

She shifted against him, her hip brushing his body intimately. His muscles tensed and desire roared through him, his body hardening at the accidental contact.

He drew her closer, letting her feel. Letting her know exactly what she was doing to him. He didn't hit on employees as a rule, ever. But she tempted him. And that was a new experience. Women appealed to him, and he desired them. But he'd never considered them a serious temptation. If it wasn't the right time, it was easy for him to leave his date standing on the doorstep and go home without taking her to bed. There had been a lot of times in his life when pleasure had had to be deferred due to responsibility, either because of his family or because of business. He was an expert at deferring pleasure if necessary. But this feeling, this hot surge of lust coursing through him, didn't feel like something that could be deferred or denied.

Her head jerked up, her dark eyes wide, her breath coming in short bursts. "That's definitely not appropriate," she whispered.

"Maybe not, but I'm enjoying it."

She licked her lips, the slow, sensual movement hitting him like a punch to the gut. She looked down again, not saying anything, but leaning in a little bit closer, her breasts brushing his chest.

Her eyes fluttered closed, her lips parted slightly and she swayed a bit in his arms. Then she went stiff, pulled back quickly, her brown eyes huge with shock.

"Did you make all the bids you were planning on making?" she asked, her breasts rising and falling with her labored breathing.

"Yes," he said, trying to ignore the ache of unsatisfied desire that was gnawing at him.

"Then we should go. We'll probably have another early morning."

She turned and walked back into the building. He shook his head. She was right to have stopped things, as much as his body rebelled against the admission. He valued her too much as an employee to sacrifice it for sex. Even if it would be incredibly hot sex.

He liked to keep his life compartmentalized. There

was work, there was his family life, and then there was his sex life, and he didn't combine them. Ever.

Though with the memory of her in his arms, how soft and sweet she'd felt there, how close he had come to tasting her lips, it was hard to remember why that was.

Lily couldn't sleep, and it was all Gage's fault. And hers. He'd nearly kissed her. *She'd* nearly kissed him. Curiosity. That was all it had been. The need to know what it would be like. She'd wondered about it. She wouldn't be human if she hadn't.

Gage was so much more than any other man she'd ever met. More successful, more driven. And those were things that appealed to her. But she had never felt so compelled to abandon all of her tightly held business principles for a few moments of…of…lust.

She hadn't wanted to pull away, hadn't felt like he was trying to manipulate her in any way. She'd felt… passion. For the first time in her life she'd experienced real, physical passion. She'd always felt passion for her work, a drive and a need to succeed, but that was where it had been contained.

Her body still felt hot and restless, unfulfilled.

"I don't want Gage," she told her empty bedroom. "I don't."

He was her boss. If she wanted a relationship, which she definitely didn't, it wouldn't be with him. Her job was too important to risk it by blurring personal and professional lines. It had never been an issue for her before.

Her clients had been almost exclusively men, and even when they'd shown interest, like Jeff Campbell, she hadn't been remotely tempted to accept. There was a clear line drawn in her mind. Work was work.

She clenched and unclenched her fists, trying to make the shaky feeling go away. The worst thing wasn't that Gage was her boss, it was how out of control he'd made her feel. She'd kissed men before—several of them—and the experience had ranged from completely undesirable to okay. None had lit her on fire from the inside out. But the near kiss with Gage made her feel like she was burning.

The worst thing was that she knew that if his lips had touched hers, that last shred of sanity would have turned to a vapor and any inclination she had to resist him would be gone with it. And when had she ever struggled with her willpower? She created her own destiny. She was in charge of her own life.

She let out a low growl of frustration and tossed off her covers before stalking over to her computer. If she wasn't going to get sleep, she would get work done.

She opened up her email account and clicked open the message that she knew contained her search engine alerts on Forrestation Inc. and Gage Forrester. It was important for her to keep tabs on what was being said about him so she could release a statement if necessary.

She scanned the message and her stomach dropped. She bit out a curse and picked up her phone, speed dialing Gage's number, not caring that it was three in the morning.

"Gage, we have a very serious problem."

CHAPTER FOUR

"This is garbage." Gage threw the printed papers back down on his desk, his muscles tense, his entire body wound up and ready to attack at any moment.

Hearing Maddy's voice, thick with tears on the other end of the phone a few moments before, had made him feel capable of very serious violence against the person responsible for spreading such venomous rumors.

It made him feel physically ill, seeing the article written with such foul accusations. Accusations directed at Madeline. She was doing well now, had graduated from college, was finally coming out of her shell and putting their neglectful childhood being her. She'd been such a quiet little girl, as if she was afraid to step out of line. Afraid he might abandon her, too. But she'd grown so much in the past few years, and now this threatened to destroy everything Maddy had battled so hard for.

"I agree," Lily said. "It's not news, and it's a shame we live in a culture that thinks it is. But the simple fact is that we do, and this story is going to be in every print and digital publication this morning, from respected newspaper to scandal rag."

"She doesn't need this. She's been through enough. She just graduated. It's hard enough finding a job, and she won't let me help her. Add this, and no one will hire her."

Lily sucked in a sharp breath and tugged on her suit jacket. "I know, Gage. Trust me. I'm fully aware of how hard it is to be a woman in the corporate world, and a…" She looked at him, her expression filled with distaste. "Sorry, but a sex scandal is hard to move past. For the woman, at least."

"She wasn't involved with him," Gage growled, skimming the article on the top of the stack again. "She swears she wasn't. She says he was her boss, she was doing an unpaid internship, and he came on to her. She refused to sleep with him, and now, now that his wife is leaving him because he's a lecherous old jackass, he's blaming Maddy to try and make her look like she was some kind of predatory female out to destroy their marriage, out to take him down and ruin his life."

"Regardless of whether she had a relationship with him or not…"

Gage's heart thundered harder, rage pounding through him. "She didn't."

Lily put her hands up in a gesture of surrender. "Okay, you know your sister better than I do, if you say she didn't, she didn't. But now that it's out like this…there's very little we can do to fight it. It's going to be everywhere. Even if she were to come back with her own version of the story, which I think she should do in the future no matter what, this is going to hit like an explosion. William Callahan is so high-profile…and his wife—soon to be ex-wife—is more famous than he is."

Gage was familiar with the man's trophy wife. She'd come on to him at several industry parties, and, despite the fact that she was a world-famous model whose looks had, literally, been memorialized in song, he'd never even been tempted. He didn't poach other men's wives. He didn't need to. But she was definitely open to playing around behind her husband's back, and clearly Mr. Callahan was no better. And they were trying to drag his sister into their sordid lives.

"Infamous is more like it," he bit out. "I'll ruin him for this."

"I don't blame you, Gage, I don't, but before you engage in serious ruination, we need to figure out how we're going to handle the media firestorm Madeline is about to get hit by."

Lily had met Maddy on a few occasions. She was a pretty brunette, petite and fine-boned, delicate and small, none of the height Gage had inherited passed down to her. She looked young, and in some ways seemed younger. It was obvious that Gage doted on her, and that, despite that, Madeline made an effort to be independent, which Lily completely respected.

She also understood the kind of dilemma she found herself in. It was hard for a woman to be taken seriously in business. It was hard to find the right balance. Dress up too much, men make assumptions about what you're there for…not enough and you would get torn apart by the other women.

"We can create our own distraction."

Lily narrowed her eyes. "No. I don't know what you're thinking, I just know it's probably going to create a big cleanup for me."

He shook his head. "It won't. But it will take the focus off of Maddy. If we can bury this story with one of our own, it will at least soften the blow."

"You have a valid point, but I seriously doubt you're

going to magically stumble upon something that over-shadows a scandal of this magnitude."

"I thought I might announce my impending marriage."

Her eyebrows shot up. "Marriage? You aren't getting married."

"No. But don't you think it would make a nice headline?"

She let out a completely undignified, involuntary snort. "No one would believe it."

"You don't think so?"

"No. You're not exactly the marrying kind."

"And why is that?"

"Marriage requires monogamy," she said. At least it was supposed to require monogamy. She'd witnessed all the drama that came when people strayed. Her mother had thrived on the drama, the jealousy...

"I don't cheat on women. If I'm attracted to some-one else, I end the relationship I'm in. I see no point in pretending to want one woman if I want another."

"You seem to change the woman you want with alarming frequency."

"And that's why it would be such a big story if I were preparing to get married. I've dated enough actresses and models to have serious headline appeal with the tabloids."

"Okay, yeah, I'll give you that. But where are you going to find a woman who won't want to marry you for real? One who will keep her mouth shut about the arrangement."

She looked back at Gage—his blue eyes were trained on her and a slow smile spread over his handsome face.

"Lily."

She didn't like the way he said her name, with intent, his low voice rolling over it, making it sound like a verbal caress. And it made her stomach tighten and her breasts feel heavy. Like last night. Like when he'd held her in his arms.

"I want you to marry me."

She could only stare at him. Words were failing her, which was virtually unheard-of. She always knew what to say. She always knew how to respond in every situation, quickly and efficiently, cutting if necessary. She was never speechless. Except she was now.

She opened her mouth, then shut it again, trying desperately to think of some kind of sharp, witty response. Instead she settled for simple. "Not really, though."

A short chuckle escaped his lips. "No. Not really. I just want you to be my fiancée."

"No." She shook her head. "No! Absolutely not."

"How much do you value your job, Lily?"

She locked her teeth together. "It's everything to me. I've worked very hard to get where I am."

"It would be a shame to have any of your hard work compromised, wouldn't it?"

"Yes," she bit out.

"I don't want Madeline's hard work compromised because she got tossed to the wolves. I don't want her to lose all of the progress she's made, all of the confidence she's managed to gain."

The threat, though he didn't state it explicitly, was certainly implied. If she wanted to keep her job, she had to play by his rules.

"And it has to be you," he continued. "You and I were seen together at the gala last night, and we were definitely breaching the boundaries of professionalism."

"We were well within normal boundaries of a boss

and employee attending an event together," she said, even as images of him holding her close flashed through her mind.

He raised his eyebrows. "Really? What else do you consider within normal employer-employee boundaries? Gotten engaged to any of your other bosses?"

"I haven't even agreed to get engaged to this one," she said through clenched teeth.

On a personal level, she was horrified by the idea. She didn't want to spend more time with Gage. She didn't want to pretend to be his adoring fiancée. But if she pushed that aside and looked at it objectively, she knew that this was the best way to throw the spotlight off of Madeline without completely compromising Gage's public image.

"You're right," she said finally. "I hate it when you're right."

"This will be simple for you, Lily. You're the consummate professional."

"If you think I'm going to fall for that, you're sadly delusional."

"What is that?" he asked, leaning back in his chair, hands behind his head, showing off his wonderful arm muscles. He knew.

"You're turning on the Forrester charm. It doesn't work on me," she said, even as her stomach tightened a little bit.

"All right, then forget the charm. We don't have another choice. If I go down, you go down with me. We have to fix this. If you walk away, it only gets worse for you. No one will hire you if they find out you left a client in the lurch when a massive scandal was breaking that related to his family. If you help successfully diffuse this, though…"

"I know." She would most likely be sworn to secrecy about the fine details, but she imagined she would earn herself an extremely glowing reference. And the best record for a PR specialist was, without a doubt, a smooth history with the press. More than a hint of scandal and her career was in serious danger. "Fine. Yes."

"Excellent." Gage picked up his mobile phone and punched in a number. "Dave? I need an engagement ring. I don't know." He looked at her. "What size ring do you wear?"

"A six."

"Six." He paused. "It doesn't matter. Make sure it's noticeable." He snapped the phone shut.

"Did you just call poor David at five in the morning to have him buy me a ring?"

"You already know the answer, why did you even ask?"

Annoyance rolled in her stomach, along with nerves that refused to be calmed. She flexed her fingers, imagining the weight of a ring there. His ring. It made everything in her feel jittery. It was such a symbol of ownership. Like he was marking her as his. Which was silly because they weren't in a real relationship and they were never going to be. But everything about marriage and relationships severely unnerved her, and it was hard to shake the anxiety that was coursing through her.

"I was just incredulous," she snapped.

"So, what's the story?"

Right. Work. This she could do. Create a press release, get the right spin. She was good at this. She grabbed her notebook of the desk. "We've been working together for a while. We've grown closer, friendship, then, well…more. And then you proposed last night after the gala, which is why I didn't have a ring yet. Because that detail would have been noticed."

"Good. Take care of it. The ring will be in your office in less than an hour then you can make the announcement."

She could tell by the way he was sitting, looking at her, that she was dismissed. "As proposals go," she said, unable to resist, "that one ranks right up there with a ring in the food."

"I thought women liked that," he said, his slightly amused.

"No. It gets the ring messy and if you don't find it you might break a tooth."

"I'll keep that in mind should I ever stage a real proposal."

"Do you actually plan on doing that?" she asked, not able to picture it.

"I don't plan to, no."

"I didn't think so."

"What about you? You're impervious to wedding bells, so you say, but do you have a boyfriend you're going to have to explain this to?"

"No. And even if I did, I told you when you hired me, work comes first. I was serious."

"You would ditch your boyfriend to further your career?"

"Yes," she said, without hesitation. "Don't tell me you wouldn't do the same to any of your past lovers."

"Of course I would. But most women don't see things that way."

"I'll ignore the most comment for now and just say, then maybe some women don't have a problem with someone else having so much control over their life, but I do. My career is important to me. It comes first.

If I was with someone, he would have to understand that."

"No man is going to understand you playing fiancée to someone else."

"Then I guess there isn't a right man for me," she said, smiling tightly. "Not in a permanent sense anyway." She couldn't resist adding it, because the last thing she wanted was to betray the fact that she didn't do relationships of any sort, at all, full stop, ever. And why should it matter if Gage knew? She didn't usually worry about it at all. In fact, she was extremely secure in her antirelationship status.

"I don't see there being a right woman for me in that way, either. Which, ironically, makes us perfectly compatible."

A reluctant smile tugged at her lips. "I suppose, ironically, that's very true."

"Now go, prepare a statement. We'll make a formal announcement this morning. Start calling media outlets and let them know we have a story. The more of them we can distract the better."

She nodded once. She could do this. It was her job. That was all. It was only business, nothing more, there was no reason why it would feel like anything else.

She clenched her hands into fists, trying not to imagine what the weight of the ring would feel like, then turned and went back to her office.

The frenetic energy of a press conference was usually something Lily thrived on. She loved everything about them. The noise, the chaos, the low hum of excitement that pulsed through the crowd. She was never nervous. She always knew just what she was going to say, or what her client was going to say.

But this morning, she felt as if she was going to throw up.

Gage took her hand and a flash of heat raced up through her fingers and into her whole body, warming her core, making her heart beat faster. She wished she could blame that on the press conference, but she couldn't. Gage had an unexpected, unaccountable effect on her body. One that made her feel like she was out of control, which she hated more than anything.

He tugged on her lightly and led her up the stairs and to the podium. Gage held her hand up and moved it out toward the light so that the massive ring, which she had placed on her own finger only a few minutes earlier, caught the light. The noise in the crowd quieted, everyone staring at them, their eyes expectant, hungry for a story.

"Thank you all for coming this morning," Gage said, lowering their hands. "Before any rumors started flying, we wanted to make a formal announcement. I've asked my public relations specialist, Lily Ford, to marry me and she's accepted."

Then, like an invisible barrier was broken, flashes from cameras went off and questions started flying at them from all directions.

"Mr. Forrester, is this in any way related to the news story about your sister this morning?"

She could feel Gage tense, his hand squeezing hers tightly. Reflexively, she reached over with her other hand and traced her fingers lightly over his knuckles.

"We are not discussing my sister or the blatant untruths that were printed about her, any more questions along that line and we're finished here."

The sound of his voice acted like a high beam in the fog of her brain. She jerked her hand away from his, horrified that she'd touched him like that. Like she had permission to do it, like it was natural.

"Do you have a date set?" This came from a woman in the crowd.

"We're still looking at venues," Lily responded.

"And what does this mean for your dating life?" one of the men asked.

"This means he's through with dating," Lily said sharply. Usually she was very cool in these situations, but she greatly resented the excessive interest in the lives of public figures anyway, and being at the center of it only added to the resentment.

"She's right about that," Gage said, drawing his thumb over the back of her hand, sending little ripples of sensation through her. "I never thought I would get married. But when I met Lily... Well, she's all that I want." He looked up, his blue eyes intent on hers. Her breath caught. He looked like he meant every word he'd just spoken, his expression sincere, his eyes trained only on her. No mystery why he scored so many beautiful women with such ease. He could do romance without breaking a sweat, and he could sound completely honest while speaking words that were nothing more than beautiful lies.

And the worst thing was that, even knowing that, even having a complete and total man embargo, it affected her. Her heart was thundering, her stomach tight, her breasts heavy.

And when his eyes dropped and his focus moved to her lips, she was silently hoping he would lean in and close the distance between them.

She shook her head sharply and tried to force the image out of her mind. She didn't want to kiss him. He was charming her. Like he'd done to thousands of other women multiple thousands of times. But she wasn't like those other women. She had standards. She knew what happened when you let a man in like that, when you gave someone else so much power in your life. She would never make that mistake. Her life was just as she liked it. Well-ordered and entirely in her control.

The rest of the questions went by in a blur and she stood there, smiling, her face placid, her manner serene. She was a professional at projecting calm when her thoughts were churning beneath the surface.

Everything in her was concentrating on ignoring the place where Gage was touching her, on where he was moving his thumb over the sensitive skin on her hand. On the heat that coursed through her from such a simple, nonsexual touch.

"Thank you, we won't be taking any more questions. We both have some work to get back to, and I'd hate to have to fire my fiancée." The crowd laughed softly at his joke. Lily tightened her lips to try and avoid grimacing.

He led her off of the stage and the minute they were safely ensconced in his limousine she jerked her hand away from him, rubbing at the spot he'd been brushing with his thumb.

"Try not to act like my touch offends you next time," he said.

She tilted her head up to face him and immediately wished she hadn't. The impact of him, his blue eyes narrowed, his expression hard, was more than she'd anticipated. After working with Gage for four months she should be used to him by now, but, while he was always in charge, no doubt about it, he didn't usually give off that level of intensity. He was completely serious about his work, but beneath it all was a definite security. He wasn't the kind of man who had to posture and get worked up over every minor detail in order to project his power. Never had she felt a hint of the intensity that she knew was just beneath the surface right now.

She knew he loved his sister, knew he was protective of her, but she hadn't realized just how much.

"I didn't act like your touch offended me," she said, looking out the window at the harbor, watching the white boats blur together. "I was perfectly composed."

"And stiff."

This was not a new refrain. She couldn't even recall the number of times she'd been called frigid, on those ill-fated, unwanted dates that had been concocted by her well-meaning friends.

Stiff was actually a little bit nicer, but she imagined the sentiment was much the same.

"Sorry, I'll work on my fawning."

"Do that," he said, his voice icy.

"No one else could tell. And if they could they would attribute it to nerves from being in front of a crowd."

"You make statements to the press on an almost daily basis."

"True," she admitted, "but not personal statements. Maybe I'm private."

"You are very tight-lipped about your personal life."

Personal life? That would be a fun conversation. The gym four nights a week. A health-conscious meal for one, and then whatever show she felt like watching on TV since there was never anyone there to complain. If she didn't have issues with pet hair she would probably have a cat, which would at least give her companionship, but would give him unfair ammo against her.

"That's why they call it a personal life, Gage, although clearly you didn't get the memo."

"Tell me this, Lily, is there any point for me to try and hide my personal life? You know how the media is, and if you aren't up front about what goes on behind closed doors they make it up, or someone makes it up for them."

"Okay, I see your point. But you tend to…flaunt."

"No, I happen to date women who are as high profile as I am, and that makes us targets. We go out, and that seems to constitute as news. We can't stay in my bedroom all the time."

The way he said that, his husky voice low and intimate in the confines of the limo, made her heart rate skyrocket. Why, *why* was he able to this to her? Why did he have the power to fill her head with images of tangled limbs and the sounds of heavy breathing, the scent of sweat-slicked bodies? Men, in a real life, personal sense, never did that to her.

She liked men, she just liked them from a distance. Like in the pages of a glossy magazine or on a movie screen. She had a sex drive, just like most everyone else, but in actual, personal application…that was what made her feel anxious. Which wasn't conducive to arousal. Orgasm required a loss of control she couldn't fathom being able to achieve, or even wanting to achieve, with another person.

But it was as if Gage was able to bypass all of her natural issues, all of her closely guarded reserve, and make her want things she'd never anticipated having a desire for. It wasn't a matter of wanting to abolish her personal barriers so that she could experience real desire and satisfaction with Gage, it was a matter of them seeming to dissolve and her desperately wishing they would return. He was her boss, and work was too important to even consider engaging in an affair that would damage that.

Fine for some women to have flings and keep themselves emotionally separate, but she was afraid she wasn't one of those women. Her mother certainly wasn't. Every man she ever slept with consumed everything she had. All her emotion, all her time, her self-respect. It had made growing up a living hell for Lily. There had been nothing she could do at the time, but now, it was up to her how she ran her life, and she chose to maintain total control.

End of story. So her hormones could just deal with it.

"I don't suppose you can," she said, teeth clenched.

"Check your alerts," he said, back to his high-handed self.

She took her phone out of her pocket and pulled up her email. She'd received a few email alerts, letting her know Gage's name had popped up in search engines. She opened the first one. "It looks like our engagement is big news. Huge news, in fact."

"How about Maddy?"

"The story's still there, and I wouldn't call it buried," she said, looking through the pages of search results. "But it's quieted."

"Good," he said.

Gage took his phone from his jacket pocket and dialed Maddy, setting the mobile to speakerphone. "Are you all right?" he asked.

"Yes, Gage. I'm fine."

She didn't sound distraught, but he could tell she'd been crying, which made his stomach tighten. "It's handled."

"I saw that," she said. "I don't want you doing this for me. I'm an adult, Gage. I have to clean up my own messes."

"Not this one, Maddy. Callahan is a bastard to drag you into this, and it's way out of your league. Let me handle it."

"Gage, you have to let me stand on my own sometime."

"I know," he said, his chest tightening. "After this."

He knew Maddy was an adult, and he understood her feeling like she needed to fight her own battles, and, if he was honest, he was more than ready to have a little less involvement with her life. But he wasn't letting her deal with this on her own.

"I'm sending you over to the Swiss resort for a couple of weeks. Just until all of this dies down."

"Gage…"

"Maddy, let me fix it."

He heard her heavy sigh on the other end of the phone. "Okay, Gage, I'll go to Switzerland. Are you still going through with your fake engagement?"

"How do you know it's fake?" he asked, looking over at Lily, who was still staring out the window, trying to ignore him. Her slight shoulders were set rigidly, her long, stocking-clad legs crossed. And they were extremely fine legs. Lily wasn't very tall, she barely skimmed his shoulder, even in her man-slaying stilettos, but those legs were long and shapely, just begging for him to run his hands over them, to draw one up so that she had it wrapped around him, bringing her closer so that he could…

He slammed a mental door on his errant fantasy.

"Because she isn't your type at all. She's too…stuffy," Maddy said.

Lily's head whipped around, brown eyes wide, full lips pinched. He swore and punched the speaker button off. "Enjoy Switzerland, Maddy. Let me handle the rest."

He snapped the phone shut. Lily was looking away again, her focus very firmly on the scenery out the window.

He wanted to touch her. To see if he could make her melt. To see what it would take to get her to loosen her hair, to get her to unbutton a little bit. Or all the way. It was easy for him to picture her naked, her perfect, petite body on display for him. She was so pale…the thought of all that milky white skin contrasting against his black sheets was the most erotic fantasy his subconscious had ever created for him.

Two things kept him from exploring the fantasy. First, she was an employee, and that was a no-go as far as he was concerned. Second, she had *serious* written all over her. He didn't do serious. Not in his sexual relationships. He'd done serious. Not in romantic relationships, but his entire childhood and young adult years had been nothing but responsibility.

His mother had done okay raising him to a point, but Maddy had been a late-in-life surprise, and his mother hadn't been willing to miss more years on the job to raise a child she hadn't wanted. His father had always put his career first and had even less time for Maddy. And that left him. He was fifteen years older and more than capable of caring for her.

When he was twenty-five, just out of college and making his first million in property development, Maddy had called and told him it had been three days

since anyone had been home, and she hadn't had anything to eat. He'd gone to get her and she'd lived with
him from the age of ten until she'd gone to college. That
was a lot of serious for a confirmed bachelor who had
his own career to try and build. Fortunately, he'd had
a network of good friends that had helped him try to
balance work and what basically amounted to sudden
parenthood.

He didn't resent it and he would never have given it
up for anything, but he was done with that. In his esti-
mation, he'd raised a child, when he'd been much too
young to do it, and he had no intention of going there
again. He'd already dealt with the angst of a teenage
girl's first crush, threatened her dates with bodily harm
if they laid a hand on her, helped her find a dress for
prom, then seen her off to college.

And despite the fact that Lily certainly didn't seem
like the kind of woman who had a biological clock ticking, she still read serious. She didn't date very often and
she was probably the kind of woman that took a certain
amount of seduction before she engaged in a physical
relationship.

He preferred women who were fun and uncompli-
cated, and if that made him shallow in the eyes of the
press, that was fine with him. He was the one who had
to live his life, and as long as he was happy with it, he
didn't concern himself with the opinions of others.

Except when it came to Maddy.

"So, now what? We have to go to galas together?"
Lily asked, her voice dry. What Maddy had said bothered her that was obvious. And if she hadn't been so
very off-limits he would have offered comfort. But he
only knew two ways to do that. One was parental, and

one was decidedly not. He imagined neither would be welcome.

"I was thinking a romantic getaway," he said, enjoying the way her lips tightened further. He wasn't used to seeing Lily flustered, but she was exactly that about the whole situation.

"And what about our jobs?"

"It will be a working getaway of course. I was planning on going to Thailand to check on the resort progress sometime in the next week. And now seems like a perfect time. Maddy's in Switzerland until the story blows over, and she'll be at one of my resorts, so the security will be tight, and with that taken care of, we can get publicity for the resort."

"And for us," Lily returned dryly.

"Doesn't hurt."

Lily's heart beat faster. Curse the man. "If Maddy is taken care of…"

"We still have to see this through. If you're caught lying so blatantly, your credibility will be destroyed. Along with the rest of your career."

And curse him again, he was right. That was always the risk with this job. There was a fine line between bending the truth and outright lies. She avoided lies whenever she could, but ultimately, her client's image— or in this case, his sister's— was her concern. But if she was caught being…economical…with the truth, the media would never take her seriously again. Credibility, once it was damaged like that, was not an easy thing to repair.

"Point taken." She put her smile on, the one she reserved for press conferences. "I guess we're going to Thailand."

CHAPTER FIVE

IT WAS late when Gage's private plane landed on the island of Koh Samui. A car was waiting for them when they got off of the plane. Lily expected nothing less. Gage was always efficient. Or at least, the people he hired were always completely efficient. Which, she imagined, brought it back around to Gage being efficient.

She took a deep breath of the humid, salty air before getting into the limo.

Gage settled in beside her. His top button was undone, his tie long discarded, his sleeves pushed up over his elbows, revealing tanned, muscular forearms that demanded an in-depth study from female admirers. He still smelled good, too, even after long hours of travel.

"Don't you find the limo a bit cliché?" she asked, running her hands unconsciously over the cool leather.

"I find it practical. I have a driver, I have privacy. I have enough room to work—" he looked at her, his blue eyes hot "—or play."

She held up a hand and tried to ignore the chip in her manicure. "I don't need to hear about your backseat exploits."

He reached across the seats and gripped the clip that

was holding her bun in place, letting her brown hair fall around her in a heavy curtain. He slid his fingers through it, rubbing the tender places that were sore from so many hours pinned back. The gentle pressure of his fingers felt so good. It was part massage, part sexual tease. She wanted to tilt her head and lean into his touch. To moan in ecstasy over what he was making her feel.

Instead she jerked her head away from his touch. "Why did you do that?"

"You may not want to discuss any of my backseat exploits, but if there are reporters waiting at the resort it wouldn't hurt you to look as though you'd been engaging in some of your own." He drew his thumb lightly over her cheek. "You're already flushed."

She let her breath out slowly. "It's hot."

His blue eyes were serious, studying, and she felt her face get even hotter. "Yes. It is." He moved away from her, leaning back against the seat.

"How is the building project going?" she asked. Anything to break the tension that had just stretched between them, so real and tight that it had seemed like a physical force. It was worse that she was sure he felt it.

But then he was a man, and she was a woman, so, naturally, if she was giving off any attraction vibes he was going to pick up on them and reciprocate. It was the way it worked. A woman didn't need to be especially desirable, only available.

"It's going well. Most of the individual villas are up and ready for use. The main portion of the resort is still under construction, but I've made sure that the villa we're staying in is totally stocked, and some of the housekeeping staff I've already hired are staying on site, so they'll be around to take care of our needs."

"I don't need housekeeping," she said dryly. "How do you think I manage in my daily life?"

"I assumed you were busy and you would have some domestic help."

Which would require her to allow a stranger in her house. Which might seem fanatical to some, but she'd done cramped, shared communal living with her mother and whatever man of the month her mother was currently attached to. No privacy. And some of the men had attempted to take advantage…it was no wonder she'd never been the kind of woman to experiment with flings. She'd had to work too hard to maintain any sort of innocence in that environment.

"We're not all billionaires, Gage."

"But I know what I pay you," he said dryly.

"But you don't know my expenses. Maybe I own beachfront property."

"You don't."

She turned to him, eyebrows raised. "You don't think I do?"

"You're too sensible."

She smirked. "As it happens I own a beachfront condo."

The West Coast, the ocean, had been her dream growing up. She'd seen the ocean for the first time at seventeen, when she moved to California, and it had been her goal to be able to see it from her bedroom window. It had taken quite a few years, but eighteen months ago she'd finally gotten the keys to her new beachfront home. A home she'd worked for. The home she'd earned. It had been the best feeling in the world.

The ultimate reward for her years of hard work, focus and independence.

"You don't seem the type."

"I don't?"

"Do you surf? Swim?"

She laughed. "No."

"That's why you don't seem the type."

"I used to dream about the ocean," she said without thinking. "In Kansas we have seas of cornfields. No ocean. I thought if I could see the ocean…it was like the world would be open to me. Endless possibilities on the horizons."

As soon as she finished she wished she hadn't said anything. She'd never told anyone that before, not even any of her friends. Her dreams had always been her own. She had a really nice group of friends, but they kept things casual, not really in depth. And that was how she liked things in general with people. Now she felt horribly exposed, and to Gage of all people, who always seemed like he could see into her, like he knew things about her even she didn't know.

"It's a good dream," he said. "And now you have it."

She nodded once. "Part of it."

"You want success."

"I want unsurpassed success in my field," she said.

"Something I understand."

"You have that kind of success, Gage."

He offered her a partial smile. "Yet, I still want more. It's never quite enough, that's the thing about ambition. But that's what keeps me going, and in business, you have to keep going. Money doesn't wait for you. If I wasn't building this resort, someone else would be, and it would be my missed opportunity. As it is, it's my payday and someone else's regret."

"You don't do regret, do you?" she asked.

"I make sure I never need to."

They pulled onto a road that was newer than the main highway, the pavement dark and smooth as the road curved around the base of sheer rock face covered with vines and moss. The road led up the mountain and the foliage grew thicker and greener and palm trees and other topical plants grew thick along the roadside.

It certainly hadn't been overtaken by Forrestation Inc., as some of the environmental groups had feared. With the exception of the road, Lily could barely make out any signs of civilization.

The partially built resort was at the top of the mountain, with a clear view of the crystalline ocean and the white sand beaches. Paths led from the main building and into the trees and, she assumed, to the separate teakwood villas.

The limo came to a halt and Lily got out without waiting for Gage, or the driver, to open her door for her.

"It has a view of the ocean," Gage said, coming to stand beside her.

She cleared her throat. "Yes, it does." It bothered her now, that he had that little piece of her. Now he knew what to say, and he knew why this place was so perfect to her. He would know what she was thinking.

She shrugged off the unsettling thought. "So, where am I staying?"

"We are staying in the house I had built for my own personal use."

The thought of staying with him did not settle well. "Why are we staying together?"

"The board is visiting. That means we have to look as cozy as possible."

"But it's a whole house?"

"Yes. More than three thousand square feet. You'll never have to see me. Unless you want to, of course."

The look that he gave her was so heated it made her body temperature skyrocket. His meaning wasn't implied so much as stated. Boldly, explicitly.

"I don't," she said, tight-lipped, knowing how uptight she sounded.

He lifted an eyebrow. "What if there's a business matter we need to discuss?"

"Then I'll look for you."

"What did you think I meant, Lily?"

She made a scoffing sound in the back of her throat. "You know perfectly well what…because it's what you were implying." He was flustering her. Honestly flustering her. That did not happen. Ever.

He didn't say anything. Didn't even try to break the thick silence with a clever comment. He only looked at her, his blue eyes roaming over her body, making her feel like he was undressing her. Like she was already undressed. Like he could see everything. Every flaw, every imperfection, every bit of her.

She looked away, throat dry. "Okay, so where's the house?"

"Just down the path."

He surprised her by opening the trunk of the limousine and taking their suitcases out himself before heading down the heavily wooded trail. She followed him, as best she could in her stilettos, which were not made for a natural path, however nicely constructed.

She wobbled and pitched forward, catching herself on his broad shoulders, her breasts crushed against his back. He stopped, his body stiff and strong beneath her weight. Her heart thundered heavily, both from the near fall, and from being so close to him again.

It was just like it had been when they were dancing. He was so solid, so hot and male. She wanted to melt into him. To chase after the riot of sensations that were moving through her body at lightning speed. To finally know what it meant to share sexual pleasure with someone else.

She pushed away from him, wobbling again, but she managed to get her balance on her own. She took a sharp breath. Just the small distance between them afforded her more clarity of thought. But when she touched him…she forgot everything. Everything but her steadily growing desire for him. Well, not really for him personally, but for his body. Gage was the last man on earth—okay, not really the last man but he was low on the list—with whom she would choose to have a real relationship. But something about him physically, probably his undeniable sex appeal, got to her more than any other man ever had.

It was raw and elemental, beyond common sense. And she really, really hated it.

"Sorry," she said, her voice breaking and, she knew, revealing just how much the encounter had affected her.

"Be careful," he said. His voice sounded thicker, huskier. That was when she knew. Knew that he was affected by her, too, that her touching him, pressing against him, was doing the same thing to him that it had done to her. And that did not make things better.

She twisted the engagement ring on her finger and reminded herself exactly why she didn't need a relationship, with Gage or anyone else. She didn't want anyone to *own* her. Didn't want anyone to control her and manipulate her with her own foolish emotions. She'd seen how it worked, what love did to you, what it asked of you. It wasn't anything she wanted a part of.

She followed him the rest of the way, more slowly and more carefully, until they reached the house. It was set up on stilts and made from solid dark teakwood with the traditional curves of Thai architecture, mixed with a modern sensibility. The large, covered outdoor living area that wrapped around the house made the most of the natural environment and the view. It appeared rustic in a sense, but she knew that inside it would have every modern convenience available, and even some that weren't available. Not to mere mortals anyway.

"I love it," she said, meaning it.

"I like it, too," he said. "I designed it, actually."

"You did?"

He shrugged. "That was how I got into property development. Architecture has always interested me. I like building resorts that are functional and beautiful, and blend in with the natural culture and landscape."

"You really have to start saying these things in public," she said.

Now she knew something about Gage, she realized. And he knew something about her. That caused strange tightening sensation in her chest.

"Why? Then your job would be easy."

She rolled her eyes, ignoring the persistent roll of her stomach. "Can't have that." She walked up the exterior stairs of the house without waiting for him and went inside.

It was gorgeous, the décor simple and traditional, a muted color palette that caused all attention to be drawn to the view outside, to the vivid colors of the beach that could never be rivaled by anything man-made.

She moved through the open living room and into the kitchen, which was outfitted, as she'd predicted, with top-of-the-line equipment. Stainless steel appliances and granite countertops. The kitchen flowed seamlessly into the dining room, which went back around into the living room.

"Where's my room?" she asked, starting to feel desperate for a little bit of space. He was making her whole body feel restless and jittery and she needed a break.

"Just through here," he said and gestured to another open doorway just off of the living room.

There was no door, just a cleverly angled wall that kept the bed from view. The bedroom was open to a massive bathroom that was, again, only private in part.

"Are there no interior doors in this house?" she asked, feeling panic start to pick at her calm, fraying the edges a bit.

"No. I thought it would compromise the integrity of the design."

"It compromises common decency. That's what it does. That's…that's my concern," she said, feeling her heart rate rise.

"I promise I'll keep to my quarters."

She hated that she couldn't play like she was fine with it. Another thing she was revealing about herself, which was one reason she valued her privacy so much. How many other twenty-seven-year-old women had such a hang-up about sharing space? Especially with a man. Most women her age shared space with men frequently and happily.

"I just…I live by myself for a reason."

"Really?" he asked, genuine interest in his voice.

Crap. She was sharing again. "I like privacy."

"I understand that."

Gage fully understood the need for privacy. Having a child—his sister—live with him for eight years had severely limited his privacy, dictating who he could have over and when. What sort of activities he could indulge in. Of course, now that Maddy was on her own, he could have women over if he chose to, but he'd gotten so used to going to hotels when he wanted sex that he'd never really adapted back.

And now that he had the privacy he wanted, the house felt empty sometimes. He still didn't want to share it with any of his mistresses. He didn't need women leaving toothbrushes on his sink. It was a level of commitment he had no desire to pursue. He had nothing to offer a woman beyond a little mutual fun in the bedroom, and he didn't see the point in making her believe otherwise. That was why neutral locations reigned supreme in his book.

Although, having Lily stay here with him didn't bother him at all. But then, Lily wasn't his mistress, and she also didn't seem like she knew how to cling or simper, which made her seem like a much safer houseguest.

"I live alone, too," he added.

"I like it," she said.

"So do I."

"I need a shower," she said, abruptly. Then her pale cheeks turned a delicate raspberry.

He couldn't help but picture her naked in the shower, water sluicing over all that pale skin as it grew rosy from the heat. He felt an ache start to build in his groin. Maybe she wouldn't be the most convenient houseguest.

Not if he wanted to keep things professional between them. Although he was starting to wonder why it mattered. He was trying to be decent. It seemed a little bit on the shady side to hit on a woman whose paychecks you signed. But decency was starting to seem less important.

Then she lowered her eyes, her blush intensifying, and he remembered why making a move on her was a bad idea. She wouldn't just be another good time. She was more than that. If she were the kind of woman who would have said she needed a shower and, instead of blushing, had given him a sultry look and invited him to join, then he would have been more than willing to forget professionalism then and there.

But she wasn't that woman. Despite the air of confidence she gave off most of the time, all it took was a touch, or a small moment of sexual tension, and the confidence melted away. She either stiffened and moved away or she blushed like an innocent. He didn't want to deal with any of that. He couldn't. He had plenty to offer women in the way of gifts and physical pleasure. But he didn't want marriage or love, he didn't see the point.

His career was too important, and he'd put it on the back burner for eight years. He wouldn't do it again. Not for a wife or a child. It wouldn't be fair to him, or them. A wife and child didn't deserve to be second. He and Maddy hadn't deserved to be second. But they had been. A very distant second. He refused to put a children through what his parents had subjected Maddy and him to. He wouldn't make them wonder what they could do to earn some attention, to gain a small about of their parents' interest.

That meant marriage was not an option.

"I'll meet you for dinner," he said, his voice rough with arousal.

She nodded jerkily. "Okay. See you then."

He turned to leave the room, fighting the urge to turn and take her in his arms and kiss her, to find out if she would be stiff against his lips, or if she would be soft and pliant.

He wanted her soft and pliant, more than he could remember wanting any woman in his life. It didn't matter that his head knew she was the wrong woman to get involved with. His body wanted her.

He tried to conjure up an image of Penny, his last mistress, the mistress he had parted ways with a very distant six months ago. He couldn't. The only woman his body wanted was Lily.

When Lily emerged an hour later she was back in her business attire, hair pinned back, makeup expertly applied. Her lipstick was a paler rose than her typical color, coordinating with her new manicure and her sky-high stilettos.

Her endless supply of colorful high-heeled shoes never failed to fascinate him. Her work wardrobe was neutral, black and gray, with the occasional brown. But she wore a rainbow on her feet. He'd dated women that wore shoes like that, but mixed with garish jewelry and flashy dresses. Their entire look was so obvious that nothing stood out. Lily knew how to dress for impact. And with a figure like hers, everything short of a burlap sack had pretty major impact. Although, he imagined a burlap sack might even pack a punch with Lily's curves to complement it.

"I'm ready to eat," she said.

"Dinner will be up shortly."

She narrowed her brown eyes. "I thought we were meeting with the board."

"Tomorrow. They've only just flown in and will be eating in their quarters so that they can rest."

"Considerate of you," she said, teeth gritted. "Although if I would have known we were eating in, I wouldn't have dressed for a business dinner." She was annoyed, but not necessarily about being out of the loop. Probably something to do with being alone with him.

"I think you still would have." He had a feeling that Lily would have added another layer if she would have known they would be eating alone together. It was clear that she wasn't immune to him, that she felt the attraction, too. Also clear that she was equally determined to fight it.

"Well, I guess technically if we eat together it's a business dinner."

"This isn't a business dinner," he said.

Her dark eyes were severe, her mouth pressed into a line. "If we were at a restaurant, I promise you I would save the receipt and write it off."

His body stirred, responding to the blatant challenge she was laying down. She wanted him, and she was determined to fight against it. He ached to release her hair from its tight confines again, to feel her lush, generous curves beneath his hands, to undo all of those little buttons, to undo her completely.

It was the wrong thing to want. But the temptation she represented was one he was finding harder and harder to resist. He didn't even want to resist it anymore.

"Sit down, Lily."

She shot him a deadly glare but settled down on the

low couch. He went into the kitchen and rummaged until he found two wineglasses and a bottle of Pinot Gris.

She took the glass, without comment, and allowed him to pour her a generous portion. A few moments later a woman from housekeeping knocked and came in with trays, setting them on the coffee table before exiting quietly.

There was a wide variety of fish, rice and noodle dishes and for a while they ate in silence. Another shock, since it was a rare thing for Lily to be silent. She always had a smart remark for every situation, and she never spared anyone her lightning-fast wit. It was one of the things he enjoyed about her.

But despite the fact that she usually filled the silence, he'd had very few real conversations with her. They kept it to work. Which was how he liked it. He'd been surprised when she'd shared about why she lived by the ocean, and felt put out when it became clear that she regretted sharing.

And it shouldn't have. It shouldn't matter. It shouldn't matter whether or not she lived by the ocean because she was a champion surfer, or if it was because she felt trapped in her home state. And yet, it had mattered.

It was easy to look at Lily and see her as a two-dimensional person. Almost an accessory to his work life, something he took inventory of. Mobile phone, laptop, Lily. And he was certain she saw him the same way sometimes. Neither of them had ever gone out of their way to connect, to know each other. He didn't see the point. When he was at work, he was at work. When he was with a woman, it was for a good time. Only Maddy and his close friends really knew much of anything about him. Even the press was ignorant of the fine details of his life. As he preferred it. If he had to live publicly he wanted to keep some aspects of his life to himself.

Now there seemed to be a shift happening in his and Lily's relationship.

It's because you want to see her naked.

That was all it was. Sex clouded a man's judgment, and while he generally thought of himself as being above that, given his amount of experience, Lily seemed to revert him back to his teenage years. Which was extremely exciting in some ways, and something part of him—the part that was below his belt, he imagined—wanted very much to explore. While another part of him, likely his brain, was telling him to ignore it.

"Have you spoken to Maddy?" Lily asked, looking at him over the rim of her wineglass as she took a sip, leaving the imprint of her glossy lipstick behind. Normally he wouldn't think anything about such a normal occurrence, but something about it, about the lingering imprint of Lily's lips, was sexy beyond reason.

"I talked to her while you were showering. She's having fun in Switzerland. No media and good skiing."

"I'm sorry she's going through this. It isn't fair. Seems to be the natural state of sexual politics though. If a woman has sex with a man, he uses it against her. If she turns him down…he still finds a way to use it against her."

"You're not the biggest fan of men, are you?"

"I like men that I know personally. Men as a species I sometimes have issues with. Or maybe, more specifically, cultural traditions that allow them to get away with pretty despicable things that women would never be forgiven for."

"Do you speak from experience?"

She slid her hand up and down the stem of the glass, the movement so erotic he felt the impact of it down in his groin. Ironic and inappropriate considering the topic of conversation. But then, he was a man. And she was very much a woman.

"Not anything close to what Maddy is dealing with, but I know what it's like for men to make assumptions."

"Jeff Campbell was making assumptions, wasn't he?"

She nodded. "Yes, he was. And I was partly glad to cancel the contract because of that. I didn't want to have to deal with another awkward conversation where I have to explain that a friendly greeting is simply a friendly greeting and not an invitation for sex."

"You called me sexist for basically saying the same thing about women I've worked with."

She frowned. "Well, you didn't have any lingering repercussions for turning your PA down."

He quirked an eyebrow. "You don't think her showing up naked in my office was over the top? What if the roles were reversed?"

She grimaced. "Okay. Point taken. People can be awful. Both genders. But I am sorry that Maddy's having to deal with this."

"Me, too. She's been through enough." He didn't usually talk about their growing-up years, or, more specifically, Maddy's growing-up years. But it seemed fair that Lily understand since she was in the middle of everything.

"She moved in with me when she was ten," he said. "My parents weren't caring for her. Not properly. So I went and got her and brought her home with me. She stayed until she went to college four years ago."

"You raised her?"

He shrugged. "More or less. I was twenty-five, no-where near ready to be a father, especially not to my ten-year-old sister, but it was what she needed. And I know I wasn't really a great substitute for a father. But I did what I could. I made sure she went to prom. And that her date—skinny kid, very annoying—got threatened within an inch of his life beforehand. A shocking number of high school students lose their virginity at prom."

It was strange to hear Gage talking like this. Like a concerned parent. Like a man who had faced things she hadn't even tried to imagine dealing with.

Lily's heart clenched tight. She'd always assumed that Gage was just a carefree playboy. The kind of man who played around simply because he had money and power and no woman would say no, and no one would look down on him for simply doing what men did.

But, just like that wildlife preserve he hadn't yet shared with the public, there was more to him. He'd raised a child. He'd been there for his sister when no one else had.

"For the record, she was back at ten o'clock on prom night," he added.

"Does that mean you let her date live?"

"I did. But I wouldn't have if he'd done anything to hurt her. Or if he'd taken advantage of her, or caused her pain in any way."

She bit her lip. "Are you going to let Callahan live?"

"Weighing the pros and cons of it."

"I didn't realize that you'd been through that with her."

He shrugged again, like he always did when things

turned personal. "I did what I had to. I wanted to do it. I love Maddy."

"It really makes sense to me now, why you're doing this, why it's so important for you to protect her. In a lot of ways you're more like a parent than a brother."

And again, she felt something shifting inside of her, felt some of her defenses weaken, begin to crumble. If he was nothing more than a carefree playboy, then it was easy to brush off her attraction to him. And while, clearly, he had strong playboy elements, he was also a good person. She liked Gage, she always had, but now she liked him more, and that complicated things, especially when the liking mixed with her steadily growing attraction for him.

She took another fortifying sip of wine and then realized that fortifying herself with the heat-inducing, slightly drugging liquid wasn't the best idea.

"I'm tired. Jet lag," she said. And lines were becoming muddled, thanks to the wine and the sudden revelation about Gage. "I should go to bed."

Gage nodded. "Good night, Lily."

Later, when she was in her bed, trying to fall asleep, she kept hearing that deep husky voice over and over again, telling her good night. And it was far too easy to imagine he was in her bed saying it, holding her close to his hard, hot body.

She wrapped herself tightly in her blanket and curled her knees up to her chest, trying to stop the ache that was pounding inside of her. The ache that was turning into a shocking feeling of emptiness that her body seemed to think only Gage could fill.

CHAPTER SIX

BREAKFAST with the board was an event. They were businessmen, so they weren't seeking public displays of affection at least, but they did want to know how the scandal with Maddy was going to affect the bottom line.

"Not at all," Lily insisted. "The incident with Maddy barely made a dent in the international media. William Callahan isn't famous worldwide. And we're going to make sure we publicize the Forrester Wildlife Preserve that Gage established here on Koh Samui."

"The cynical might argue that I set aside all of that land to keep my competition out," Gage said when the members of the board had left the table, off to a golf game Gage had arranged for them.

"Yes, the cynical might," she said. "But your motives aren't important."

"Do you really believe that?"

"In this context, yes, I do. As far as life application goes, of course motivation matters. But this is for a sound bite, a press release. They can speculate about your motives all they like, but the important thing is that you did it. At least that's how those concerned about environmental impact will see it."

"Interested in sightseeing today?"

She raised her eyebrows. "Don't we have paperwork to file, or something?"

"Not today. I thought you might enjoy seeing some of the island. The main focus of this resort is simply bringing people into the natural beauty of Thailand. That's why, at my resort, I haven't made a golf course and built bars along the beach. It would be good PR if you were familiar with the place."

She sighed. "Using my job title against me. Shameless."

He looked at her. "I can be."

Silence, the thick tense kind, settled between them again. Lily licked her suddenly dry lips, and his eyes dropped, following the movement. A rush of pure feminine pride raced through her. That she could affect a man like Gage was nothing short of incredible. She had no experience at all and he had likely slept his way through the phone book.

But she wasn't imagining it. He was feeling it too. The insistent beat pounding inside of her, demanding satisfaction.

She looked away and tried to steady her breathing, tried to think logically. They were adults, and that meant there was only one place an attraction like this would end if it was acted on. And that was in bed. All fine for most people, but she had less experience than most teenagers, and Gage was a thirty-seven-year-old man with years of experience. It was an incongruous, insane combination.

"Bring a swimsuit," he said finally, breaking the tension between them. Most of it anyway.

"I don't have one."

He frowned. "You didn't bring a swimsuit to an island?"

"It's a business trip."

He lowered his voice, his blue eyes intense. "I think it's a little more than that."

She shook her head. "No. Don't say that. Don't talk about it."

"Because if we don't talk about it we don't feel it?"

"Because it's stupid. We work together." She didn't even pretend to be ignorant of what he meant. What would the point of that be?

No matter how much she wanted to deny it there was an attraction between them. An attraction that, if she was honest, had been there, smoldering since that very first interview, the one that had not resulted in her being hired. Which was why, even though she'd been put out that he'd chosen someone else, she'd been relieved that she wouldn't be the one who had to work with him every day. Because he'd affected her in ways no other man had, and it wasn't something she'd been prepared to deal with. She still wasn't, she just didn't have a choice now, since she was stuck in a foreign country with the man, pretending to be his fiancée.

"I don't swim, actually," she said, the thought of being that exposed making her feel jittery. It was less a matter of revealing her body, and more a matter of losing her image, her business suits and killer shoes, which always helped her amp up her confidence.

He arched an eyebrow. "You don't know how to swim or you don't swim?"

"Is there a difference?"

"A pretty big one. The difference between whether or not I have to jump in and save you if you fall overboard."

She narrowed her eyes. "Okay, I know how, I just

don't." Not in front of him anyway. "And anyway, if I fell overboard, you know you would jump in after me."

A slow smile spread across his face. "Maybe. I'll have a member of the staff track down a swimsuit for you. You'll enjoy yourself. Trust me."

The boat ride out to the small island just off the south side of Koh Samui was incredible. The water was completely clear, the depths of the ocean clearly visible as they floated over the surface of the water.

Lily found herself relaxing, even in Gage's presence, which was a strange feeling. But the scenery was so gorgeous and the small yacht skimmed so smoothly over the small waves, that it was simply impossible to fight the effects.

Even the swimsuit, a barely there bikini held together with tiny strings, no longer had her feeling so tense. Of course, she was covered with a T-shirt and shorts, so that helped.

She'd worn a bikini once before. Something she'd purchased herself for her sixteenth birthday. Her mother's boyfriend had seemed to think it was some sort of invitation. She felt incredibly lucky to this day that he'd been more of a jerk, rather than being outright evil. At least he'd listened when she'd said a very emphatic no. But the lingering memory of his alcohol-flavored kiss was more than enough to remind her of where men sometimes saw invitation and opportunity.

She didn't really believe Gage would do anything like that, though. She never had. He would never need to force himself on a woman. He wouldn't anyway. She was confident in that. But the bikini itself wasn't the biggest worry. Without her business clothes, without that reinforcing barrier between them, she was afraid she might forget why she couldn't give in to the attraction they both very clearly felt.

So don't forget.

Gage steered the yacht into an alcove that was surrounded by a sheer rock face that created a natural wall of privacy around what looked like a small swimming area. The water was clear here, too. Lily could see silver flashes beneath the surface that she knew were fish.

"I can definitely see why you built a resort out here," she said.

"I visited Thailand for the first time when I was in college. I knew I wanted to do something here then. I was just waiting for the right time."

She sat up in the deck chair she'd been lounging on. "You built the business up by yourself?"

He nodded. "Started small, with residential homes that I fixed up. Then I found some land to subdivide and built a neighborhood, which got me off to a pretty good start. I started looking for investors after that."

"Why resort properties then?"

"Because they're more profitable. The industry is more stable. There's a class of people that will always vacation no matter what."

It sounded like her own reasoning for her job. It wasn't as though she loved public relations more than anything. But she was good at it, and she made good money at it. It served her sense of ambition, her drive to succeed. Her need to put more and more distance between the new Lily and the Lily she'd left in Kansas.

"How about you, Lily? Did you start your business by yourself?"

She nodded. "Yes."

"No help?"

She laughed. "No one in my family would have known how to help. Actually, I don't have all that much family. Just my mother and whatever man she's shacked up with at any given moment."

More than she'd intended to share. How did he do that? He had a way of making her want to bare all to him. Wanting to make him understand her, when she really should care.

"It takes a lot of drive to make your own success," he said, looking at the island in front of them instead of at her.

"Yes, it does. Why didn't your family help you, Gage? Your parents had money."

"I wouldn't take money from them. Not after what they did to Maddy."

The glint of rage in his eyes was so intense, so feral, that if it had been directed at her, she almost would have been frightened of him. There was so much more to Gage than she'd originally assumed. Carefree playboy. Was that really how she'd seen him just a week ago? Oh, she'd always sensed a level of intensity beneath the surface, but she'd thought that was just ambition, drive for his career. It was more. A lot more.

"At least she had you," she said softly.

There hadn't been anyone for her. Her mother had been too caught up in the soap opera of her life, and there certainly hadn't been an ally available in the scores of men her mother had lived with over the years.

A flash of a feeling, a strange longing, shook her. What would it be like to have someone support her? Stand by her no matter what? To have someone in her life that cared about her in the sacrificial way that Gage loved Maddy.

She blinked. There wasn't anyone. And she didn't

need there to be anyway. That was what made her mother so weak. Her mother needed someone else to make her feel complete, needed drama and loud fights and passionate sex to feel alive. Lily made herself feel alive. She pushed herself, supported herself. She was the only one she counted on for anything, and that was the way it had to be. If she let herself down, there was no one else to blame, and there was no one else hurt. It all came down to her.

Usually, those thoughts left her feeling fortified, but not now. It just made her feel lonely. She used to ache like this all of the time. Wish that someone would care for her, care about her. She'd let it go so long ago she hadn't realized that those old longings still existed… they were buried, but still there.

She inhaled a sharp breath of the hot, damp air.

"Of course she had me," Gage said, his voice hard. "I would never leave her to fend for herself."

A tightening sensation curled in her stomach. Envy, she realized. Envy that Maddy had someone who cared for her so much, to love her so much, even if her parents hadn't. Lily hadn't had anyone. She still didn't.

"Let's swim," she said, the words leaving her mouth before she had a chance to process them. She didn't really want to reveal her body to Gage. She valued her image, the shield she'd put up around herself, too much to make herself so exposed. But she realized that if she didn't do something she was in danger of doing something much stupider than that.

"I didn't think you swam."

"It's too beautiful to resist."

Gage dropped anchor on the boat and stepped back down on to the deck, gripping the bottom of his T-shirt and pulling it off in one fluid movement.

Lily felt her jaw go slack, and she knew that she looked as awestruck as she felt. She'd never seen Gage without a shirt. She'd mostly seen him in business attire, which was a massive treat for the eyes. And then, in preparation for the yacht trip, when he'd changed from his suit into pair of well-worn, well-fitted jeans and a threadbare T-shirt that revealed hints of his musculature beneath the soft, thin fabric, she'd found him incredible.

But now, standing in front of her with nothing but those jeans, low-slung, revealing lines that seemed to point straight down to a part of his body that should be completely off-limits to her, even in her mind, he had the power to stun her completely.

His chest was essentially mind-numbing. Acres of golden skin with just a slight dusting of dark hair, his muscles well-defined, shifting and bunching as he moved around the yacht, tying off ropes and making sure everything was secure for them to disembark.

When he straightened she couldn't help but watch the play of his ab muscles, shifting, rippling.

Oh, my...

Her heart thundered and her mouth went completely dry.

She owned beachfront property. She saw half-naked men every day of the week. And she even liked looking at them. But never, ever, had she been unable to do anything but stare. But she couldn't tear her eyes away from him.

Now she really needed a swim. And she hoped the water was cold enough to jar her out of whatever stupor her hormones were lulling her into.

He unsnapped the top button of his jeans and the

intensely provocative motion shook her back to reality. "What are you doing?"

He didn't say anything, only gave her a wicked grin and lowered the zipper on his pants, shrugging them down his slim hips, revealing his swim shorts.

She narrowed her eyes and grabbed the hem of her T-shirt before hauling it over her head. She tugged her shorts down and tossed them onto the chair before the full impact of what she'd done and what she was wearing could hit her.

His eyes raked over her, his expression mirroring everything she was feeling, although he didn't have the dumbfounded look she was sure had been etched onto her face. No, there was nothing confusing about any of this for him. His expression showed nothing but intent. He knew what he wanted, and he knew what to do about it, and suddenly she felt as if she would trade anything, even half of her kingdom so to speak, for an ounce of that surety. To feel confident. To know she could have what she wanted and suffer nothing for the indulgence.

Her self-imposed strictures had never bothered her before. She'd been happy simply putting her head down and working, climbing the ladder, doing everything she could to put miles between herself and her past.

Now, for the first time, she wondered if she'd missed something somewhere along the way.

Part of her wanted to give him the disclaimer that she never wore such revealing swimwear. But another part of her, the more stubborn part, didn't want him to know that she felt totally out of her depth being alone with a man in the middle of a tropical paradise, wearing little more than a few strings tied together and passed off as swimwear.

Instead she reached up and released her hair from its clip, letting it fall down over her shoulders in a wave before she headed over to the ladder that led to the water below them.

She could feel him watching her, could feel the heat of his gaze, touching her like a caress. A shiver ran through her. Her breasts felt heavy and she knew, without having to look down, that her hardened nipples were clearly visible through the thin fabric of her bikini.

She turned and put her foot on the first rung of the ladder, very determinedly not looking at Gage. She made it halfway down the ladder when Gage dove over the side of the boat, his perfect entry barely making a ripple in the clear pool of water.

She rolled her eyes and continued down the ladder. "I'm very impressed," she quipped when he came back to the surface.

"I am, too," he said, not bothering to hide his frank appraisal of her.

Embarrassment warred with pride and arousal. It was the strangest thing. Men had liked her looks before. Men—adult men—had been making passes at her since she was a freshman in high school. Her first, immediate response had always been to discourage. It always made her feel defensive.

But this didn't feel like something she was being subjected to. She felt a part of it, like they were both trapped in the same swirling undertow, unable to escape the pull. She felt like she knew Gage's thoughts, knew them and shared them. That their desire mirrored each others.

She dropped into the water, shocked at how warm it was. Gage swam to her, and put his hand over hers, over where she was still clinging to the metal ladder.

"You can swim, right?"

She nodded. "I just haven't in a long time."

His touch was doing all kinds of things to her, making her ache, making her want, but also, offering comfort. It wasn't like anything she'd ever felt before, and she hated that she was feeling it for him. That she was feeling it for her boss.

He smoothed his thumb over her ring finger, over the ring that was settled there. His ring. "Don't lose this. I don't want to have to send a dive team out."

She looked at her hand. "Oh!" She hadn't even realized the ring was still there. And it had felt so heavy at first that she'd been conscious of it all the time. She didn't even want to know what that might mean. "I can go put it back."

"I've got it."

He took her hand from the ladder and slid the ring off of her finger, climbing quickly back onto the boat.

She flexed her fingers. Now they felt bare. It was an irony she didn't enjoy.

Gage came back down the ladder and she moved to the side as he slid back into the water beside her. "Can you swim to the shore?"

She nodded with more confidence than she felt.

"Let's see if you can beat me," he said.

She couldn't fight the slight smile that tugged at the corner of her mouth. "You know me so well. How can I resist a challenge?"

"I knew you couldn't."

He turned and swam toward shore, smooth strokes barely making a splash in the crystal water. She followed, trying hard to keep up, but she couldn't. He must have known she couldn't or he wouldn't have issued the challenge. He probably swam competitively or something.

She gave up trying to preserve her makeup and slipped under the water, knowing she would be faster that way. When she finally surfaced to get air, Gage was already on shore, lying on the beach, the white sand a light dusting on his golden skin.

When she finally got to where her feet could touch bottom she walked the rest of the way onto the warm sand. "That was cruel," she said, wiping water, and what she was certain would be trails of black mascara, from beneath her eyes.

"You should always carefully consider challenges."

"I accept every challenge."

"Which is why you lose some of them."

She scowled at him and sat next to him, the heat from the sand burning her partially exposed backside.

Gage was having trouble drawing breath, but it had nothing do to with his recent physical exertion, and everything to do with the woman sitting next to him. He'd seen Lily polished to perfection, ready to tackle the press. He'd seen her dressed for an art gala, her hair and gown perfectly pressed. But he'd never seen her like this.

Her brown hair hung wet and curling, her makeup washed off by the saltwater. He could see a light sprinkling of freckles over her nose and across her high cheekbones. She looked softer, more touchable.

And then there was her body. A body that had inspired him to get into the water as quickly as possible so he could avoid revealing to her the effect she was having on him.

Her curves were always flattered by whatever she

wore, but seeing them revealed by the bright red bikini was an entirely different experience.

Her pale breasts, high and firm, her nipples puckered and tight against the wet, clinging fabric of her top, her long, exposed legs, more perfect than his mind could have ever imagined them to be, had him hard and aching. He wanted her, and all of the reasons for him not to have her were becoming less and less significant.

She leaned back, took a deep breath, her breasts rising and falling, his eyes drawn to the pale, creamy skin. "I should take vacations. Or go outside of my condo and go the beach once in a while. You make time for recreation and you're a lot more successful than I am."

"I lived eight years with very little personal life. I've learned to make the time," he said.

"I need to, I think. I didn't before we came here, but…now I do."

She rolled to her side, propping her head up on her elbow. His heart leapt. There wasn't a single swimsuit model that could possibly be more beautiful than Lily, with her unconscious, uncalculated sensuality. It was a provocative pose, her breasts nearly spilling out of her top, her waist seeming even smaller, her hip rounder, in that position, yet he could see nothing in her eyes that even hinted at any knowledge of it.

Lily wasn't sheltered. She wasn't naive. But she seemed so unaware of the power she could wield over a man. Of the power she had over him now.

"I think I… My life is so focused on work. On getting further and further ahead. I never even give myself a chance to enjoy anything else in life. I love my job, and I enjoy work, but…I never date."

"I find that hard to believe."

"Okay, I've dated," she said. "In fact, recently I've had several very disastrous dates set up by well-meaning friends."

"Why would you have your friends set you up? Why not just date someone you meet and are attracted to?"

She laughed softly. "That would require getting out of my house or the office on occasion."

"You could have any man you wanted," he said, his voice rough.

She looked at him, her dark eyes unveiled for a moment, the heat in their dark depths calling out to him, making his body ache for her. Making him ache for her in more than just physical ways. "I haven't really wanted any men."

"You want me," he said, not seeing any point in skirting the issue.

"I…sometimes I think I do," she said, her voice a whisper. She looked away from him then. It was strange, seeing her unsure, seeing her vulnerable. He wanted her to be bold, to show confidence, to give him some kind of sign that she was open to a purely physical fling.

If her take-no-prisoners attitude from the boardroom carried over to the bedroom, she would. But when it came to attraction she seemed to lose all of the boldness. All that hardened attitude turned soft. It made him want to comfort her. To just hold her against him until the tension left her body and she softened against him, softened for him.

He sucked in a breath, consigning the consequences of his actions to hell, and leaned in, brushing his lips against hers. He waited, waited to see what her reaction would be. That wasn't his usual style, but she was nothing like his usual women.

She looked at him then, her dark eyes unsure. He

kissed her again, more insistently this time, his hands skimming the dip of her waist, the curve of her hip. When he slid his hands around to her backside and slipped his fingers just barely beneath the waistband of her bikini bottoms she sucked in a shocked breath, parting her lips, giving him the chance to slide his tongue into her mouth.

She brought her hands up to his arms and gripped his biceps, clinging to him. She moaned softly as he abandoned her mouth, pressing kisses to the soft, tender column of her throat. Kissing the pulse that fluttered at the base of her neck.

Then he captured her mouth again, moving both of his hands to her backside and bringing her so that she was resting partly on top of him. Her thigh was pressed against his erection, the slight pressure pleasure and torture at the same time.

She pulled away, her eyes wide, her breathing harsh. "Oh…" She rested her head on his chest, her heart pounding hard enough that he could feel it against his stomach. "How do you do that?"

He chuckled, despite the persistent ache in his groin reminding him they were nowhere near finished, and ran his fingers through her hair. "Do what?"

"You make me forget why this is a very bad idea. You make me forget why I decided it can't happen. I can't think of anything when you kiss me."

"That's a good thing, Lily."

"I don't know that it is."

Lily slithered away from Gage and stood on wobbly legs. She felt light-headed, like she might pass out. She'd never, ever, been kissed like that. Oh, she'd been kissed, she'd been pretty thoroughly kissed in fact, but it had never felt anything like that. It had never made her forget where she was, who she was, why she shouldn't be kissing him.

Usually, when she was being kissed, she was wondering if the guy was going to ask to come in for a cup of "coffee," and how she was going to turn him down. But she had a feeling Gage could have stripped off her insubstantial swimsuit and she never would have noticed, or been upset about it. In fact, she had a feeling she simply would have embraced it, the mind-numbing pleasure of his touch, and gone after something they would likely both regret later.

She sucked in a sharp breath. "We've already been over the fact that neither of us does the serious thing," she said slowly. "Which means...which means if we were to have sex it would be a fling. An affair."

He stood up, too, his arousal still blatantly pressing against the front of his shorts. She tried, valiantly, not to look, but failed. She'd never seen such an aggressively male sight in her life. And he was tempting her all over again.

She didn't need tempting. She needed a moment of sanity.

Gage nodded. "That's how I conduct my relationships, Lily."

She looked at the water, at the waves lapping against the shore. "What about my job?"

"Your job isn't in jeopardy either way."

"Then I guess the only question is whether or not *I* can do a fling."

"You think you might want more?" he asked.

"No. I don't want more, I know that. I like my life as it is. But then..." She'd seen her mother on the brink of insanity over men, crying when they didn't call, crying when they did. Throwing things when they cheated, screaming when they broke up with her.

Lily had worked so hard to never be that person. She'd avoided relationships, avoided any kind of deep, emotional involvement. Part of her was afraid that, while she knew she didn't want to enter into relationship hell, she would forget that as soon as she crossed that line with a man.

Sex seemed to have some sort of strange power over women, a power than went beyond the simple pleasure it provided. She didn't want to be subject to that.

"You're concerned it would be awkward working together?"

"Yes." *Among other things.* "And my job is very important to me. I don't think it's worth compromising that for a fling."

He moved to her, cupping her cheek, stroking her skin with his thumb. "It would be a very good fling."

She closed her eyes, fighting the rising tide of heat and trying to lay claim on her own body again. "I'm sure of that."

Fear warred with common sense and desire. She wanted him, but she was afraid. Afraid of who this desire might make her become. Afraid of losing control. Of giving any of her hard-won control to him, both in the bedroom and in her life in general.

She hadn't been worried about that when he'd been kissing her though. She hadn't been able to worry about anything.

She felt like she was standing on the edge of one of the rocky cliffs that surrounded the island, poised to jump into the water, unsure of how deep it would be. She could turn and walk away, and never know, but everything would be back to normal, back to her life as she knew it, as she had made it to be. Or she could jump, not knowing what would happen, not knowing if she would survive.

"I…I can't." It was too much. He made her feel too much.

She saw a flash of frustration in his blue eyes, but it didn't linger. He cupped her face with both hands now, his touch tender. "If you change your mind, you can always come to me," he said, his voice strained. "But you will have to come to me. I don't force my attentions on women who don't want them. I have no need to."

He turned from her and waded back into the water, swimming back to the yacht.

A feeling of sadness washed over her. She almost wished he would have promised to seduce her. Now that it was up to her she knew she would never find the courage. And she hated that. Hated that she still lived with so much weakness. Weakness she'd been able to ignore, been able to deny, until she'd met Gage. Weakness she was still too afraid to try and overcome.

CHAPTER SEVEN

LILY disappeared into her room when they arrived back at the vacation home and reappeared a few hours later, her armor back in place. Her hair was pinned perfectly into place again, her makeup covering her freckles.

"Any plans for tonight?" she asked, her high heels clicking on the wooden floor as she moved across the room, keeping her distance from him as she settled onto the low couch.

"We're treating the board to a traditional dinner on the beach. Complete with traditional dancing."

"I love that idea. Will you be doing it for regular guests, too?"

He nodded. "Yes. When I first visited Thailand I was backpacking with friends, no luxury resorts or anything. We ate in the marketplaces and avoided the tourist traps. I want to bring that element into the resort. Luxury, but with a chance to experience the culture."

She shot him a severe look, her lush lips pulled into a tight line. "We're putting that in the press release when the resort opens. I don't understand why you're so reluctant to give the public some information about the good things that you do."

He let out an exasperated sigh. "As you said, Lily, they call it a private life for a reason. I don't see the

point in sharing every aspect of myself with the press.
I don't talk about the fact that I raised Maddy because
I'm afraid it would embarrass her. She feels like she
must have been unlovable for our parents to neglect her
like they did, and I'm not about to let the public know
the circumstances of her life. It isn't fair to her."

"And the other things? The sanctuary? Your respect
for the Thai culture?"

"Personal."

"But it's not really. It relates back to your business,
to your image. And really, why not let people know
you're actually a decent person?"

He laughed. "My parents made so many charitable contributions they were hailed as the most generous couple in the San Diego area. They have plaques
on schools and hospitals. It didn't make them good
people."

Gage knew, better than most, that public image and
private image were not the same thing. His parents
were the most self-absorbed, selfish people he'd ever
encountered, and that included every one of his past
mistresses.

All of the flash, all of the grand gestures, meant
very little when the only thing behind it was a desire
for more publicity. His parents didn't care about anyone,
or anything, beyond their own ambitions. He'd worked
all of his young adult years to establish his business.
He'd been so determined to impress them with who
he'd become.

He'd made his first million, his first two million, and
still he'd waited. Finally he'd stopped caring. Probably
on the day Maddy called, telling him she hadn't eaten
for three days, not because his parents were too poor to
provide her with food, but because they were so busy

living their very important lives they'd forgotten their daughter. That was also the day he'd brought his sister to live with him.

"The fact that my parents were willing to spare the time to write a check to boost their likability, to gain more business, didn't make them good, or giving, or caring," he growled, rage coursing through him at the memory. "I don't play that game."

He didn't know what it was about Lily that made him say those kinds of things. She made him want to explain. If it were any other woman, any other employee, he simply would have let them think what they wanted, no explanation offered. But she wasn't just another woman, and she wasn't just an employee, either. He wasn't certain how he felt about her falling outside of those clear, distinct categories.

"I understand that. I understand how much parents can motivate what you do and don't do." She looked up, meeting his gaze for the first time since they'd kissed on the beach. "My mother...growing up with her was difficult. Her relationships and all the drama they came with were the most important things to her. They consumed her and I hated it. I hated seeing her so controlled by this twisted emotion that she called love that made her do and accept the most horrible things."

"That's why you don't do relationships."

She nodded in confirmation. "That's why I don't do relationships. Ever. I don't want to turn into that. I don't want anyone or anything controlling me like that."

"I wouldn't, Lily, you know that. I don't do the toxic relationship thing. Women I date are free to be their own people. I'm not looking to force anyone to fit into my lifestyle, because I'm not looking to add anyone to my life permanently."

Lily bit her bottom lip until it hurt. She was tempted, again, so very tempted, to take Gage up on his offer. She'd come out of the bedroom with the best of intentions, her protective shield in place, ready and willing to resist him and carry on like she always had. But that was impossible. She *knew* now. She knew about the power of desire.

Wanting sexual satisfaction was entirely different than wanting another person. It wasn't simply about wanting to reach the peak of pleasure, it was about wanting to touch him, taste him, explore him. It wasn't about just wanting a man. That would have been much easier to cope with. This was about wanting one man specifically. She wanted Gage. No one else.

But the fear wasn't gone. Being with him was complicated, and not just because he was her boss. Sleeping with him would mean no barriers. There would be no way for her to stay in control the whole time. She knew that just from one kiss. Ironic since she'd always thought that when she did choose to have sex with a man her problem would be forcing herself to give up her control.

She'd imagined she would find it impossible to reach orgasm because she would be too concerned about being vulnerable, out of control. She hadn't anticipated the man being able to rob her of it as neatly and quickly as Gage was able to.

When he was touching her, she *wanted* to surrender, wanted to simply allow him to sweep her off her feet and take her on the journey her body was begging to go on. And that was frightening.

She closed her eyes and swallowed hard. "Give me until after the dinner tonight," she said. "I'll decide by then."

Gage's expression didn't change, his firm jaw set, his eyes unreadable. "Decide?"

"Whether or not I'm ready for a fling," she said then added, "a fling with you."

"I didn't imagine you meant with one of our distinguished members of the board," he said, his voice husky.

She laughed shakily. "I wanted to make sure. I know how people can spin things. I work with the media, remember?"

He leaned in, so close she could feel his breath fanning over her cheek. She closed her eyes as a shiver slithered through her body, starting in her shoulders and spreading everywhere, leaving her nipples tight and aching, her body wet with wanting him.

"This isn't really your thing, is it? You're not a fling kind of girl."

Her eyes fluttered open, reality crowding all the lovely arousal that had been making her feel warm and languid and brave. "You don't think so?"

Of course she wasn't. She was a twenty-seven-year-old virgin, but that admission wasn't about to escape her lips. She didn't want him thinking he was special, or that there was something wrong with her, or that she was suddenly going to start salivating whenever she saw a diamond ring. This wasn't emotional for her, not really, this was about physical need.

She trusted Gage, in a certain respect, but that was the only emotion involved. Still she'd had the opportunity to observe how Gage was in relationships. He wasn't controlling, or manipulative. He was honest about what he wanted and both parties in the relationship ended up satisfied in more ways than one. That was what she wanted, all she wanted.

And she had to do this. She had to take control of her life, her body, her sexuality. Now that she realized how much of her life had been controlled by her mother's actions, now that she saw just how much power she gave to the many men that had paraded through her mother's life, to the drama and the fights and the tears, she knew she had to move beyond it. This was her chance. If she was brave enough to take it.

"I haven't had time to have one since coming to work for you." The honest truth, even if it was misleading.

"Just don't forget that it's only a fling. Women can be emotional about sex and if it's been a while for you…"

She met his gaze, her heart pounding hard. "Gage, have I ever seemed like the kind of person who doesn't know her own mind? Let me worry about it. I promise you, I don't have one single repressed fantasy about love and happily ever after anywhere inside of me. I'm far too practical." She stood from the couch, trying to keep her expression cool, trying to ignore her rapidly beating pulse. "And anyway, it's only a fling. I'll probably forget about it in a few years' time."

Gage crossed the room, his expression intense. He bent down and hooked his arm around her waist, bringing her into a standing position, hauling her up against him. "You won't forget me, Lily," he said, his voice rough.

He leaned down, his mouth urgent on hers. There was nothing slow about this kiss, nothing like the kiss they'd shared on the beach. This was fire and urgency. This wasn't a slow tasting, this was a feast. She parted her lips for him, meeting his tongue thrust for thrust, lacing her fingers through his short dark hair, pulling him even harder against her.

His big hand cupped her bottom, bringing her tightly against his body, letting her feel the hard ridge of his erection pressing against her stomach.

He pulled away from her suddenly, his breathing harsh, his chest rising and falling. When he withdrew completely and stepped away from her she was afraid she might melt to the floor without his arms to support her.

She put a hand on her lips, feeling how hot and swollen they were.

"After the dinner, tell me what you want," he said gruffly. "Be very sure."

"I know what I want now," she said with a boldness she didn't feel. "Do you want me? I mean *me*, not just sex." She didn't know why, but that seemed important. She didn't want him picturing one of his little blonde heiresses while he was in bed with her. That was a matter of pride.

He took hold of her wrist and pressed her hand against his chest, against his raging heartbeat. "Does that feel like I want you?"

"Yes," she whispered. She looked down and saw, very clearly, the outline of his rigid erection pressing against his jeans. She swallowed. There was no room for her to be timid. He wouldn't want a shy little virgin in his bed, that much was obvious from the type of women he chose to date. Which meant she'd have to be a confident virgin, a virgin who could fake more experience than she had. Well, experience she might not have, but she had desire.

She slid her hand down his chest, moved her palm to cover the hard ridge of his arousal. He let his head fall back, his breath hissing between his teeth. "So does this," she said.

"Careful," he groaned. "Or neither of us will be making it to dinner."

A sliver of pleasure wound its way through her, along with a surge of adrenaline. This was a new kind of power, power she hadn't anticipated. She'd assumed, because of the way her mother behaved, that when it came to sex, men held all the cards. But she knew now that wasn't true. Right now, holding him in her hand, she was in control. She was the one driving him crazy with desire, pushing him beyond his control.

"Well, we can't have that. I'm really looking forward to dinner."

He leaned in, pressed a kiss to her neck, to where her pulse was fluttering rapidly. "I'm looking forward to dessert."

The flickering light from the bonfire, the lingering heat from the day, combined with the slow, seductive music, made Lily feel like she was under a spell. Maybe she was, because she had no idea what sort of magic had bewitched her into thinking she could have a no-strings relationship with Gage. But even now she wasn't afraid, not even after having time to reflect on what it would mean for her. What it might make her feel.

She wanted him. Why should her dysfunctional childhood keep her from having something she wanted? She'd never given it that sort of power in any other area of her life. In fact, she'd been determined to overcome it no matter what. But when it came to men, she'd let it hold her back.

It wasn't as though there were any missed opportunities she regretted, no men she wished she'd been able to take the chance on. But if she didn't find out what it was like with Gage, she knew she would regret that.

It would be a holiday romance. Not even a romance, it would be nothing but holiday sex. She would find out what it was like, satisfy her curiosity, satisfy the flame that burned low in her body, and move on. And so would he.

They were adults, there was no reason they couldn't be adult about it. No reason at all.

She looked at Gage, at the way the orange flames highlighted his sharp cheekbones and angular jaw. He was such a gorgeous man, and she'd kissed his perfect lips. Anticipation made her feel restless, edgy. Needy.

Soon she would know what he looked like without clothes covering his amazing body. Soon, every part of him would be hers. To explore, to touch, to taste.

"I think this is an amazing investment opportunity you have here, Mr. Forrester," one of the board members, she wasn't sure which one, said.

"It is," she said, sitting up straighter. "And what Gage is doing here goes well beyond simple tourism. He's offering a true, authentic experience, with as little or as much luxury as the guest would like to experience."

The older man gave Gage a sly smile. "Not a bad idea, Forrester, getting your PR specialist so sweetened up."

Gage scooted closer to Lily, looping his arm around her waist. "Lily has more professional integrity than anyone I've ever met. Myself included. Our relationship has nothing to do with the quality of her work. I'd recommend her business to anyone."

Lily was shocked to hear Gage give her such an emphatic endorsement, and she said as much when the members of the board were either too intoxicated to pay attention, or had gone back to their rooms.

"It's true," Gage said, shrugging. "You're great at

what you do. My attraction to you has nothing to do with how well you do your job."

"And when our relationship is over you're planning on pawning me off? Professionally speaking, I mean." She hated the insecurity in her voice, hated the slight quiver that made her sound weak. What did it matter if he was planning on letting her go? As long as her next job paid as well, it didn't matter whether she stayed with Forrestation or not. She'd done a wonderful job for his company, and there was ample evidence of that.

"Not at all. I'll have no problem working with you after things end, Lily. It's never been an issue for me. I'm still on good terms with most of the women I've had relationships with, and if I'm not, it's because of them, not me."

"After we leave Thailand, it's over," she said, with much more finality than she felt. But it was vital, absolutely necessary that she put a limit on it. That this was madness brought on by a sensual setting. Madness that did not move into the office with them.

He raised his eyebrows, his mouth quirked in a sardonic half smile. "Shall we sign a contract?"

She sniffed. "I don't think that's necessary, but I don't see the point of bringing it back into the office, either."

"You drive a hard bargain, Ms. Ford."

"I learned from the best, Mr. Forrester."

He leaned in and kissed her on the forehead, his lips warm, the feeling of comfort it brought her making a flutter of panic spring to life in her belly. He wasn't supposed to make her feel things. He pulled back and ran his hand over her smooth, neatly tied hair. "You need to wear your hair down for me. It's sexy."

She searched for some witty, off-the-cuff reply, but

she lost the ability to think when he leaned in again and kissed her, the pressure of his lips tender at first, then more urgent. She put her hand on her cheek, slid her tongue over his bottom lip. Yes, she was making the right choice. She wanted this. She wanted something beyond business, something just for herself. No one had to know. Actually, everyone would believe it had happened now, with their fake engagement making headline news, whether it happened or not. Which made it all the more tempting to indulge.

Just now the only thing she could feel was a throbbing urgency that started at the apex of her thighs and radiated out. Made her feel empty and excited all at the same time.

"I think we should go back to the room," she whispered, kissing his neck, tasting the salt of his skin.

"I think that's a very good idea."

Now that Lily was standing in Gage's room, looking at the big bed in the corner, she didn't feel as confident as she had on the beach. As she had when he was kissing her. She still wanted him, but all of her insecurities were back. She wished she had something to help boost her confidence.

Sexy lingerie would have helped. Clothes always helped her slip into her role, helped her create the image she was striving to project. She used it for work to great effect and she needed it desperately now. Needed something to help her be that confident woman that she always tried to portray in the office.

But she didn't have any lingerie. She hadn't really been expecting to have wild island sex with her boss... or anyone, for that matter.

Gage came up behind her, put his arms around her,

kissed her neck gently, letting her feel the evidence of his arousal against her back. It was very compelling evidence.

She let out a slow breath. "Turn the lights off," she said.

He spun her around so that she was facing him. "I want to be able to see you. I've fantasized about how you might look. What color your nipples are. I want to see your face when I make you come."

Heat flooded her cheeks and she knew she was blushing like the virgin she was.

"Does that bother you?" he asked, his dark brows drawn together, his expression tight.

She shook her head. "It's…it's okay. I liked hearing you talk like that." She was surprised to discover that bit of information about herself.

Yes, hearing him say things like that was embarrassing in a way, and she knew she wasn't going to be able to give him anything like it in return, but hearing him talk like that…it was enough to help her get lost, to forget who she was, who he was, and just embrace the desire that was rolling through her in waves.

"But I would feel better with the light off," she said.

He cupped her chin with his hand, ran his thumb lightly over her bottom lip. "Do you always make love with the light off?"

Make love. It was the first time he'd called it that. Maybe he thought it was too crude to call it what it was now that they were in the bedroom. Maybe that was his version of gentlemanly conduct. She wished he'd just stick to the basics and not muddle things. Not make her feel like they might be about to *make love* when she knew they were just going to have sex.

"I…" She tried to come up with something that wasn't a lie. "I prefer the lights off." There. She was being economical with the truth, but she wasn't out-and-out lying.

He came back to her kissed her gently on the lips before walking over to the other side of the room and turning the main light off. The windows were still open, casting silver moonlight over the bed, but it was better than the full glare of a sixty-watt bulb.

Her heart thundered hard when Gage walked to the bed and started to unbutton his shirt, his movements quick. Now she understood why he'd wanted the light on. She wished she could see him. But then she would lose her covering, and she wasn't prepared to deal with that.

He shrugged the shirt off and it fell to the floor. She could see the outline of his muscles, the moonlight highlighting the ridges and valleys on his body. She swallowed, her throat suddenly dry.

"Come here, Lily," he said softly.

She moved toward him, heart thundering. She was shaking, with nerves, with need, with the enormity of everything. It shouldn't be such a big deal. It was only sex. People had it every day, and then afterward, they walked away. She would do the same.

"Kiss me," she said. "Now." Because when he kissed her, everything made sense, everything seemed right.

He didn't move, he only offered her a half smile that she could see in the pale moonlight, the rest of his handsome face hidden in the shadows. "I told you, Lily, you have to come to me."

She sucked in a breath and walked toward him, putting her hands flat against his chest, his body hard and hot, so masculine. She slid her hands up to his shoulders, his coarse chest hair rough against her palms. She leaned in and kissed him on the corner of his mouth, a move she hoped would tease him, because it was teasing her.

He turned his head and captured her mouth with his, the kiss turning hungry in an instant. She wrapped her arms around his neck, pressing her breasts tightly against that hard, broad chest, the action helping to soothe the sting of her aroused nipples.

He moved his hands around to cup her breasts, to tease the hardened buds. She moaned into his mouth, the sound beyond her control, an expression of pleasure she couldn't have held back if she'd been conscious enough to try.

He wrenched his lips away from hers, pressing a hot, openmouthed kiss to the side of her neck, the touch so erotic it made her knees buckle.

"I have wanted you," he said, kissing her collarbone, "from the first moment I saw you." He kissed the curve of her breast. "I've wanted you naked, in my bed, flushed with desire."

"Now you have me," she said, the words escaping before she could turn them over in her mind, before she could really analyze what she meant. What they might mean to him.

"Yes," he said, his blue eyes glinting, "I do."

He unbuttoned the top of her shirt then took care of the rest of the buttons with a practiced ease she was thankful for. He made it seem so easy, so smooth, that she forgot to be nervous when her shirt fell open, revealing her lacy bra.

He made quick work of that, too, both items of clothing falling to the floor. He moved his hands back to her bare breasts and teased her hardened nipples. Her head fell back, more uncontrollable sounds of pleasure coming from her mouth. All she could do was simply enjoy what he was doing to her, because she had no hope of doing anything else.

He replaced his hands with his mouth, sucking her nipple deep inside, before laving it with the flat of his tongue. "You taste as good as I imagined you would," he said.

Kneeling down in front of her, he undid the closure on her shorts and pulled them down her legs, taking her panties with them. He leaned in then, his breath hot on her just before he claimed her with his mouth, his lips and tongue working magic on her clitoris. She gripped his shoulders trying to steady herself, trying to keep from dissolving into a whimpering puddle at his feet.

Tension started building in her stomach, so tight she thought her legs might buckle. She took a breath, trying to fight the growing sensation of pleasure. She knew what it meant. She was on the brink of orgasm, her whole body trembling with the effort to hold it at bay while he continued to subject her to an onslaught of pleasure.

She threw her head back, fought the rising tide that was threatening to overtake her, threatening to drown her. He'd brought her up so high that if she went over the edge, she was afraid of what might happen. Of what she might do. Of what he might make her feel.

"Enough," she panted, desperate for respite, needing a moment to capture her sanity again.

"You don't want it like this?" he asked, standing and flicking the snap of his jeans open and shrugging them off.

She shook her head, her eyes glued to his body, what she could see of it in the dim lighting. She'd never seen a naked man in person before. He was almost awe-inspiring. His body so different from hers. He was so masculine, muscular, his erection thick and tempting. It scared her how much she wanted him. How much she wanted to feel him inside of her. How necessary it suddenly seemed.

She sat on the bed, her legs shaking, her whole body shaking, inside and out.

Gage got onto the bed, leaned over her and moved his hands behind her head, unclipping her bun and weaving his fingers through her hair, spreading it out around her. "I fantasized about this, seeing all of your beautiful hair fanned over my pillow. It's sexier than I could have imagined."

Lily hadn't imagined that there would be so much talking involved in sex, but Gage knew just how to say the right things to make her feel like her body was going up in flames. His words worked with his touch, bringing her to the edge again, making her feel like she might burn to cinders if she couldn't have him.

And this time, there was nothing she could do to stop it. It was like her body belonged to him, like only he could control it. Like he had to power to elicit whatever response he wanted. She closed her eyes, shutting out the thought. Shutting out everything but the desire that was coursing through her.

"I want you, Gage," she said. "I need you." She slid her hands over his back, over his tight butt. His body was perfect, everything a man's body should be. And he was all hers, for tonight at least, to explore and touch. To have his body joined to hers.

He reached over to the nightstand and rummaged for a moment before pulling out a condom packet, tearing it open and rolling the protection on in one swift movement. Then he kissed her, parting her thighs gently and settling between them.

She loved the feeling of having him over her, of feeling his naked body pressed against every naked inch of hers.

He nudged at her damp entrance with the head of his erection and she spread her legs wider, hoping it might help her accommodate him. He put his hand underneath her backside and lifted her slightly before thrusting into her.

The flash of pain shocked her, but it was over quickly and then she just felt full. So deliciously full. Never in her life had she felt so complete, yet so needy at the same time. Having him inside of her was wholly satisfying, while also managing to create a deep need in her that she knew only he could answer.

"Lily?" His voice was rough, the tendons in his neck standing out, a testament to the strain it caused him to speak, to keep himself still.

She kissed him, and she felt his body shuddered inside of her, his shaft growing harder, increasing the feeling of fullness. Increasing her growing pleasure. "Gage, let me have you."

She knew the exact moment he lost his control. He withdrew before thrusting full back inside of her. She arched into him, the feeling so exquisite she thought she might break apart. She gripped his buttocks as he rode her, wrapped her legs around his calves as she moved against him in rhythm. Her climax started to build, the tension inside of her reaching heights she thought were impossible.

If the peak she'd nearly reached earlier had been frightening, this one was completely terrifying. All-consuming. Her entire being trembled, the need for release pulling her muscles tight, making her entire body tense. She couldn't fight it. Didn't want to fight. She needed to finish it, no matter what. There was no other choice. Her control was given over to him.

"Oh, Gage, oh, please," she breathed, not knowing quite what she needed from him.

He moved his hands to her breasts, brushed his thumbs over her nipples, the added stimulation just what she needed to push her over the edge. The dam that had been holding back the flood burst and pleasure rushed through, overtaking her. She froze, her back arched, her mouth open on a soundless scream as her body tightened around his. He thrust into her, harder, more wildly, his movements lacking any control. Then he found his release on a masculine groan of pleasure.

On the heels of her release, of the amazing burst of pleasure, came a wave of emotion so strong it made her ache. She held on to him for a while, feeling his heart beat against her chest, listening to the sound of his broken, labored breathing. Her body shook and she felt warmth on her cheeks. She put her hand up and touched her face, feeling the wetness left by her tears.

CHAPTER EIGHT

GAGE looked at Lily, flushed, satisfied and crying, tears rolling down her cheeks, little sobs making her body shiver beneath his.

"Are you hurt?" he asked, his chest tightening. He'd never been with a virgin before, but even without the experience, he was certain that Lily had been one. And it was causing a riot of emotions to roll through him, emotions he'd never dealt with in his life, and didn't want to deal with now.

"I…" She sucked in a shaking breath. "No."

He withdrew from her body and rolled over so that he was still close, but no longer connected to her. He needed at least that much space, that much of a chance to regain his sanity.

He drew her into his arms, let her cry. His muscles were so tense he felt like they might seize up. Everything in him wanted to run, but he forced himself to stay, to hold her until the tears stopped falling.

She pulled away from him, scrubbed her arm across her cheeks, leaving her face red and puffy. It was rare to see Lily look anything less than perfect, and even rarer to see her when she wasn't composed. Those moments when she'd come apart in his arms, she hadn't been composed or businesslike. And now, with her nose cherry-colored from crying and her brown hair tangled from their recent lovemaking, she was still beautiful to him. Possibly more beautiful than she'd ever been.

"I'm sorry," she said stiffly.

"Why didn't you just tell me? Didn't you think I might want to know?" he said, the clawing feeling in his stomach making his voice harsher than he'd intended.

"No, Gage, I didn't. My experience, or lack of it, is none of your business."

"I told you, this is temporary."

She turned her head sharply, dark eyes glittering. "And I told you that we're finished when we leave Thailand. Nothing has changed. I didn't tell you that I was a virgin, which is what I assume your issue is, because it was a nonissue to me. Therefore, I wouldn't think it would matter to you." She blew out a breath. "I should go to my own room. This was a mistake."

She moved to leave and he took her arm. "No. Lily, you're not leaving. You're staying with me, in my bed." And why that should matter to him, he didn't know. He wasn't the kind of guy who cuddled afterward. In fact, he usually left the hotel sometime after his lover had fallen asleep. If they didn't leave first.

But it didn't seem right to take Lily's virginity and have her sleep alone. A litany of curse words scrolled through his mind. He didn't want it to matter that he was the first man she'd been with. He didn't want her to be different in any way. She was right, it was her choice. She was a twenty-seven-year-old woman, not a young girl that he'd seduced.

"I would feel more comfortable in my own room."

"Too bad. Clause five of our fling contract says we share a bed when we make love."

"I don't remember approving that."

"And I don't remember seeing anything about you being a virgin."

"I told you, it doesn't matter."

He blew out an exasperated breath. "It does, Lily, whether you think so or not, it does. You didn't know you would cry. You didn't know how it would make you feel."

She shrugged. "It was a release. It just happened to release tears, too. I'm not going to lie, it was a fantastic orgasm." He noticed that she angled her face away when she said it. Her voice was casual, but it was obvious that she didn't feel casual.

"The last thing I want to do is hurt you, but I can't give more than I've offered."

"Honestly, Gage, I don't want more than you've offered. Why do you think I was a virgin? It wasn't because I was saving myself. It's because I didn't want the hassle."

She gathered the sheets up and moved to climb out of bed.

"Lily, stay with me. I'm not going to turn this into something that seems sordid and dirty by having you go and sleep in your own room."

She stayed still for a moment, her expression cool, her dark eyes focused on a point other than his face. But after a moment she settled back into bed, pulling the sheets up as high under her arms as she could.

He leaned in and kissed her bare shoulder before rolling out of bed and walking into the bathroom to dispose of the condom. His heart was still pounding from the force of his release. He walked back into the bedroom and climbed back into the bed. After a moment's hesitation he pulled her into his arms.

She deserved that much. It didn't mean anything,

it couldn't. But it had been her first time, and she deserved to have nothing but good memories from it. She deserved more than he'd given her. More than he could ever give her.

He'd been counting on a second time, after he'd gotten the hot and fast out of the way. But he didn't want to cause her any pain.

In every possible way, he wanted to spare her pain. And he was worried that it was too late for that.

It was still dark when Lily opened her eyes. Gage's arm was snaked around her waist, holding her to him, her backside pressed against his hard erection.

She looked at the clock. Nearly five.

Panic fluttered in her stomach. She didn't want him to wake up and see her like she was. She needed her armor, something to help her be cool and calm when she had to face the man in whose arms she'd come apart. The man who knew she had been a twenty-seven-year-old virgin. The man who had held her while she'd cried in the aftermath of her release.

She slid out of the covers and she tiptoed out of the room and across the house, into her room, wishing, again, that there was a door so that she could close it behind her.

The first thing she did was check her email for new alerts and cursed creatively when she saw one pop up about Maddy.

She brainstormed ways to divert the new details Callahan and his wife were dishing while she showered, trying not to linger on the parts of her body that still felt sensitized from Gage's touch. She shivered as the hot water sluiced over her skin and tears pricked her eyes. Again. She shut the flow of water off and dried quickly, before applying her makeup, fixing her hair and picking out a freshly pressed skirt and button-up blouse.

She was sitting on the edge of the bed, fastening the dainty buckles on her blue kitten heels, when Gage's voice broke into her thoughts.

"You have the most interesting taste in shoes."

"I like shoes," she said, her heart fluttering wildly. She gritted her teeth and tried to calm her body's response to him before she looked up.

He was standing in the open doorway, leaning against the frame, wearing last night's jeans, riding low on his lean hips, and nothing else.

"Why aren't you in bed, Lily?" he asked, his voice so seductive it ought to be outlawed.

"I get up early," she said tightly, rising from her position on the bed. "And I'm not really a lounge-around-in-my-pajamas kind of person."

"I wouldn't guess you were. But I had hoped you were a walk-around-in-nothing-but-a-smile kind of person." His blue eyes were hot as he looked at her, his expression making it clear that, even though she'd gone to all the trouble to dress, he was envisioning her naked.

She sucked in a breath. "Nope, not that, either."

"Lily, come here."

She found herself walking toward him, even though she didn't remember telling her feet it was all right to move. He pulled her to him and kissed her, gently, seductively, sensually. She pressed her palms against his chest, intent on pushing away, but instead, her hands just lingered there, enjoying the feeling of all that hard, masculine flesh.

He pulled away slightly, resting his forehead against hers. "We aren't done," he said, his voice soft, but uncompromising.

Her whole body tingled, her nipples tightening, her core aching for his possession. They weren't done. There was no way she could leave it at one night, not when he still had the power to affect her like he did.

They had to let the fling run its course. That was what had to happen. They had a few days until they were meant to leave Thailand, and in that time they would be able to get it out of their systems. She was certain of it.

"I know we aren't," she whispered.

"When I wake up in the morning, I expect you to be in my bed. And I don't want you to be dressed." He moved against her, his arousal blatant, the intent in his eyes obvious. And she found herself responding to it. Very few men spoke to her that way. They found her intimidating. Gage didn't. And for some reason she found it incredibly sexy, hearing him say just what he wanted. "I want you naked. And I want you ready for me."

"I expect the same," she said, finding boldness much easier to come by when she had her appearance put together. It was easier to find her confidence when everything was in place. She felt more in her element, like this was a business negotiation and she had bargaining power.

"Those are terms I can readily agree to." He kissed her neck and she melted against him. "So, there is an advantage to you wearing your hair back. I can kiss you like this." He demonstrated again and she trembled beneath his erotic touch.

"I have some work to do this morning," she said, not sounding terribly convincing, even to herself.

"Do you?"

"Yes," she gasped as he nipped her lightly then soothed the sting away with his tongue. "A witness has spotted us venue-hunting for the wedding."

He stepped away. "Have they?"

She frowned. "I know. It's mildly horrible. But there are new details coming out about Maddy's supposed affair with William Callahan. If the media is intent on reporting that as fact with no more proof than they have, then I don't feel too guilty for misleading them."

"They're vultures. All they want is to feed off of the misfortune of others. To make a profit off of someone else's misery. I say lie away," Gage said, his expression fierce.

"Anyway, I just need to cultivate a convincing story and send it using one of my alternate email accounts."

"That's why I pay you so much."

"For my evil genius?"

He smiled, and her heart leapt. "Among other things." He cupped her cheek and her leaping, traitorous heart compounded its sins by pounding harder when he brushed his thumb lightly over her skin. "I'm going to go and check my email. I'll meet you afterward, for breakfast."

She could only nod as he turned and walked back out of the room. She sank onto the bed, hand on her chest, and tried to catch her breath. When he'd smiled like that…it had made her feel as if her heart was too big for her chest.

It's just the sex. Nothing more.

She walked over to the desk and sat at her laptop,

determined to push all thoughts of Gage from her mind and focus on her work. After all, the fling with Gage would only last a few more days. Her job was the constant. It was what mattered and she wasn't about to compromise that by trying to make more of their relationship than there could ever be. She didn't want it anyway.

The new physical connection they had was enough. She had no desire to get in any deeper. Part of her still wondered what she'd been thinking to give in to the attraction that burned between them. Part of her wished she'd just walked away from the edge of the cliff instead of jumping into the unknown.

He was right about one thing. She hadn't known. She'd thought sex would bring pleasure, but she hadn't realized the connection it could forge between two people, not really.

Of course, she hadn't been thinking when she'd agreed to the fling. She'd been following her most base desires instead of her intellect. Which had been her first mistake. But it was too late now. Now she *knew*. Now she felt like she had to let it reach a conclusion or it would always feel like it did now. Mysterious, almost too good to be real. Like she might cry just from thinking about the moment when Gage had joined his body to hers.

She finished dashing off the email and hit Send then leaned back in the chair, trying to breath deep enough to make the tightness in her chest go away.

She pushed away from the desk and stood. It was too late now. It was done. She'd made the decision, and she would accept everything that came with it. There was no point in regretting it. All she could do now was see it through. And when it was over she would be back to living like she always had, with the memory of how wonderful a few stolen moments in Gage Forrester's arms could be.

She managed to hold the tears back the second time they were together, until she escaped to her room on the excuse that she wanted a shower, and that she didn't want to share. Then she let it out. Tears tracked down her cheeks as she stood beneath the water.

She didn't know what it was that made her emotions, always so under control, release completely in the aftermath of a climax with Gage. She shut the water off and dried quickly, wrapping the towel tightly around herself before returning to the dark bedroom.

He'd honored her request for darkness this time, too, pulling down the shades likely because he knew just how inexperienced she was now. But he'd been merciless in his pursuit of giving her pleasure. He'd driven her higher, further, than she'd ever imagined possible.

And when she'd reached the peak, she'd screamed her pleasure. She cringed at the memory of how completely she'd lost her control. He'd always been able to do that to her. Even if it was just by getting her to talk about things she normally kept to herself.

She tiptoed back into the bedroom, hoping that Gage was asleep.

"You're beautiful," he said, his voice husky and enticing in the darkness, proving that her hopes for sneaking back in unnoticed were in vain.

A lot of men had told her she was beautiful, but never while she was naked. Not that he could see her all that well with the lamp switched off, the only light in the room filtering in from behind the edges of the shades. She was used to men drooling over her looks, but being told she was attractive had never affected her in the slightest.

It didn't matter what someone thought of her if she didn't have any interest in them. But hearing it from Gage made new heat bloom in her belly, made her ache to have him again, despite the strength of her earlier release. Physically, she was ready anyway. Emotionally, she didn't think she could go through it again.

She didn't respond, she only slid back into bed, her heart hammering already, just from being near him. She rolled over to her side, facing away from him, her arms crossed tightly over her breasts.

"You don't like to be told that you're beautiful?" She felt the mattress dip as Gage shifted and moved nearer to her, putting his arms around her and drawing her against him.

"Thank you," she said softly.

"You're so tense, Lily." He moved one hand to her shoulders and kneaded her tight muscles gently.

"I'm still not used to this."

Inwardly, Gage berated himself for putting both of them in this situation. He didn't know what compelled him to draw her closer, to want to comfort her when she was obviously in distress. It wasn't what he was looking for. But he couldn't resist the urge to hold her, either, even as slight panic gnawed at his stomach.

It was the responsibility that came with bedding a virgin. He'd never done it before that first night with Lily, and he wouldn't have done it if he would have had any idea that such a confident, sensual woman could have so little in the way of sexual experience.

Whether she believed him or not, she would remember him. Even he remembered his first lover and it had been nearly twenty-two years since the encounter. And it had only happened once. Like it or not, it was up to him to make sure she remembered her first times positively, since it would probably affect her future relationships.

He curled his arm more tightly around her as a fierce possessiveness, like nothing he'd ever felt before, coursed through him. He didn't want to think about Lily being with another man. Ever. She was his.

Mine.

He loosened his hold on her and rolled onto his back, gritting his teeth. She wasn't his. He didn't want her to be. She couldn't be.

He was having some sort of unforeseeable, uncontrollable response to being her first lover. Something he hadn't imagined he was capable of. He wasn't a traditional man. He was all for women being just as liberated as men when it came to sexual pursuits. Unless, of course, the woman was his sister. But he'd always sought out and preferred experienced women, so to have Lily's lack of experience mean anything to him didn't make any logical sense.

That he was bothered by her holding a part of herself back didn't make sense, either. But he was. He gave himself over to pleasure when they were in bed together, but he never engaged his emotions. For him, that wasn't a matter of holding back, that was simply how it was.

But after that first time, after that first, unexpected explosion of emotion, he sensed her fighting something, fighting him, each time they were together. He didn't want that. He wanted to draw the biggest response from her that he could, wanted to take her to new heights of pleasure every time. He wanted to steal all of her inhibitions, wanted her to make love to him in the bright light of day with her hair down and her body revealed to him.

He shouldn't want any of it, and none of it should matter. He had nothing to offer her. If he offered marriage what sort of prize would he be? A man who put his work before everything else. A man who would likely be just as good of a husband and father as his own father had been.

He drew her close to him again. Her virginity, her tears in the wake of a climax, none of it should matter. But it did.

CHAPTER NINE

THEY were leaving Thailand tonight, flying back to San Diego. Back to real life. Back to being boss and employee. Unless of course they were anywhere near where the media might be, then they were still an engaged couple. When they were really just a…not even a couple…just two people who had ended a recent, temporary, only physical fling.

Lily sighed and leaned back in her reclining chair, pretending to relax. That's what they were doing, relaxing, out on the island where they'd shared their first kiss. But she wasn't relaxed. She was aching inside and she wished, more than anything, that she wasn't. She wished she didn't feel anything. Maybe she should feel something, wistfulness maybe, a slight sadness that her incredible nights of pleasure were nearly over, but not this heaviness that had settled in her chest and made her entire being feel as if it was filled with lead.

Gage had been swimming, and she had been content to watch, studying his movements, his athleticism. Now, he was walking through the waves, making his way toward shore, his trunks resting low on his lean hips. And she couldn't help but admire him. Her lover. Her lover whose body she'd barely seen because she'd only ever consented to make love with him in the dark. She knew the feel of his body, though, knew the taste of it. Her heart tightened, and she ignored it.

He moved to her and sat beside her, his gaze roaming over her body, his eyes hungry. She wasn't as embarrassed this time, for him to see her in the bikini. She didn't even feel terribly self-conscious with her makeup washed off and her hair damp and curling thanks to her brief swim. She didn't need the shield as much as she had before.

"We're leaving tonight," he said, his voice husky.

"I know." She didn't look at him.

"Do you still want to end things when we leave Thailand?"

"It's for the best. We had a four-day fling, and it's over now. When we get back to San Diego it will be business as usual. And that's how it has to be, especially with everything going on concerning Maddy. I can't afford to be distracted, and neither can you."

"I do find you very distracting," he said. He leaned over her, brushed her hair from her face. "You're beautiful. I like the way you dress for work, but I like you like this, too. I especially like your freckles." He ran his finger lightly along the trail of dots that were sprinkled across the bridge of her nose.

She felt her cheeks heat. "I've never liked them."

"They're a part of your beauty." He brushed her cheek with the back of his hand and continued on, moving his knuckles lightly over her cleavage, barely hidden by the skimpy bathing suit. Her nipples puckered against the damp fabric, the slight chill created by the breeze not to blame for her response.

When he reached behind her and undid the knot on the halter top of the bikini she clamped her hands to her chest. "What are you doing?"

"Lily, I want to see you." His blue eyes were intense, compelling, his square jaw set.

She lowered her hands and let the fabric fall slightly, the lingering wetness keeping it from falling completely away.

"You don't need anything to be beautiful, sweetheart. All you need is to be you. You're the single most gorgeous woman I've ever seen."

His words were so sincere, and she felt them hit her straight in her heart, right at the source of the unbearable ache that had claimed her body for its own, reminding her that this was likely her last time with him.

The other times she'd been timid. She'd tried to hide behind darkness, behind her makeup, behind her business suits. But she wasn't going to hide anymore. She didn't need to. She was going to take this moment with Gage, this last moment, and she was going to simply feel all of the pleasure he could make her feel.

She pulled her top down the rest of the way and reached around behind herself, releasing the last knot holding the swimsuit on, the last thing keeping her from revealing her breasts.

Gage sucked in a sharp breath, his jaw clenched tight, his eyes hot on her, making her nipples ache for his touch. She hadn't realized how she would feel. She'd thought she would be relinquishing power by being naked, being so vulnerable in front of him. But instead, she just felt an incredible rush of power. The same way she had felt when she'd first realized how much he really wanted her.

He flexed his hands, tightened them into fists, and she knew that it was taking all of his restraint not to touch her, not to rush her. She met his gaze, arousal streaking through her, the abject desire so obvious in

Gage's eyes, in every tense line of his magnificent body, making her bold.

She moved so that she was on her knees and pressed her palms on his chest, still slick with water, hot from the sun, his heartbeat raging against her hand. "Take those off," she said, looking down at his shorts, at his erection, straining against the wet fabric.

He grinned at her, the wicked smile spreading slowly across his face as he moved his hands to the top of his shorts and pushed them down his spare hips, revealing his body fully to her for the first time.

She reached out and circled his shaft with her hand. "*You're* beautiful," she said.

"Now you," he said roughly.

She abandoned her hold on his body, gripped the sides of her bikini bottoms and dragged them down her legs, leaving them in the sand, any embarrassment she might have felt earlier completely absent now. She was lost, in the moment, in her feelings. In Gage.

She stood and wrapped her arms around his neck, kissing him, leading the kiss for the first time, adrenaline and desire pumping through her. "You have a condom, right?" she asked, panting heavily when she abandoned his mouth.

He chuckled and bent down, retrieving his shorts and producing a thin, plastic packet. "I wasn't a Boy Scout, but I take the motto very seriously."

"I'm glad."

He gave the condom packet to her and she tore it open without hesitation, hoping that the sense of confidence she was feeling would help where her inexperience might make things awkward. She was able to roll it onto his thick member without too much effort, the feeling of his hard flesh beneath her hand a thrill that she knew she could never tire of.

She kissed him, keeping her hand on his erection, squeezing him gently. He moaned into her mouth, his obvious appreciation more than enough to fuel the flame of her growing need.

"I want to be on top," she said, unsure if she'd really spoken the words out loud. But this was Gage. She had always spoken her mind to him. Why not now? This was her last chance to have him, and she wanted to have him on her terms. She wanted to have the control.

Gage was afraid he might be in danger of a heart attack, top physical condition or not. Lily, his shy lover, wasn't being shy now. He'd known she was beautiful, had admired what she'd allowed him to see of her body, and hadn't pressed for more out of deference to her inexperience. But now, she was gloriously naked in front of him, in the bright Thai sunlight, her breasts round and full, the tips peaked and aroused, rosy like her lips. A temptation he could not, and did not want to, resist.

He cupped them, teased them, teased himself until she whimpered with pleasure. "I want that, too, Lily," he said, his throat almost too tight for him to speak.

He gripped her around the waist and sat himself down on the sand, bringing her with him and settling her gently on top of him, her loose, wavy brown hair shielding them, creating a curtain around them.

He lifted his head and captured on of her perfect nipples between his lips and sucked gently. She gripped his shoulders and moved her hips, her feminine core sliding over his hard shaft. He cradled her hips and lifted her slightly, helping her find the right position. She sank down onto him gently, her head falling back and a moan of delight escaping her lips as he entered her fully.

It was a battle for him to stop himself from coming as soon as he was inside of her body. But the incredible feeling of being joined to her, combined with the full, unshielded vision of her gorgeous body, had him teetering on the brink.

His blood pounded through him, hard and hot, reckless. And when she began to move over him, setting a rhythm that was slow at first, then faster, more aggressive as she found exactly what pleased her, he could only hold tightly to her, using her hips to keep him anchored to the earth.

He felt her slick core tightening around him, felt the beginning of her orgasm. She bit her lip and tossed her head back again, fighting the release as she always did, before giving in and shuddering out her pleasure. As soon as she reached her peak, he gave himself permission to go over, giving in to his own release with a groan that he couldn't suppress.

She lowered her body onto him, her head resting on his shoulder, her breasts pressed tightly against his chest, her breathing harsh, shaky. He smoothed her hair back and wrapped his arms around her, enjoying the moment. He had never felt anything like that before, not in all of his years of experience.

He had always enjoyed sex, but it had been strictly physical. When he was with Lily it was beyond that. It went to a place that he had never imagined possible. A place he had never imagined could be remotely desirable.

He felt a strange tightening in his chest. She hadn't held back this time. She had been aggressive. She had given herself to him, not just her body, but something more. She had put serious insecurities to rest, and she had done it for him.

Part of him had wanted that, had resented that she'd withheld from him.

Now, with the unwanted tenderness swelling inside of him, all he could do was be thankful that this was their last time together. He couldn't afford for things to go further. For her to get in too deep with him. Because how could he ask all that he had from her, when he had nothing to offer in return?

It was impossible to sit next to Gage only hours after having him naked and beneath her and not have those images flash through her mind. He was back in his business suit, settled into his seat on the plane, his laptop open as he went over some of the specs for the hotel he was having built in England. Thoroughly in boss mode. And still she couldn't do anything but relive those last, powerful moments when she'd shattered over him, when only his tight grip on her hips had kept her from flying into a million pieces.

She hadn't cried that time. But everything in her had felt raw and exposed. She had felt so powerful at first, so amazed that she had been the one to make such a sexy man shake with need. But when her orgasm had crashed in on her she'd realized that if she had a hold on him, he had an equal hold on her. She'd thought she was in control, but it had been a false hope.

She'd also thought that a few days in Thailand would be enough to satisfy her curiosity, scratch her itch, or whatever she'd been imagining it to be. It was so much more complicated than that. She hated that it was, but the absolute truth was that she hadn't remained detached, and she didn't feel the same about him as she had when they'd first arrived in Thailand.

She didn't know how she felt, and, honestly, she didn't want to explore it. But she felt something.

"What are you working on?" she asked, feeling stupid and so much like the kind of silly female she'd always tried to avoid being. She knew what he was working on. It was a sad state of affairs when she was reduced to that kind of ridiculous behavior to make conversation.

"Just going over everything for the Hayden Hotel. Making sure everything I have in my database is the same as the report the contractor sent me."

"Oh," she said.

"It's getting late and we have to be in the office when we land in San Diego. You should try and get some sleep in one of the bedrooms."

By herself. Which she should be thrilled with since it was exactly in line with the deal they had made, and even if they were still involved in their purely physical relationship, she valued her space. But she wasn't thrilled. It made her chest ache, something she couldn't stop or understand.

"Okay. You should sleep, too." She didn't know why she'd said that. She sounded more like a nagging wife than an employee, or even a lover. *Attractive.*

He looked up from his computer and her breath caught. She blinked. He was handsome. He had been before they'd slept together, and he would undoubtedly continue to be handsome. He would probably only improve with age, since, unfairly, men seemed to do that. She couldn't afford to let him affect her every time he so much as glanced her direction.

"Later," he said.

There was no veiled promise in his words, no hint of anything more, like there would have been yesterday, or even earlier that day. He meant that later he would sleep, that was all.

And that was exactly what she would do, too.

She rose from her seat, brushed past him and went to the bedroom that was at the back of the plane. She selected the smaller of the two rooms, since it clearly wasn't the master bedroom, and that way she wouldn't run the risk of accidentally winding up in Gage's bed. Again. Not that any of the other times had been an accident.

Her heart rate kicked up at the thought, her breasts growing heavy, her body getting ready for another erotic encounter.

"Too bad," she said to the empty space.

She kicked off her shoes and lay down in the bed fully clothed, unwilling to go back out into the main part of the airplane and find her bags, which she'd forgotten to bring back with her.

She stretched out, telling herself that having the entire bed to herself was welcome, since she'd been forced to share her space for the better part of a week. But it didn't feel spacious, it felt cold and empty.

And she hated that, after only four days, it was stranger to be without him than it was to be with him.

CHAPTER TEN

"I THOUGHT you could use this," Lily said, setting the large coffee cup on Gage's desk. They were both suffering from jet lag, and even less sleep than usual. At least she was.

He, of course, appeared entirely unaffected as he looked up at her and offered a nod of thanks before accepting the coffee and taking a long drink. Only his closed eyes and slight sigh gave away just how much he needed it.

"What have you got for me this morning?" he asked, his eyes trained on his computer screen.

She took a breath. It was going to be fine. Easy. She was back in her element, not away at some sensual, tropical resort that was basically designed to make the patrons lose their minds and surrender to seduction.

"Nothing new regarding Maddy, but I wouldn't call off the engagement yet. Too obvious." She lowered her eyes and they settled on the ring, still in its place on her left hand. Her heart squeezed tight.

"Of course."

"Your wildlife sanctuary on Koh Samui is being hailed as a great act of conservationism. It's all over the news this morning."

"Good."

She gave him a hard glare. "You don't sound enthused."

"I told you, Lily—" he looked up at her "—my concern about my image begins and ends with the way it affects the bottom line. On a personal level, it isn't a priority." He looked back at his work.

"You're bullheaded, Gage Forrester," she mumbled, sitting in her chair and trying to ignore the rapid flutter of her heart that had been tormenting her since she'd woken up that morning.

"I see no real problem with that."

"What's wrong with people knowing you're a nice person?" she asked, exasperation edging its way into her voice.

"What's wrong with people I don't know and don't care about not knowing?"

She lowered her eyes and stared at the white lid on her coffee cup. "It doesn't make you like your parents just because the public knows about the good that you do in the world."

"We don't need to bring my parents into anything." She looked up into his ice-cold eyes. "It doesn't relate to the work we're doing here. You just stick to doing your job, Lily, and I'll do mine."

His parents and his past clearly wasn't open for discussion anymore. Not now that she was only an employee. When she'd been a potential lover he had shared with her, but now...now she wasn't fit to speak of it apparently. She sucked in a sharp breath. It didn't matter. He was right. It was personal, and this was business. What she'd learned about him during their brief relationship, if it could be called that, had nothing to do with what happened in their professional association.

She would just have to pretend that she didn't know

he'd sacrificed so much of his life to raise his sister, a sister he still felt responsible for. She'd have to pretend she didn't know exactly what he looked like under those perfectly tailored business suits.

Of course, it wasn't any kind of challenge for Gage. Temporary sexual relationships were par for the course for him. Which was one reason she'd decided to give a sexual relationship with him a try, so having an issue with it now was just contrary.

"All right, Gage, but it makes my job easier when you do as I advise you to do."

"I gave you my permission to make the announcement about the sanctuary," he said, his voice conveying just how unconcerned he was.

"Yes," she said tightly, "and it's helped. As I knew it would. Letting people run stories about you that are full of conjecture and false information isn't right."

"Of course, you have no trouble feeding the press false information."

She gave him a steely glare. "They had false information to begin with. And you didn't have a problem with it, either."

"To protect Madeline? Of course not. And we're going to continue on Saturday."

"Oh, really?" Her heart sped up.

"Yes. A very valuable client's daughter is getting married and holding the reception at the San Diego Forrester tomorrow. I've been asked to make an appearance, and of course that means my lovely fiancée should be on my arm."

She looked down at the ring that still glinted on her left hand, her entire body getting stiff with tension. It had been one thing to play happy couple with Gage before they'd been…intimate together. But it was quite another thing to try and pull off when that segment of their relationship was over.

She would have to touch him. Hold his hand. Maybe kiss him.

They hadn't held hands in Thailand. Not casually, not by themselves. It was an odd realization, and it was even stranger that she cared. It was simply a telling example of what their relationship had been. Purely sexual. Those little gestures that actual couples used to convey affection didn't apply to their four-day fling.

"Okay, that works for me." It did. It would. It had to. It was her job to protect Gage's image, and if she didn't go with him, questions might come up, which meant she had to go with him, and she had to turn in the performance of a lifetime.

It had meant buying a new dress—a short, black one with a low V-neckline that had a slight ruffle to help conceal some of the cleavage that the dress put on display—but when she walked into the San Diego Forrester on Gage's arm, her engagement ring sparkling in the overhead lighting, she felt like she belonged there. Like she belonged with Gage.

It was a dangerous feeling, but it was one she had to embrace, at least for the night. There was no other option. Tonight she was Gage Forrester's fiancée. She would try not to focus on the fact that she was really Gage Forrester's discarded leftovers.

Who asked to be discarded.

She took a deep breath and tried to rid herself of the tightness in her chest.

The hotel was decorated beautifully, every table covered with a crimson tablecloth, white orchids in white vases acting as centerpieces. And the tablecloths matched her shoes, which was a very nice and convenient surprise.

Maybe if she focused on that she would survive the evening with some semblance of sanity intact.

Gage put his arm around her waist the moment they fully entered the reception area and she had to fight the urge to melt against him. It was so strange, how natural it was to want that. How easy it was to want to lean on him.

She managed to stop herself. She wasn't about to cling to him, even if his touch did feel better than she remembered. And he smelled amazing. She'd always noticed that about him, from the very first time they'd met. But it was different now, more intimate. Now she picked up on the subtle scent of his skin…clean, but beneath the scent of soap and aftershave, the slight musk of his skin. She could pick it out so easily now, now that she'd been so close to him, now that she knew just how his skin tasted.

The thought made her want to moan out loud, but she managed to hold it back.

Gage sought out the father of the bride and he introduced Lily as his fiancée, then talked to the man for a while about the reception, and offered a free round of drinks. After that, he was fielding requests to hold events at the hotel from every third guest they encountered.

"That was clever," Lily said as they took their seat at their own private table.

"My hotels are popular for a reason."

"You know how to give good service," she said lightly, not realizing the undercurrent in her words until it was too late. And then their eyes met and her stomach tightened.

She licked her lips, but as soon as she slicked her tongue across them they were dry again. She wondered if he could see the signs of her arousal. He knew her so well in that way. She could see his. His eyes darkened, a muscle in his jaw jumped, his hand tightening around his wineglass. He wanted her, too, even though their fling was over.

He'd been cool on the plane ride back to the U.S. and in the office over the past week, but it had been a show. She'd assumed he was done with her, that he'd consigned their affair to a pleasant memory and hadn't thought of her that way, hadn't wanted her, since the moment they'd left Thailand.

"I meant, your customer service is outstanding," she said tightly, trying to ignore the pounding of her pulse and the rush of blood that was making her body feel ultrasensitive.

"Of course," he said, his voice rough, his arousal obvious to her.

"This is really beautiful," she said, trying to recover from her foot-in-mouth moment.

"Yes, it is." His eyes were fixed on her, his gaze lingering on the swell of her breasts. She'd chosen the dress partly for that reason, she was ashamed to admit. She'd told him once that she didn't pick her clothes based on someone else's desires, but she had today. She knew that he liked her figure, and she'd set out to elicit a response from him.

But it was so frustrating, seeing him the office, burning for him, while he seemed to feel nothing but professional courtesy. She was frustrated with him, and she was frustrated with herself. She didn't know what she wanted, didn't know what response the wanted him to give her. She just knew she was unhappy, that at night her bed felt cold and empty. That she no longer found solace in her beachfront apartment and her solitude.

"Gage…"

He reached across the table and captured her hand in his, stroking it lightly with his fingers. She closed her eyes and let out a slow breath, electricity sparking in her body, her heart beating double time, everything in her shaking with desire.

"I've been thinking a lot about you, Lily. About our time in Thailand."

"Don't," she said sharply, pulling her hand back and putting it in her lap.

"You tried to deny the attraction between us before, Lily, and it couldn't be done."

She swallowed hard. "We can ignore it. I can ignore it."

He looked at her, those blue eyes more temptation than she could handle. "But do you want to ignore it?"

"No," she whispered.

"Then what do you want?"

He was going to make her say it. For the first time in her life she wished someone would make things easy for her. That he would just sweep her into his arms and carry her up to one of the suites. But he was making her choose. He was leaving the consequences up to her, which meant that later, she wouldn't be able to blame him if things exploded on them.

"I want you," she said, her voice low, "but I don't want to want you."

"That does amazing things for my ego, sweetheart," he said, offering her a slight smile.

Her heart tripped and a short laugh escaped her lips. "You know I'm not into ego stroking, Gage."

"That's a shame." Their eyes caught and held, tension and electricity arcing between them.

"One more night." Her words were rushed, the blood roaring in her ears.

"One more night," he said, standing from the table, taking her hand and drawing her up with him.

"Isn't it rude to leave this early?" She cast a backward glance at the full reception, at the cake that had yet to be cut.

"It's not as rude as my stripping your dress off of you and having my way with you in front of all those nice people would be."

They headed down one of the long hallways to a row of elevators.

"You wouldn't do that," she said, going for censorious, but only managing breathless.

"I never thought I would, Lily, but you make me feel things…" He trailed off and stopped walking, turning her so that her back was to the wall. He stepped in, put his hands on her waist and leaned in, taking her mouth, devouring her as though he was starving. "You make me do things," he said. "I don't know myself sometimes when I'm with you."

"Same here," she said weakly, the wall and Gage's hands the only thing keeping her from sliding to the carpeted floor.

"My apartment is here," he said, "at the hotel."

"Really?"

"It made things easier to manage, especially in the beginning. I've never left." He punched the "up arrow" button on the wall and the elevator doors slid open. "Spend the night with me."

"Yes."

He stepped into the elevator and pulled her in with

him, holding her tightly against his body, kissing her neck softly.

"Gage," she whispered, wrapping her arms around him and taking his lips with hers. She'd missed him, much more than she'd realized, much more than she wanted to face.

He backed her up against the wall, the kiss growing urgent, hungry. She gripped the knot of his tie and jerked it hard to the side, loosening it so that she could reach the top button of his dress shirt and unfasten it with her shaking fingers.

She slid her hand inside his shirt, curling her fingers when she came into contact with his hot, hard flesh. He growled and gripped her hips, drawing her tightly against him. There was no restraint in him this time. Always before, he'd held back, but now he was unleashed and she was experiencing the full force of his desire. She gripped the edges of his shirt and tugged, sending buttons scattering across the elevator floor.

She slid her hands down his stomach, over his perfect ab muscles. He was so beautiful to her. Her heart thundered and she felt an intense well of emotion stir in her stomach, mingling with the intense desire to have him inside of her, to be joined to him again.

Gage gripped the sides of her dress and bunched it up in his hands, and Lily felt the hem rise higher. "Are you trying to kill me, Lily?" he groaned when his hands made contact with the bare space of skin between her black thigh-high stockings and her thong panties.

"That wasn't my goal. If you're dead you'll be of no use to me."

He laughed wickedly and kissed the curve of her neck, his fingers edging beneath the thin fabric of her underwear. She gasped when he moved his fingers over her clitoris.

"Is that good?" he asked, his lips brushing against her sensitized skin.

She could only nod as he continued to work magic on her with his hands. He slid one finger inside of her and felt a surge of pleasure, a tightening in her pelvis that she knew meant her climax was about to crash in on her.

"Come for me," he whispered, adding a second finger, and she was powerless to do anything but obey.

She gripped his shoulders, her hands still beneath his destroyed shirt, her nails grazing his sweat-slicked back.

When she finally came back to reality she realized they were still in the elevator.

"I stopped it," he said, gesturing to the control panel.

She adjusted her dress and patted her hair with a shaking hand. "Good." She had forgotten. She'd forgotten everything but how much she wanted him. She'd forgotten self-preservation, common decency, everything.

And she couldn't regret it. Not yet. Because even though her body was still tingling with the aftereffects of her orgasm, she wanted more. She wanted him. All of him.

He pushed the button for the top floor and the elevator began to move again. When they reached the top floor he keyed in a code and the doors slid open, revealing an extremely masculine, modern apartment space.

She stepped out of the lift on wobbly legs. She felt a slight smile tug at the corners of her mouth. The whole place was very Gage. Furniture with clean lines, neutrals accentuated by pops of color that reminded her of the beach. It was beautiful and opulent, and surprisingly functional.

It felt more intimate now, being in his home. It was one thing to have an affair at a vacation spot, but another to actually come into where he lived. To sleep in his bed.

Panic nibbled at her, her stomach about to explode in a flurry of nerves. But then Gage put his arm around her and dipped his head to give her a light kiss on the lips, and she couldn't worry anymore. Relationships, feelings, commitment, all of it scared her, made her want to run. But Gage didn't. Somehow, no matter what the feelings between them were, she couldn't be afraid of him.

"Would you like something to drink?"

She laughed. "Not yet. We have unfinished business." She looked at him, at his gaping shirt that was still tucked into his slacks. "I like the look," she said.

"I was attacked by a shameless hussy in an elevator," he said, taking her hand and leading her down the hallway.

He had pictures on his wall. School pictures of Maddy. Her high school and graduation pictures. It hit her again what a wonderful man he was, the things that he chose to hide. Part of her wanted to find out everything, but so much of her wanted to ignore everything she already knew, and didn't want to find out any more. This was about sexual satisfaction, a slight extension on their fling's deadline. This wasn't about finding out what an incredible person he was.

His bedroom was a definite man cave. A large bed, wall-mounted TV and very little else. Not the den of seduction she'd always imagined. She'd sort of thought he might be the type to have a Jacuzzi tub and a stripper pole in the middle of his bedroom. She was relieved to see she'd been wrong. Not that it should matter.

He shrugged his shirt off and tossed it onto the floor, his slacks and underwear following. She reached around to grab the zipper tab on her dress.

"Wait a second," he said, coming toward her. "Let me."

He turned her around gently so that she was facing away from him, his hands possessive on her hips. She leaned back against him, reveling in his heat, his strength. In him.

He slid his hands up beneath her dress and gripped her panties, dragging them down her legs. She stepped out of them and kicked them aside, trying to make sure they didn't get caught on her heels.

He moved his hands to her waist, slid them over her hips, back up to her breasts, not really touching, not the way she wanted. It was as though he was tracing her curves, memorizing her shape.

Then he slowly pulled the zipper down and she let her dress fall to the floor. A masculine groan of appreciation rumbled in his chest. "You're gorgeous," he groaned. "The most beautiful woman I've ever seen. I'll never get enough of looking at you."

Her heart thundered, her body quivering with desire. "Gage," she choked out.

"Get on the bed," he said, his voice rough, commanding, thrilling.

She complied, trying to turn and face him.

"No," he said, moving behind her and taking one of the pillows from the head of the bed, then another, stacking them and moving her over them so that her upper body had some support.

Her blood rushed through her veins, hotter, faster. She knew what he was going to do, and it thrilled her, excited her and frightened her, all at the same time.

"Do you trust me, sweetheart?"

She could only nod, the lump in her throat too much for her to speak past. But she did trust him. In this moment she did. She was giving him more than she'd ever given to anyone else, and as much as it scared her, it also felt as necessary as breathing.

She heard him tearing a condom packet, protecting them both, as he always did. She was grateful for that. She knew a lot of men didn't care enough to do that, but Gage never acted as though it was a sacrifice, as though it should be up to her.

She felt the blunt head of his erection probing her slick entrance.

"Are you ready for me?" he asked.

"Yes," she managed to choke out.

He thrust inside of her, deep, deeper than she'd ever felt him before. She curled her fingers around the bed-spread, trying to hold back the hoarse cry of pleasure that was climbing her throat.

He held her hips tightly, his movements strong and sure, nothing tentative about his claiming of her body. Because that was what it felt like. It was more elemental than their other times together, and in a lot of ways, she had less control. She was at his mercy, and yet she couldn't be afraid of him, and he wasn't harming her, he was only giving to her. Giving her pleasure while he took his own. While they shared in it.

He reached around and stroked the source of her desire. Already she could feel another orgasm building, this one stronger, more intense. She whimpered, and clenched the comforter tighter, the tension too much for her to bear because she knew when it broke she would shatter with it.

She felt his muscles start to shake, felt his fingers dig into her hips. He was close, too.

"Lily," he said, as he went over the edge.

His fingers worked her faster and she followed him, her body tightening around him as he pulsed inside of her. Their orgasm went on and on, blended together until she was sure they were feeling the same thing. Until it almost felt as though they were one body.

And when it was over, he turned her and took her in his arms so that she was facing him, so that he could brush her hair out of her face, his other hand continually sliding over her curves.

"Did you like that?" he asked. There was no arrogance in his voice. He didn't behave as though he already knew the answer, he wanted to know. And that made her heart squeeze tightly in her chest. Gage wasn't the kind of man who questioned himself, and that he would do it for her…it was impossible to feel nothing.

"Very much. It was incredible."

He circled her waist with his arms, bringing her closer, and she curved her leg over his thigh. They just lay there for a moment, catching their breath, letting their heart rates return to normal.

"This isn't the way I pictured your bedroom," she said finally.

"Really? What did you picture?"

"Stripper pole."

He laughed and kissed her hair. "Sorry to disappoint. For you, I would have one installed, trust me. The possibilities are fascinating."

She smiled against his shoulder. Surprisingly, the idea of putting herself on display for him like that didn't horrify her in the least. How could it when they'd shared so much?

"I don't bring women here," he said.

"Could have fooled me."

"You're actually the first woman I've had here since Maddy came to live with me. I got used to conducting my affairs away from my home. I don't even have them in my own hotels."

"Why is that?"

His body tensed slightly. "Probably for the same reason we both live alone."

"Then why...why did you bring me here?"

He shrugged. "You're different. I know you. I was feeling very impatient."

Her stomach tightened. His words thrilled her and scared her. She was different. He knew her. He had brought her back to his apartment, a place he didn't bring other women.

She wasn't supposed to be different. She was supposed to be another in a long string of purely physical affairs, a woman he wouldn't want anything from. And she was supposed to feel the same way about him. He wasn't supposed to matter.

Of course she liked him, but there couldn't be anything beyond that.

She should get up. Get dressed and go home. He would probably expect it. He should expect it. It was different when they were both staying in Thailand. But here in San Diego they both had their own houses, their own space.

But he was still cradling her against his chest, and for some reason, even though he was the source of her fear, he was also a source of comfort. She wrapped her arms around him and rested her head on his chest. Nothing had changed. It was just a part of their fling. It couldn't be anything more.

CHAPTER ELEVEN

"I THOUGHT you could use some." Gage held a mug of coffee out to Lily and she sat up straighter in the bed, letting the covers fall around her waist.

"Thank you," she said, taking it and inhaling the heavenly scent. She was such an addict, but at least he understood. Understood and shared in it.

It was an interesting reversal of their morning routine. And an interesting setting for it. She'd always thought there was an undercurrent of domesticity in their office routine, but this took it to a whole new level.

He sat on the edge of the bed, his own mug in hand, dressed only in a pair of jeans, his chest still bare. There were certain aspects of this that were a definite improvement to their office mornings.

"What are your plans for the day?" she asked, a little embarrassed once the question had escaped. Was it really any of her business what he was doing? It wasn't a workday and they didn't have a real relationship.

"Nothing. A total rarity. Usually I try to visit Maddy on Sunday, but she's still in Switzerland, and having a lot of fun. She says she's been totally untouched by the scandal there."

"That's great, Gage." She could see the relief on his

face and it made her feel the same feeling, swelling inside of her. She knew how much he loved Maddy, knew even more now. She felt as though she could feel his emotions sometimes, as though her own matched his.

Gage was enjoying Lily's newfound boldness in bed. Even now she was sitting up with her breasts bare, acting as though she hardly noticed. He noticed. She was truly the most beautiful woman he'd ever seen naked. And he'd seen his share.

Usually, after a few encounters, the mystery had worn off and he wasn't as captivated by his lover's beauty. Or, as was the case when plastic surgery was involved, sometimes a woman actually looked better in her clothes than out of them.

But not Lily. She fascinated him. Clothed or naked, dressed up, or in a bikini.

He kept waiting to regret bringing her back to his apartment, letting her into his personal space. But it hadn't hit him yet. It felt better, having her here than it would have felt taking her to an anonymous hotel and having sex with her on a bed that was there almost solely for that purpose.

It had never bothered him before. That was how he'd always conducted his affairs. If it weren't for those years raising his sister, his room may very well have ended up with a stripper pole in it. But he *had* raised his sister, and that had changed things. It had likely changed some things for the better.

He didn't know what was happening with Lily. Didn't want to know why it felt right to have her in his home, when he had never wanted to bring another woman here before. Didn't want to know what it meant that he couldn't imagine ever tiring of her.

Last night had been the hottest night of his life, hands down. The only other experiences that came close were the other times he'd been with Lily. She wiped memories of other women from his mind. He couldn't even remember what appeal those other women had ever held. They were too blonde, too tanned, too thin, too surgically enhanced. There was nothing genuine about them.

They weren't like Lily. Lily, who was soft and beautiful, who didn't cling to him. Lily, who he gladly held all night long, when he'd never wanted to do that with any other woman.

"I need to go home," she said suddenly.

His first thought was that he didn't want her to leave. And he'd definitely never felt that way about a woman before. He hated to admit that that first reaction, the desire to hold her to him, keep her with him, scared him.

There was no point in caring. No point in wanting.

"Why?"

"I don't have any clothes. I only have that dress." She gestured to the black fabric pooled at the foot of his bed. "And when I leave, everyone's going to know what was going on. No one wears a dress like that on Sunday morning."

"My simple solution is that you could forgo clothes altogether."

"No."

"I'll drive you back to your place. Is there anything else you need?" he asked.

"I usually work out today."

He wasn't surprised to know that she worked on her body. She took a lot of care with her appearance, not to the point of obsession, but just enough that she projected a very polished image. That was one thing that made ruffling her so much fun.

And if he could just focus on the fun and ignore all of the other things, their affair could continue for as long as they both wanted.

"I'll go with you. I work out on Sundays, too."

She nodded slowly, but he could tell she wasn't thrilled with the idea. She was extremely cagey and very closed off with her emotions, something he normally wouldn't notice or care about, but for some reason, with her, he cared.

When they were in bed together, or on the beach, her walls started to come down, and he reveled in those moments. He shouldn't. There was nowhere for their relationship to go. Even if he wanted love and marriage, she was the wrong woman. What could they bring to a marriage? A mutual obsession with their own businesses, their own lives? And if he didn't have his business, what other attraction could he possibly offer?

In business, they were well-suited, in bed, they were incredible. But that was all it would ever be. That was all it could ever be.

"Remind me never to work out with you again," Lily said, rubbing her shoulders as she settled into Gage's low-slung sports car.

"Too much for you?"

She groaned and leaned her head back against the seat. "Normally, I don't like to admit defeat, but in this case, I'll concede."

"Are you hungry?" Gage asked, maneuvering the car into traffic.

"Very."

"Do you want to go out?"

She grimaced. After a workout that intense, she wasn't fit to be out in public. "I can cook for you. My condo is close."

Gage hesitated for a moment before changing lanes and heading in the direction of her home. She didn't know what she was doing, why she was inviting him to come home with her. Because she was certain that he would end up staying. That they would end up in bed together, and she was sure that was the wrong thing to do. She should have told him to drop her off at home, should have tried to start putting distance between them.

But she hadn't. And even now that she recognized what she should do, she wasn't going to do it. She wanted to be with him. Maybe she should stop analyzing everything and just be with him.

"It's a two-car garage," she said when he pulled into the lot of her condo. "Just stop here for a second."

She got out of the car and keyed in the code for the garage and the door opened. She got back into the car while Gage drove it inside, parking next to her little commuter vehicle. For a moment, it seemed shockingly comfortable, to have his car parked next to hers, almost like they shared the space.

She shook her head and got back out of the car and moved to unlock her side entrance. Gage followed her in. She had always been proud of her house, and had hosted a few dinner parties for her friends when she'd had the time, not since she'd started working for Gage. It wasn't as luxurious as his house, but it was hers.

"You have a view of the ocean from here?" he asked.

"From the bedroom."

"I'll have to take a look," he said, giving her a wicked grin.

"Later," she said, "but now I'm hungry."

"Later," he said, hooking his arm around her waist and bringing her in for a kiss. He hadn't kissed her at all today. They'd spent the day together but he hadn't touched her, hadn't acted like there was anything between them. She was surprised by how much she'd missed it.

"Definitely." She moved away from him and went into the kitchen and started rifling through the produce drawers in her fridge. "Stir-fry?" she asked.

"I didn't imagine that you would cook."

"I have to eat."

"My mother didn't cook."

Lily laughed, but there was no humor in it. "Neither did mine." She put a head of cabbage on her cutting board and began to slice it. "I learned when I moved out here. Otherwise I existed on frozen pizza and whatever my friends' parents fed me when they felt sorry for me."

"Do you have any family here?"

"No. I left home at seventeen. My main requirement was that none of my family be where I went," she said, hearing the bitterness edge into her voice.

"And you wanted to be near the ocean," he said.

"Yes. I did."

"Did the men your mother dated hurt you? Is that why you avoided relationships?"

She took a breath and tossed the sliced cabbage into the wok on the stove. "They didn't hurt me in the way that you mean. But my mother was so dependent on them, and most of them were terrible. She let them control everything she did, and by extension, everything

I did. We always lived in these tiny little houses with no privacy. I could always hear them fighting, or making up. I'm not sure which was worse."

She put the rest of the vegetables and some pre-cooked chicken into the wok and pushed them around vigorously with a spatula for a few minutes before turning the burner off.

"Not all relationships are like that," he said.

"Not all of them are like your parents', either."

He didn't say anything to that. Conversation turned back to business, and she was thankful for that.

She served their dinner in the dining room and Gage sat in the chair next to her, instead of sitting across from her, his hand on her thigh, stroking her absently. It was very domestic, the two of them eating a dinner she'd cooked. It certainly didn't fit in to the parameters of an affair.

Neither did sharing the gory details about a dysfunctional childhood. But Gage had always made her want to open up. It had always been easy for her to say too much to him.

They ended up watching a movie in the living room before heading to her bedroom and making love. It was amazing, like it always was, and, like always, she felt a little piece of the wall around her heart crumble when she came apart in his arms.

And when he gathered her against him she felt tears trailing down her cheeks again, all of the emotion rising up inside of her again, needing a way to escape.

She didn't know what it was that made her feel this way. Not for sure. She had a suspicion, but she hoped, more than anything, that she was wrong.

* * *

They drove to the office together the next day, despite her protests. She also conceded to packing an overnight back, just in case. She shouldn't have. She shouldn't have left it open. She should be ending it. They'd had an agreement and they weren't sticking to it.

The relationship, because it was growing into that, was now beyond her control. She wanted to be with Gage almost more than she wanted her next breath, but she didn't want to want it. She didn't want to want him.

She was sitting in her spot in his office, notebook in hand as he briefed her on a new resort property in Goa, India.

"Any concerns regarding the location?" she asked.

"Not that I can foresee. It's an older resort, and basically we'll be renovating it and bringing some more tourism into the area."

"Excellent. I love it when you make my job easy." She looked up at him and her heart fluttered in her chest.

There was no compartmentalizing. She had thought that Gage, her lover, could be someone different in her mind than Gage, her boss. After all, she'd always been able to set everything aside and focus on her work. But it wasn't possible. Whenever she looked at him she was flooded by memories of them making love, of him looking at her, his expression tender.

"And I don't do it very often," he said.

"You're getting better."

"Don't let that get out."

She smiled. "I won't."

Gage stood from his desk and walked around to where she was sitting, coming to stand behind her before leaning down and kissing her lightly on the neck. "You're a terrible workplace distraction."

She closed her eyes. She knew he was making a joke. But it was true for her. He was distracting. She couldn't think about her job when she was with him. She could only think about him.

"I want to take you out tonight," he whispered, his hands moving over her shoulders, sparking a fire in her belly.

"You took me out a few days ago. To the wedding reception."

"No, I want to take you out on a date. Not to a work event designed for networking."

"Why? So we can have our picture taken together?"

"It wouldn't hurt."

It was important, of course. Gage was always seen in public with his woman *du jour*, and it wouldn't do for his fiancée to be the exception.

"All right. What do you want to do? And do I need a new dress?" she asked.

"It's a surprise, and I've taken care of everything for you. You'll come home with me after work, just like we planned."

She moved away from his touch and stood. "Then I'd better get to work."

He cupped her chin and kissed her lightly on the lips. "See you later."

She smiled, and she was afraid it was a little bit of a punch-drunk smile. "See you later."

She didn't need to buy a new dress, because there was already one waiting at Gage's home for her. It was on his bed, zipped up into a garment bag.

"Did you pick this out or did David?" she asked, turning to face Gage, who was standing in the doorway.

"David has terrible fashion sense. I chose it at lunch, but I sent a picture of it to Maddy to make sure it was right."

It felt a little strange letting him pick out her clothes. She'd never liked it when any of her friends chose an outfit around a boyfriend, or let him dictate their wardrobe. Of course, she was already starting to think of Gage when she shopped. And he wasn't even her boyfriend, not really. *Boyfriend* was too insipid of a word for a man like Gage. *Lover* was more accurate, and more fitting. More arousing.

"I want to see how it looks on you." He stood there, eyes fixed on her.

"Not with you standing there."

"I've seen you naked before," he said dryly. "I hope that's not a shocking revelation for you."

"It's different than getting changed in front of someone."

"It is?"

She nodded. "Yes, it is. So…" She gestured for him to go.

"I'll go, only because I was taught it was polite not to impose on a lady, but, and this is a promise, I will be stripping that dress from your delectable body later, which renders this show of modesty entirely worthless."

"Then it's worthless." She turned away from him, then said, "I hope you're a man who keeps his promises."

"Always." The door clicked shut behind her and she turned again. Gage was gone, giving her the privacy she'd asked for.

She bent down and unzipped the bag. And laughed. It was bright red, made in a heavy satin fabric, the exact opposite of the type of thing she normally wore. No black, no navy, nothing flowing. Of course. She would have been annoyed, but she appreciated his humor too much.

And the dress was gorgeous, which further absolved him. The sweetheart neckline was sexy, but not overt, which earned him major points since he could have gone plunging. The hem fell just above her knee and there was exquisite pleating at the waist that was extremely flattering to her figure.

There were shoes, too. Black, of course, to defy her usual affinity for colorful shoes. And she found she liked the shoes as well as the dress.

She emerged from the bedroom dressed, her hair down, another style choice she didn't usually make. "Will this do?" she asked.

Gage stood from where he was sitting on the couch, his expression intense, his eyes roaming over her, the hunger in them compelling, undisguised.

"You're gorgeous," he said. "Have I mentioned that?"

Yes, he had, and every time it felt more and more real. "Once or twice."

"I thought you might appreciate the color choice."

"It was clear you had my tastes in mind when you picked it. And then decided to go with the opposite. But I do like it."

"I'm glad, because I'm a big fan."

He stood and walked over to her, looping one arm around her waist and then moving his other hand to her loose hair, sifting it through his fingers. "You have beautiful hair. I'm captivated by it."

She sucked in a breath. "You're an easy man to captivate."

"No," he said, his face serious, "I'm not." He lowered his head and kissed her lightly, the gesture somehow more romantic than if he'd ravished her mouth.

"I'm almost ready," she said, knowing she sounded as breathless as she felt. "Makeup."

He followed her into the bathroom and grabbed his razor from the medicine cabinet while she rummaged through the bag she'd brought with her and found a shade of red lipstick that would work well with the dress.

He shaved away his five-o'clock shadow while she put the finishing touches on her look, and the whole time her hands were shaking. It was the sort of thing a married couple would do. At least, the sort of thing she imagined a normal married couple might do.

"I'm ready," she said. Anything to get away from the house, from this domestic scene that was making her whole body ache with longing she didn't want to feel.

All eyes were on them as they made their way to a trendy San Diego nightspot. It was because of Gage, she was certain. He drew the attention of men and women. It was more than just his incredible looks, though they were certainly a factor, it was the aura of power that he projected.

He went straight past the maître d' and led her to a table in the back. "My table," he said, as he pulled her chair out for her. It was secluded, set back into an alcove that had a curtain just barely drawn back so that the main portion of the dining room was mostly hidden from view.

"You come here often?" she asked facetiously.

"It's one of my favorite places."

She wasn't sure how she felt about coming to a place he went to with other women. She couldn't feel anything about it. It couldn't matter. They were here to get attention from the press and the fact that it was one of his usual places made it a good choice to accomplish that. Everything else was moot.

But it didn't feel like it. It felt vital somehow.

"Our food will be here shortly," he said.

"You ordered ahead? And without asking what I wanted?"

"No, I always get whatever fresh item they're featuring on the menu and they know that."

The little flutter of panic that had been ready to take flight in her stomach calmed slightly. It was only food, but there was the dress, too, and the shoes. It was the kind of thing she'd always worried about when it came to men and relationships.

He reached across the table and squeezed her hand, just as the waiter was coming with their dinner. She had to wonder if he had done it because he wanted to, or if it was part of the show. She couldn't worry about it though, not when he was looking at her like she was the only woman he wanted. Like she was the only woman he'd ever wanted.

He was the only man she would want. She couldn't imagine being with anyone else. Couldn't imagine wanting to be. She'd never met a man to equal him before, and she doubted she ever would. She ignored the trickle of fear she felt as she acknowledged that. Until that moment she'd been pretending that she would simply find someone else when she was ready. When she had physical needs again.

It was a reasonable thought. If she and Gage were

only fulfilling a physical need for each other, then wouldn't anyone do?

No.

"It's hard to enjoy dinner when all I want is to take you back home make love with you."

Lily blushed, something Gage found infinitely attractive. That she was capable of the act at all was a novelty, but that wasn't what it was. It was more than that. With Lily it was always more. He'd attributed it to her being a virgin, but it wasn't so simple.

Tonight, when she'd walked out of the bedroom in that red dress, he'd known for sure there was more. He wasn't entirely certain what he was going to do about it, a first for him, but he knew that she wasn't simply a temporary diversion. Knew that it wasn't about distracting the press anymore, or even a simple fling. They had passed that point a long time ago.

She looked at him, her expression wicked. "I'm having similar fantasies involving your shirt."

"You've already ruined one of my favorite shirts."

"It's for the greater good," she said, a smile curving those lush red lips.

He loved talking with Lily, loved the way her mind worked, her wit, her sense of humor. Her company. There had never been anyone in his life who added so much. She understood his business, she was wonderful to talk to, and in bed…he had never experienced anything like what they shared when they were together.

Usually by now, he would be bored with a lover. But he couldn't imagine Lily boring him in any way. And he didn't know what that meant, what purpose it could possibly serve. He didn't know how to give love, didn't know how to receive it. There was Maddy, but she loved him because she'd always needed him. He had no experience with the emotion otherwise. He seriously doubted he was capable of giving it or getting it.

But for now, it didn't matter. He wouldn't let it. Tonight he would lose himself in her body again. Tonight he would be inside of her, and when that happened, nothing else seemed to matter quite so much.

They both ate quickly, all thoughts of a photo-op for the press forgotten, and as soon as he paid the check they made a mad rush for his car.

He took her hand and she laughed, walking quickly in her heels. He spun her to him and kissed her, his stomach tightening when she pulled away and he got a good look at her gorgeous face, at her beautiful smile.

"We should hurry," he said, his constricted throat making speech a near impossibility.

"I agree."

CHAPTER TWELVE

BEING with Gage, making love with Gage, was always amazing. But it had never been like this. His hands moved over her curves, his touch reverent, his lips soft but urgent on her skin. And when he claimed her, surged into her body, she truly felt as though she didn't know where she began and he ended.

She dug her nails into his shoulders, locked him more tightly against her by wrapping her legs around his hips and she arched into him and gave in to the pleasure that was coursing through her body. But it was more than that. More than just a physical reaction brought on by sexual arousal and release.

His body went taut above hers, the tendons in his neck standing out, a hoarse grunt signaling his orgasm. She held him to her, felt his heart beating hard against her chest. It was so much more than sex. So much more than a fling.

And she didn't think she could face it.

Before she and Gage had started sleeping together, they'd been colleagues, they'd almost been friends and then they'd moved into being lovers. But now it had moved beyond that. There was so much more. It made her heart feel like it was too big for her chest, made her entire body ache. And it also made her feel more alive than she'd ever been. And it terrified her.

She shifted beneath him and he rolled off of her, settling beside her. She squeezed her eyes tightly, hoping that she wasn't about to embarrass herself by crying postclimax again. Only this time it wouldn't simply be due to the release. It was all about the feelings that were exploding inside of her.

Gage gathered her close and she went willingly into his arms. Even though it seemed necessary to her control that she have some distance, she just couldn't bring herself to leave. She wanted to be with him.

He laced his fingers through her and kissed her shoulder, the gesture one of tenderness, caring. A gesture that made it hard for her to breathe.

"Thank you for what you've done for Maddy," he said, his voice rough, his breathing harsh.

She felt a twinge in her chest. She didn't want what had just happened between them, what had been happening between them for the past couple of weeks, to be her thank-you for helping out his sister.

"Of course," she said, trying to keep her voice steady.

"She's had to deal with enough without adding this...I can never forgive my parents for what they've done to her." He tightened his hold on her. "The worst part is, I would be an even worse father than my own was."

She turned to face him. "Why do you think that?"

"My work is my mistress. And just like a real mistress, it tends to get in the way of your real family."

"But you raised Madeline."

He nodded. "I did. And I wouldn't trade it. She's

wonderful. But I put a lot on hold for her and if I were going to have children I would have to do it again."

She nodded. "That's true."

"You don't want kids, do you?"

She bit her lip, the flow of emotion that was pumping through her a mystery. "No. I have the same problem with my job that you have."

She'd never planned on having children, never wanted to get married, but suddenly, the idea seemed sad to her. Listening to Gage outline just why it was impractical for either of them to ever have a family made everything seem so final. And he was right.

But for one crazy moment she wished that he weren't. She wished they were different people. People who knew how to have relationships. But if time weren't the issue, it would be something else.

"Maddy and I...we love each other. We grew to depend on each other out of necessity. But...I don't think I have any more to give," he said.

She looked at him. His eyes were closed now, his body relaxing, readying for sleep. She'd fallen asleep next to Gage every night this week, listening to his deep, even breathing. And someday that would be gone. It would have to be. There was no future for them.

Pain hit her square in the chest, stole her breath.

She loved him.

She loved him, and she didn't want to. She didn't want to be in this relationship, didn't want to have to sacrifice her ambitions, didn't want to deviate from her life plans. There was no way either of them could make anything like a marriage work, not when their businesses took up all of their time.

Not when she was afraid of what it meant to be in love.

What if they grew to hate each other as much as they cared for each other now? When the misery set in, misery because they'd had to compromise too much, because Gage was tired of her, what would she be left with?

She almost laughed. She might be in love, but Gage wasn't in love with her. He'd said more than once that he didn't do serious and for him, this was just another fling, another strictly physical relationship. And now he'd outlined, in clear detail, why he wasn't meant for fatherhood or marriage.

She'd fooled herself into thinking she wanted a fling, but it had always been about more than that. She'd wanted to move past all of the issues that still hung over her head. Wanted to erase her mother's influence in her life if possible.

And instead she'd landed herself in a mess her mother would have reveled in. She loved a man who would never love her back. She loved a man she didn't want to love. She was in the relationship she'd never wanted.

She slid out of his arms and went into the living room, clutching her arms, trying to keep herself from shivering.

It didn't matter how she felt about Gage.

She laughed out loud into the empty room. It did matter. Now that she knew what her feelings meant, she knew she had to finish with him. She shook her head. She'd done what she'd promised herself, and him, she wouldn't. She'd fallen in love with her first lover.

She sank onto the couch and drew her knees up to her chest, her heart pounding so hard she thought it might break. The pain so severe she was certain it already was.

She couldn't do it. She couldn't stay. Not feeling like she did.

A tear slid down her cheek.

She was so afraid that if she stayed, she would give him everything. Everything she'd learned to hold inside, all of the emotions she'd learned to carefully suppress. And they wouldn't be enough for him, either. She wasn't enough. She never had been. Her love hadn't been enough for her own mother, why would it mean anything to him?

She pressed the heels of her hands hard against her eyes and tried to block the flow of tears. She had to be strong. She had to end it. Before he did it for her.

It was 4:00 a.m. when Gage woke up and found Lily's side of the bed cold and empty.

Lily's side of the bed.

Any other time, it would have bothered him to think of anything in his home as belonging to someone else, especially a woman he was seeing. But with Lily, it seemed natural.

He didn't feel claustrophobic when he thought of spending an indefinite amount of time with her. He wanted her, and for now that was fine. He could continue to enjoy her until the arrangement no longer benefited either of them.

He pulled on a pair of dark boxer briefs and went out into the living room. Lily was sitting there on the couch, a cup of coffee in her hand, a blank expression on her face. Her hair was pulled back into a bun and she was dressed in a fitted skirt and jacket, her work uniform.

"Did something happen with Maddy?" he asked,

thoughts of the media hounding his sister his first thought.

She shook her head, her lips pursed. "No. Maddy's fine. At least, I haven't seen anything about her in the news."

She lowered her eyes and gripped her coffee tighter. He'd spent a lot of time with Lily over the months she'd worked with him, more since they'd started sleeping together, and he knew her moods. She was upset and she was trying desperately not to show it.

His first crazy thought was that she might be pregnant, though he had been vigilant about protection. Still, a thousand images rushed through his head. Lily, her belly rounded by pregnancy. Lily, holding their baby.

The very idea should have terrified him. He'd never wanted to be a father. Not because he didn't want children, but because he didn't want to become his parents. He had the same kind of ambition both of his parents had shared, and so did Lily. They'd discussed as much only that evening. So when would they see their baby? Between work and work-related events?

But if it had already happened, there was nothing that could be done. If she was pregnant, he would face it, and he knew that she would, too. Neither of them ran from things. They faced things head-on, which was why they had more than they occasional clash.

A baby. A small surge of exhilaration rushed through him. Maybe this would be his chance. His chance to have everything he didn't believe he could ever possibly earn.

"Lily, whatever it is, you can tell me," he said, his voice tight.

"I can't do this anymore, Gage."

Her words hit him with the impact of a brick. His

stomach contracted and his chest squeezed tight. Pain ripped through him before it was washed away by a tide of anger that washed it away.

"You can't do what?" he asked, his voice soft, because he knew he was on the edge, and unless he kept himself under careful control, he might lose it completely.

"This. This relationship. Whatever it is we have. We agreed to a fling, and this—" she gestured around his home "—staying at each other's houses and going on dates and you buying my clothes, that's not a fling."

"Yes, Lily, this is a fling. It certainly isn't anything more." The pain in his chest compelled him to lash out, made him want to shatter that composed look on his face, find a break in the calm, smooth voice.

It was an incredible crash, thinking that he'd found a way to hold on to her forever, and finding out she was slipping away from him. He had nothing to hold her to him, nothing to make her want to stay.

He swallowed hard, trying to block out the incredible pain that was lashing at his heart, making him feel raw, wounded. This was why he didn't simply give emotion, didn't do caring. He had loved his parents, and it had meant nothing to them. And then, even with all of his achievements, he hadn't been enough.

He wasn't enough for Lily, either.

She looked up at him and for a moment, he was certain he saw pain in her eyes, until she masked it again with the blank expression she'd been wearing when he walked into the room.

"Then why prolong it?" she asked, standing. "I'll get a cab."

"Why? You have to be at work soon. I can drive you," he ground out.

She looked away from him. "I don't know…"

"It's just a fling, Lily," he bit out. "And we always knew that it would end. And we agreed you would continue to work for me."

She sucked in a sharp breath. "Of course. My job is important to me. Another reason why I don't think it's smart to prolong this. I don't want it affecting our work."

Something about the way she said that made his stomach burn. Her job was important. What had passed between them wasn't.

He couldn't even believe that only moments before he'd been imagining having a baby with her. Had even thought they could make it work. But she was no different than his parents, and when it came right down to it, neither was he. He might have thought, for a brief moment, that he could be someone else, that he could have another life than the one he was meant to have. But it was not possible.

"I'll get ready," he said and turned away, headed back into the bedroom and shut the door behind him. He pounded his fist hard against the wall, hoping that it might loosen some of the pain that had settled in his chest.

He shook the lingering sting from his hand and went to his closet. His chest still hurt. He wanted to back out and take her in his arms and tell her they weren't finished. He wanted to take her back to bed and pleasure her until neither of them could think. Until she didn't want to leave him.

But there was no point. This was always the way it was going to end. It was what he wanted. What he had to want. He didn't do permanent. He didn't want to be tied down for the rest of his life, to have to put himself, his job, second. He'd been there, he'd done that.

But he didn't feel a sense of freedom at the thought of ending his affair with Lily. He only felt like there was a hole inside of him. And he had no idea how he would fill it without her.

Lily sat in the chair across from Gage's desk, pen in hand, taking notes. She was gripping the pen too tightly and her hand hurt. But everything in her body hurt. To be with Gage—without being with him—was almost pure torture.

But she had agreed to it. She had agreed to the fling in the first place, and then she had instigated its demise.

But she had done it for all the right reasons. Gage had said, unequivocally, that their relationship was nothing more than a casual affair. And she had fallen in love with him.

She just needed some time away from him. Not that she was going to get any real time away from him. Not when she had to see him every day. But she wasn't about to self-destruct her career just because she'd made the stupid mistake of sleeping with her boss. And falling in love with him.

She didn't even want to be in love, so the fact that she was absolutely heartbroken over him was even worse. But what would they do in a relationship? Get married? Have a family?

It was laughable. They weren't suited to it. Neither of them wanted it.

Her heart burned in her chest. If she didn't want love, then why did the thought of having it with Gage make her ache like it did? Why did her heart feel like it was going to shatter? Why did her life, her perfect life that she had worked so hard for, suddenly feel empty?

Lily's bed felt empty. She only wished her heart could feel as empty. But it was full. Full of pain, love, need.

She rolled out of her bed and walked out onto her balcony. She could hear the waves crashing on the shore, smell the sea as the crisp wind blew over the surface of the water and carried it to her.

This was what she had worked so hard for. This view. Her home. A home that was hers alone, a life that was hers alone. One that wasn't controlled by her mother.

A tear slid down her cheek. She didn't feel free anymore. She'd imagined, for so long, that she was. Had believed that because she'd left, because she'd quit caring whether or not she was enough for her mother, that she had left it behind her.

But she hadn't. She had carried it with her. It had motivated her, made her successful in her professional life as she'd moved further and further away from her painful childhood, and made more of herself than her mother would have thought her capable of.

It had made her successful in some ways, but she had allowed it to stunt her in so many other ways. She was still letting it stop her.

She closed her eyes and breathed in deeply. She wanted Gage. She didn't know if he wanted her, not in the same way she wanted him. She didn't know if he could ever love her.

Her own mother hadn't loved her half as much as she'd loved the various men that had paraded through her life.

It galled her to find out that the thing that had kept her from a relationship, from love, was the fear that she wasn't good enough. She hid it by focusing on things she excelled at, and she simply ignored everything else, so that she didn't have to face it.

She wasn't going to do it anymore. She felt as if she was back on the edge of the cliff again, the ocean at the bottom, a swirling sea of uncertainty beneath her. She could turn and run, as she had done before, or she could face it head-on. She'd managed to do that with business, to face down opponents in the media, without breaking a sweat.

It was her personal life, her feelings, that she'd been afraid to face.

She took a deep breath, trying to lighten some of the weight that had settled in her chest. She didn't know what Gage would say if she told him she loved him. He would probably turn and run the other way. But she knew that she had to tell him. She wasn't going to live in fear anymore, not with the fear that she was unlovable, not with the fear of what might happen if she gave herself over to a relationship.

Gage had asked her once if she trusted him, and she'd said yes. But she'd lied. She hadn't trusted him. If she had, she would never have felt the need to run before he had the chance to end the relationship.

Because that was what it came down to. She was running. She'd been running since she was seventeen.

She wasn't running anymore.

Gage was at his desk at five that morning. He couldn't sleep. Not without Lily in his bed. Without her in his arms.

And she had left him. Women never left him. He was always the one to end a relationship. But not this one. Lily had left him.

He wanted her back, but if he had her, he had no idea what he would do. What he could do. Frustration roared through him. He wanted something he could never have, wanted to give Lily things he wasn't certain he knew how to give. Wanted her to feel those things in return when he knew she simply didn't.

It was not the first time it had happened to him. His parents had not wanted him, they hadn't wanted him even with all of his achievements. Why should Lily want him? He'd let her walk away because he'd always believed, deep inside of himself, that he was not a man who someone could love. And so he had set out to become a man who didn't need love. And when Lily had left, he'd told himself it was for the best.

But there was a war being waged inside of him. A war that pitted what he'd always believed about himself against his heart's newfound desire. No matter the outcome, it made him want to take a risk, to dive headlong into all of the things that Lily made him feel. Things he hadn't imagined were possible for him to feel.

He had always been the man who took care of things. When Maddy had needed him, he was there. Always. There had never been a situation in his life that he hadn't believed he could find the solution to. But there was nothing he could do now.

He wasn't the kind of man who admitted to needing. To needing help. To needing someone else. But he needed her, and there was nothing in his own power that could bring her to him, that could make her want him the way he wanted her.

He looked around his office. He had always considered this his biggest achievement, yet now, it felt like nothing. He would gladly give it up in that moment, for Lily.

He thought back on the years he'd spent raising Maddy. They had been stressful, and trying, and sometimes too much for a twenty-five-year-old man to deal with. But they had been fulfilling in a way his life hadn't been since.

There was something he could do. Something he had always vowed never to do. Not since he had told his mother he loved her when he was five and she had simply stared at him in stony silence. He could tell Lily. He could put himself on the line, his heart, his pride. What did it mean if he didn't have her?

He blew out a harsh breath and stood from his desk just as the door to his office opened. Lily stepped in, hair in a knot, prim and proper outfit skimming her curves like always. Making him want to see the beauty that lay beneath.

She turned on shut the door, the lock clicking softly.

"Gage," she said softly, her voice shaking.

He thought of the first time she'd walked into his office for a job interview. Her manner had been confident, her voice steady. She looked far removed from that woman now. There was vulnerability, real emotion.

"I didn't expect you this early," he said.

"I couldn't sleep."

"I couldn't sleep, either." Their eyes caught and held, and he knew they had both been sleepless for the same reason.

"I thought…Gage, I have to tell you," she said. "I thought that not needing anyone made me strong. I didn't want to be like my mother and need things from other people all the time. So I avoided relationships. And then I met you, and I wanted you, I wanted you enough that I thought I could take the chance and have you, and because you were only interested in temporary, you wouldn't ask anything of me."

She took a shuddering breath and continued. "But you did, Gage. You asked everything of me. You challenged me, and you asked me to do things that were hard. You wouldn't let me hide."

She reached back and pulled on the tie that was holding her hair in place and let it fall loose around her shoulders.

"I still tried to hide," she said. "I didn't want to expose myself to you. To anyone."

She unbuttoned the first button on her top, then quickly undid the rest, letting her blouse fall to the floor. Her hands shook as she undid the catch on her bra and let it fall down to the floor, too. Then she pushed her skirt down her rounded hips, leaving her standing before him in nothing more than a pair of tiny panties and some bright blue shoes.

"Image is important," she said, dragging her panties down her legs and kicking her shoes to the side. "I've always said that it was because image is a part of my job. But I was using it to hide. As long as I had all of this—" she gestured to the clothes around her feet "—I could play the part. I could pretend I was confident. Like I had everything together. But I don't. I was just afraid." She laughed. "I am afraid. But I'm not going to give you the image anymore. I'm just Lily Ford. I wasn't born with money. I worked for everything I have. And I'm afraid of being in love. Of being in love with you. Because I'm afraid that I'm not enough."

He looked at Lily, his heart hammering in his chest. Then he crossed the room and took her in his arms, her body warm and soft against him. "You're everything, Lily. Don't ever doubt it." He smoothed her silky hair, sifted his fingers through it. "I love you. When you're in your business suits ready to take on the world, and when you're crying after we've made love. I love everything about you. Every part of you. It's all you."

He felt her shoulders shake. "You love me?"

"Yes, Lily. I love you. I was as scared as you are, because I think I've loved you for a very long time, but I didn't know what to do with it. I was afraid that I wouldn't be enough for you. That I wouldn't be able to give you what you deserved. That I wouldn't be able to give our children what they deserved. I was afraid that I was like my parents, that things would always come before people. But I would give it all up today if it meant I could have you."

"I would, too," she said, her voice muffled by tears. "None of it matters if I can't share it with you."

"You don't have to give anything up for me, Lily. I love how ambitious you are. I love your wit, your humor, your drive. I would never ask you to be someone else. I want the woman you are."

"I would never ask you to change, either."

"Work isn't my life anymore," Gage said, looking at her beautiful, tearstained face. "You are. Our children will be. When you told me you were done…right before, you looked so serious, I was certain you were going to tell me you were pregnant. And I was scared, because I didn't know if I could be a good father. I didn't know if I could love a child properly, not after how I was raised. I didn't know if that child could love me. But I knew if I was going to have a child, I wanted it to be with you."

"Gage…" She put her hand on his cheek. "Our children will love you. And I love you. I can't help myself. Our parents were screwed up, but we don't have to be."

"No, we don't."

"Of course, you know that if we get married, I'll have access to all of your dirty laundry, and my job will only be more difficult, since I'm going to have to hide all of your flaws from the public, when I'm aware of every single one of them."

He laughed and smoothed his hands down her back, over her bare curves. "You love my flaws."

She whimpered. "I do. And you love mine."

"More than I love my own."

"We can do this, Gage," she said, her voice trembling. "We can have this."

"Of course we can, Lily. Love isn't what your mother had, love isn't what my parents gave to my sister and me. This is love. What I feel for you. All of the things I'd worked for suddenly meant nothing without you to share them with."

"That's exactly how I felt. Everything that I was happy with before was empty if you weren't there. I always liked empty before I met you, Gage, but now it just feels hollow."

"Lily, I think we need to sign another contract."

"Really?"

"I do. One that says we're going to stay together, for better or for worse, for all of our lives."

"I would definitely sign that," she said, smiling through her tears.

"Was that an agreement?"

She kissed him, long and hard, with all of the passion and love they felt coursing between them. "Yes, it was. But I'm not thinking a handshake is how I want to seal the deal."

"Oh, no," he said. "I can think of so many better ways to celebrate this union."

"Show me," she whispered against his lips.

"For the rest of our lives."

Hot reads!

These 3-in-1s will certainly get you feeling hot under the collar with their desert locations, billionaire tycoons and playboy princes.

Now available at
www.millsandboon.co.uk/offers

24 new stories from the leading lights of romantic fiction!

Featuring bestsellers Adele Parks, Katie Fforde, Carole Matthews and many more, *Truly, Madly, Deeply* **takes you on an exciting romantic adventure where love really is all you need.**

Now available at:

www.millsandboon.co.uk

The World of Mills & Boon

There's a Mills & Boon® series that's perfect for you. There are ten different series to choose from and new titles every month, so whether you're looking for glamorous seduction, Regency rakes, homespun heroes or sizzling erotica, we'll give you plenty of inspiration for your next read.

By Request

Back by popular demand!
12 stories every month

Cherish™

Experience the ultimate rush of falling in love.
12 new stories every month

INTRIGUE...

A seductive combination of danger and desire...
7 new stories every month

Desire™

Passionate and dramatic love stories
6 new stories every month

nocturne™

An exhilarating underworld of dark desires
3 new stories every month

For exclusive member offers go to
millsandboon.co.uk/subscribe

WORLD_ M&Ba

Which series will you try next?

Discover more romance at

www.millsandboon.co.uk